Moon Isle
The Oracles
Broken Harbor
The Gates
Sun Isle
Singing Mountains
Agora
Hive
Sky Isle
Abbey
Bay of Teeth
The Last Tower
The Craters
Star Isle
Lightlark

NIGHTBANE

ALEX ASTER

LIGHTLARK #2

AMULET BOOKS • NEW YORK

Cataloging-in-Publication Data has been applied for and may be obtained from the Library of Congress.

ISBN 978-1-4197-6090-7

Text © 2023 Alex Aster
Book design by Chelsea Hunter

Printed and bound in U.S.A.
10 9 8 7 6 5

Amulet Books are available at special discounts when purchased in quantity for premiums and promotions as well as fundraising or educational use. Special editions can also be created to specification. For details, contact specialsales@abramsbooks.com or the address below.

Amulet Books˙ is a registered trademark of Harry N. Abrams, Inc.

ABRAMS The Art of Books
195 Broadway, New York, NY 10007
abramsbooks.com

For Rron—
you make the real world better than a fictional one

My bane and antidote, are both before me.

—J. Addison, *Cato: A Tragedy,* 1713

VAULT

Isla Crown tasted death on the back of her tongue.

Moments before, she had unlocked the hidden vault in the Place of Mirrors. Inside, power churned, whispering in a language she didn't understand, calling to something deep in her marrow. It felt urgent, obvious, like the answer to a question she had somehow forgotten.

The rest of the abandoned palace was falling apart, but this door had remained closed throughout the curses. Her ancestors had fought to keep it a secret. Her crown was the only key and Isla thought, as she pulled the door open with a scream of a creak, that they must have hidden it away so thoroughly for a reason.

Her heart raced as she peered inside. But before she could get a look at anything good, a force battled through the gap, struck her in the chest, and sent her careening across the room.

The door slammed closed.

For a moment, there was silence. Peace, almost, which had become the most coveted and rarest of luxuries. It was all she dared wish for nowadays. Peace from the pain that pulsed through her chest, where an arrow had split her heart into two. Peace from the thoughts that ravaged her brain like insects feasting on decay. So much had been lost and gained in the last few weeks, and not in equal measure.

For that one second, though, she was finally able to empty her head.

Until it cracked against the stone floor, and her peace was replaced by a vision of carnage.

Bodies. Bloodied. Charred. She couldn't see what realms they were from; she could see only their skin and bones. Darkness spilled around the corpses like knocked-over pots of ink, but it did not settle, or puddle, or disappear.

No. This darkness devoured.

It finished off the rest of the bodies, then turned its attention to her. The tendrils climbed, cold and damp as lifeless limbs. Before she could move, the shadows parted her lips and forced her to drink them. She gasped for air, but all she tasted was death.

Everything went black, like the stars and the moon and the sun were just candles that had been blown out, one by one.

Then, the darkness spoke.

"*Isla.*" It had his voice. *Grim's* voice. "*Come back to me. Come back—*"

A blink, and she was back in the Place of Mirrors, all refracted sunlight and skeletal branches scraping against the remaining glass, reaching for her like hands.

And Oro. He was there in an instant, cradling her in his arms. He was not one for dramatic reactions, which only made his expression of horror more concerning.

Isla reached up and found blood running from her nose, her ears, her eyes, down her cheeks. She looked at the blood on her fingers, and all she could think about was what she had seen.

What was that? A vision?

A warning of what Grim would do if she didn't return to him?

She didn't know, but one thing was clear: as soon as she had opened that door, something had slammed it closed again. Something was in that room.

And it didn't want Isla to find it.

TRUTHS AND LIES

It rejected me," Isla said. It didn't make sense. The power called to her; she could feel it. So why had the door slammed closed again?

The king's golden crown gleamed as he tilted his head back, studying her. He was standing as far from her place on the bed as the room allowed.

It didn't matter. Even from feet away, she could sense the thread that tied them together. Something like love.

Something like power.

Oro finally spoke. "You're not ready. I don't think your crown is the only key. If it wasn't meant to be easily opened, the vault's door could be charmed to admit only a Wildling ruler."

"I *am* a—"

"One who has mastered their abilities."

Oh.

Isla laughed. She couldn't help it. Of course the island would continue to come up with ways to make her feel inadequate. At this point, it was like a game. "If that's true, then I guess it will remain closed," she said, staring intently at a spot on the wall. The only Wildling masters still alive were her guardians—and if she ever set eyes on them again, she would kill them for murdering her parents. And for all the lies they had fed her.

Silence came to a boil and spilled over. She could almost *feel* Oro's concern in the air, a heat tinged in worry. She resisted the urge to roll her eyes. Of all the things she had been through, being swept across the room by a snobbish door was far from the worst.

She hated his concern, and she hated herself for the anger that had hardened inside her like a blade, that struck out at even something as innocent as worry. Lately, though, she couldn't seem to control any of her emotions. Sometimes she woke up and didn't have the energy to even get out of bed. Other times, she was so angry, she portaled to Wild Isle just to have a place to scream.

"I will teach you," he said.

"You're not a Wildling master."

"No," he admitted. "But I have mastered four realms' powers. The abilities are different, but the execution is similar." His voice was gentle, gentler than she deserved. "It was how I was able to use *your* power."

It was how he was able to save her. She would have been boiled alive by the core of the island if Oro hadn't used the bond between them to claim her powers in the Place of Mirrors. That had been the moment her feelings for him were revealed. The fact that he could access her abilities meant she loved him.

Though she didn't even know what that—love—was.

She had loved her guardians.

She had loved Celeste.

She had, at some point, loved *Grim*.

The vision. Death and darkness and decay. Was it a threat? A glimpse of the future?

The weight around her neck felt even heavier now. The necklace Grim had gifted her during the Centennial had been impossible to remove, and yes, she had tried. It had a clasp, but so far it had refused to open. It seemed there was no real way to take it off. Only she could feel it. Oro didn't even know it existed.

Isla wondered if Grim was like that necklace—insistent and refusing to let her go. Would he kill people just to have her?

"I have to tell you something." She considered keeping it to herself. If it had involved only her, she might have. She had broken the curses. She deserved more time to recover. Her cuts and bruises from the Centennial

4

had disappeared, but some wounds were invisible and took far longer to heal than broken skin and bones. "In the Place of Mirrors . . . there was a vision."

He frowned. "What did you see?"

"Death," she said. "He—" She found herself unwilling to speak his name aloud, as if that alone might summon him from the shadows, bring him to life in more than just her mind. "He was surrounded by darkness. There were dead bodies everywhere. The shadows were reaching at *me*—" She winced. "It looked like . . . war."

It looked like the end of the world.

Sharper heat swept through the room, the only sign of Oro's anger. His smooth face remained expressionless. "He won't stop until he has you."

Isla shook her head. "I chose *you* . . . He feels betrayed. He might not even care about me anymore." Oro didn't look convinced. She closed her eyes. "Even if he did, do you think he would start a war over me? Risk his own people?"

"I think that is exactly what he would do," Oro said, his gaze faraway, as if lost in thought. "Isla. You need to start your training, and not just to get into the vault."

Training. That sounded like far too much effort, she decided, for a person who had to bargain with herself just to leave her room every day. She didn't use to be like this. Training had been hammered into her like gemstones into a blade's hilt. It was part of her very essence.

Now, she was just tired, more mentally than physically. All she wanted was time to recover, and why did even thinking that make her feel like the most selfish person on Lightlark?

Luckily, she had an excuse other than her own unwillingness. "You know I can't." As king, Oro was the last remaining Origin who could wield each of the remaining Lightlark powers—Skyling, Starling, Moonling, and Sunling. It was supposed to be impossible for anyone other than his line to be born with more than one ability. According to

Aurora—whom she had once thought to be her best friend, Celeste—her Wildling and Nightshade gifts were tangled together in a way that made them largely useless unless a Nightshade released them. "My powers—"

"I have a plan for that."

Of course he did. Her teeth stubbornly locked together. "I don't have time to train. I have to get back to the Wildlings."

"They will need you to be at your utmost strength."

Why was he so set on her training? And why, truly, was she so against it? "It's a distraction," she tried. "I can learn later. After they're taken care of. After we've figured out the Nightshade threat, if my vision is even real."

"You have the power of a Starling ruler now, Isla," Oro said gently.

When Isla killed Aurora, she had used an ancient relic called the bondmaker to steal all the Starling's power. The action served as a loophole to fulfill the part of the prophecy that stated a ruler had to die to break the curses. A ruler's power functioned as the life force of their people. All Starlings would have died along with Aurora, if Isla hadn't stolen that power.

Now, she was responsible for two realms, when she wasn't even qualified to rule one.

"Your Wildling and Nightshade powers might have stayed dormant all this time," he continued, "but this will not. The abilities are too great. If you don't learn how to control them, they will control you."

That seemed unlikely. In the last couple of days, she had casually tried to use her Starling powers. To move a quill. To make a burst of energy off her balcony. Nothing. She would have doubted that the bondmaker had even worked if the Starlings weren't still alive.

"Isla," Oro said, and the tender way he said her name dulled the defensive edges of her anger and pain, just a little.

"Yes?"

He took a step, then another, until she was bathed in his warmth, even though he was still farther than she would have liked.

Oro studied her from the foot of her bed. "Say you'll train with me. And mean it."

"Fine," she said quickly, just because she knew it was what he wanted to hear. Just because nowadays, she would do anything to stop thoughts about the Centennial and what had happened. "I'll train with you. I mean it."

"Your excitement is overwhelming," he said flatly.

"I *am* excited," she said through her teeth.

His look sharpened. "You do realize I know you're lying?"

Of course he did. That was his flair, the extra power rulers often carried from distant bloodlines. She imagined fate laughing at the irony of their pairing: a liar loved by someone who could sense the truth.

Instead of glaring at Oro, she was happy to turn the attention back to him. Curiosity made for the best distraction. Wasn't that all life was, she reasoned, painful moments strung together by distractions? "What does it feel like?" she asked, sitting straighter on the bed.

The thin sleeve of her dress dipped down her shoulder. She watched him track its fall.

"What does what feel like?" he asked, eyes lingering on her newly bare shoulder.

Something thrummed in her chest. She hadn't often noticed Oro staring at her. Until the moment when Aurora confirmed the king loved her, she hadn't even thought he had *liked* her.

One of her bare legs ran the length of the bed, slowly, until her toe reached the floor. Her dress rode high up her thigh, and she could feel the heat of his eyes on her. She did the same with the other leg, until both feet were by the bedside.

He studied her, top to bottom, and suddenly the vault was forgotten. Her inadequacy—forgotten. The betrayals? Forgotten.

Part of Isla wondered if he was still just looking at her to see if she was okay, but no, no, it was far better to believe he was watching her for other reasons.

"When someone lies to you. What does it feel like?" She drifted over to him, barefoot, her back slightly sore from her rough landing. Her head pounded in pain, the wound just recently healed by her Wildling elixir, but she ignored it.

He remained very still as she stopped before him.

"Does it hurt?" She tilted her head. "Does *anything* really hurt you?"

The look he gave her made it clear he wasn't going to answer the second question, so she tried the first again. "Do the lies hurt?"

Oro was so tall, he had to crane his neck down to look her right in the eyes. He reached out and ran his thumb across the divots of her crown. "It depends on who's telling them."

Guilt sank its teeth into her chest. The idea that her lies had hurt him inexplicably made her hurt as well.

Was that what it meant to love someone?

She had lied to him throughout the Centennial, but he had never lied to her. She knew that now for certain. He was the only person she trusted in the world, though she realized trusting anyone after what had happened was astronomically foolish.

Was *that* love?

Isla placed her hand on his chest and felt him stiffen. He was warm in a comforting way that made her want to feel his bare skin beneath her fingers. He did not move an inch as she got closer—and closer still.

They had barely talked about the connection between them, the undeniable thread. He had let her have her space. She had wanted to take things slow. Not rush in, the way she had with Grim.

But at that moment, she didn't want any space between them.

She stood on her toes, wanting to bridge the gap between her lips and his, *finally*, but no matter how long she stretched her neck, she couldn't reach him.

Oro stared down at her and frowned. "Is this your attempt to distract me?"

Absolutely. She didn't want to master her powers. She didn't want to think about any of her newfound abilities. Once she started, she would have to think about things—and *people*—that had scarred her, perhaps beyond repair. "Yes. Let me?"

He lowered his head. His golden crown winked in the light.

Then his hands were on her waist. His fingers were long across her back; she arched into his touch. He grabbed her, so tightly she gasped—

But before she could wrap her legs around his waist, he carried her to the bed . . .

. . . and dropped her back onto the sheets.

By the time she made a sound of protest, he was at the door. "Rest, Isla," he said. "The dinner is in a few hours." She groaned. It was the first time representatives were all meeting, to discuss the aftermath of the curses. "Then, we'll begin our training."

FLOATING FEAST

Make me look like a sword," Isla had told the Starling tailor Leto. "One that's more blood than blade." A mixture of Wildling and Starling. That was what she wore as she swept into the dining room.

The Sunling nobles had arrived early with their ruler. They were already seated when Isla walked through the doors, and when their eyes went straight to her—sharp and hungry—she had the unnerving feeling of being the very thing they had come to pick at and consume.

Before, she might have cowered under their scrutiny, but now she strode to the table like she didn't notice. What could anyone on this island do or say to her that they hadn't already done? Moonling nobles had tried to assassinate her. The others had already judged her down to the bone. In the marketplace, most people avoided her, still hating Wildlings because of their bloodthirsty curse, even after it had been broken. Her new red, metal-woven dress whispered against the smooth floor, feeling almost like chain mail, fighting against the silence shrinking the room.

She quickly marked the Sunling nobles as she passed them by. A man with long golden hair tied into a braid and dark skin, wearing a solemn expression. A tall woman, made up of about a thousand freckles, her hair the color of rust. A man who looked old—remarkable, given that even Oro looked young, and he had been alive for more than five centuries—his spine curved toward the table as if emulating the top of a question mark. He smiled at her, light skin crinkling, but it tipped more toward amused than friendly.

Oro sat at the head of the table, and he was also watching. The king would have looked exactly like he did at the beginning of the Centennial, at that first dinner, if not for his eyes. Back then, his eyes had been hollow as honeycomb.

Now, they burned right through her with an intensity that made any previous thoughts unspool around her. He almost imperceptibly traced her with his gaze. Her bare, tan shoulders. The silk-and-steel corset. The slit in her dress revealing knee-high boots she'd had made, because they were more practical than her heels or slippers. Her long brown hair, with tiny red flowers woven through the ends. She watched him back, for just a second. His broad shoulders. Golden hair. The sharp panes of his smooth face. He had been paler before, after so many years without sunlight, but now he was glowing, radiant. He was so beautiful, it almost hurt looking at him.

She didn't remember noticing how attractive he was at that first dinner.

Was *that* love?

Oro looked away quickly.

As she took her place next to him, the doors opened, and a breeze blew her hair back, bringing with it the comforting scent of pine and the prickling chill of mountain air. Azul swept in with the current, feet never touching the floor. He was joined by two others, not nobles but elected officials. Skylings ran their realm as close to a democracy as was possible in a system where rulers were born with the bulk of the power, power their people's lives hinged on.

While Azul's hair was as dark as his skin, the woman behind him had hair the color of the sky itself, complete with a bit of white mixed in—a sign she was ancient, just like the curved-over Sunling. Unlike the old man's, though, her posture was perfect. Her skin was deep brown, and she was small in stature.

The Skyling next to her was built like a tombstone, as solid as if he were carved straight from the Singing Mountains. He was white as the

cliffs of Lightlark, and so tall Isla couldn't see the color of his hair from the way his face was angled as he stared straight ahead. He was large enough to carry three swords on his belt comfortably, and he dwarfed all of them. Isla had the unpleasant thought that her own sword would look something like a quill in the giant's grip.

Azul came around the table to greet Isla, though his seat was on the other side of Oro. "Your style has changed," he mused.

His, happily, had not. The ruler of Skyling was wearing a tunic with shards cut out of its sides and bulbous sapphires in place of buttons. He wore a ring on every finger.

It was her first time seeing him since the Centennial had ended. *You should have sought him out,* her mind whispered. Another failing.

She wanted to ask how he was doing after watching the specter of his long-lost husband disappear once the storm cleared. She wanted to apologize for believing even for a moment that he was her enemy. She wanted to ask him how the Skylings were faring in the aftermath.

Before she could get a word out, Azul said, "We could make time to meet, if you would like."

"I would like that very much," she said.

"Good." He dipped his chin and whispered, "Beware. Someone is always watching."

He was right. Conversation had started up, but she could still feel attention fixed firmly on her. In the days that she had spent in her room after the end of the Centennial, Oro had told the island's nobles and representatives that Isla had broken the curses and gained the power of a Starling ruler. The news had swiftly spread among the people of Lightlark.

The leaders sitting around her now had watched her stumble her way through most of the Centennial's trials. They must have wondered how she, out of all the rulers, had been the one to finally put an end to the curses.

Just as Azul was seated, the doors opened once more, and a single Starling walked through. She had light brown skin, dark eyes, and a sheet of shining black hair. Her clothes were faded silver, more storm cloud than freshly sharpened blade. She froze as everyone turned to face her. Less than a second later, she recovered, walking with her head high. Because of their previous curse, Isla knew for certain that the Starling was younger than twenty-five, close to her own age.

They locked eyes, and the girl frowned. Still, Isla felt an understanding pass between them. Two people who felt remarkably out of place.

"Maren," the Starling said simply before being seated, by way of introduction, and then she proceeded to focus very intently on the curved edge of the solid gold table.

Only one chair remained empty. Cleo's.

It didn't seem like the Moonling would be joining them. Chimes rang through the golden room, marking the hour. Oro stood. "After five hundred years of suffering, the curses plaguing our realms have been broken, thanks to Isla Crown, ruler of Wildling." She felt eyes on her again. "Over the last centuries, our priority was survival. Today, we meet to discuss how we move forward. I see an opportunity for growth in every sense of the word. To get there, we must deal with the aftermath of five hundred years of our people divided and our powers constricted in the face of new threats." He looked around at them all. "First, let us celebrate the end of much of our suffering by sharing a meal."

Oro was seated, and conversations began, but Isla focused only on her unsteady breathing. Nerves rolled through her stomach. The attention had already been turned to her. Soon, there would be questions. What if she answered wrong?

No one knew about her past with Grim. No one knew she was secretly also a Nightshade. If they did, they might have imprisoned her right then and there. Nightshade had been their enemy for centuries. They had been at war right before the curses. If her vision was to be believed, they might soon find themselves in another battle against them.

"We are monsters, Hearteater," someone said in her ear. "Or, at least, that's what they think."

Grim. He was here.

She startled. Her heart hammered. Her gaze darted around the table, expecting to find him close by or to see some reaction from the others.

But he was nowhere. Maybe he was invisible. Her eyes strained to see even the smallest ripple in the air that might give him away. She waited for him to appear before them. Her hand inched toward Oro to warn him—

Nothing.

She knew what she'd heard. Or did she? It could have been her own mind. Grim had said those same words more than a month ago, when he was still pretending not to know her.

The truth was, he had known *everything* about her. They had a year's worth of memories together that he had made her forget, to suit his own agenda at the Centennial. He had cut part of her life away as easily as Leto shearing excess fabric.

She didn't know what she would do if she ever saw him again, but she didn't need to worry about it at the moment.

Grim wasn't there.

She had imagined it, then. Perhaps her mind had made up the vision in the Place of Mirrors too. It couldn't be real. Grim wouldn't kill innocent people to get to her.

She saw flashes of that vision again. Death. *Children*—

"Breathe," she said to herself, before taking a deep breath, knowing how ridiculous it was that she had to remind herself, vocally, of a body's basic function. Her nails dug into her palms, trying to keep herself in the moment, as if she were clinging to an anchor instead of becoming unmoored yet again in the shifting currents of her mind.

"Don't forget to exhale too." Oro.

Under the table, he placed his hand on her knee. His thumb stroked the inside of her thigh. She knew he meant it as a comforting gesture,

but for a moment all her senses sharpened to his touch. Her eyes met his. He removed his hand.

A special drink was prepared, a Sunling specialty. Flaming goblets were served on floating platters by Starlings, who moved objects using their mastery of energy. Isla noticed they smiled at the Starling representative—Maren—in a friendly way.

Oro casually drank from the goblet, and the flames extinguished, not burning him in the slightest. The Sunling noble with the dark-red hair downed hers in an impressively short amount of time.

Would it burn her if she wasn't Sunling? No, of course not. Oro would never serve his guests something that would harm them. She was the next one to drink from her own flaming goblet.

It tasted of honey and burned like liquor. The flames licking the edge of the goblet stroked her cheeks as she drank, then sank into the dregs of the drink before simmering away completely.

The first food course was pure Skyling. It was a floating feast, served in a flowerpot—miniature vegetables still tied to the roots, flying about, that one had to pin down with their fork to eat. She couldn't place every food by name, but one had the familiar texture of potatoes, was violet in color, and had a surprising bite of sweetness. Some of the vegetables seemed to have minds of their own and playfully evaded capture, flying within the confines of their root leashes. Oro watched her try to pin down an especially active beet, amusement touching the corners of his mouth.

The second course was Starling. The fine silver plates contained a single orb. Once all were served, the Starlings snapped their fingers in unison, and the orbs exploded, revealing a cut of unfamiliar meat, carved into precise pieces. Large saltlike rocks formed a circle around the protein. Isla bit into one and startled when it burst like a firecracker in her mouth.

The Moonling course arrived last.

The Starling attendants mumbled apologies as they delivered the dishes, though they were clearly only following orders. Blocks of ice

were presented with live fish still swimming within them. Their eyes were wide as they tried to navigate their quickly melting confines.

Isla felt the heat of Oro's anger—almost enough to set the fish free—though his expression remained impassive.

Before Oro could say a single word, the doors of the room burst open. Isla expected to see a dramatic entrance from Cleo.

A Moonling stood at the entrance . . . but it was not the ruler. The man had long white hair that reached the middle of his torso, nearly the color of his skin, and a staff in his hand.

"Soren," Oro said. "How nice of you to join us. I presume this is your idea of a joke?"

The Moonling man—Soren—pursed his lips. "More of a statement. Excuse my late appearance, but I find I have no appetite when I consider the state of the island, not so unlike the blocks of ice before you."

That made them the fish.

"Cleo sent you in her stead?" Azul asked.

Soren nodded. He took the empty seat that had been set aside for the Moonling ruler.

Oro stood, and the entire center of the solid gold table dropped, forming a basin. The blocks of ice rushed to the middle, then melted, filling it. The fish swam in relieved circles.

With a look that was befitting of the cold king Isla had believed Oro to be before the Centennial, he looked at Soren and said, "Now that dinner has ended, why don't you begin by telling us where Moonling stands?"

The Moonling's longest finger slipped across the gem atop his staff. "You are of course aware that we have severed our bridge to the Mainland."

"Another statement?" Oro asked.

The Moonling shrugged a shoulder. "As well as a protective measure. The curses kept people in check . . . and we are aware we have enemies on the island." His gaze landed on Isla.

She almost wanted to laugh. *That* was the reason he was going with? *Her?* Moonling nobles had tried to assassinate her, and Cleo had, personally, nearly finished the job. She supposed it wasn't a leap to think she, with her newfound power, would be set on revenge.

It was still a ridiculous excuse.

Oro gave him a look. "And your armada of ships?"

The Moonling noble took a leisurely sip of the flaming goblet that had now been set before him. "So we can sail to the Moonling newland, of course," he said. "To unite our people once more."

That might have been partially true, but it wasn't the only reason, and Isla didn't need Oro and his flair to know it. Cleo had begun building her army of ships during a time when faraway travel was a death sentence for Moonlings.

"Unite them how?" Azul asked. "To bring those on the Moonling newland to Lightlark? Or bring those on Lightlark to the newland?"

The room was silent, charged with energy. This was the big question, she knew, from speaking with Oro. After the curses were cast, most of the realms had fled Lightlark to create their own newlands, hundreds of miles away. Some people had remained on the island. Would the rulers decide to move back, now that the curses were over? Would they leave Lightlark for good?

"My ruler has not decided yet," Soren said smoothly.

Oro turned away from the Moonling in dismissal to face Azul. "And the Skylings?"

Azul motioned toward his representatives. "These are elected officials Sturm"—the giant nodded, his eyes never leaving the opposite wall—"and Bronte." The petite woman gave the ghost of a smile.

"Every Skyling will have a choice," Bronte said. "To remain on the Skyling newland, or join us here on Lightlark."

That seemed in keeping with their realm.

Sturm nodded. "We have already begun teaching the newer generations the art of our flight, though the journey to or from the newland

is still too long. We have contraptions that offer flight by harnessing wind for that purpose."

Oro nodded. He made to face his own representatives when Azul said, "There is something else. Rebellion on the island is brewing. Our spies have heard the whispers, carried along the wind."

Oro frowned. "What do those whispers say?"

"The people are not pleased with how long it took to break the curses, or our decisions as rulers."

"Which realm?" Oro asked.

"All of them. The ones on Lightlark, at least," he said. His gaze shifted to Soren. "Yes, even Moonling."

Rebellion. Would the people of Lightlark really attempt to overthrow Oro, or any of the other rulers? Without heirs, their rule represented a total monarchy. Rebellion was futile, when killing a ruler would result in the death of everyone in their realm.

Their expressions were grave, but no one looked too surprised. It made Isla think rebellion was not a new concept on Lightlark.

"I plan to visit all the isles and newlands to address the people directly," Oro said, his eyes meeting Soren's. "Hopefully, it will give everyone a chance to air their grievances."

He nodded at his representatives. "Enya, Urn, and Helios join me," he said. Sunlings didn't have a newland—all of them had stayed, along with Oro, who was both ruler of Sunling and king of Lightlark. "As many of you know, they serve the Mainland court as well. We are focused on shifting our infrastructure and routines back to normal after being nocturnal for five hundred years." His eyes briefly met Isla's before he said, "We are also preparing our legion. With the curses broken, we can only assume Grimshaw will take it as an opportunity to attack."

This was in response to her vision, Isla knew. Oro was taking it seriously.

Soren frowned. "You believe he has the same ambitions as his father?" Grim's father went to war against Lightlark, Isla knew, decades before the curses. Nightshade wanted control of the island.

"Perhaps," Oro said. "All we know for certain is that Nightshade is more powerful than ever now that the curses are broken and our realms are divided. We must work together again to present a united front."

There were murmurs of agreement, and hushed whispers that sounded curious about the idea of a Nightshade attack.

"Speaking of working together . . ." Soren said. His attention turned to Isla. "All of the Wildlings fled Lightlark. How is your realm faring?"

After the curses, Isla had injected power into her lands, to save her people while she recovered. Late at night, with her portaling device, she had visited them in secret. "Wildlings have begun shifting their primary food source." She saw clear disgust on Soren's face, which she guessed had to do with the fact that her people had previously subsisted on human hearts. "My people have already started harvesting their own crops, but we will need aid to achieve an assortment of diet and agriculture now that they are dependent on farming. I—"

"How many of you are left?" Soren interrupted.

She frowned. "I'm not sure. As you know—"

"You're *not sure?*" Soren asked, eyebrow raised.

She could feel her face go hot. It was a reasonable question. The kind a good ruler would know the answer to.

"Do most of your people know how to wield power?"

"I don't know."

"How is housing? What has the rate of reproduction been in the last century?"

"I will have to find out," she said through her teeth.

"Do you—"

"Enough," Oro said. He turned to the Moonling. "Soren, I'm sure Isla would love to have you visit the Wildling newland if you are so curious about her people."

Soren looked like he would rather stick his fork in his eye, but he went silent.

Isla's gaze didn't leave the table. Her throat felt tight. Her breathing was constricted, as though her lungs had shrunk to half their normal size.

She didn't deserve to be a ruler. She had known that for a while, but Soren's line of questioning had thrown her lack of wisdom in sharp relief. Poppy and Terra had ruled the realm while she trained for the Centennial, and now they were gone. She had banished them.

For the first time, Isla wondered if that had been a mistake.

The Starling representative who had announced herself as Maren cleared her throat. There was an intensity to her, an energy that coursed through the room. "For centuries, we have been an afterthought. A blip in your ancient lives. We have been treated as disposable by many. Taken in the middle of the night. Subjected to labor, and torture, and sometimes worse." She looked at the king. "You executed those found guilty, but so many fell through the cracks." She grimaced. "Star Isle is in ruins. I can't imagine the newland is faring much better." She looked to Isla. "We need a ruler."

How could the Starling seriously be looking at Isla for help, after seeing how badly she had just recounted her own realm's condition?

Soren frowned. "What you ask is impossible. One cannot be the ruler of two realms."

"She did receive the full power of a Starling ruler," Azul remarked.

Soren barked out a laugh. "The girl can't even rule her own realm. Now you're ready to give her *two*?"

"The *girl* has a name—and a title," Oro said, his voice cutting through the room. "You will address her with the respect you give all rulers, or I will use you as kindling for the castle hearth."

Isla stiffened. Oro's defense had been sharp. She glanced at the faces around her, but they looked abashed rather than suspicious.

Soren's eyes flashed, but he bowed his head in respect. "Forgive me, King."

"Don't apologize to me," Oro told him.

Soren begrudgingly turned to Isla and said, "I apologize, Ruler." Isla just stared at him. He turned back to the king. "With respect," he said, his *s* pronounced in a particularly serpentine manner, "it does not seem wise to give a single ruler that much power . . ." He hesitated, considering his words. "*You*, King, are the only one meant to preside over multiple realms."

Oro's look at the Moonling was just one shade away from casting flames. "Azul is correct. She has the full powers of a Starling ruler, and, might I remind us all, is the sole reason any of the Starlings are still alive." He turned to Isla. "The responsibility is hers to accept."

Isla was silent. She couldn't decide like this right now. As much as she wanted to put a dagger through him, Soren was right. She had just demonstrated, very publicly, that she had no idea how to properly rule a single realm, let alone two. Two of the weakest realms, the most ravaged by the curses; the ones currently in need of the most support.

"How would that work?" the woman with the dark-red hair said. Enya. Her voice was raspy and deep. She carefully appraised Isla, tilting her head to the side. "Would she be coronated? Officially announced as ruler? She already has the power; it would simply be a matter of ceremony."

"The public will not like it," the Skyling woman—Bronte— murmured, though not unkindly. She was simply voicing a fact.

"Of course they won't like it," Maren murmured under her breath. "It would make it more difficult for them to continue to exploit us."

"What was that?" the old Sunling said, a touch too loudly, genuinely seeming as if he had not heard her.

"This is all going very well," Soren said offhandedly to the giant Sturm, who did not so much as blink in recognition that he was being spoken to.

"I said," Maren started, her voice growing in intensity, frustration and anger building in her expression—

"I'll do it," Isla said, standing, putting a bookmark in the plaited conversations.

Silence.

"Are you certain?" Oro said, holding her gaze. He looked at her like they were the only two people in the room.

"Yes," she said, not certain in anything but the fact that Maren clearly knew Isla was not the best leader . . . and she had asked for her help anyway. The Starlings must be desperate. She was not the right choice for this—of course she wasn't.

No, that wasn't right. She would *become* the right choice.

Isla couldn't deny them, especially now after she'd heard of the atrocities that had gone on for the last few centuries. Who was she, if she sat and did nothing after learning of that horror? What would be the point of killing her best friend and breaking the curses if Lightlark and its people descended into chaos soon afterward?

"I will officially become the new ruler of Starling," she said, meeting Soren's eyes. "I will have a coronation."

CHOICES

I don't know how to rule," she admitted. Azul sat in front of her in Juniper's old bar. The spheres of liquor behind the counter were still filled. The curved chairs and tables hadn't collected even a spot of dust yet. The body and blood had been taken care of, but Isla was almost back to that day, weeks before, finding him dead. With Celeste.

Aurora.

The barkeep who kept secrets had died because of her. He had helped her. He was one of the *only* islanders who had helped her.

It made her want to be better—worthy of his sacrifice.

"A very dramatic declaration you gave. I quite liked it." Azul leaned back in his chair, a glass of sparkling water glittering in front of him, bubbles popping and releasing a berrylike scent. "Do you *want* to rule, Isla?"

No. That was her first response. But it seemed too selfish to say aloud, so she said, "Do I have a choice?"

The Skyling ruler raised an eyebrow. "You *always* have a choice."

Skylings valued choice over all else, as evidenced with their democracy. It was an alluring principle, Isla thought. What she wouldn't give to hand off all this responsibility to someone else.

"Do I?" she said, her voice more grating than she had meant it. "I have ruling power from Starling now, and Wildling. Who else could rebuild them?" Azul just looked at her, so she continued. His silence angered her for some reason, because all these questions were *real* ones, ones she wanted answers to. "Hmm?" she said. "Should I just go back to my room and let them all die?"

"You could," he said. Azul shrugged a shoulder, looked at a perfectly manicured nail. Every part of him was immaculate, as always. "But you're choosing not to." He met her eyes. "Right?"

She had requested he meet her. She had declared to the nobles and representatives that she would have a coronation. She had made not just a choice but *choices*.

"Right," she murmured.

He flashed his perfect teeth at her. "Good. Now that that's clear . . . Of course you don't know how to rule, Isla." The compassion in his tone caught her off guard. "When I was in my twenties, I was too busy flying off with boys and drinking every shade of haze to even think about anyone other than myself." His smile turned sad. "When you make the choice to rule, you are making a promise that you will put your people's well-being and happiness above your own."

Isla frowned. It shamed her how awful that sounded.

She didn't *want* to put others first, not after everything she had just been through. A person could only take so much. Her trust had been broken, along with her heart. There wasn't much left of her to give. She wanted to be selfish with the parts that remained. Didn't she deserve that?

"I see," he said.

"See what?"

Azul began humming to himself, and the wind seemed to mimic it. Somehow a current was moving through the room and jostling her hair, even though all the doors and windows in the bar were closed. "Of course."

"Of course *what*?"

The Skyling ruler folded his hands in front of him. "Are you close to your Wildling subjects, Isla?"

"No."

"They didn't know you believed yourself powerless?"

She shook her head.

"What was your relationship to them?"

Isla lifted a shoulder. "Nonexistent. My guardians made all the decisions. They ruled. Because of my . . . *secret* . . . I was kept far away. Only paraded on special occasions, at a distance." She bit the inside of her mouth, a habit that would have made Poppy flick her on the wrist with her fan. "If I'm honest, they are my blood, they are my responsibility, I would do anything for them . . . but they feel like strangers."

Azul nodded. "Of *course* they do," he said, and the way he validated her feelings . . . the compassion in his voice . . . it was beyond anything she had ever experienced. "And the Starlings here, they *are* strangers. You don't care about them." He shrugged. "You don't care about this island."

His voice was without judgment. His eyes held no disgust. Azul only shook his head. "How could you? You've only been here a few months. The worst moments of your life were likely spent right here on Lightlark. You don't have fond memories before the curses to look back on, and most of the people hate you, because of their perception of Wildlings."

Everything was said so matter-of-factly. Isla couldn't tell if his even tone made the words hurt less or more.

"Are you going back to the Wildling newland, Isla?"

"I plan to." She told him about her portaling device and how she had visited. She offered to portal him to the Skyling newland when needed.

Azul's eyes only glimmered with curiosity. "Charming," he said. "I appreciate your offer, but I meant . . . are you returning to the Wildling newland for good?"

For good. Before, when the Centennial had ended, Isla could not fathom staying on Lightlark. Now, things were different. *She* was different.

"No."

"Then this is your home now," Azul said. "Your *chosen* one." He stood, his light-blue cape billowing behind him in a breeze only he seemed privy to. "Learn to love it, and your two realms. It is up to the leader, not the subject, to connect." He outstretched his hand. "Come with me."

She took it without question, the rings on both of their fingers clashing together like wind chimes. "We're not flying . . . are we?"

Azul smiled. "Do you trust me?"

"I do," she said, and it was the truth. It was stupid, she realized, to trust anyone after everything. She knew that, but what was the alternative? Closing herself off forever? Ever since the end of the Centennial, she had felt a wall harden around her. If she wasn't careful, it would become impenetrable.

She had asked Azul for help. The least she could do was let him in.

They stepped out the back door of the bar, into an alleyway. He offered his other hand. "May I?"

She took his hand.

Then she was in the air. And Azul's flying was far smoother than Oro's had ever been.

In the aftermath of the curses, Sky Isle was transformed. The city built below had been abandoned for the one floating above, just as most of the Skyling people had promptly deserted walking in favor of flying. A castle sat nestled comfortably in the clouds, with spires pointing at the sky like quills ready to decorate a blank page. A waterfall spilled from the front of the palace in an arc that reflected every color imaginable, into a shimmering pool below.

And they were all *flying*.

It looked natural, like the air was so much empty space finally being put to good use. Isla had only ever seen Oro fly—and now, Azul. She hadn't expected there to be so much flourish. Flying seemed to be a bit like handwriting; everyone had their own signature. Some were graceful, like Azul, to the point of making it all look like a choreographed dance. Others were more like Oro, brusquely taking steps in the sky, as if walking on an invisible set of bridges no one else could see.

Some weren't really flying at all. They glided on contraptions with wings, using their control over wind to power the inventions.

Azul had wrapped her in wind. She floated right beside him—with her hand fully clenched around his wrist, just in case—taking it all in as best as she could.

"Your realm's curse . . ."

"Was one of the better ones," he filled in.

Not being able to fly for five hundred years certainly must have been terrible for a society that had clearly woven their power through the fabric of their day-to-day, but it wasn't nearly as bad as dying at twenty-five or eating hearts to survive. That didn't mean it wasn't deadly, though. "Azul. The day it happened—"

"We lost many of our people. They all just . . . fell from the sky."

Isla closed her eyes. The thought of them, without explanation, falling to their deaths . . . She clutched Azul's wrist harder.

"Flying comes naturally to us; even those with the smallest shred of power can do it. Those who weren't skilled enough—or quick enough—to use wind to cushion their fall . . . perished."

They had reached the castle. Instead of landing in the clouds—which Isla didn't trust in the slightest—they continued floating, right through the entrance.

The ceiling was nonexistent. One could float right in and through the palace in one smooth motion. The castle had hallways but no stairs. To get to the different levels and out of the main atrium, one had to fly. She could see why this palace had been abandoned after the curses.

Isla wondered how many important resources Skylings had suddenly had no access to, for years, because of their curse. The first time she had visited Sky Isle, she had marveled that the highest building in the city had a spire that reached the very bottom of the castle above it. Now, she realized that was the only way for them to reach what had been lost. They'd had to build to it.

The air felt thinner so high up, and it was cold enough to make her skin prickle, though the Skylings didn't seem to mind it. They all wore light blue in honor of their realm, in fashions with much more

range than she had seen from other realms. Dresses didn't seem to be so popular, which she imagined was a practical choice. Even now, Isla was grateful her dress and cape were heavy enough to keep her modest as she floated around.

Skylings nodded at Azul with respect, with joy, smiling, clapping him on the back as they passed him by. Most nodded at Isla as well. Some stared curiously. Others smiled openly.

They flew to the top of the castle and through its ceiling to view the palace and its floating city from above. He motioned toward the hundreds of people in a market that looked miniature from their height, then to a string of mountains miles away. Sky Isle went on and on, farther than she could see.

"They are my purpose," Azul said. "It was not easy to leave Lightlark after the curses, but my people voted, and most wanted to leave the uncertain future of the island. I'm proud of the Skyling newland, and all we created in the last few centuries, but there is no doubt that our power's heart is here." He took a deep breath, like he could smell and taste and feel that very power, thrumming across the isle. He looked at her. "I can't teach you how to rule, Isla. You must figure that out yourself. All I know is that I put their interests and well-being far above my own. Every day. They are what kept me going, even in my grief." He glanced at her sidelong. "Now that the curses are over, there will be pressure for you to have an heir."

Isla whipped her head to face him. "What?"

"Your people will want to secure their future." He sighed. "Many precautions were put in place in the last few hundred years to ensure the safety of rulers. My people voted for me to almost constantly be surrounded by a legion for protection. I was not permitted to travel to other newlands."

That made Isla's own travels with her starstick seem that much more reckless. For a moment, she began to understand why Poppy and Terra had been so strict.

Isla did not want to create an heir.

She wasn't ready. Did that make her horrible? Even more selfish?

She also didn't want to live the rest of her life insulated and heavily guarded, knowing her death would mean the end of all her people . . .

"There are other ways to have an heir, beyond the obvious," Azul said. "It is possible for rulers to transfer power, through a love bond, or special relics." *Like the bondmaker*, Isla thought. "The cost is high, however. Permanently transferring ability shortens a ruler's life significantly."

That didn't seem like a viable option either. She had barely had a life. She wanted to be able to live it.

"You look like you're about to be sick," Azul said.

"It's the height."

Azul made a sound like he knew the truth. "It is an honor to rule but not always a pleasure, Isla." He squeezed her hand. "Go, visit your people. Face them. Be honest with them. You are their ruler. Whether or not you have deemed yourself worthy, you are all they have."

That, Isla decided, was what she was most afraid of.

CORONATION

There were fewer Wildlings left than she thought.

Months before, she had addressed her people. Now, only a fraction remained. They looked weak. There were details she hadn't noticed before, when she had been so focused on her journey to the Centennial. Now, she saw the signs clearly. A woman with short hair, crudely cut, wore a torn top that revealed all-too-visible ribs. Another looked far too pale, lips chapped, face devoid of color. They had learned to make enough food; she had seen them. She supposed it would take some time for consistent nourishment to make them healthy again.

Some details were the same. A portion of her people had animal companions near them, just like the day she left. Wildlings were known for their affinity with creatures. Poppy had a hummingbird that flew around her hair. Terra had a great panther.

She had always wanted an animal companion. It would have made her life far less lonely.

Terra had always said no.

Isla opened her mouth to speak. Before she could, they did something she couldn't have expected. Didn't deserve.

One by one, they bowed.

"No, I—"

They had never done that before. Isla had never demanded it. It wasn't a custom she was used to.

She didn't like it. Anxiety thrummed across her skin, and she wanted to yell that they should be screaming at her, calling her names, telling her everything she had done wrong up until this point. They looked like they were still *dying*. She was a failure, not a hero.

Isla stepped back, words caught in her throat, when a woman with a capybara next to her said, "You broke the curses. You did what all other rulers for centuries could not."

She frowned. "How do you—how do you know that?"

"Terra told us."

Terra? The name was a dagger to the chest. How had her guardians even known she was the one to break the curses? Why had Terra told them, after being banished?

Had she defied Isla's order? Was she still here, on the newland?

"Where is Terra now?" the woman asked. "She was here . . . and then she vanished. And Poppy?" *No. Not still here.*

"I don't know," Isla said honestly. She thought about telling them about the banishment, but she needed to first get a sense of their allegiance. Would they be loyal to her . . . or to the guardians who had mostly ruled the Wildlings since her birth? "Please stand," she said. She told them everything else. That she'd believed she had been born without powers. That she had a device that allowed her to portal at will. That she now had Starling power. When she was finished, she said, "I have not been a good ruler. I don't know your struggles. Speak candidly, please. I know you must have questions. Ask them. Tell me what you need."

Something flickered in her vision. Isla turned, and for the slightest second, she saw Grim, standing among the crowd, watching her.

She froze. Panic dropped through her stomach.

A blink, and he was gone.

Someone asked a question, and she didn't hear it.

She shook her head. "Sorry, what did you say?" Her ears were ringing. First, the vision in the Place of Mirrors. Then, his voice in her head. Now, she was seeing him . . . What was next?

What was wrong with her?

"I asked what is happening on the island."

She wondered how much she should say. "There is uncertainty on Lightlark right now. The realms are divided. There are signs of rebellion. We also have reason to believe Nightshades might try to attack Lightlark, like they have in the past." She attempted a smile. "Once all of that is dealt with, I hope to have us all back on Lightlark one day," she said. "This has been our home for five centuries, but it is weakened. Lightlark is where we have always belonged."

There were some murmurs, but no one spoke out against her. She hoped that was a good sign.

She answered their questions as best she could, then sought out a woman who wore purple flowers through the ends of her hair, the color of leadership. She was tall, with light skin, dark hair, and sharp eyes. Her name was Wren, and Isla learned she led one of the larger villages on the newland.

"Why are some people standing apart from the rest?" Isla asked. Her people were not as united as they had seemed months prior. Some were huddled together, but others stood on the outskirts.

Wren looked at her for a moment. "I mean no disrespect," she said. "But you didn't have the curse. You don't know what it's like to have to kill others for food. To go hungry because there simply wasn't enough." She shook her head. "Most of us did things we're not proud of to survive."

Tears burned Isla's eyes. All her life, she had thought it a horror being locked in her room and training so rigorously. It was nothing compared to what her people had gone through; she knew that now. "What do you need?" she asked. "How can I help you?"

Wren pressed her lips together. "We have slowly learned to make food. It has been good for us, I think, figuring things out on our own. Any challenge now . . . it is a mere shadow of what we endured."

"You must need something," she said. "Some of you still look starved. I can bring more food. Bring people to help teach you to make other crops or help reconstruct houses." She had seen the state of the villages

during her travels with her starstick. Some buildings had stood the test of time, and others had fallen to pieces. "I can—"

Wren cut her off. "How are the Starlings?"

"I don't know. I've asked, but I haven't yet visited the newland or isle."

"Help them," she said. "We are resourceful. Older. They are so young. They need you more than we do." She smiled sadly. "It would help," she said. "With the guilt. To know in some way, we are aiding another realm, instead of . . ."

Killing them.

Isla nodded. "I'll be back," she said. "With help and resources, after my coronation."

Wren nodded. "We will be waiting."

Bells rang at a distance. The air was sharp with salt from the sea and burned honey from the fair that had cropped up at the base of the castle, all carts filled with varieties of roasted seeds and bands holding their instruments, but not playing them, not yet.

Isla stood at the top of the stairs, just beyond the shadow of the doors, just out of view of the thousands of people waiting below.

It was the day of the Starling coronation, and it seemed everyone on Lightlark was in attendance.

Well, almost everyone.

"No sign of Moonling," Ella said quietly behind her, because Isla had asked her to look. The young Starling had been her assigned attendant during the Centennial. Now, Isla employed her to be her eyes and ears wherever she could not see or hear.

The bells came to an end. It was time.

Isla stepped forward.

Strings of silver beads made up a dress like spun starlight. Her cape glistened in a ripple behind her as she walked down the stairs.

It was still a shock to wear a color she had only dared to use on her prohibited excursions beyond her own realm. It felt wrong, it all felt so *wrong*, like she had taken her friend's life, robbed her of her silver, and put it on herself.

Was that what these people thought? That she had killed Celeste—Aurora—for the power?

She looked to the crowd for answers, stomach tensed, braced. Their faces were a mosaic of surprise, curiosity, hate, disgust, trepidation, vitriol—

Breathe.

Isla took another step, and her foot nearly missed the stair completely. She briefly considered gathering her gown in her hands and running back upstairs, locking herself in her room and going anywhere, *anywhere,* with her starstick.

She wasn't worthy of any of this. She didn't deserve to rule anyone. She didn't even know herself. Part of her past was missing, and that person—the one who had supposedly loved a Nightshade—felt like a stranger. She was sad all the time, and there were so many emotions pressed down, in the deepest depths of herself, that she knew one day would overpower everything else and claw their way out—

She felt it: a thread of heat, steadying her. It was honey in her stomach, a beam of sunshine just for her.

Him. She met Oro's eyes. The king was her destination. He stood tall and proud and golden, at the very bottom of the steps. There was a silver crown in his hands.

He looked at her like it was just them, no crowd, no crowns.

She took another step. Another. Until she was standing in front of him.

Oro didn't say anything. He didn't have to. She could read a thousand words in his amber eyes, like *you can do this. I'm here for you.*

The past few days, she had been avoiding him, knowing he would want her to begin her training. She felt ashamed. Her people needed her to be strong. He just wanted to keep her safe.

He raised the crown high above her, not wasting a moment, knowing she wanted this to be over as soon as possible.

"As king of Lightlark, I name you, Isla Crown, the ruler of Starling." He placed the crown on her head. It was done.

There was a rumbling.

Oro had turned to address his people, but he paused, his brows coming together slightly.

Nervous murmurs spread through the crowd. There was a second of stillness, the island righting itself, and the people silenced, their momentary curiosity instantly forgotten. But Isla watched Oro, and his expression remained the same. Her hand inched toward the blade at her side.

Before her fingers reached the hilt, the island broke open.

The ground beneath her feet parted like a screaming mouth. She would have been swallowed if she had not been on its edge, on a part that rose like a sharpened tooth. Her body soared back with the force; she closed her eyes. Pain across her side was the only sign she had landed.

Screaming sliced the air in half as a scar tore across the castle steps in a rippling sweep, stone crumbling and falling away.

Both were drowned out by the screeching.

Winged, monstrous creatures howled as they barreled through the open fissure.

Their necks were short, their limbs long. Their tails were nearly non-existent. Their anatomy almost resembled people, except for their faces—which were pure reptile—their black scales, and, of course, their wings.

In a few moments, they were everywhere.

Dozens of the creatures dropped down, aimed at the crowd. Isla put a hand above her, as if it would be any type of shield against the teeth that curved out of the beasts' mouths like slanted blades.

Before the beasts could reach them, a blanket of flames erupted into a barrier. *Oro.* The heat was scalding, steaming Isla in her clothes.

When the fire was pulled away, the creatures were gone, reduced to ash that rained upon them. Dozens were killed.

Before anyone could run for shelter, more creatures emerged.

The scar had to be closed. The beasts were rising in endless sweeps, squeezing through the gap. Groaning, Isla pushed herself up to her arms.

Oro was leaned over his knees, clutching his side. Any injury to the island hurt him as well. It must have felt like he was also being peeled open. Face twisted in pain, he lifted his hand and created another barrier, but the creatures closed their wings together in response, making themselves into sharpened arrows, talons at their fronts like blades. With cries that threatened to crack the sky into shards, they barreled through the protective sphere—

And feasted on them all.

Bones crunched, blood splattered, limbs were torn away. The beasts crashed down, undisturbed by Sunling flames, Starling sparks, or Skyling wind. Their talons tore through flesh as easily as swords through sand.

Azul shot up into the air, with a legion of Skylings surrounding him. They fought with bursts of wind, shooting the creatures down from the sky or slamming them against the island until they went still. Sunlings wielding swords covered in flames guarded people huddled behind the carts in the fair. All the islanders fought back, but many were no match for the creatures, whose hides resisted most uses of power. Before their strategy could be changed, most of them were torn in half by powerful jaws. Some islanders stopped using their abilities altogether, as it marked them as targets, and pressed themselves to the ground or ran.

Just like at the ball months before, Isla watched it all unfold, a helpless spectator. No. They might hate her, this might never feel like home, but she had to do something.

Isla stood on weakened legs, blood hot on the side of her face. She placed a hand over her heart. The heart that had been torn in two by

an arrow. The one that was healed by the heart of Lightlark itself, the one that was linked to Oro's own ability.

A heart that had, more times than not, failed her.

"Please," she whispered, eyes on Oro, who was oscillating between killing swarms of beasts attacking his people and trying to close the scar the winged creatures were still flying through in droves.

She could help him. Wildling power included controlling rock and land. If she could manage to grasp some of that power, she could help all of them.

Isla closed her eyes. She focused on her breathing.

Nothing.

She stretched out her trembling hand. "Come on."

Nothing.

The powers she had been born with were twisted together, making them harder to access. Her Starling abilities were not, however. They were there, just below the surface. She summoned them.

Nothing happened.

Perhaps she could focus on the link between her and Oro instead. Use *his* power. She looked at the king, whose arms were both shaking with effort, one outstretched at each side.

She felt it. Tried to grasp it. *Nothing.*

She shook her hand toward the cut in the ground, picturing herself sealing it shut with ice or burned rock or energy, willing with every bit of her being for it to close. "Come on!" she bellowed.

Nothing.

Her yell had attracted the attention of the closest winged creature. It opened its mouth, and a severed arm fell to the ground.

Then, it lunged at her.

Isla didn't have a chance to scream or attempt to use power again. With just a flap of its wings, it was right above her. She saw the creature bare its teeth, open its massive jaw.

An inch from swallowing her head whole, the creature froze. Its wings moved slowly as it closed its mouth and lowered its face, as if to inspect her.

Isla didn't know why, but she reached toward it, until the very tips of her fingers grazed the space between its eyes—entirely too aware eyes.

The beast blinked. Then, it opened its mouth again—

And screeched. The sound nearly popped her ears, and everything around her muted. She gritted her teeth, readying herself to be eaten alive.

But the creature only turned its head and left, with another screech.

The rest followed.

Isla watched them flee to the horizon, calculating the direction they were going. Nightshade. They were going toward Nightshade.

No. She remembered her vision in the Place of Mirrors . . . Grim attacking with shadows that killed everything in their path. She had convinced herself it was a figment of her imagination, but—

Maybe it was real.

By the time the beasts were just a smudge in the distance, Oro had closed the opening in the ground. Screams still pierced the air, along with the metallic scent of blood. The back of Isla's throat burned with inhaled ash. The injured . . . their wounds didn't look normal. Their skin looked ravaged by shadows. The lesions were growing, moving, slowly decaying everything in their path.

"You did this."

The voice sounded smothered, faraway. Isla turned. A woman was standing in a sea of bodies, not far at all, pointing a finger right at her.

"It didn't attack her. She was communicating with it!"

She took a step backward. "What? I didn't—"

A man joined the woman. "I saw it. She's allied with the Nightshades, isn't she?" Isla shook her head. "This ceremony was a setup, so we could all be here at once. So the beasts could attack us."

"No, of course not," she said, barely hearing her own voice, taking another step back.

No one was listening to her.

Isla's heart was beating too fast; she was hyperventilating, and still none of the air seemed to be reaching her lungs, and she was suddenly light-headed—

"Enough." The word was an order and silenced the crowd. Azul dropped down from the sky, landing in a crouch that shook the ground with power. He had one of the creatures' heads in one of his hands, cut neatly by the sword on his waist, dripping in dark blood. He turned to look at Isla for just a moment, and she worried his face might be full of suspicion, but he only looked curious.

A hand hot as fire gripped her shoulder. She turned to see Oro, searching her face, looking her over, checking for serious injury. Only when he seemed satisfied did he turn and begin yelling orders. Isla could barely hear a word that came out of his mouth. The world had started tilting. In response to one of Oro's dictations, Azul flew from what was left of the steps in the direction of the isles.

"Wildling elixir," she said to herself, knowing this was how she could help. People were dying all around her—they needed to be healed. She had never seen injuries like this, but the healing serum had never failed her. If she could get to her starstick, she could portal to the Wildling newland and get more. She made her way up the steps, narrowly avoiding the closed scar, walking over corpses of the creatures that Oro had killed. They sat charred and steaming.

She didn't even make it to the doors of the castle. At the top of the steps, Isla fell to her knees. Her legs had gone numb. Panic closed in around her. She couldn't breathe. Blood. Everywhere. So many dead. She hadn't been able to save them.

If she hadn't been so selfish, so weak; if she had started training like Oro had insisted, she could have helped, she could have been more than just a blight.

She thought of her vision again and Grim's voice. *Come back to me,* he had said. That was what he wanted.

The creatures were clearly summoned by Grim. There was a reason they hadn't hurt her.

Her breathing was labored. She heard Ella saying her name, attempting to pull her up. Her eyes closed, and all she saw in her mind was the woman pointing at her, declaring her the cause of all their suffering.

Isla couldn't help but think that maybe she was right.

INSIGNIA

The Insignia glowed faintly as if whispering a welcome. Isla hadn't stood on the marking since the day she had first arrived on the island. The symbol was simple—a circle that contained illustrations representing all six of the realms. This was a neutral place to meet and speak on the Mainland, with the castle standing watch, a beast of stone, towers, and fortress walls.

Isla shifted on her feet, over the rose of Wildling. Oro was across from her, on the sun. Azul stood on the bolt of lightning.

Cleo emerged in a crashing wave, straight from the ocean. Seafoam still puddled at her feet.

The last time Isla had seen her, Cleo had tried to kill her.

The Moonling turned to look at Isla, and her eyes gleamed, as if she was relishing the same thought. Her white dress had a high neckline and sleeves that ran all the way to the floor, covering the etching of the moon.

Whatever she hoped to find in Isla, she was clearly disappointed, because Cleo frowned and turned to Oro. "How, exactly, did she stop it?" Her voice sliced through the silence and a wave crested high behind her as if to meet it. She commanded the seas. All the water in the world bowed before her.

"I'm standing right here," Isla said. She was more than capable of speaking for herself.

Cleo only slightly shifted direction to face her again. She smirked. "How did *you*, once supposedly powerless, now all-*powerful*"—the ruler made even the word *power* sound pathetic when related to Isla—"stop the dreks?"

Dreks. Was that what they were called?

How did Cleo know what they were?

She probably should have come up with a response to the question if she was going to insist on being the one to answer it. She swallowed. "I—I don't know. I touched it."

Cleo said every word like it was its own sentence. "You touched it."

"Yes," Isla said through clenched teeth.

The Moonling turned back to Oro. "How many more do you want us to heal?" she asked the king, and Isla understood that she had been dismissed.

Forty-five people were dead. More were still fighting for their lives. She had gotten Wildling healing elixirs from the newland, but they needed more help. Oro had summoned Cleo through Azul, and she had taken her time arriving to the palace.

"Fifty-four are critically injured," Oro said.

"We will provide healers."

Oro nodded. "You've visited the oracle, I presume. Were you able to wake her?"

The oracle was on Moon Isle and only rarely chose to unthaw. The Moonling shook her head no.

Oro would know if she was lying. "We all know this was likely an attack from Nightshade. We need our realms united. Where do you stand?" he demanded.

"I haven't made my decision to stay or to leave."

Oro's expression did not shift an inch. He had been expecting this. "What is the true purpose of your army and ships?"

"To protect Moonling's interests when I do make my decision."

"Make it soon," Oro said. "This is not the time to flee to your newland."

Azul spoke up. "Cleo, you aren't actually considering leaving."

Cleo whipped to face him, her dress a white puddle beneath her feet that shifted, liquidous. "We have long been too dependent on this land.

42

The curses are broken. It could be an opportunity for more. Perhaps the island should fall."

Azul stared, unbelieving. "If Lightlark falls, the realms will follow. Our power is strongest here. Our future is here."

Isla remembered what Azul had told her during the Centennial—Cleo hadn't attended the previous one.

This was not a sudden decision. Cleo had thought about leaving for a while. Why? It didn't make sense.

Oro's eyes were pure intensity. "If we go to battle with Nightshade, which side will you be on?" Leaving Lightlark for the Moonling newland was one thing . . . choosing to stand against it was another.

Cleo raised her head. Her chin pointed in the king's direction, sharp as her tone. "The winning one."

A hundred-foot wave crashed against the cliff, spilling onto its lip, right over the Moonling ruler.

When the water pulled back, she was gone.

The Moonling healers had never seen anything like the drek wounds. They were able to slow the decaying of the skin, but, in the end, her Wildling elixirs were what was able to remove the marks completely. She portaled back to her newland several times throughout the night, and her people had willingly given their own stores of the elixir. They were down to just a small patch of the rare flowers.

Most people were saved. The rest had succumbed to their wounds. Isla walked to her room slowly, Oro at her side. The moon trailed them both through the windows as they made their way up the castle stairs.

She leaned against her door when they reached her room. "Cleo called them dreks. Have you heard of them before?"

"No. Moonlings have always prized their histories and historians. She might have read about them." He was studying her again. She had caught him doing it, every few minutes, since the attack. It was as if he needed to constantly reassure himself that she was uninjured.

"I'm fine," she said gently. She looked down at herself and winced. She was covered in blood, after helping the healers. It wasn't hers.

"I know," he said, but his brow didn't straighten. Worry was etched into each of his features, and not just for her, she knew.

"You did everything you could," she said, reaching up to touch his face, because she was known for giving far more grace to others than to herself. Her fingers were covered in blood—she dropped her hand before it reached his cheek. "Those creatures . . ."

Oro closed his eyes. She would bet he was replaying the events in his mind. When he opened them, she saw guilt in his expression. He blamed himself for every single death.

She wanted to take that pain. She wanted to think of anything that could make him feel better.

Before she could say anything else, he brushed his lips to the crown of her head and said, "Goodnight, Isla."

RISING UP

It was the middle of the night when the balcony doors to Isla's room burst open. The ocean rose like a hand, and it dragged her out of bed.

She gasped in shock, salt water scorching her throat and nose and lungs. Her shirt scrunched up, her stomach raked against the stone terrace, and she had enough good sense to cling to the balcony pillars, but the sea was too strong. It pulled her hundreds of feet down, straight to its depths.

She choked on lungsful of water, sure she was going to die, until her vision went dark.

When it returned, she was on her knees, hearing the word, "Now," and then the water was being pulled back out of her as quickly as it had been inhaled, salt scraping against her throat.

The high ceiling was stone. Stalactites hung from the top, sharp as icicles. She was underground. No one would hear her screams. Her eyes still burned from the sea, but she blinked frantically past the sting, looking for a way out. Shadows glinted all around, and suddenly her captors came into focus. They were wearing masks—monstrous red masks that hid their faces completely.

Her kidnapper and the one who had revived her were clearly Moonling; they had to be, to use the sea to their advantage as they had. The rest were not.

Isla spotted the blue hair of Skyling. The gold and red tresses of Sunling. No Starlings she could see. Their clothes were all the same shade: beige. A color that had not officially been claimed by any of the realms.

"Are you sure?" She could just make out the words of a muffled voice. "Perhaps if we waited—"

"There's no time," another, louder voice said. "The drek attack is just the beginning. This happens now."

At first, Isla's mind had gone straight to Cleo, but now she wondered if the rebels were behind this, the ones Azul had mentioned at dinner. Did they think she was responsible for the dreks? Is that why they were hurting her? Isla opened her mouth, to say anything, but her throat was raw. Nothing came out.

She had no weapons. She was already covered in blood, the skin of her stomach scraped clean. Salt stuck in the wounds. If her hands weren't tied together behind her back, she could have reached for her invisible necklace, clutched the stone, and watched Grim turn all of them to ash.

Should you ever need me, touch this. And I will come for you, he had said when he had given it to her.

The fact that she was even considering it worried her.

Isla should have listened to Oro from the beginning. Her life was not her own.

Were none of them Starling? Why would they want her to die, when it would mean the death of so many others? She heaved again.

"Don't move," someone commanded as some in the group inched forward. She watched them approach and counted her last moments down in her mind.

Cold hands gripped her raw skin—

The world exploded.

At their touch, energy rippled out of Isla like the consequence of throwing a stone in a still pond. Power burst in every direction, sending everyone around her soaring. She heard the crunch of bones as some were catapulted against the stone walls. Screams. She saw the red of the masks mixed with blood.

Someone had been thrown directly into a stalactite, pierced right through their skull.

"I didn't—" Her voice was barely a rasp. She hadn't tried to hurt them, even though they'd clearly intended to hurt her.

She didn't wait to see if they recovered. The energy had torn through her restraints. Isla ran.

The tunnels were dark and musty; she heard the crash of the sea somewhere nearby. There were multiple directions, but she made a choice and kept going, eventually on an incline. She needed to reach the surface. The rebels—were they right behind her? She didn't stop to listen. Sharp stones stabbed her bare feet until everything began to go numb. Her clothes were drenched in blood, fabric stuck against her wounds.

Just when she wondered if she would be trapped forever beneath Lightlark, there was a path so vertical, she had to climb it on her hands and knees. A wooden door, barely the size of a cupboard, was at the top.

She burst through, into an abandoned shop, covered in cobwebs, dust, and broken glass. Some of it cut her feet as she ran through the door, right into one of the forgotten corners of the agora. The harbor was to her left. She saw the broken ships, some on their sides, some no more than a pile of wood.

Down. She needed to go down to the heart of the market. For a moment, her fingers inched toward her necklace, her mind going there again.

The rebels could be chasing her. Grim would end them all in a moment.

A shiver snaked down her spine. That was the problem.

What was wrong with her?

Isla dropped her hand and raced down the narrow stone road, past shops long closed.

It was late, and the streets were empty, except for a patrolling Sunling guard. When he saw her, his eyes went wide in alarm, and Isla wondered if she should be afraid. Could he be working with the group that had taken her? Some of them had been Sunling, after all.

Before she could worry too long, the guard swept off his golden cloak and draped it over her shoulders. Only then did Isla realize she was in her soaking nightclothes, her body nearly completely visible beneath them.

The cloak was warm, and Isla sank to the ground wrapped inside it while panic spilled around her as more Sunling guards were called. Someone shouted to alert the king.

She knew Oro had received the news when a tidal wave of heat raged across the island.

When Oro had found Isla, shaking and raw skinned, he had looked like he wanted to bring the entire island down. The very ground beneath their feet had shaken as he had said, very calmly, "Who did this to you?"

By the time he had ripped the abandoned house to pieces, the rebels were gone. He had ordered his guards to search the tunnels, and they had found hundreds of passages that no one officially knew existed.

Now, in the throne room, everyone was quiet with fear. Isla had never seen Oro so angry. The only person who dared even look at her was Soren.

"Treason has been committed," Oro said, his eyes pure fire. His voice thundered through the room. He was standing in front of his throne, addressing a hall filled with all the nobles and representatives across the island. Azul stood down the steps, to his side.

Isla was next to him. Her skin had been scraped away; parts of her stomach had needed Wildling elixir to piece back together. The salt water had made the pain unbearable. Every sweep of the fabric of her dress even now was torture, but Isla wanted to stand here, in front of them, as a demonstration of strength.

"A ruler was attacked. Let it be known that anyone who is found associated with this group of rebels will be strung across the cliffs in the Bay of Teeth." It was a torturous death, according to Azul. Sea creatures as large as entire parts of the castle lived there, in waters so deep it was

rumored no one had ever seen their bottom. "Any ill will toward the Wildling realm stops now. A Wildling broke your curses. *This* Wildling is the reason Lightlark still stands. You will treat her and her realm with respect, or you will find another place to live."

The representatives quickly filed out of the throne room when the king was finished. Soren was last to leave, and Isla had the unsettling feeling that he was going to talk to her. In the end, he simply turned and left.

Azul approached, with two guards behind him. "This is Avel and Ciel," he said. "Two of Sky Isle's best warriors. They have volunteered to be in your service for as long as you require them." Guards. They wanted to keep her safe. Avel was a towering blond woman, with her head shaved nearly all the way down. Ciel was the same height, with the same color hair, though his grew long. Their features were almost identical. Twins, she assumed.

The idea that someone outside of her realm, who had no link to her at all, wanted to help her . . . it made her eyes burn with emotion. Not everyone on this island hated her because she was a Wildling, she thought. Not everyone wanted to hurt her.

"Are you sure?" Isla asked them.

In unison, they knelt in front of her, bowing their heads and offering their sapphire-tipped daggers. "You broke the curses, Ruler. We are forever in your debt."

Isla shook her head. "No. No—you are *not*," she said. She thought about the rebels and their attack. "But I will accept your services, at least for the time being."

She thanked Avel and Ciel, then asked them for privacy. They stood watch outside the doors of the throne room.

Only she and Oro remained inside. By the time she walked up the steps to Oro, he was sitting slouched over, his head lowered. One of his hands dragged down his face. He startled as she knelt before him, so their gazes could be level.

His eyes were bloodshot and devastated.

"I will find them," he said.

She put her hand on his cheek. For a moment, he stiffened, like he wasn't used to being touched—who would dare touch the king?—but a second later, he leaned into her palm. "I know," she said.

"If they had *killed* you, I—" He closed his eyes, and the heat of his anger was like a wall, mixed with the tinge of something heavier. Sadness.

"I know," she said again, because she would feel the same way if something happened to him. Their love was a shining link between them. She felt it, lustrous, as she leaned her forehead against his. "I'm here. We're both here. We're both fine."

His eyes dipped to where her dress had partially fallen open, showcasing some of her remaining scars, including the one over her heart, where an arrow had pierced her during the Centennial. No amount of elixir had been able to fade it. She leaned back so the dress fell closed again.

"The healers said I won't even have a mark from the attack by the end of the week." She had been treated by some of the Moonlings who had remained in the castle with those injured by the dreks.

"You shouldn't have a mark to begin with."

"Oro," she said. He didn't meet her eyes. He was looking past her, likely imagining the dozens of ways he was going to torture the rebels once he finally found them. "I want to start my training."

That got his attention.

"With the dreks, I tried—" She winced against the memories of limbs being torn away, of screeches blowing out her eardrums. "I attempted to use the powers. I really did. Even with people dying around me, I couldn't summon my abilities. I couldn't save them." She grimaced. "But then, underground . . . I didn't even try, I didn't even *think* about it, and I became a weapon. I'm glad I did, but you were right. I want to learn to control my powers so they don't control me."

He nodded, looking determined, relieved, like she had given him something to do to help keep her safe.

"You said you had thought of a way to attempt to untangle them?" she asked.

His relief faltered. "Yes," he said. "But you're not going to like it."

UNLEASHED

Remlar was grinning like someone who had boldly declared the future, then watched it come true. Oro's glare did nothing to dim that smile.

"I told you she would return willingly," the winged man said. During the Centennial, he'd told them, *I want the Wildling to visit me. Once this is all over . . . she will come willingly, I assure you.*

He had known, Isla realized. Back then, when he had said that she was *curious . . . born so strangely*, she had believed Remlar was talking about her secret, her powerlessness, but now she understood. He had known then she was Nightshade.

"Tell me, King, you weren't that naive," Remlar said. "She is so very clearly touched by night."

"Enough." Oro's voice was sharp. "Can you unravel her powers?"

Remlar nodded. He was an ancient creature. Isla didn't know the extent of his abilities, but she sensed he was older than she could even imagine. He had dark hair, like Grim's. Was he truly a Nightshade? How was that possible?

"Do it," Isla said.

Oro looked at her. "You have a choice. You don't have to—"

"I know," she said. Then, again to Remlar she said, "Do it."

Before Remlar could move an inch, Oro took a step toward the winged figure. "If you hurt her," he said, voice lethally calm, "she will kill you. And then I will find a way to revive you so I can kill you again with my own bare hands."

The threat made Isla's own mouth go dry, but Remlar, who clearly had put a very low value on his life, just grinned wider. "I would expect nothing less, *King*," he said. "But she has nothing to fear from me. She's one of us."

Us.

It was foolish, but something in her swelled at the word. When so many had rejected her, someone—even someone like Remlar—claiming her . . . it felt good.

He walked over to her, clicking his tongue. His wings twitched as he studied her, mumbling to himself. His skin was the blue of a bird's egg. His stride was feline, graceful, and his eyes were as sharp as his teeth.

His grin became wicked. "You might want to run," he said casually to Oro. "Or, better yet, fly."

Isla didn't know if Oro heeded his warning. With one rapid motion, Remlar placed one hand against her forehead and another against her heart, and her vision exploded.

Pain tore her in two. Her scream was a guttural rasp; she could hear it even above the ringing in her ears. Tears swept down her cheeks.

She fell to her knees.

Her left hand struck the ground, and darkness erupted from her fingers. It ate through the nature in its path; everything living became cinder. Trees fell and disappeared; the air went gray with swimming shadows.

Her right hand landed, and from it a line of thousands of flowers billowed, rising from the ground in waves, blossoming in rapid succession. Roses, tulips, marigolds—they made a blanket across the forest, color streaming.

The world died and came to life in front of her, and she kept screaming until her voice disappeared in a final croak. It might have been seconds or minutes, but eventually, everything settled, and she stood.

One side of her was total desolation—the other the very definition of fertility.

Oro was in front of her in a moment. "Isla," he was saying, but it was just a whisper at the end of a tunnel.

She took one step forward. Teetered.

"Look at me, love," he said.

Love. She held on to the word like an anchor, but the thread between them slipped through her fingers—

Darkness won the war and swallowed her whole.

BEFORE

Isla took the steps two at a time—she really shouldn't have come. How had she been so foolish?

Terra had always warned about Nightshades. They were the villains in all her stories. The monsters.

She really hadn't meant to. She had meant to portal somewhere else entirely, but one thought, while her puddle formed—

Here she was, in the most dangerous place in the world. Running from a group of guards, around dark stone corners, in halls that echoed and closed around her in cavernous arches.

Isla turned into a narrow hallway and crashed to her knees. "Come on," she growled, pressing her starstick firmly against the ground.

No puddle formed.

Isla didn't want to wonder what would happen if she wasn't able to travel home. Nightshade lands were thousands of miles away from the Wildling newland . . . It would take *months* to return by ship, and how would she even pay for passage? She didn't have any jewels on her. Now that she thought about it, no one in their right mind would agree to take her anywhere, anyway.

If anyone figured out who she was . . . she was dead.

The Centennial was just a year away. The Nightshade ruler was a monster. He had been invited to attend the event for the first time, according to her own invitation.

What would he do to her if he found her? Kill her immediately as the first step in breaking the curses? Imprison her? Torture her?

She swallowed. She had thought of her own room as a prison . . . how foolish she was. There were much worse places to be trapped.

Yells. Steps. The clatter of armor.

Instinct took over. She lunged for a door—and it was unlocked. Before the guards could spot her, she threw herself inside.

Another hallway.

Voices outside. Already. There were several more doors. She tried all of them.

Locked.

Locked.

Locked.

Locked.

The voices were closer. Without thinking, she started pounding on the last door, desperate, frantic—

It opened.

A woman stood there. Her arms were crossed.

"You're late," the woman said. "Put this on and join the rest."

Isla had no idea who the woman thought she was, or who the rest were, but she knew luck when she saw it.

The woman all but shoved her into a different room. And Isla was so grateful, so afraid for the guards to find her, that she stripped off her clothes in the dark and put on whatever the woman had given her—fabric that was tight against her body. All Isla cared about was that it would make her look like the rest of the Nightshades. Even if the guards *did* find her here, she would blend in. Especially if she was joining people wearing the same thing.

The door swung open, and Isla nearly brandished the dagger she had kept strapped to her thigh, alongside her starstick.

It was just the woman. She had paint on her finger, and before Isla could object, she unceremoniously smeared it across her mouth.

"Go," she said, pushing her toward another door.

A dozen other women were waiting on the other side. All dressed like her. She nearly sighed in relief. She blended in perfectly . . . especially with the red on her lips.

All she had to do was find her way back outside, where she could try her starstick again—

"Into position!"

Position? The women suddenly straightened into a line, one she quickly joined, wondering what in the world was happening.

Was this a fighting legion?

If so, why were they wearing dresses?

Was this some sort of rehearsal?

She swallowed. If it was, she would be found out momentarily. She obviously wouldn't know any lines for a play, or choreography for a dance . . .

"I hope I'm chosen," a woman to her left whispered to someone who seemed to be her friend.

"I hope *I'm* chosen," she replied. "This is my fourth time hoping to get noticed. It would be an honor to be part of the ruling line."

Ruling line?

Isla turned to the women to ask them what was happening, and why they looked so excited, when the door in front of them opened.

He walked in.

Isla froze.

She knew who he was instantly. Something about the way the air moved around him, about the resonance of his step. He was the tallest man she had ever seen, a foot and a half taller than her at least. He had relatively long black hair like spilled ink, falling across his forehead, curling around his ears. His mouth seemed set in a permanent frown. Unimpressed.

He was the king of nightmares, a demon.

The ruler of Nightshade.

She was dead. He had found her out. They had trapped her; the woman must have recognized her somehow, alerted the guards—

What an idiot. Poppy and Terra had taken such great pains to keep her safe, and she had disobeyed their orders, for what? To experience something new? How selfish she was.

Her fingers inched toward her thigh. She wouldn't have a chance against the ruler of Nightshade, against *any* ruler—no matter how well she could handle a blade, power was power—but she would die with dignity. Fighting.

Just as her pointer finger found the smooth metal, his eyes met hers. She stilled.

His look was strange. There was no hint of fury, or even satisfaction. Just a slight widening of his eyes—a curiosity.

That didn't make sense. If he was about to kill her, wouldn't he announce his intention? Slay her where she stood, in front of all the others?

"You," he said.

He was staring at her. He meant her.

She didn't move a muscle. His eyebrows rose just a fraction of an inch. Surprise. Another unexpected emotion.

The woman from before all but shoved Isla forward, toward him.

The Nightshade ruler stared down at her. She didn't breathe. Then, he turned and walked back through the door.

She was expected to follow him. She knew that for certain when the woman from before gripped her wrist and said, "*Follow*," so fiercely that she actually did.

Her steps echoed through the empty hall. His were almost silent in front of her. All she saw was his back. Her own shoulders were small—tiny slopes.

His were wide cliffs.

He had perfect posture. The posture of a warrior. She swallowed. How many thousands had he single-handedly taken down? Even in her

glass room, she had heard whispers about his malice. Some Nightshades could kill with a single touch—wasn't that the rumor?

A shiver worked its way down her spine . . . and turned into a pit in her stomach when he led her into a dark room.

Was this where she would be executed?

She tugged her dress up while his back was still turned and risked a look at her portaling device. It was still dark, lifeless.

No.

Isla needed a plan.

The voices in her head crowded, wicked, quick to attack. What plan could she possibly come up with to have a chance against him?

She was a fool. A powerless fool.

The door closed behind her, and she jumped.

The ruler of Nightshade—*Grimshaw*—turned to face her. He looked her over quickly. Was he sizing her up? Deciding how he would make her suffer?

She swallowed. Took a step back.

He lunged for her.

Isla should have grabbed her dagger, but she was more shocked than she had ever been in her life, so she froze.

Froze as he pressed her against the wall, and—

He . . . he lowered his face until his lips were mere inches from hers. His eyes were hungry, full of desire. He wanted to kiss her. That didn't make any sense.

Suddenly, all the pieces came together. Why the women in line looked so excited. Why they were speaking of hoping *to be chosen*. Becoming *part of the ruling line*. They had all clearly volunteered to be presented in front of the Nightshade ruler. He thought she wanted this. He thought she had *signed up* for this.

He didn't know who she was.

She could have pushed him away. Told him the truth. But she didn't. She was a fool. That had already been established, hadn't it? Her entire

life, she had been locked up. She had never been this close to a man before. She had never *felt* this way before.

His hands, so large, so callused, gripping her so strangely. His *height*. His eyes, dark and gleaming. *Hungry*. His hard body, pressed against hers, his muscles and her curves lining up so naturally. Those seemingly unimportant things—much less important than who he was, and what kind of weapons were inches away from her—became all she could think of. She went very still.

For a moment, she forgot herself. And him. She forgot everything she had ever been taught.

"Is this okay?" he asked, looking down at her. He was leaning lower, his breath grazing her lips. A shiver worked its way down her spine.

This was her chance to say no. Instead, she found herself saying, "Yes." And meaning it.

Then, his lips were on hers.

Isla had never been kissed. Didn't *want* to be kissed by her enemy, her rival, the filthy, deadly—surprisingly attractive—Nightshade. Then why had she said yes? She should push him, say something, but his lips were a key, unlocking things she had never felt. Heat, pulsing every-where. Sparks, dancing across her skin, as his thumb pressed against the palm he held against the wall. As his teeth skimmed her lips, as his lips dipped down her neck . . .

She kissed him back. She held him just as tightly as he held her.

Her hands ran through his hair, and it was so much softer than she would have imagined. She felt her way down his neck, his chest, and he felt hard and cold as stone. His tongue swiped against the hollow of her throat, and she made a sound that shocked her.

Sensing her excitement, he made some sort of growl and hauled her up, against the wall, as her legs locked around his middle. She gasped, because in this position, she could *feel* him . . . *all* of him. Right against her. Right against her—

All at once, she remembered herself.

Remembered who he was, how she needed to get out of there *now*.

He was her enemy. The moment he found out who she was, he would hurt her. This could be a trick. Surely, he was going to attack her at any moment.

She needed to strike first.

Just as he deepened their kiss, she grabbed her dagger from where it was holstered on her thigh. Gripped its hilt.

And stabbed him through the chest.

There was a moment of quiet. The Nightshade ruler met her eyes, right before his chin dipped, and he slowly looked down to his chest, where the dagger still stuck out, inches from his heart.

Then, he released her.

There was no time. No time to turn around, to check if the warmth across the front of her body was shame or fear or his blood.

She ran out the door, grabbed her starstick, which somehow, mercifully, now glowed.

She drew her puddle of stars—

And was gone.

FAVORITE

Isla awoke soaked in sweat and panting. Oro was there, hand behind her head. The rest of her was draped across his lap. They were still in the forest, framed by life and decay. She imagined Remlar was lurking, watching.

She pressed her forehead to Oro's shoulder and cried. Her Nightshade powers had been awoken, and they had begun to unravel her mind. Undo what had been done. She thought of what Grim had told her, weeks before, after the Centennial.

Remember us, Heart. You will remember. Then you will come back to me.

She would never go back to him. Nothing would change his betrayal. Nothing would change the fact that Grim seemed intent now on killing innocent people. One thing was for sure, however.

She was starting to remember.

Her powers were detangled, and Isla wondered if they would have been better left alone.

She had been going in and out of consciousness, but now all her senses came flooding back, far too sharply. They were in the Mainland woods. Oro must have flown them here. Her memory still clung to the corners of her vision, as if it had claws.

A blink, and she saw Grim again, his hands curled beneath her—

No. She pushed the image away. She wouldn't tell Oro about it. It was the past. It didn't matter. She had been vulnerable while her power had been unleashed, she told herself. It wouldn't happen again.

She felt Oro's hands smoothing down her back. "There you are," he was saying, meeting her eyes, frowning as he checked her temperature with the back of his hand. "How are you feeling?"

Her head pounded like the sea against the cliffside, and there were *voices*. Whispers everywhere, from every direction. Something had filled her body to the brim. She was an overserved goblet, wine spilling down the sides.

"I feel everything," she said. Tiny threads all around her, waiting to be pulled. Whispers from the vines beneath her hands, from the towering trees around her, from the shadows beneath them. "There are a million voices, all fighting for my attention." Power was like a seed in her chest she had swallowed whole, and it was growing roots within her.

All her life she had wondered what it would be like to have power. All her life she'd had it, hidden deep inside. Now, it was free.

"We can find you a Wildling master," Oro said, his voice a blade through the chaos. "I can get your portaling device. We can take you to the Wildling newland." It made sense to train there, with her own people, but—

"No," she said quickly. "I don't want to risk harming them. I—" Her touch had killed an entire forest. It was just like her Starling power exploding out of her. She had no control. Panicked, her eyes darted around. "Take me somewhere else. I don't want to hurt anyone."

With three separate powers—Wildling, Nightshade, and Starling—the abilities seemed to be battling. When she had gotten her Starling abilities, she had felt strange but nothing like this.

In an instant, she was in Oro's arms, and they were in the air. When they landed, she immediately stumbled away, afraid that if he touched her for too long, she might hurt him.

"You can't kill anything here," he said simply. "Everything is already dead."

He was right. They were on Wild Isle. The voices had quieted, just a little. Still, the skeletal trees called to her, the dirt beneath her

feet hummed, and she could still hear the Mainland woods even from far away.

She needed those voices out of her head—it was already a crowded place to begin with. She needed to stop feeling pressure against her ribs, like the seed of power was going to burn right through her chest. "It's too loud," she said. "I can't—I can't escape it."

"When you gain a hold on your power, you won't hear them anymore," he said. "Right now, you are inadvertently summoning everything—the world is simply answering your call. It will get better as you begin to gain control."

She shook her head. How long could that take? "I can't, I can't—"

One more step, and she sank to her knees and said, "I think I'm going to be sick," before she did just that. Her throat was still coarse and sore from the ocean water; it burned like a skinned knee.

He was behind her, his heat a welcome warmth, his hand gathering her hair in a single fist. "It's going to be a rough few days as your body adjusts," he whispered. "I'll be right here with you."

"Please don't leave me," she said, her voice frail and pleading. For just a moment, she wanted to cry out for Terra, her teacher for her entire life. *She* was the one who should have been teaching her this. But Terra had betrayed her, and besides Oro, she was alone.

"Never, Wildling," he said.

She retched again.

The Place of Mirrors became their temporary home. Avel and Ciel moved in as well. They helped coordinate getting furniture, food, and supplies, alongside Ella, who brought clothing and Starling soup. The Skyling twins took turns guarding the entrance to Wild Isle. No power other than Wildling could be used in the Place of Mirrors; she had learned that during the Centennial.

It gave her an added layer of protection. Isla was more vulnerable than ever, but she felt safe here against the rebels—and with Oro sleeping right beside her.

She wished she could enjoy that fact a little more, but for the next few days, she was always either clenching her teeth against pain, being sick, or sleeping.

A fever turned to chills. She felt nauseous all the time. Oro fed her pieces of bread and soups and got her to drink water even when she cried, because everything hurt, and would he please make it stop?

He looked as pained as she felt.

She fell asleep holding his hand every night, and every morning when she awoke, with a headache worse than the last, he was already there, looking like he hadn't slept at all.

"You can go," she said weakly one night, as he very badly attempted to brush her hair and tie it with one of her ribbons. Ella typically helped her, but she had sent the Starling home early that night, since she had been working around the clock for days. "I'm sure you're needed elsewhere."

Oro just looked at her, the corners of his lips twitching in amusement that didn't reach his eyes. "I was given strict orders not to leave your side."

Isla managed to smile, before grimacing as a new wave of pain washed over her. "Oh? I didn't know the king of Lightlark took orders from anyone."

"Not just anyone."

She stared at him, her pain abating just a little. A wavy lock of hair came loose, and Oro cursed, starting over.

"You have many skills," Isla said, a faint laugh escaping her even as every part of her ached. "Doing hair isn't one of them."

Oro began to smile in earnest. "Here I thought I had another talent." He brushed through her locks again and said, "I like your hair."

"You do?"

He nodded. "It . . . shines nicely in the sun. I didn't know that until after the curses." She smiled, despite the pain. The fact that he noticed something that specific about her, that he was paying that close attention . . . it made her feel warm inside, for just a moment, before the nausea returned.

"I like your eyes too," he offered, studying her face, as if wanting to make her smile again. He quickly returned his attention to her hair. "They're my favorite color."

She raised an eyebrow at him. "My eyes happen to be your favorite color?"

Oro paused, looking a little like he regretted starting this conversation in the first place. He stared intently at the ribbon between his fingers, and it looked almost physically painful for him to get the next few words out. "No. It . . . it *became* my favorite, after . . . after—"

He was flustered. Isla couldn't believe it. The king of Lightlark, the cold ruler of Sunling she had heard about her entire life, was *flustered*. It was adorable. Isla's chest felt like it was being cracked in half, but she couldn't help but tease him. "Really?" she said. "Please. Tell me everything you like about me, slowly, in detail."

Oro gave her a look that made her certain he knew she was reveling in his discomfort.

She pressed her lips against another smile. "Do I encompass any other favorites? Am I your . . . favorite liar? Favorite incapable ruler?" Her tone slowly became bitter, because in truth, she couldn't imagine being anyone's favorite anything. "Your favorite weakling who can't go a few hours without retching?"

Oro turned to her, then. He looked her right in the eyes as he said, "Isla. You are my favorite everything."

Her lips had been parted with another self-deprecating and annoying statement, but she closed them.

That couldn't be true.

What was there to like about her? She was weak. Foolish—

She looked away. Suddenly, she was the one who was uncomfortable. Oro didn't lie, but she couldn't imagine anyone saying good things about her, when her mind told her the opposite. "I feel better," she lied. "You can leave for a bit, if you want."

"Is that so?"

"Better than ever, actually."

"Right." He lightly brushed away another strand that had come loose—because he was truly hopeless at tying her hair—and she knew he was also subtly checking her temperature. "Well, Wildling, even if I couldn't naturally tell that you're a liar, your skin is so warm, you could pass for Sunling."

Oro should be with a Sunling. Someone more like him. Someone who wasn't such a mess. "Do you wish I was?"

"Sunling?"

She nodded, and it didn't do anything to make her head feel better. Before he could respond, she added, "Do you wish I wasn't . . . everything I am?"

He was quiet for a moment. Her eyes slowly began to close, suddenly heavy. Fighting against sleep was useless in this state. "No, Isla," he finally said. "It's the parts you don't seem to like about yourself that I love the most."

Love—

She wanted to accept it, savor it, clutch it, let the word swallow her whole and make her happy. But instead, she drifted off, into the waiting arms of sleep.

BEFORE

S he was kicking off her shoes, rubbing her toes. No matter how many times Poppy made her stride in straight lines, or even forced Terra to make her train in the ridiculous heeled shoes, she would never get used to them.

And the *dresses*.

The ones with all the ties and buttons hell-bent on not letting her breathe. Each stitch and clip of her corset was conspiring together to suffocate her, she was sure of it.

Your face and words will be just as important as your blades and swords during the Centennial, Poppy said.

Isla highly doubted it.

She had all the buttons down the back of her dress undone when she noticed a shadow in the corner of her room. A shadow that *flickered*.

In a moment, the dagger she kept hidden beneath her vanity was in her fingers, and she whirled around, only to be face-to-face with the shadow now as it rippled then settled.

Grim was standing over her, eyes trained on the dress that hung from her shoulders, not her blade.

"Hello, Hearteater," he said.

He had found her. She had foolishly hoped it would take him longer to figure out her identity. Or that her stabbing had wounded him enough to buy her a few weeks to figure out a plan. She knew it wouldn't kill him. She had just wanted to incapacitate him long enough to make her escape.

Now here he was.

Impossibly, in her room, in the Wildling newland. Here to kill her.

Before she could breathe, his hand was wrapped around hers—the one that held the dagger—so painfully that she flinched.

Isla grunted, adrenaline rushing through her, as she tried to wrestle herself away. That only made him angry. He growled and shoved her against the glass wall of her room. It felt nothing like before.

No, this time he twisted her arm painfully, so that her own knife was at her throat.

She writhed beneath him, heart pounding, arm flashing in pain. All he did was frown down at her, eyes fixed in a glare.

"You cursed hearteater"—he spat the word like it disgusted him—"dare to come to *my* realm, disguised, to assassinate me." The blade dug against her neck. She had sharpened the tip herself; it was so sharp that it immediately cut into her skin. She smelled her own blood. He was going to kill her, stab her just like she had him.

She wasn't like him. She didn't have power that would delay her death.

Isla flicked the wrist that he wasn't holding. The weapon disguised as a bracelet unveiled its spike. She stabbed it through his thigh.

The Nightshade ruler roared, and her dagger dropped to the floor—but before she could take her chance to escape, the blade to her neck was replaced with an invisible grip.

She choked as she floated in the air, clawing at her throat. He stood there, focused, as she was hauled farther up the wall.

Isla gasped for breath, but the grip didn't loosen. She saw stars. Could barely hear him as he said, "Was this your plan to keep me from the Centennial? To try and break the curses? Did you mean to make a fool of me?" The pressure gripped even tighter, and her vision went white. "Who are you working with?"

Isla tried to speak, but her words sounded like whimpers.

"How did you travel to Nightshade so quickly?"

At that, Isla glared at him, enraged, exasperated. How was she supposed to answer all his questions when he had her throat in an invisible fist?

Like he could read her thoughts, he bared his teeth—

And released her.

Isla fell to the floor in a heap, gasping, her fevered forehead and hands flat against the cold ground. Her unbuttoned dress slipped down her shoulders.

It took what seemed like a lifetime to catch her breath. Once she did, she gripped the dagger from the floor, scuttled to the corner of her room, away from him, that monster, that filth—

He had almost killed her.

Across the room, Grimshaw frowned. *Frowned.*

It was her turn to bare her teeth at him. She lifted the dagger in his direction, with a shaking arm. "Monster," she said, her voice just a rasp against the back of her throbbing throat. She spat at him.

He had the nerve to laugh. He took a step forward, and she had to force herself not to flinch.

"*I'm* the monster?" he said. Another step. "When Wildlings eat the hearts of men?" He looked down at her with disgust.

He didn't know, then, that the curse didn't apply to her. That was good.

Her hand went to her neck, and she winced. The skin there was tender.

Grimshaw followed the trace of her fingers. "Do I need to remind you that you *stabbed* me?" With a furious motion, he tore his shirt up to reveal an angry scar just inches from his heart.

Isla swallowed. Stabbing him had been a mistake. She had been panicked, acting on instinct.

Now she knew how foolish it had been. If he hadn't been her enemy then, he certainly was now. Grimshaw would be at the Centennial if he decided to accept the invitation. He would kill her.

The Nightshade ruler took a step closer. Prowled, really. His chin bent low, he looked at her with eyes dark as charcoal, squinted into a glare.

She scuttled back an inch. Another.

"How did you get into my realm?" he demanded.

Panic spiked through her chest. She forced her eyes not to dart to the floorboard where she hid her starstick. Her spine was drenched in fear, but she used all her strength to sit up straight, to meet his gaze.

The Nightshade ruler's voice became eerily calm. "How," he said, taking another step. "Did." Another step. "*You.*" The word held the same poison as his look as he regarded her, splayed against the greenhouse glass like a weakling. "Get. In."

He bent down low, eyes never leaving hers. By the time he was almost nose to nose with her, she used that fear as a cover. As she cowered beneath his shadow, she gripped the blade still in her hand.

Before he could take another breath, its tip was resting just below his chin.

Her nostrils flared. Her voice shook, out of not just fear now but anger. Anger at herself for being so weak.

"Get," she said, matching his tone. "*Out.*" Something in his expression flinched at the spit flying from her mouth, from the intensity of her words. Good. "Of. My. *Room.*"

She pushed the blade into his skin for emphasis, waited to feel the heat of his blood on her hand.

But before she could apply enough pressure, he vanished.

She collapsed fully against the floor, shaking like a child, wondering how the Nightshade seemed to have the same portaling ability as her starstick.

KEY CLICKING
INTO A LOCK

Isla startled awake. *No.* Oro was still clutching her hand, but he was finally sleeping, head leaned to the side. She didn't want to wake him.

A single memory was one thing. *Two?*

She had been so weak. Cowering. Now that her abilities were unraveled, she refused to ever feel that way again.

That day, Isla left her bed. She bathed in the small tub Ella had set up. The water was freezing, as Oro couldn't use his abilities in the Place of Mirrors to heat it, but she gritted her teeth against the chill. She put on the dark-green pants, long-sleeved shirt, and high brown boots Leto had made her.

Isla began her training.

The dirt was dead in her hands.

Isla sat in the middle of Wild Isle, fingers curled into the soil. The headache and voices hadn't gone away, but she forced them to the corners of her mind. She had been trying and failing to use her powers for nearly an hour.

"I don't understand," she said. "Before . . ." All she'd had to do was place a hand on the forest floor and it had exploded with life and color.

Oro was standing a few feet away, leaning against a half-rotted tree. "Raw power is like a beast. Without mastery, it lashes out unpredictably. Not always when you want it to." The memory of the rebels touching her skin flitted through her mind. "That's why learning control is so important."

"And difficult?" she asked, finally pulling her hands from the dirt.

"And difficult," he agreed. "Using it in a directed way requires intense focus."

Focus.

Her mind was filled to the brim, a thousand thoughts running rampant. She couldn't focus on a single thought if her life depended on it.

"It might," Oro said, and only then did she realize she had said part of that aloud. He bent down and grabbed a rock. He placed it in front of her. "Instead of just trying to force your power out, focus all of your mind and energy on this," he said. "Move it."

He got up and left.

She whipped around. "Where—where are you going? I thought you were going to train me."

"I am," he said.

She watched him walk back to the Place of Mirrors.

Her first impulse was to yell at his back that he had promised not to leave her, but no. She could do this.

Isla dug her fingers into the dirt again. She took a deep breath. Dropped her shoulders. She tried to focus on the sensations around her. The dryness of the ground. The heat of the sun warming the crown of her head. The slight wind making the loose hairs around her face go wild.

It took only a few moments for focusing to feel almost physically painful. Then it slipped, and thoughts poured into her mind like high tide. Worries. Anxieties.

Him.

No. She shut him out, closed her eyes tightly. Dug her fingers deeper into the ground. "I will get this," she said. "I will forget, and I will focus."

Would she, though?

Her powers needed a strong vessel. She was a half person. Walking through life carrying the weight of her past around with her.

She tried to force it all away. She sat and curled her fingers even deeper, until dirt ran far up her fingernails.

Nothing happened.

For days, she sat in silence, then went to bed frustrated. Some hours, she could hold her attention in small spurts. Others, distractions would dive in like vultures. Sometimes, the voice in her head was cruel. It was like there was a blade in her mind, feeling around for where it could hurt her the most.

The rock never moved an inch.

When Oro came to meet her that night, she was exhausted and frustrated. "I cannot just spend days staring at a rock," she said.

"Learning to wield takes time."

"How long did it take you?"

Oro raised a brow at her. "To master? Years for each power."

Years. She didn't have years. Her vision of Grim's destruction could happen at any moment. She wondered if she should have told the other representatives and rulers about it. Would they trust her at all? Would they believe she was working with Grim, like the woman after the drek attack?

He must have seen her face drop because he said, "It won't always be hard. One day, something will give. Some of a ruler's mastery of power is like a key clicking into a lock."

Breath caught in her throat. So far, she had felt no such key. It was another rejection. First the vault. Now this.

"Isla," he said, coming to stand in front of her. "What's wrong?"

"You don't get it," she said quickly. "Control was probably easy for you. You never knew what it was like to be *alone* in your incompetence, to not be in total and complete control of—"

"I killed someone," he said, and his voice was so serious, she tensed. "By accident, with my abilities. When I was a child."

"What?"

"Power usually develops later in life, but I set my crib aflame when I was just a few months old. My mother found me sitting in the center of the flames, just staring at her. They were forced to train me as soon as possible, as they feared I would destroy the castle with a tantrum. I was far stronger than I was supposed to be, as a second child."

"Stronger than Egan," she said, speaking his brother's name. The former king, who had sacrificed himself, along with all other rulers, for the chance of a future.

Oro nodded. "I was sent to the isles every few years, to master each ability. Control was the first lesson I ever learned as a child. Control your emotions, or you could bring the palace down. Control your heart, because allowing anyone access to that power would be ruinous. Control your tongue, because you are not the firstborn, and your opinions don't matter."

Isla's heart broke for the little boy Oro had once been. She took his hand.

"I did all of it," he said, staring at the ground. "There was another ability, though, that hadn't manifested in centuries." His eyes met hers. "Since I didn't know about it, I couldn't control it. I had been playing with my friends, having too much fun, and, before I knew what was happening, I turned an attendant to solid gold." His voice had become lifeless. The mistake still seemed to haunt him, centuries later.

Isla couldn't imagine the pain. If she killed an innocent person by accident, because of her lack of control, she would never be able to forgive herself.

"I felt such guilt and shame, even as my parents celebrated my power. The only thing that got me through my training were the people I met. I had—*I have*—really good friends."

He did? Isla felt ashamed that she had never even asked him much about his life before the curses.

"For years, I didn't wield," he said. "I was ashamed of my abilities. The guilt ate at me. I hated myself for a long time."

Tears stung her eyes. He couldn't know how similar she felt now, for different reasons.

"It was only after I was able to forgive myself for the mistake I made as a child that I could start living again." His thumb grazed the back of her hand. "You will get this, Isla," he said. "It might not be today, or tomorrow, but I will be here with you until you do. You are not alone."

You are not alone.

It was early the next morning when she snuck out of the Place of Mirrors, shoes crunching on the leftover glass on the floor.

She took the rock to the edge of the isle. Legs hanging, she watched the sun climb from the horizon like a phoenix, dying every day, only to rise again.

She closed her eyes.

For once, instead of trying to keep everything down, Isla dared her mind to do its worst, and it did. Her pain came flooding through the walls she had put up, and it hurt, *it hurt so much,* but it was almost a relief to have her emotions spilling out of her, instead of keeping them all pressed down.

She thought about her parents. Born enemies. A Wildling and a Nightshade. Life and death. They really must have loved each other, she thought, to not only get together . . . but also have a child.

Would they be ashamed of her? Would they think her weak?

She allowed herself to grieve the little girl who had grown up locked away like a secret. The one who had bled countless times to be the best possible warrior. Terra had taken the approach of breaking her first, so that the world would not. All she had ever wanted was to be accepted. To be good enough. To be *loved*—

It had made her the perfect person for Celeste—*Aurora*—to target and take advantage of. That name in her thoughts made her ache. Her *friend*. She had been her best friend.

Finally . . . she thought of him. *Grim*.

The memories were like pulling the stitches of a wound, making it bleed again.

After hours of letting her thoughts go wild, Isla took a breath and began to forgive herself for some of her mistakes. She pictured the little girl, sitting alone in her room, and thought, *She doesn't deserve this.*

When she focused on the rock again, she realized that besides her crown, her powers were the only thing that connected her to her ancestors. To her *mother*.

She closed her eyes and found the incessant, anxious, cruel thoughts weren't so strong anymore, as if letting them run wild had caused them to lose their energy.

Isla had never known her mother, but she wanted to make her proud. She wanted to help her people. She wanted everything that she had already been through to be worth it.

She wanted to be better, for that little girl sitting in the glass room.

Her arm lifted, her gaze trained on the rock.

Something in her chest thrummed, coming to life, then caught—a key clicking into a lock. She didn't dare blink as she outstretched her hand.

The rock began to vibrate. It squirmed beneath her gaze.

She reached back, then threw her arm forward.

It moved—

Along with the five feet of island beneath, which was carved out like a giant had dipped its finger into Wild Isle and dug a path right across it. Isla now had a clear view all the way to the water from where she stood. She was covered in dirt.

Isla was breathless. It was sloppy, and far from controlled, but she'd done it.

. . .

From then on, they trained from the first sunlight to the last. In the mornings, she and Oro ran on the beaches below the Whitecliffs. He said it would help clear her mind, and it did.

She practiced moving large and small objects. She practiced manipulating the dirt and rocks around her. Every day, he came up with new tests, new ways to sharpen her control. In the evenings, they had dinner together, just the two of them. Afterward, they would sit on the floor, drinking tea, trading stories about their childhoods, until Isla inevitably fell asleep. She always woke up in her bed, though, meticulously wrapped in blankets.

Since she hadn't been able to visit the Starlings after the coronation, Isla asked Oro to station guards at the Star Isle bridge, to prevent the attacks, and to provide any immediate assistance they might require.

"Consider it done," he had said, and it made her feel a little better about committing all this time to training.

Little by little, control became natural. The power within her, unruly and vast like the sea, began to sharpen into a single stream of ability.

Today, Oro pulled a blindfold from his pocket. "Is this okay?" he asked.

She nodded, and he tied it tightly around her head. "Bring back any memories?"

He laughed, the sound low and scraping the back of her mind.

"Did you want to kill me that day?" she asked, remembering how she had knocked the crown from his head with one of her throwing stars. How it had clattered noisily in the shocked silence.

"No," he whispered somewhere close to her ear, the shade of his voice making her arms prickle, even though it was scorching outside. "Quite the opposite."

"Really?"

"Really. That night, all I could think about was your annoyingly smug face when you took off the blindfold."

The corners of her lips twitched. "I was pretty impressed with myself." She frowned. "Though my demonstration wasn't nearly as impressive as your gilding." She said the last word carefully. With what he had shared with her, she imagined his ability to gild was still tinged with pain. Tainted. Hundreds of years had gone by. She wanted to take the pain associated with the ability away.

Was *that* love?

She reached up and moved the blindfold so she could see him. "You know," she teased, "for someone who can make anything into gold . . . I would think you would have already gifted someone you love at least a golden apple. Or a golden . . . blade of grass."

Someone you love . . . She surprised herself with the boldness of her words.

He tensed. She only got a glimpse of his surprise before he tugged the blindfold down over her eyes again. His hand did not leave her face. His thumb slid down her temple, and it sent shivers through her body. He sighed and leaned down to whisper in her ear, "When all this is over, I'll gild you an entire castle. Is that sufficient?"

"That's a little excessive."

Another sigh.

He stepped away, and his voice became serious. "Wielding power means feeling it around you, not simply seeing it. Even with your back turned, or eyes closed, you should be able to sense a threat."

A rock hit the side of her head, and she whipped around, baring her teeth. "Really?"

"It was a pebble. I'm reaching for a rock now. Focus."

Isla couldn't see a thing behind the blindfold, but she focused, and the tiny threads that had annoyed her so much previously began appearing, a million little links around her. She had blocked them out the last few weeks, but now they all came rearing back, especially since one of her main senses had been taken away. The more she mentally searched her

surroundings, the louder everything became again. It was like endless noise; she couldn't focus on anything—

By the time she sensed the rock, it had already hit her shoulder.

She winced. The bruise was sure to look like a storm cloud.

"Focus."

"I am," she said through her teeth.

Another rock hurtled at her. She sensed it and shot out her hand but missed. It hit her hip.

Isla felt something rising through her ribs, uncurling in her chest.

When the next rock hit her in the stomach, it unleashed.

"Put your arms down, Isla."

Were they even up? She ripped the blindfold off, only to see sharp blades made from branches, dozens of them, levitating in the air, all pointed at Oro. Rocks hovered between them, vibrating with intensity.

Isla gasped, and they fell to the ground with a lifeless thump.

She took a step back. "I—I'm sorry." She hadn't even realized what she was doing. Her power had taken over.

Oro stepped toward her. "I was never in danger."

But what if she *did* hurt him one day? When he was asleep? When she wasn't paying attention?

"You need to work on controlling your emotions when using power," he said. "But." There was a but? "That was impressive."

"It was?"

"It was focused, at least. A lot more controlled than when Remlar initially released your powers," Oro said.

"So, what you're saying is, I am getting more efficient at trying to kill you," she deadpanned.

"Precisely." His expression turned serious. "Emotion undoes control," he explained. "When you're emotional, your power has no constraint. It might seem like it makes you more powerful, but it can be dangerous. It can drain you completely until there's nothing left."

Isla trained harder. She tested the limits of her control, working to keep her emotions steady. Her life narrowed to just her, Oro, and her Wildling power. For over a week, there were no more memories. No more voice inside her head. No sightings.

The shadow of Grim had disappeared, and Isla hoped she never had to see him again.

ENYA

I want to continue my training on the Wildling newland," Isla said.

They had worked together for weeks. She was still far from a master, but she felt in control enough that she wouldn't be a danger. It had been too long since she had visited her people. She needed to make sure they were taken care of, then she needed to start preparing for the inevitability that Grim was coming for her. He had likely orchestrated the drek attack.

What was next?

"And I need help. I don't just want to bring them provisions. If it's possible . . . I would like to see if anyone would volunteer to teach them skills they didn't need before. How to prepare different types of foods, for example, and a dozen other things I can't think of. I don't really . . . I don't really know—"

"I know someone."

"What?"

"I know someone who will know some of what they will need," Oro said.

Her brows came together. "Who?"

"Do you remember Enya?"

Isla remembered the tall Sunling at the dinner with the dark-red hair and freckles. She hadn't looked unfriendly but not exactly friendly, either. Appraising, maybe.

"She taught Sunlings how to survive in the dark, after the curses. How to set up systems that allowed for crops to still grow, and life to still happen, even though we couldn't be outside in the daylight. She's good at coming up with solutions for problems that don't even exist yet."

That person sounded perfect. "It sounds like she has been a great Sunling representative."

"More than that."

She raised an eyebrow at him.

"Remember I said I had friends?" Oro said.

"It was the shock of my life."

He gave her a look.

"She's one of them?" she asked, incredulous. They hadn't seemed that close at the dinner, but she supposed it had been a serious function.

He nodded. "She's one of them."

The Sun Isle castle looked dipped in a pot of gold. Enya sat at the head of a long dining table, with her feet propped up on the chair beside her. Her red hair was tied into a braid. She had an orange peel and a knife in front of her.

They had met before, but Isla was suddenly nervous. She hadn't known that she and Oro had been friends. Would the woman judge her? Did she know about Oro and Isla's . . . connection?

He placed a gentle hand against her lower back, as if sensing her nerves. His touch was fire. It was such a simple gesture, but it immediately made her feel better. She looked up at Oro and found him watching her. His fingers flexed against her spine—

"It's a wonder either of you train at all, with how much you look like you want to bed one another."

Her eyes snapped back to the woman sitting across the room.

"Enya . . ." Oro said smoothly. "At least give Isla a few minutes before she's wishing I hadn't brought her to see you."

Enya shrugged and swung her legs around. She wore dark-gold—almost brown—leather pants, and a gold metal corset over long-sleeved

chain mail. Armor, it looked like, though somehow casual. Her metal-plated boots clanked against the floor as she walked over, beaming.

"Well, you look different," Enya said. Isla was wearing her training clothing, instead of her usual dresses. Her crown was in her room. Before Isla could say a word, Enya pulled her into a hug. Into her ear, she whispered, "He's almost intolerable, isn't he?"

"I can hear you," Oro said.

"Of course you can, that's the best part," Enya said.

"How—how do you know each other?" Isla asked. They bickered like siblings. But no . . . Oro's entire family was dead.

"Our mothers were best friends," Enya said. She stepped to stand next to Oro. Her height was impressive, but she was still short enough to lean her head against his shoulder. He did not so much as move a muscle in response. "Whether he liked it or not, that meant I would be by his side forever."

Oro sighed, but Isla could see fondness there, beneath his frown. "Enya has been one of my Sun Isle representatives since before the curses. She often acts as my proxy, and attends meetings in my stead."

"Like Soren," Isla said, almost to herself.

Enya made a gagging noise. "Nothing like him, Isla. But yes, a similar role." The Sunling got straight to business. "I hear you need help on the Wildling newland. Volunteers. Infrastructure. Some organization?"

"Everything."

"Good. I've taken the liberty of, and I hope you don't mind"—she looked to Isla like she really did care if Isla had an objection to what she was about to say—"rounding up a group already. All of them are respectful of all realms, including Wildling. They don't know what it's for, in case you don't approve, but—"

"Once she gets something in her head, she is relentless," Oro said.

Friendship, for more than five hundred years. Since childhood. Part of Isla wondered if she should be jealous, but she just . . . wasn't. Isla

was grateful that Oro had had someone he could count on when he lost his family. Someone he could trust.

Enya shrugged, not even trying to deny it. "I can get obsessive. At least I know that about myself . . ." She shot a wicked grin at Isla, then turned to Oro. "*Some* people are far less eager to admit their faults." She led them through the palace to a room that looked like it was used for strategy. There was a circular table inside, decorated like a sun. At its center was what looked like a pile of ash.

"Would you mind sketching the Wildling newland for me? I already have a rough idea of how many people we will need, and where, but it would be helpful to see."

Isla just stared at the pile. She turned to Oro, and he smoothed the ash into a thin layer. "Here," he said. He traced lines in the ashes with his finger, and a moment later they hardened, becoming three-dimensional figures. Interesting.

She dipped her finger inside and felt like a painter, with a canvas and paint that both came to life. There was a time when Isla hadn't known much about her lands, but she had explored them through portaling many times since.

When she was finished, Enya reached over and grabbed the map. It came off in her hands. She looked at it from all angles, then set it down again.

"Very well. We'll be ready in three days. I've organized my schedule so I can stay there for a week, to make sure everything goes smoothly. Does that sound acceptable?"

Acceptable? Isla wanted to bow at the woman's feet.

"It sounds perfect," Isla said.

"Oro tells me you have a portaling device?"

She nodded.

"How many people can it transfer at once?"

"I'm not sure. The most I've tried is two."

Enya waved away any worry. "No matter. We will go in small groups. We'll make it work."

Isla believed her. She would believe anything that came out of her mouth.

"Thank you," Isla said, and, unexplainably, her eyes stung. She felt such gratitude . . . Enya didn't even know her, and she was helping her. Her people.

"Thank *you*," Enya said, and her eyes sparkled mischievously. "For showing us that our dear Oro does indeed still know how to smile."

Enya had gathered a dozen volunteers. They all stood together on the Mainland, with supplies between them. She quickly explained the usage of the starstick, and the volunteers looked curious, but no one questioned it.

Isla drew her puddle of stars as big as she could, and they all barely fit inside. Then, they were in the Wildling newland.

One of the volunteers was immediately sick. "Sorry," she said. "I should have warned you about the nausea."

Isla had portaled them to Wren's village. The tall Wildling stepped out into the street within minutes. At first, she looked alarmed, but slowly, her expression calmed. She dropped the hand that had instantly gone to her blade. Isla realized then that she hadn't properly prepared her people for visitors.

"This is Oro, king of Lightlark," Isla said. By then, a few Wildlings stood in the streets, watching the volunteers warily.

At once, they bowed their heads.

Isla introduced Enya, then Ciel and Avel, who rarely left her side, then the rest of the volunteers. Her people stared at them with varying levels of wariness.

The volunteers looked a little frightened too. The Skyling to her right was smiling, but her gaze kept darting to the monstrous hammer one of the Wildlings carried on her back.

Isla stepped between her people and the visitors. "We are here to help," she said. "*All* of us."

She worked with the volunteers to hand out supplies from the Mainland castle stock. They would need more for the rest of the newland, but this was a good start. Wren proposed the Wildlings be temporarily consolidated into a few key villages, so help could be centralized. A vote was conducted, and every person agreed to host their neighbors for the time being. Many Wildlings gave up their own homes to the volunteers for the week they planned to stay. Lightlark chefs began teaching Wildlings how to safely prepare meat.

"I'd like to do this for the Starling newland too," Isla told Oro. "If Enya wouldn't mind." She had portaled there a few times, to check on them, in secret. They could use this just as much as the Wildlings.

Isla stayed up until the early morning speaking to her subjects, learning their names, their habits, their lives. She fell asleep on a bench in the middle of the modest village square to the lullaby of laughing, building, and sizzling cooking. Oro must have flown her to bed, because she woke up in her old room a few hours later and startled.

She gasped, tensed. She was back in this prison, this glass cage—

"Breathe, Isla."

Oro was leaning against her doorframe, nearly filling it with his height. His golden hair was slightly damp from rain, like he had only just walked back inside. Something about the sight of him made her feel like she couldn't breathe properly.

It felt criminal for someone to actually look good with limited sleep. Had he even slept at all?

She assumed he had just been at the village. "How are they?" she asked, her voice a little strained.

"Good. Enya has a new system for storing water and food and tracking who can wield."

"Of course she does," Isla said, not unkindly. She was in awe of the Sunling's organization.

It was hot and humid in the Wildling newland, and Oro had placed her in bed wearing her clothing from the day before. She began to peel off layers, without really thinking, until she looked up, and found him watching her, eyes slightly wide.

Isla held his gaze as she slowly removed her long-sleeved shirt, leaving her in just the thin sleeveless fabric she wore beneath. It clung to her skin, outlining her every curve.

She could have sworn she felt the room get even warmer, as he lost hold of his Sunling abilities. His control slipped, for just a moment.

Oro stared at her, and she watched him swallow—

He was the one to look away. "Are you ready for training?" he asked the wall.

She sighed. Training was the last thing on her mind at that moment. She wanted him in her bed; it would be so easy to just let the world disappear for an hour—

"Isla?"

Her name on his lips made her burn even more, but she said, "Yes."

"Good," he said. "Today, we're growing something."

POISON

Oro made an orange rose sprout from his palm. He reached over and put it in Isla's hair. "Your turn."

Isla sat and stared at her own hand for several minutes, without any results.

They were sitting at the edge of a stream. The sound of water rushing over rocks was a balm rubbing against some quiet corner of her mind. The stream was framed by hill faces on either side, some parts jutting out more than others, creating a curved, somewhat narrow river, making it impossible to see exactly where it led. Thin waterfalls fell off some of the cliffs, sheer and frayed like curtains of hair.

Isla had always wondered what it might feel like to swim here but had always feared Terra and Poppy seeing her wet clothing or hair and not being able to explain it. Visiting the stream at night might have been an option—her guardians at least gave her privacy when she was supposed to be sleeping—but then she would have been at the mercy of a forest draped in darkness that she had learned the hard way had no mercy at all.

The woods had not hurt her when she walked through it this time. No, the nature had leaned down toward her, as if the trees had wished to whisper their secrets into her ears.

"Close your eyes," Oro said. "Let your mind go still. Find nature in the world around you. Form a connection to it. Siphon that energy exactly where you want it. Think of the rose, blooming in your hand."

She followed his directions, but her heart was beating too fast. Her lids fell closed far too easily. She wasn't sleeping more than a handful of hours a night, and she was starting to feel it.

"Breathe, Isla," Oro said.

She breathed and started the process again, focusing her thoughts. When her eyes opened, she found the smallest of flowers blooming in her palm.

Before she could smile, the rose shriveled up and died, as if poisoned.

She was the poison. For she was born not just with the power to give life . . . but also to take it away. "I cannot be Wildling without Nightshade," she said, her voice brittle. "I will always be death. I will always be darkness."

"You decide what you are, Isla," Oro said. "No one else."

It might have been a comforting thought, if Isla didn't immediately think that she would only have herself to blame for her own mistakes, should she make them.

No one else.

Tears streamed down her cheeks, shocking her.

Oro was instantly inches away. "What is it?" he asked, fire already flaming in his palms, as if he was ready to reduce anything that made her upset to ash.

What was wrong? Why was she crying? All she knew was that now that it had started, she couldn't stop. A sob scraped the back of her throat.

Oro always demanded the truth. She gave it to him.

"I . . . I don't want to rule. I don't want my life tied to thousands of others. I don't want to have all this responsibility." She shook her head. "And I know that makes me selfish and awful, and I have no right to be so upset, but I am. I want a life, Oro. Worse than all that is I don't deserve any of this power. I am no one."

"You are not no one," he said steadily. "You are Isla Crown, and you are the most powerful person in all the realms."

She choked out a laugh that sounded more like a sob. "I am *a poison*," she said. "I have almost no control of these powers. They are wasted on me." She shook her head. "Take them. *You* take them, Oro. I'm serious. Use them. Steal them, with the bond. You open the vault."

Oro frowned. His anger seemed to burn through his previous hesitance at giving compliments, because he said, "Love, you seem to be under some delusion that you are anything less than extraordinary. Who did that to you? Your guardians? Did they make you feel like nothing you did would ever be good enough? Or was it him?" *Grim.* The woods heated with his anger. "Tell me, Isla. Did someone else break the curses? Am I mistaken?"

She clenched her teeth. Tears swept down her jaw, getting lost in her hair.

"Damn the vault," he said. "Damn the powers. You had nothing, and you broke the curses. *You* are the key. You see that, don't you? We were broken before you came. With you, we were saved. You are not a poison, Isla," he said, his voice filled with intensity. "You were the cure."

Isla shook her head. "I shouldn't have won," she said. "It should have been someone else."

Oro cursed. He knelt before her and gently took her face in his hands. "Is this what's been worrying you? Is this why you haven't been sleeping?" He had noticed, then. Ever since she'd had the second memory, she had tried her best to hold off on deep sleep. She rested only a handful of hours a night, not long enough for her to slip into another memory. So far, it had worked.

She didn't respond, and he studied her expression. Sighed. "I wish you could see yourself the way I do. You would never doubt yourself again."

Isla closed her eyes.

What if she tried to believe him? What if she put the negative thoughts to rest once and for all?

He was right. She had survived the Centennial. She had *won*. She had defended herself against the rebels. This power was alive, somewhere inside her, and she was going to claim it fully. She wasn't going to let anyone—or *anything*—use her like a puppet again. She had saved everyone else. Now, she just needed to save herself.

"Isla," Oro said.

He was looking down at the hands in her lap.

In them sat a blooming rose. Minutes passed, and it did not die.

For the first time, Isla sneaked out of the Wildling palace through the front door.

She had woken up early. It had been like almost every other morning in her life before the Centennial. Taking a bath. Tying her hair back into a braid. Strapping herself into her light-brown fighting clothes, fabric wrapped around and around her arms. She slipped on simple shoes.

Before she could lose her nerve, she stepped into the forest. Oro was right. She was more capable than she gave herself credit for.

She refused to be the person who believed in herself the least. She refused to keep being her own worst enemy, letting her own mind get in her way. It stopped now.

The weak girl who had been raised here, who had feared the forest, was gone. It was time to bury her for good.

These woods had never felt like home. She had trained around these same trees for years, her own blood had been shed here, but never had she felt any sort of attachment to it.

Until now.

Isla leaned down and took off her shoes. She took a step forward. The moment her bare foot hit the ground, a shock went right through it, up her leg, her spine, into the crown of her head and up toward the sky.

Oro had spoken about forming a link with her power source. A trust. A connection clicked into place. The woods knew her.

There was no wind, yet the trees rustled in greeting. She took another step, and the dirt trembled around her toes, as if power surrounded her. All thoughts drained from her mind.

She placed a hand against the nearest tree, and moss flowed from her fingers, rippling down to the grassy forest floor. The grass grew to a wild height that reached a branch that sprouted bright-purple wisteria. The flowers spiraled down the branch in bunches like bracelets, until the end, where an acorn grew, drooping like an earring. It became so large that it fell, right into Isla's palm.

This was what it meant to be Wildling.

She took off running. The world stepped to the side to let her through. Trees moved their branches, vines on the ground curled back toward their roots, animals waited for her to pass. A group of birds followed her path, their chirps sounding like encouragement. Flowers sprouted as soon as her feet left the soil, filling her footprints. A blanket of marigolds and roses bloomed in her wake.

She jumped into the air, hand outstretched, and a vine soared to meet it. She swung, careening through the forest, landing in a tree. She didn't stop, she kept running, and a bridge of branches formed before her, spanning across the top of the woods in a pathway.

It was a flow, a heightened state, a different awareness. She tasted the forest on the tip of her tongue, moss and dew and pine. A warmth traveled through her bones, as if parts of her that had been dormant were now awakening, a flower in her chest finally blooming under the sun. The woods uncurled at her proximity.

The forest was alive—she could see it now as she ran across its back. It was on her side. It would never hurt her again.

It was part of her.

She ran and ran, climbing higher. Nature raced to meet her every need, without her even having to think it. Her focus was complete, she had given all of herself to the woods. In that moment, they were one entity—she could feel it around her, a heartbeat, an ever-changing and flowing force.

It felt like nothing could break that concentration, until she looked down and saw Grim standing far below, watching her.

Isla gasped. Her focus fell, and her pathway along with it. She crashed through the treetops. A branch hit her back, stealing her breath. Her vision swam with shadows. Her head knocked against another branch, and the pain was blinding. She reached for anything to hold on to, but her fingers were sweaty, and she couldn't get purchase.

The forest would save her, wouldn't it?

Her connection had given out. She was a stranger, yet again.

No. Her powers would lash out. Surely, they would save her. Her Starling abilities. Wildling. Even Nightshade.

They wouldn't let her die—

She gasped, watching the ground rush up to meet her.

Just before she hit the forest floor, two strong arms caught her.

Avel was panting over her. Her pale face was flushed red and sweat dripped down her cropped hair. "You fall fast, Ruler," she said, out of breath.

Isla's eyes were wide. "You were there?" She had thought she had sneaked out of her quarters successfully.

She was such a fool. One drop, and her people would have been dead. How could she be so careless?

She had felt so in control. So powerful.

Control was fickle, she realized.

"We're always here," she said, and Ciel came crashing through the trees to land next to them. His face was flushed too. In that moment, they looked identical.

"Thank you," she said, though those words would never be enough.

Avel and Ciel took her back to the Wildling palace, and Isla watched the forest floor for any sign of Grim.

LYNX

By the time the volunteers left, the Wildlings had their homes fixed, a steady food supply, new skills, and resources. Isla decided to stay behind for a couple of days, to spend time with her people. She sent Ciel and Avel back to Lightlark, to help in Azul's search for the rebels. Oro had insisted on staying, not wanting to leave her alone, but she knew he had spent too much time on her already. She told him to trust her, and he did. On the Wildling newland, she felt safe.

She got to know each of the Wildlings in the village and ventured to other settlements close by. Wren took Isla into the forest and taught her a few Wildling wielding techniques, including stances, arm movements, and uses of ability. They spoke for hours.

At the end of one of these lessons, she caught Wren studying her, and said, "What is it?"

Wren shook her head. "It's just—we always wondered why you never came to see us," she said. "I know why now, but before . . . we were confused. Your mother is the only other ruler I've ever known, and she was always there. Playing in the village. Talking to us. She knew everyone. Everyone loved her."

Her mother.

"What—what was she like?" Isla asked, her voice small. She felt like a child again, clinging to any mention of her mother. Terra and Poppy almost never spoke about her.

Wren smiled. "She was extraordinary," she said. "Fearless. Reckless, at times." Her smile faded. "We grieved her immensely and hoped to

know you too. But . . ." She shrugged. "I suppose we did know something must be going on," she said. "We were curious . . . when you didn't take a bonded."

Isla's brows came together. "Take a what?"

"A bonded," Wren said. She lifted her arm, and a massive hawk with a stripe of orange on its back came soaring down from the treetops, landing on her sleeve. The bird blinked at her with its sharp eyes.

"Oh, an animal companion," Isla said.

"A *bonded*," Wren repeated. Isla didn't know why it seemed to be important to Wren, but if taking one showed that Isla was a Wildling, even though she hadn't had their curse or powers up until recently—

"I'll take one," Isla said. "If it's not too late." It might be a pain to transport the creature with her everywhere, and she didn't know how Oro would feel about an animal residing in the Mainland castle, but she would figure that out later. Gaining her people's trust was more important.

Wren seemed surprised. "You would do the ceremony?"

Isla didn't know anything about a ceremony, but she said, "Of course."

Wren smiled. "Then I will announce it," she said. She looked around, felt a leaf between two fingers, and studied the treetops. "Tonight is a good night . . . yes, tonight will work."

Tonight.

Okay. Isla could do tonight. "So . . ." she said. "I can pick anything? An insect"—that would be easier to carry around—"a bird"—could be useful to transport messages—"a . . . butterfly?"

Wren shook her head sharply. "A bonded reflects the disposition of a person. For *rulers*, it represents their power and strength."

So, Isla would be expected to bond with a larger animal. Great. That would make things more difficult, but she couldn't very well back out now.

"And *you* don't pick your bonded," Wren continued. "It's the other way around." Her eyes were fierce. "The bonded chooses you."

. . .

Isla was wading in water up to her knees. The ceremony, it turned out, was far more complicated than she had anticipated. This was a sacred part of the newland, Wren told her, the oldest part, born of seeds and creatures taken straight from Lightlark. It was a swamp, with grass that grew taller than her, water lilies as large as rugs, mud that seeped between her bare toes, and slick creatures that moved below the dark water, smoothing around her ankles.

She was at the very front, a leader who had no idea where she was going. She should have asked more questions, she thought bitterly, though they would have revealed how little she knew about her people and their customs.

She risked a quick look over her shoulder and saw the Wildlings silently wading behind her, faces illuminated by the fireflies they held in their palms. Their bonded were with them, swimming alongside, flying above, or watching from the thin strips of bare land at their sides.

One of them caught her eye, and she whipped back around. Her head was beginning to itch. She scratched just below the crown of flowers her people had made her for the occasion—purple larkspur, in honor of her ancestor, Lark Crown, one of the three original creators of Lightlark. She had spent hours sitting still as her people made bracelets down her arms from the rare varieties of larkspur, its color so concentrated, it stained parts of her skin purple, an honor reserved for a ruler. It was a valiant color. The color of a leader and warrior.

Isla didn't feel like either as she carefully stepped across the muddy ground, wincing anytime her foot sank too deep or connected with something solid. She was so focused on stepping around a strange clump of rocks that it took her a while to notice the wading behind her had all but quieted.

She turned to see the Wildlings were retreating, the light of their fireflies getting dimmer and dimmer.

Only Wren approached. "This is where we leave you," she said. Perhaps it was Isla's eyes widening, but Wren seemed to sense she needed more instruction. Her head dipped low. Her tone was sharp. "You don't come back until the morning. You don't come back without a bonded." Isla swallowed. What if none of the creatures wanted her? Wren handed her a bow and a single arrow.

"What is this for?"

"It's tradition, for a ruler's hunt for their bonded. For the rest of us, we simply must catch our animals, to show our worthiness. Rulers must put an arrow through theirs." Wren's eyes darted around nervously, and that's when Isla's stomach began to sink in earnest. The Wildling looked afraid.

Of what?

"I thought—I thought you said the creature chooses me."

"It does," Wren explained. "The creatures out here . . . if you're able to wound one . . . it's because it *allows* you to."

Isla took the bow and single arrow with trembling fingers. As soon as they were out of her hands, Wren gave a sharp nod, then began to hurry away, toward the others.

She watched them go, her confidence shrinking along with their silhouettes, until she couldn't see them anymore.

With a shaking breath, she turned around to face the heart of the swamp.

The swamp turned back to forest, though none of it was familiar.

She climbed out of the water and stilled—the trees lining the marsh . . . they were in the shape of people. Their arms made up the main branches, green sprouted from the crowns of their heads, their bodies formed the trunks, and their legs, the exposed roots that went straight into the dark water. They were frozen in strange movements, their faces carved into the wood. Some had mouths stretched far too wide, like they had been screaming.

Isla swallowed and kept moving. Wren had been clear. She couldn't return without a bonded. It would make her look weak, unworthy of ruling her realm.

The forest was quiet. She walked until she reached a massive tree that had tipped over on its side. Its branches were large enough to be entire pathways, rising into the air, going as far as she could see. They were covered in a thin layer of moss. She jumped, gripping the soft edge with her fingers, then pulled the rest of her body onto the lowest one. With a quick assessment of her surroundings, she followed the path, into the core of the tree.

It was far too silent. Isla had the uncomfortable feeling that there were eyes everywhere, watching her, yet every time she turned around, she was alone.

Alone. No one understood her, not really. Oro tried, he really did, but there were parts of her she would never let him see.

She wondered if a bonded animal would be able to sense every aspect of her—the good and the bad. The potential. The idea of someone or something seeing her for what she could be, instead of what she was . . .

Or maybe the creatures of the forest had already assessed her, and rejected her, just like the vault. It wasn't enough for *her* to feel the connection. According to Wren, the animal decided.

For now, it seemed, they had decided against her.

A rustle, and she turned to find herself facing a wolf, covered in moss and greenery instead of fur. Its tail was made of long reeds. Isla raised her arrow. Hope built in her chest. The wolf wasn't large, but at least it was something.

Before she could let her arrow loose, the wolf was gone.

Her fingers curled painfully around the bow. Slow, she had been too slow. Is that why it had run away?

What if she didn't see another creature?

Moments later, she realized that wouldn't be an issue. A spider with legs as tall as trees walked by, its body casting a thick shadow around

her. Isla didn't even raise her weapon. The spider was massive, but she felt no connection to the creature whatsoever.

She just needed to keep going, she told herself. There was a bonded for her here. She just needed to find it.

Her bare feet were soundless against the moss of the branch. Tiny flowers bloomed with her every step, painting the greenery. The occasional bird swooped down to study her, before flying away. She walked down the path as it curved into a forest floor shaded by a massive canopy of treetops. A giant rib cage greeted her, with flowers growing out of its bones—the remains of a creature so large, she couldn't even imagine what it had looked like alive.

Just then, a stag with branches for horns stepped into her path. It stared at her, tilting its head in wonder.

It was beautiful. Something in her chest thrummed to life as if welcoming the connection. She slowly raised her bow, clicked her arrow into place—

The stag stepped toward her, then froze. Its eyes focused on a place behind her. It shuffled back in fear.

What was—

A deafening roar shook the trees at her sides. Birds flew away, in the opposite direction. Hot breath heated her body as she was covered in spit.

Slowly, arrow still raised, Isla turned around and looked up. And up. And up.

A giant bear stood on its two feet, with a crown of horns that could skewer her in a moment.

Was this her creature? It would certainly mark her as a strong ruler. Isla released the arrow, trying her chance, but the bear knocked it away with a paw, breaking the wood in two.

Her only arrow, gone.

Isla wasn't thinking about the fact that she wouldn't be able to find a bonded now. Panic had taken over. She dropped the bow. The bear

roared again, getting close to blowing out her hearing, and Isla realized why Wren had seemed so intent on leaving the swamp.

Venturing to this area of the newland was a risk. Her people were endangering their own lives by letting her complete the ceremony.

This was the first step in them trusting her, she realized. A leap of faith. They believed she was strong enough to survive it.

So, she would.

The bear was too large, there was no hope in outrunning it. Just as it reached back its clawed hand to rip her to ribbons, she darted between its feet and ran up into the treetops. The bear couldn't climb; it was too heavy, it would break the branches. That was what she told herself as she climbed as fast as ever, purple rings of flowers down her arms seeming to glow in the dark.

She scurried up, higher and higher, and risked a look behind—

Only to see the bear's horns inches away, as it climbed after her.

Nature. She was in nature. Her heart was beating too wildly to form a connection to the woods the way she had before. She gritted her teeth, trying to focus. Her arm shot out, and she managed to make a few smaller branches fall in the bear's path, but it did nothing to slow it down.

She needed to break the branches below the bear. That way, it would fall through the treetops. She threw her powers out, but panic had clouded her mind, weakening her hold on her abilities. The branches creaked but did not crack.

The bear growled, and Isla began climbing once more. Heart echoing through her ears, she squinted through the night and saw that the branches became much thinner farther up the tree. She threw out her power, and one broke. It would have to be one of those, then.

Isla reached for the next branch—and roared as the bear's horns flayed the back of her calf open.

Her scream echoed through the woods, and she continued to climb, dragging herself up, one of her legs now useless, fighting her way to the top. If she could just make it a little higher. A little—

A crack. The first crack beneath the bear's weight as they traveled up to the thinner branches. It didn't seem to notice as its horns broke through the foliage, as it bared its teeth, chomping at the air.

Her leg was on fire; she couldn't think around the pain. She felt her grip on her powers almost completely slipping. She didn't have the strength left to break several branches. It would have to be one strategic cut. She stopped climbing and watched the bear get closer. Closer. She took a breath. In. Out. Attempted to focus as much as she could. Narrowed all her energy to one spot, one particularly thin branch, right in the bear's path. It kept going. It was just feet away. Then inches. She outstretched her hand. Nothing.

Come on.

Nothing.

She felt its breath on her face, saw its tongue in its mouth as it parted its teeth and roared—

Snap.

Her power split the branch in half, and the bear immediately fell out of view. Cracks sang through the woods as the bear broke everything in its path, and then there was a final thunderous echo as it landed.

Silence.

Isla panted. Too close. She risked a look down at her leg and tensed. The skin was split and she could see muscle. Blood was smeared across the tree. Other creatures would find her—

Just as she had the thought, two large eyes glowed through the night, in the tree across the way. They were looking at her. She scrambled back on her branch, arm raised, willing any of her power to rise.

The creature stepped out of the shadows, and Isla gasped.

It was a massive black leopard. Standing, she wouldn't even reach the top of its leg. It had bright-green eyes and teeth the size of her skull.

She looked down at her calf, then at the creature. It had smelled the blood. She was injured, an easy target.

It stalked toward her, head bent low, assessing. It looked ready to lean back on its haunches and strike.

She tried her best to focus on the forest, to form a connection, to beg it to protect her, but the pain in her leg had become a complete distraction.

The leopard should have been too heavy for the branches, but it leaped gracefully until it was right in front of her.

Isla's entire body shook as it leaned down far too close—and sniffed her.

She swallowed, hoping for the life of her that she smelled unappetizing. It opened its mouth, revealing its monstrous fangs. Then, it did something unexpected.

The leopard begrudgingly leaned its head down, as if bowing before her.

Isla blinked. Had it . . . had it accepted her?

She didn't have her arrow . . . the bear had split it into two. She couldn't—

The leopard made what seemed like an annoyed sound as it waited. What did it want? It leaned down lower, and no . . . it couldn't . . .

Did it want her to get on its back?

She was bleeding too much; she needed the wound closed soon. She fought to stand, gritting her teeth against the pain, and limped over to the leopard's side. She tried to climb up its fur, but she kept slipping, her blood getting everywhere. Eventually the leopard seemed to get tired of waiting, because it gripped the back of her shirt with its frightening teeth and flung her over. She landed painfully on its spine and fought for purchase, gripping its dark hair in her fists.

The leopard didn't give her even a second to get used to it. Before she could test her position, it leaped off the branch.

Her stomach was in her throat, her eyes burned against the air, she was floating off its back—then roughly landing again, her leg roaring in pain.

With a few jumps that made her want to retch, the leopard finally landed on the forest floor. It stalked around, head bent low, as if looking for something. Finally, it paused and tipped over to the side. Isla slipped off its back in the most undignified way imaginable.

Exasperated, the leopard motioned with its head toward something on the ground. Her arrow. Half of it, at least.

It was telling her to complete the ceremony. Somehow, it knew that to claim it, she had to shoot it.

The bow would be useless now. She leaned down, grabbed the broken arrow, and approached the creature.

It watched her warily.

"This is . . . this is going to hurt . . ." she said.

The leopard regarded her in a way that hinted at disdain. Great. Her own bonded didn't seem to like her.

Then why choose her? Why let her do what she had to do next?

Isla winced before reaching her arm back and putting all of her remaining strength into stabbing the leopard in the leg with the arrow.

It didn't even move or make a sound. It simply reached down, grabbed Isla by the back of the shirt again, and threw her behind its head.

"Hey!" she said, wincing. "Stop doing that! It—"

Before she finished her sentence, the leopard took off. She yelped and held on tightly, ducking her head down, lest a branch behead her. The leopard raced like lightning, jumping over roots, traversing around trees. The world moved so quickly around her, she buried her face in its surprisingly soft fur, until the leopard finally slowed.

It had brought her to the center of the village. She sat up as the leopard walked down the streets and watched as her people left their homes, staring at her in clear wonder.

It stopped in front of Wren, whose eyes were wide. Her voice was thick with emotion. "I wondered . . ." she said. "I—I didn't dare hope."

Isla slid off the leopard's back and nearly collapsed on the road, her leg covered in fur that had stuck to the blood. She looked from the animal to Wren. "Wondered what?"

"Isla," Wren said. "Lynx was your mother's."

REFLECTION

Her mother. This leopard . . . was once bonded to her. Isla was losing a lot of blood, but she turned and looked the creature right in the eyes. For a moment, the disdain faded, and she saw only unfiltered sadness.

The cat grieved her mother. That was why it had chosen her.

"We need to get you healed," Wren said. Other Wildlings rushed forward. There were calls for the healing elixir. "He'll follow, don't worry."

Wren was right. Lynx remained by her side. He was so large he couldn't fit through the doors of the palace, so she used her starstick to portal him into her room, which he didn't like one bit. He made a disgruntled noise before he went to the corner, curled, and sat down, making the ground tremble and taking up a large portion of her space. Wren pulled the arrow out of his leg, then put healing elixir on it. Everyone left her to rest.

Through the darkness, Isla saw his bright-green eyes gleaming. Then, as they closed, the world went dark again.

The next morning, Isla portaled to Oro and said, "I need to show you something." She took him back to the newland with her.

He now stood in her Wildling room, staring at the creature that was staring back, many feet above his head, baring its massive teeth.

"You have . . ." Oro was saying.

"An animal companion," she said. "A bonded." She motioned toward the great leopard. "His name is Lynx, apparently."

"Right." He reached out a hand, not seeming too concerned that the leopard could tear it off, and Isla watched as the leopard sniffed him. Tilted his head. Then leaned down, allowing himself to be petted between the eyes.

Isla was outraged. "He likes you more than he likes me!" she said. The leopard's eyes slid to hers, unimpressed, before looking at Oro again.

Oro smiled, and the sight was so beautiful, her hurt all but shriveled up. "What an impressive creature," he said. "I've never seen anything like him."

She frowned. "Not on Lightlark?"

He shook his head. "We have lions and tigers on Sun Isle, but none remotely this size."

That seemed to please Lynx. He made an approving sound, and Isla shot him a glare. "I told you this morning how impressive you were, and you turned your back to me," she said.

Lynx didn't even bother looking at her.

She sighed. "He was my mother's bonded, according to Wren."

"Ah," Oro said. He pressed his hand against Lynx's lowered head. "You must miss her," he said to the cat, and he made a thrumming noise.

Isla's throat worked. She wished the cat could speak, so she could ask him all about her mother. Now, though, she had to think of the practical. "I don't know what to do," she admitted. "There's nothing like these woods on Lightlark. I don't want to trap him in a castle . . . if he even fits in the hallways."

Lynx gave her a scathing look.

Fine. If he could understand her, let him decide. She stood in front of the leopard and said, "I can take you back with me, to the castle. Or I can leave you in this forest and come back to visit soon. I can start making a place for you on the island."

Lynx stared at her for half a second, before turning toward the window. His choice was clear.

A pang of disappointment shot through her chest, though she understood it was the right choice. She didn't know why she was so surprised. Lynx had clearly chosen her out of obligation, not fondness.

Oro rubbed his hand down Lynx's lowered head again before turning back to Isla. She watched him study the circles under her eyes. She had only slept a handful of hours last night. He sighed and said, "There's something you should know."

Upon their return to Lightlark, Azul and her Skyling guards were waiting.

"The rebels were spotted," he said.

Isla's chest tightened, remembering the pain of that night, being swept away under the water, so helpless—

Never again. She could use her Wildling power now. She might not be invincible, but at least she had a fighting chance.

She also wasn't alone. Ciel and Avel moved to her sides immediately.

"Where exactly?" Oro demanded.

"Their whispers were heard by our spies, coming from Star Isle. We tracked them down from the sky, but they just . . . vanished. Underground. We found more tunnels, but they all had dead ends."

Ella spoke from her place at the back of the throne room. "It's true," her attendant said. "I saw them for a moment. There are Starlings among them, I'm almost certain."

"Who?" Oro demanded. Isla remembered his threat. He would string any of them up across the Bay of Teeth. "Give me names."

Ella did not hesitate. "I didn't recognize anyone specifically. They wore masks. They must have Starlings among them, though, because no one else knows about the tunnels in the crypts."

Oro frowned. "Crypts?"

"They were built during the curses. To house the many dead. And hide us from the rest of the island." Anger curled in Isla's stomach as she remembered hearing about the abuse of the Starlings. "We kept them a secret, because of that. They're the only reason some of us are still

alive . . . and they're the only way to get past the creatures that took over the east side of Star Isle."

"What do you mean, creatures?" Isla asked.

"Monsters. No one goes there anymore, except through the tunnels to gather supplies. Anyone who goes too far . . . never returns."

Guilt swirled in Isla's stomach. She had been so focused on her powers and the Wildlings, she had abandoned the Starlings beyond asking Oro to send guards and provisions. She should have gone to Star Isle sooner. She should have made sure they were okay.

She wouldn't waste another moment. "Ella. Will you send word to Maren? I'm going to Star Isle."

"I'm going with you," Oro said.

She turned to face him and said in a low voice, "I need to go alone." He frowned.

"Not alone," she clarified. "Ciel and Avel will be there." Her Skyling warriors inched closer.

Isla imagined Oro would demand to speak to every Starling and interrogate them over any information about the rebels. That wasn't what they needed. That wasn't the way Isla wanted to first address her new people.

Oro nodded, but he didn't look happy in the slightest. He turned to Azul. "Did your spies hear anything else about the rebels? Has anyone else been attacked? Threatened?"

Azul shook his head. "No one else."

That couldn't be true. Why only target her?

If what Ella said was correct, that there must be Starlings among the rebels . . . that didn't make sense. They had hurt her. They could have killed her, which would have led to the deaths of all Wildlings *and* Starlings.

Something wasn't adding up.

Isla caught up with Ella before she left the Mainland castle. She felt awkward asking her these questions, but she had to know. "Are the

Starlings . . . are they disappointed that I'm their ruler now? Are they angry that I still haven't visited?"

"No. They know you were attacked and that you've been busy since."

Isla frowned. "They must resent me, though. They must—"

Ella laughed. Isla didn't think she had ever seen the Starling laugh before.

"Isla," she said softly. "All of us grew up accepting that our lives would be short and likely miserable. Few of us had any dreams. Or goals. Or hope. *You* gave us a chance to live. To most of us, you are a god. A savior."

As she walked back to her room to change into her training clothes, Isla repeated the words she had told herself in the Wildling newland woods. She was strong. She was the ruler of Wildling.

And the ruler of Starling.

Isla closed her wardrobe after getting a dress and froze.

In the mirror, there was Grim, standing in a full suit of armor. He held his helmet loosely in his hand. Ready for war.

She spun around and shot her arm out. A branch from the tree of her room snapped off, then sharpened into a blade. It stabbed right through the room.

But it was empty.

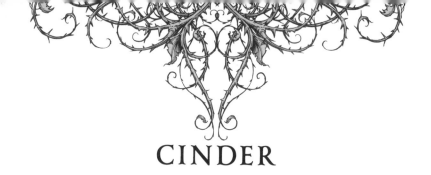

CINDER

Star Isle was in ruins. Its castle looked long abandoned. Towers lay in the sparkling silver dirt. Windows had been blown open. The pathways were covered in rocks and trash. Ciel and Avel flew above, circling so high up she had to squint to see them. Ella was at her side.

Maren, the Starling representative from the dinner, met them at the entrance of the crumbling castle. There was a little girl with her, with the same shining dark hair, wide eyes, and light-brown skin. "My cousin," she said curtly. The cousin stared at Isla and opened her mouth to say something a few times, but Maren gave her a look, and the little girl went quiet. "They're all in the throne room."

"Is everyone all right?" Isla asked. The Sunling guards at the bridge hadn't seen the rebels. There were Skylings in the rebel group—they must have flown in from another isle. Their motivations were a mystery. Why only target her? "Did the rebels . . ."

"We're safe. Thankfully, it seemed they were just recruiting. Or, perhaps, looking for something."

She frowned. "Why do you think that?"

Maren raised a shoulder. "Why else venture through the crypts? They're dangerous. All Starlings know that. No one goes inside them unless they're desperate."

When she walked into the castle, Isla's stomach plummeted.

Much of the room was empty, and everyone was breathtakingly young. Children, mostly. Only a few dozen looked to be around her age.

They watched as she walked through the crowd, to the front of the throne room. There were no seats, and because they were all standing, so did she.

"I don't know what I'm doing" was the first thing that came out of her mouth, and she almost instantly regretted it.

They just stared at her. There was just silence, until a voice said, "No one here does," quite cheerfully.

"Cinder!" Maren said, shooting her cousin a look. "Forgive my cousin, Ruler." The girl couldn't be more than eight years old, and she didn't stop beaming, even when Maren elbowed her side. Some people around her nodded.

"It's okay," Isla said, smiling at Cinder. She felt a little better . . . and worse. It might have been a relief to get here and see that someone had everything taken care of. "How many Starlings are left on Star Isle?"

"There are a hundred or so more," a man closer to her age said. He looked to be one of the oldest among them, with a strong jaw, messy silver hair, and white skin. "Give or take."

She frowned. "Did they know about the meeting?"

The man smiled without humor. "They knew." There was something in between his teeth that he was chewing, long and glimmering.

"Okay." Isla wove her fingers together and drew in a breath, straightening her spine. She wouldn't let opposition deter her; it was to be expected. First, then, the simple questions. "Where do you all live?" She waved a hand around the throne room. "Here? In the castle?"

There was a bubble of laughter somewhere in the crowd.

"*Some* of us do," Maren said, looking pointedly at a group of Starlings Isla could now tell apart from the others. Their clothes were nicer. They wore fine strings of constellation-like diamonds around their necks and wrists.

The nobles. Of course. She recognized some of them from the Centennial. There were eight of them in the group, all with different features, hair textures, and skin tones. Unrelated, it seemed. The last of their lines?

She turned back to the group. "And the rest?"

The man with the reed between his teeth lifted a shoulder. "We can show you."

Yes. That would be better. She still had so many questions. How did they source food? Did most of them know how to wield power?

Celeste—*Aurora*—had demonstrated her realm's capability for making weapons during the Centennial. Did they have stores of them?

Before she ended the meeting, there was something she needed to say.

"Your ruler was my friend, I thought. I took her power to save this realm." She lifted her palms. "I didn't want to be your ruler. But I will be what you need me to be," she said, surprising herself with her words. "Right now, things are difficult. Starlings died in the attack of the dreks. We are preparing for the possibility that it was one of potential future Nightshade attacks. Rebels were spotted just yesterday." She looked around. "I am here for you now, and together we will navigate this new chapter. Your ruler's death will not be a waste. Tell me what you need."

There were whispers. No one spoke up, though, not for a minute.

Then, Maren said, "What we need most is for you to stay alive. You gave us a chance at a long life. We intend on using it."

Isla asked Ella to stay behind and write a list of any immediate grievances and necessities. She figured the Starlings would be more comfortable telling someone familiar what they needed.

Maren and the man chewing the reed between his teeth—Leo—led her to where they lived. They were bickering in front of Isla in a familiar way.

Maren's cousin fell back to walk by Isla's side. She could feel Cinder's eyes on her, and after a few minutes of clear staring, Isla finally turned to look.

"Yes?" she coaxed gently.

"What's the king like?"

Isla blinked, startled. It wasn't the question she'd been expecting. No one on the island knew that they were . . . she didn't really know what they were.

Of course, the little girl didn't know that. As a ruler, Isla would obviously have been in contact with him. She was just curious.

"Brooding," she replied, giving Cinder a wink. Maren must have heard, because she snorted in front of her, unexpectedly. Within a moment, she was back to her rigid posture.

The little girl's eyebrows came together. "What's brooding?" she asked. Before Isla could respond, she yelled to her cousin, "Maren, what's brooding?"

Her cousin ignored her and started fighting with Leo again. "He's just . . . serious," Isla explained. There were a thousand other things he was that she wouldn't tell the little Starling girl. "Haven't you seen him?"

She shook her head so hard, her short, wavy hair hit the sides of her face. "No. Maren doesn't let me go on the Mainland and keeps me inside when he visits. What's the Mainland like?"

Isla frowned. "What? Why—"

Maren turned around and said, "That's enough, Cinder. Stop bothering our ruler," before taking her wrist and pulling her ahead.

They led her to a row of abandoned buildings composed of towering silver columns, broken stairs, and missing cobblestones.

Isla watched as Starlings darted into different structures, walking expertly over the smashed steps.

Maren, Leo, and Cinder turned into one of the buildings, and Isla followed, careful of her footing. Silver vines and leaves curled through every gap in the place. The ceiling was high and vaulted. Centuries before, it must have been a royal assembly hall. Now, it housed dozens of makeshift houses. Some were built of wood and stone. Most were a mixture of different fabrics and hides, pulled taut.

Isla stopped in her tracks. "This is where you live?" She couldn't keep the shock out of her tone.

Cinder studied her face a moment, then said, "What's wrong with it?"

"Go find Stella," Maren said, motioning an unwilling Cinder away.

"But I don't *want*—"

"*Go*," Maren said. Cinder pitched her shoulders back and walked away in slow, dramatic despair.

Maren turned to Isla. There was a sharp look in her eyes, as if she might scold her, if she wasn't her ruler. "Two years ago, a fire burned down where we used to live." She looked quickly over to where Cinder had wandered off to, still slowly making her way to wherever she needed to go. "This is where we went."

"This is where *some* of us went," Leo clarified. "Others went their own way." Someone called his name, and he nodded at Isla before jogging over to the other side of the structure.

Isla shook her head. "I don't understand. Star Isle is massive, and there aren't many of you left. Why didn't you simply go to a different set of houses? Or live in the castle?"

"The castle belongs to the nobles," Maren said. Isla was about to object to that when she added, "And the specters. They're too troublesome to live among . . . dangerous too." Isla remembered the specter that had entered her body, and had wanted to stay in there forever, and immediately understood. "Most of the residences are on the far side of the isle, and we don't go there anymore."

"Why?"

"Creatures took over, centuries ago. Anyone who goes east of the forest never returns."

The creatures Ella had mentioned.

Anger surged in Isla's chest. Aurora had visited the island every hundred years for the Centennial. She had known about all this and had done nothing. Of course she hadn't. She'd clearly never cared about anyone but herself.

Isla shook her head. This isle needed far more help than she had realized.

A thought prodded at her. "Why haven't you let Cinder leave Star Isle?"

Maren looked at her with what could only be described as contempt. "I told you all during the dinner. During the curses, the other isles treated Starlings as disposable. Our lifetimes are—or have been—just a blink compared to others'. We were often taken. Abused. Killed, even. Especially since many of us haven't learned to wield . . . there's not much in the way of protecting ourselves."

"Not anymore," Isla promised. "I won't let anyone harm any of you," she said, and she meant it, though she didn't know how she was going to keep that promise.

Maren smiled, but it was tight, like she didn't quite believe her.

When she returned to the castle, Oro was waiting for her. His posture was rigid, as if worry had hardened his body into stone. His eyes lit in relief when she approached. "How did it go?" he asked.

She let him into her room and told him everything. He listened and asked a few questions, but she could feel him studying her. Finally, he took her hand. Smoothed his thumb across it. "I'm worried about you," he said.

Isla frowned. She motioned toward herself. "Oro, I'm fine—"

"You're not sleeping well . . . it doesn't seem like you're eating well either . . . You seem haunted," Oro said. "What is haunting you, Isla?"

Her mouth fell closed. She wanted to tell him. She really did. But part of her thought if she said the words aloud, it would make the memories more real, and they would come at her at full force. She didn't want to remember. She just wanted them to stop.

Oro was right, though. She was being haunted.

It wasn't what was haunting her, but who.

She didn't want to think about Grim right now. The only time her thoughts of him stopped was when she was with Oro.

She took a step toward him, and she changed the subject. "I missed you, the last few days," she said, and it was the truth. Spending time with the Wildlings was important, but she had started to expect Oro's presence. He was always there for her. So patient when they practiced. Even now, he recognized the signs that she wasn't fine, when no one else did. He knew her.

Isla wanted to know him.

"I missed you too," Oro said, looking surprised the words had fallen out of his mouth. He frowned, clearly frustrated that she had shifted the conversation.

She stared at his mouth. *That mouth*. How was it possible that they both knew they loved each other, yet they hadn't so much as kissed?

Her heart began beating unsteadily. She wanted to know what it was like to touch him. She wanted to feel his heat against her bare body as they explored each other's every inch in the dark.

Before she could say or do any of the things that had raced across her mind, Oro pressed his lips against the top of her head, said, "You need to rest," and left.

She might have been more annoyed if he wasn't right. Her body felt like it weighed a million pounds.

That night, she was so exhausted, she fell into her deepest sleep in weeks.

BEFORE

Isla was a fool.

That was what her own mind told herself, anyway, repeatedly, its favorite lullaby. Terra might have judged her harshly, but Isla was her own worst critic.

She was trying to be nicer to herself lately, so she might have convinced herself she was *not* a fool if she wasn't objectively doing something astronomically foolish.

Her puddle of stars rippled before her, a slice of midnight. Her guardians were away for the day, visiting a local village. This was her chance. Before she could stop herself, she threw herself through, right into the Nightshade ruler's room.

It was just how she remembered it.

Black marble floors. High, vaulted ceilings. A bed with simple black sheets.

Only one thing was missing: the towering ruler who had pressed her against that very wall, and—

She shook the thought away and gripped the vial in her hand. She was here for a very specific, *very stupid* reason. A few days prior, the Nightshade had appeared in her room and tricked her into revealing her portaling device. Before he could take it from her, she had cried and begged him to let her keep it. It hadn't been one of her proudest moments.

Grim had called it his, and after witnessing his portaling power, she could only conclude that he must have enchanted it. Objects could be infused with power, she knew. It had a cost, though, shortened life, depending on how much ability was given.

Why had Grim made a portaling device? And how had it ended up in her room?

In the end—shocking her and likely him—he had disappeared, without taking it . . . which made her feel inexplicably guilty about having stabbed him in the chest. She didn't like to be in someone's debt, so she had brought something for him, as a peace offering.

So where was he?

Isla stood in the center of his room for half an hour, pulse racing, expecting to find a blade against her throat at any moment. Every minute that passed convinced her more how foolish this errand was. The starstick was *hers* now, but somehow she had convinced herself that him not stealing it from her was something to be thankful for.

Stupid. The more she thought about it, the more ridiculous it seemed. She was just about to form her puddle of stars and retreat to her room when she heard his voice.

It was joined by another. A man. She could barely make out their words. They were discussing some sort of strategy.

And both were getting closer. Closer.

Her starstick was lifeless in her lap. Of course it was. Of *course*. No time to try to coax it into working. She had to hide.

There was barely any furniture in the room. No desk to duck beneath. The bed didn't have enough room under it.

But there was another door. She threw herself through it just as the men entered the room.

A bathroom. All black as well, though here the black marble floor was threaded through with silver veins. A massive onyx tub sat at the center. Its spout was located on the ceiling, twenty feet above. Under normal circumstances, Isla might have marveled at it—it truly was a beautiful concept, a stream of water falling from such a height into a tub, like a miniature waterfall—but right now, it was her hiding place. She tucked herself into the basin and brandished the starstick.

It was dead in her hands. Something about this place must make it difficult to use, she thought, which she probably should have considered before portaling herself here.

"Stupid," she called herself as she willed the starstick to glow again. "Not you," she whispered. "You're brilliant." The enchantment still didn't light up. "Unless, of course, you don't work—then you're stupid too."

The starstick was still dim when the bathroom door suddenly creaked open.

Isla didn't dare take a breath. She closed her eyes tightly. Listened. *Leave, please leave . . .*

The opposite of leaving. The sound of something light hitting the floor. A pause.

One step. Another.

Then, the stab of something sharp right through her chest—

Isla screamed.

Her dress was soaked through. But not with blood. She had been pierced by the cascade of water.

The stream abruptly shut off, and Isla sat up, only to come face-to-face with a ruler with a horrified expression on his face.

"Have you lost your mind?" he asked, the words sharp and filled with malice. He was shirtless.

Isla quickly looked away. She held something out toward him, palm open. "I—I came to give you something. As a thank-you—" No, she had already decided she didn't need to thank him for not taking the thing she held most dear away from her. "—I mean, a peace offering. Here."

She threw it in his general direction, and the only indication that he had caught it was the fact that no glass shattered against the smooth floor. After a few moments of silence, she dared look back at him. He was frowning down at the vial, which looked laughably small in his hand.

The elixir was something the Wildlings had been developing. The bud of a certain rare flower, when extracted correctly, produced an

elixir that healed all wounds. There were only two problems. The first was that each flower produced only a tiny amount of useful nectar. The other was that the serum did nothing to remove pain.

"It's a healing ointment. For—" She motioned toward his chest and winced. "For that." Silence. He looked like a sculpture she had seen in a Wildling garden, perfect and almost scarless except for that massive cut right next to his heart. It was clear he had a Moonling treating him, or that would have been impossible. So, why hadn't he fully treated this one yet? "For the scar," she clarified, thinking he must be confused. "Listen. I didn't mean to portal here before; it was a mistake. I didn't plan on stabbing you. It was just—an instinct?" She spoke too quickly, trying to get the words out. "I came to offer peace. We don't need to be enemies."

I don't need you as an enemy was what she didn't say. *The Centennial will be hard enough for me as it is.*

The Nightshade didn't say a word as he dropped the vial into the sink. She winced as the glass shattered.

Then he said, "Get out."

The venom that filled his voice . . . He was disgusted by her. So disgusted, he had refused her gift. No, he had *ruined* it.

This was her fault. She was a fool to have wasted it on him.

She wanted to follow his command, get out and never come back. But, as insufferable as he was, she needed him to agree to peace. She didn't want to live looking over her shoulder, waiting for the Nightshade to exact revenge. "What do you want, then?" she asked. "What can I give you?"

He paused. He was already halfway to the door, and she watched the muscles in his back tense. Without turning around, he said, "You are incapable of giving me anything of value."

His words were like a slap to the face, because they were true. She was a powerless ruler of a steadily dying realm. But he didn't know that.

"Then let's settle it with a duel," she said, the words tumbling out

of her before she could stop them. "If I win, all ill will between us is forgotten. We can begin anew at the Centennial."

That made him turn around. He was glaring at her. "Only a fool would believe they could best me in a duel." He looked her up and down, his distaste only deepening.

She glared back at him, even as her confidence wavered. He was right. Why did she suggest this? It seemed impossible to beat him, but now, she had to try. "Wildlings are warriors, just like you."

His lip curled with humor. "No, Hearteater," he spat. "Not *just like me*." He picked up his shirt from the floor and slipped it back on. "Fine. When I win, you will never return here again. I've tired of you."

Demon. An easy promise to make. She slowly climbed out of the tub, and walked with as much dignity as she could muster in a wet dress, until she was right in front of him. He roughly took her hand. His hands were freezing. Enormous.

"My swords are in my room," she said.

A moment later, she was back in the Wildling newland.

Impossible. He really did have the power of her starstick. That was how he had appeared so easily in her Wildling palace, twice now.

"How—" she said, but he was dropping her hand like her touch was poison.

"I have more important matters to attend to," he bit out.

She didn't need to be told to hurry. Isla reached for her favorite sword.

"Let's go into the forest," she said. It was still day. She estimated they had about an hour of sunlight left until the Nightshade had to be indoors again.

He walked steadily toward the glass wall, toward the woods—then walked *through* it. Another rare Nightshade ability she had heard about but that seemed impossible until she had seen it with her own eyes.

What would she do with a power like that? She would never be trapped in her room again. She wouldn't need to sneak through the

very inconvenient and nearly too-small window like she did now, on her stomach, the bottom of her still-wet dress catching and ripping on the way out.

Grim stared down at her, unimpressed, then walked into the forest like it wasn't a mess of vines and roots that could suffocate him if they wished.

With every step the Nightshade took, the shadows in the woods seemed to lengthen toward him.

If Isla had Wildling power, would the plants reach toward her the way the shadows did for him? Did he notice that they didn't?

Grim whipped around and struck.

He would have sliced her right across the middle if she hadn't practiced every day for nearly two decades for the Centennial. It was one of the few times she was let out of her quarters and permitted to enjoy the castle grounds. She had thrown herself into it, relishing the way her body moved more and more deftly at her command.

Instinct made her own sword—her favorite, a blade half the size of the one the Nightshade was using—meet his own.

A clash, another, and the Nightshade advanced so forcibly, Isla wondered if he was trying to ensure she would never bother him again, not by winning the duel but by killing her. She was forced to retreat farther into the forest. Only knowing the maze of this slice of the forest kept her from tripping over vines. This was where she and Terra trained, almost every day. The forest might not listen to her, but she knew its every detail.

Grim frowned as he followed her. "This is a duel, not a scenic stroll," he said.

Isla tried her best to stand her ground. At the force of his next hit, she dug her heels into the dirt instead of retreating. She felt the strength of his blow in her teeth.

Maybe she wasn't as good at swordplay as she thought. What was she thinking, suggesting a duel?

He'd had five hundred years and active experience in battle to perfect his fighting. Where Isla had to think about each move, his every advance seemed mindless, simple, natural. She gritted her teeth, but he was expressionless, like this wasn't taking even a scrap of his energy.

Her skill was nothing.

A sharp sting across her arm—she'd been cut. She didn't dare look down at it; she couldn't afford even half a second of distraction.

You need to win, the voice in her mind said. *Grim is too strong to be an enemy at the Centennial. Or an enemy at all, really.*

But winning seemed impossible.

No—not impossible.

She knew the forest. That was her advantage.

Isla's mouth twitched. This forest was dangerous. And Grim was about to find out how.

"You look far too confident for someone with such a lack of skill," he said.

And he looked far too smug for someone who was about to be flat on his back, Isla thought.

Renewed with determination, she matched each of his blows, again, again, again, their swords clashing together like lovers, the sound of metal against metal echoing through the forest. The Nightshade didn't even seem to notice that they were moving in a specific direction. He didn't even look at the ground until it was too late.

Isla swept around a tree, inviting him to lurch forward in attack—

Straight into a slice of bog sand.

It decorated this forest in patches, strong enough to trap animals in its clutches.

And, apparently, surly Nightshade rulers.

Once he was in it to his ankles, Grim couldn't move his legs. He made to move, then startled, staring down at his feet and still annoyingly blocking her advances. He wasn't even looking! When he realized he would no longer be able to move his feet while they dueled, he bared his teeth at her.

"You know I could portal out of this," he said. "If I believed it would in any way impact my chances of winning."

"I believe that would be considered cheating."

Grim gave her an incredulous look. "And trapping me in this vile substance isn't?"

Angry, he swung his blade harder than ever, and she met him stroke for stroke, her feet just inches away from the bog sand's clutches. The tree hunched above them was trimmed of some of its leaves as their blades clashed at an impossible speed. Isla was afraid to blink lest she miss one of his blows, and by the set of his eyes, Grim almost looked . . . *impressed* that she could keep up.

Then, without warning, he reached his other hand between their blades, grabbed her by the front of the shirt, fell back, and pulled her atop him.

She would have been skewered on his sword if he hadn't been holding her up with a firm hand against her chest. His blade's tip was positioned right against her heart.

He had won.

"I don't ever want to see you in my lands again," he said.

Then, he vanished, leaving Isla to fall face-first into the bog sand.

GOLDEN ROSE

Isla awoke on the floor, having fallen out of bed. Sunlight streamed through the gap in her curtains.

No. Another dream had turned into a memory. They were getting stronger. Longer.

They had dueled. The match they'd had during the Centennial hadn't been their first. Grim's skill hadn't been nearly as impressive then. She'd been so pleased with herself, being able to best an ancient warrior. But no . . . she knew now he had clearly been holding back. He'd wanted her to look strong in front of the others, so they would think twice about attacking her.

Her hands curled into fists as the realization settled into her mind. "The demon let me win."

If Isla couldn't stop the visions, she could at least replace them— make new memories to erase the past. Erase *him*.

Oro and Isla had just finished training. She had managed to roll a boulder across a field without touching it at all. The heavier the object, the more concentration it required. She'd rushed to move the rock, to finish the lesson early. Because afterward—

It was time to do something bold. Make clear exactly what she wanted.

She had just taken a shower. Her hair was still damp. She had summoned Oro to her room, and when she stepped out of the bathroom, he was waiting, freshly showered himself.

Isla might have laughed at the expression on Oro's face if she wasn't so nervous. She had never seen him go so still. She wasn't sure he was even breathing.

His gaze was a brand as it traveled up her bare legs, to the red lace that left little to the imagination.

Oro rose from the seat he had been waiting on, his movements slow, like he was using every ounce of his well-practiced control. He walked one, two, three steps, eyes never leaving hers, until he was before her. "Are you trying to torture me?" His voice was thick.

She repeated the same words as before. "Yes. Let me?"

He didn't even smile at her attempt at humor. He just stared, then closed his eyes tightly. "*Isla,*" he said, her name a prayer.

She waited for him to sweep her off her feet, to crush her against the wall, to feel every part of him against every practically bare part of her.

But he did not move an inch.

Isla shook her head. "I don't understand. I can feel it. You love me. Why—why won't you touch me?" She had tried to touch him multiple times—had tried to kiss him, to get close to him, to make clear what she wanted. Every time, he had rejected her. The realization came at her like a sword hilt to the temple. "Are you—are you not attracted to me?"

He said nothing, and she suddenly felt ridiculous. Of course he could love her without wanting her in that way. Various shades of love existed. She was so stupid, so foolish for just *assuming*—

"I'm sorry, I—"

Oro had her pressed against the wall before she could say another word. He was looming over her, eyes filled with a burning intensity that made heat pool everywhere. "Isla," he said. "*Attracted* does not begin to describe what I feel for you."

She swallowed, and his eyes went to her throat. He reached out a tentative hand and traced a line over her collarbone. Lower. Down her chest, across the mark where an arrow had pierced her heart.

"Every time I see you, I think the gods must play favorites. Every time you're near me, I am overcome with the urge to bed you, to have you, again and again. I want to devour every inch of you, until you're all I taste, until you are shaking with pleasure in my arms. *That* is what I want."

Isla had never wanted a person more in her entire life. She pressed against him. "Then do it. All of it."

She glanced down, and the evidence of his want was clear. It made her heart race to an impossible speed. With shaking hands, she unbuttoned the clasp of her top until it dropped. He looked at her like he wanted to spend a week with her, locked in this room.

But he only closed his eyes and said, "Isla. I want everything with you. But not now."

"Why not?" she asked, tears hot behind her eyes. She willed them not to fall, knowing she looked pathetic enough already.

His expression softened. "You're struggling, love." He took her hand. "I feel like I'm watching you fade, day by day, and I don't know what to do." He surprised her by going down on one knee, his gaze never leaving hers. The king of Lightlark was kneeling before her. "Tell me how to help you. I'll do anything. Give you anything. Just tell me."

The tears fell freely now. "I can't," she said.

He rose and cupped her face, smoothing her tears away with his thumbs. His palms were hot as coals, and she leaned into them. "Whatever it is, you can tell me. You are not alone. You do not face the world alone anymore."

Isla closed her eyes. It was hard to swallow; it was like her throat was swollen and raw, trying to keep the words down.

This secret . . . It was too much to bear. The memories were trickling in against her will; she was defenseless against them. Isla had told Oro she trusted him. That was true, wasn't it? If she couldn't tell him what was happening to her, then who?

Her eyes were still closed as she said, "I'm starting to remember."

She felt him stiffen in front of her. She opened her eyes, and Oro . . . his gaze was fire. He was angry, so angry—

Isla squirmed beneath his hands. Was he mad at her? She suddenly felt deeply ashamed for some reason, laid even more bare than she already was. "I'm sorry," she said, and she wasn't sure why.

Oro's eyes softened immediately. "Isla, don't ever apologize for something that isn't your fault." A muscle in his jaw shifted. "This is his fault."

She understood now. Oro looked murderous because he wanted to kill Grim. He was the reason she was suffering.

She nodded. She agreed, and she hated him, *hated* him. She needed Oro to know that. "I despise him," she said, words shaking in her mouth. "He is a monster, and I . . . I don't want to remember." She shook her head. "I'm trying my best to block them out, but with my powers untangled . . . I tried not to sleep, and it worked, for a while. But . . . I think things are starting to remind me of him, unlocking those memories. He went into my room during the Centennial; I don't think that helps. He was in my *mirror*. It's driving me mad. All I see when I close my eyes is *him*—"

"Move into my room," Oro said immediately.

Isla blinked. "What?"

"He's certainly never been there." Lest she suggest moving into any other room that wasn't his, he added, "It's the most protected place in the castle, should he be trying to reach you through other means. You can take it. I'll stay somewhere else."

Isla didn't want him to stay anywhere else. The fact that she was wearing only lace in front of him was proof of that. But Oro wouldn't hear of it.

By that afternoon, Oro had her stuff moved into his chambers and his moved out.

The memories stopped after Isla moved into Oro's room, and she was able to peacefully sleep through the night. It was as if the proximity to

the king's belongings, sleeping in his *bed*, was enough to smother all thoughts of Grim. She found a drawer that had been forgotten, filled with his clothes, and claimed one of his shirts. Then another. And another. They were massive and comfortable, and wearing them to bed helped her feel less alone.

At training, she was better able to focus. Every day, she grew stronger, her power inching forward, the blade within her sharpening.

What had started as a reaction to an attack, a desperation to open the vault and prepare against the next crisis, had started to become . . . fun.

They were sitting in a forest on the Wildling newland, Lynx watching them as they trained. She visited the leopard often, bringing gifts, all of which he rejected. She would wait at the edge of the forest surrounding the Wildling castle, offering in hand. Eventually, he would prowl out to meet her, sniff what she had brought, and walk back into the woods.

She was convinced the only reason Lynx had stuck around this long today was because Oro was here.

They were telling each other what to make, back and forth.

"A yellow rose," Oro said, and she made it bloom in front of them.

"A sunflower," she told him, barely containing a smile. He rolled his eyes and made it.

"A twenty-foot vine," he said, and she made it hang from a tree, so long it wrapped in spirals on the ground.

Her lips twitched.

"What?" he asked, voice flat.

"A—a—" She couldn't say the words before bursting into laughter. And it really wasn't that funny. Truly, it wasn't funny at all.

But she didn't know how long it had been since she had truly laughed. A week had gone by without any memories. She felt lighter. Freer.

Oro seemed to like her laugh. He tried not to smile and failed, until his face was overcome with it. And she was no match for the brightness

of that smile, like sunlight was filtering through his skin. His warmth grew, engulfing her like a blanket.

"What is it, Wildling?" he said, shaking his head as he watched her try to regain her composure.

She closed her eyes. Looking at his face would just make her laugh more; she was suddenly stuffed with joy. With happiness. With . . . love.

Sitting here, in front of him. Sharing a power between them. His patience, as he had helped her learn.

She breathed slowly, trying to stop herself from going into a fit again, and said, "A—" She laughed silently, shoulders shaking. "A golden blade of grass."

She heard Oro sigh in his long-suffering way. She heard shuffling in front of her.

Her eyes were still closed when he lifted her hand, opened her fingers, and left something in her palm.

It was not a golden blade of grass. Or a golden apple.

It was a tiny rose, turned into solid gold. Petals frozen. Bulbous and beautiful. It was perfect.

Her lips parted as she looked up at him. He was smiling.

Isla had never seen him look so happy.

"Oro," she said.

"Yes, Isla?"

Emotion made her throat go tight. Her voice was thick. "Everyone I've ever loved has betrayed me—"

His eyes gleamed with flames, the heat of his emotions burning the space between them.

"Except for you."

She stood and walked in front of him. For the first time, she was towering over him from his place on the ground. He looked up at her, the sun illuminating the sharp panes of his face. He was beautiful. She'd known it from the first time she saw him—though she wouldn't have admitted it to herself back then—but now she saw more. The set of his

eyebrows, the way they were always straight, unless he was smiling. The way his frown seemed deep-rooted, his mouth nearly perpetually turned down. Except when he was with her.

"I want to burn all of them alive," he said simply. "Everyone who ever hurt you. I want to watch them go up in flames."

She raised an eyebrow at him. "That's not very noble of you."

"I don't care."

By the set of his jaw, she knew he was thinking about one person in particular.

"Ask me," she said.

"Ask you what?"

"Ask me if I still love him." During the Centennial, she had developed feelings for Grim. When it mattered, though, he couldn't access her abilities. Still, Oro knew she was starting to remember their history. He must have wondered if it had changed anything.

Oro grimaced at the ground. "It isn't a fair thing to ask."

"Ask me anyway."

He paused. "You don't have to answer."

"I know."

"Do you love him?"

She didn't hesitate. "No."

Isla could see the little signs. She recognized them now. His shoulders settling. Jaw loosening. Relief.

She was telling the truth.

Isla didn't love Grim. Perhaps she had, at one time. But that was in the past. Now she was completely focused on the future.

He was her future. He was her friend. The person she trusted. The person she was happiest with.

He finally stood, towering over her. She looked up at him and said, "Oro. Oro—I love you."

He knew that. He had known for months, thanks to the thread between them. She had almost said the words before.

He went very still anyway.

Then he broke out in the most beautiful smile she had ever seen. "Say it again," he said. "I missed it."

"You did not," she said, laughing. Then she took a step closer to him. "I love you."

He closed his eyes, like he was taking every word in, committing this moment to his mind. "Again," he said, like they were in training.

She took a step closer and whispered it right in front of him. "I love you . . ." she said. "Even though you've never taken me on a date . . . even though you've never so much as kissed me."

Oro opened his eyes and peered down at her. "You want to be kissed, Wildling?" he said.

She shrugged. "Among other things."

He shook his head at her, but then he raked his long fingers through her hair, cupped her by the back of the neck—

And kissed her.

His lips were hot as flames. Their first kiss was soft. Loving.

Their second was not. He pulled back to look at her for just a moment, then seemed to forget they were in front of Lynx, who made a sound of distaste. In a quick motion, he lifted her to his height by the waist, turned, pressed her against the closest tree, and kissed her desperately.

He parted her lips, and she could taste him—he was summer and heat and fire, and when he bit her bottom lip, she groaned into his mouth. She couldn't get enough of this; her heart felt like it might burst inside her. Her chest tightened as she felt his warm, muscled body pressed against hers.

His grip kept her firmly against the tree, but his thumbs swept under her shirt, making circles against her lower stomach.

Fire flowed through her veins at his every touch. She lowered her head and brushed her lips against his neck and kissed against his pulse.

It quickened—his hands suddenly curled beneath her, and she locked her legs behind his back.

Want bloomed deep within her. His eyes were rooted to hers, flashing with intensity. She reached for his shirt—

Lynx growled in warning.

Oro laughed silently, then carefully took the hand that had tried to undress him in his. He pressed their intertwined knuckles against the tree, next to her head.

His lips swept down her neck. "I love you too," he said against one of her collarbones, and then he kissed her again.

WILDFLOWER

The kiss had been its own sort of key. It unlocked emotions she had pressed down deep within her soul. Positive ones, for once. She hadn't realized how much good had been buried beneath the gloom. Love was a wildflower, she realized. It grew best in secret.

Love made her bold. "I have an idea," she told Oro the next morning. "Two ideas, really."

"Tell me."

"First—I want to celebrate Copia. Here, on Lightlark." She imagined Oro had heard of it when Wildlings lived on the island. It was a day of celebrating abundance and creation. Isla had only ever seen the celebrations from far away, as a figurehead, but even with her people in a weakened state, she remembered flowers in hair, trees growing fruits, music, and dancing. "Not to the full extent, of course. But just with a dinner. Here, in the castle gardens." She shrugged. "It seems like a good way to introduce the people here to the idea of Wildlings potentially coming back. And to showcase my powers in public. Show the rebels that I'm not afraid of them."

"Would you want to bring your people here for the celebration?"

Isla had considered it. None of the Wildlings alive had ever stepped foot on the island. And the people here were . . . unwelcoming, to say the least. She didn't want to bring the Wildlings to a place where they would be ogled, and judged, and potentially harmed. Especially with the rebels still at large. "No. Not yet."

"What is your second idea?"

She smiled. "When my people do end up being ready to come

back . . . I want them to have a place to come back *to*. I want to make a place for Lynx, if he ever decides he likes me."

Oro flew them to Wild Isle. She started with a hand against the ground. A rosebush, blooming from the dead dirt. "I want us to bring it to life again," she said. She reached for his hand. "Together."

Using her power, Oro made an oak. Another. Isla turned to a mummified tree and ran her fingers up its peeling bark. At once, it exploded in color and leaves. She went around, painting Wild Isle in vibrant hues, shades of green and red and purple and blue and brown. Flowers, everywhere, in every shape. Trees, huddled together like gossips, their branches scraping in the wind.

By the time the sun came down, part of the isle was alive, so alive. She beamed.

Isla had created hundreds of little lives, little threads, all reaching toward her, glimmering, shining.

And—as if it had never happened before, like the Nightshade power in her had withered away—nothing died.

Every time Oro used her power, she felt it, like a hand stroking down the rivers of her ability. It was an intimate experience. He had used her power before but never for this long. Today, they had worked for hours. By the time they reached his room, she had never felt closer to him.

"Tonight . . . stay with me," Isla said.

Oro looked down at her, and she didn't think he had ever looked so exhausted.

"Nothing needs to happen," she said, her voice a smooth whisper. "We can talk. We can sleep. We can dream, side by side. That's all, unless you want more." And, even though she wanted him now more than ever, it sounded like more than enough.

"This is what you want?" His eyes searched hers. "This will make you . . . happy?"

She nodded.

He entered.

Isla went to the bathroom to change. She wore what she had been wearing to bed every day for the last week or so: one of Oro's shirts. He had a lot to spare. They all smelled like summer, and soap, and faintly of citrus.

She didn't even really think about it until she stepped out of the bathroom, and Oro looked at her as if she had stepped out naked.

He looked almost horrified.

"I—I'm sorry." She moved one foot back into the bathroom. The marble was cold beneath her feet—everything was cold compared to him. "I found them in your room. I didn't think you'd mind. I can change."

Oro laughed.

He *laughed*.

His hand slid slowly down his face, then curved to the back of his neck. He groaned. His voice was dark as midnight as he said, "Don't you dare. Don't you dare wear anything else." She had never heard him so . . . possessive before. It made the bottom of her spine curl, made her think about them, and the bed, and the fact that they would soon be in it, together—

Any hope that something would happen between them died when Oro changed and slipped beneath the covers before she could diligently study what he wore to bed. Then, the flames of the room were extinguished.

She squirmed beneath the covers. Her nerve endings were on fire; she felt *everything*. The sheets against her legs, her shirt against her chest, prickling with need, the fabric of that shirt riding up, nearly showing the lace she was wearing underneath.

Oro was silent behind her. Warm, as always. She tried to even her breathing. Suddenly her heart was beating far too quickly.

Isla slowly smoothed a leg across the sheets until it met his, scalding her in heat that dropped right through her.

He was there. He was always there for her, wasn't he?

"Oro." The word was swallowed by the dark silence of the room. Seconds passed.

"Isla," he said, his voice free of sleep, like he had been awake this entire time as she had shifted uncomfortably with need. Need for *him*.

She turned around to face him. "I—" she said. She closed her eyes tightly. What was she doing?

He reached a hand to her shoulder, likely to comfort, but she wanted more than *comfort*. She immediately placed her hand over his.

She found his amber eyes in the darkness, clouded with concern. No, she wanted them to be filled with something else. She looked him right in the eye as she said, "I need you."

Oro stilled. He swallowed. His gaze sharpened, suddenly on high alert.

"Isla—"

"No." She shook her head. "Please, don't tell me that it will confuse me, or it's the wrong time." She shifted closer. "I want you. Right now. I *need*—"

Intimacy. Pleasure. Those were the words she didn't say, but the way his eyes closed for just a moment, his jaw clenched, told her he knew her meaning.

Her body shifted closer, until the hand that he had placed on her shoulder fell to her hip. She slid the sheets down, so he could see her, all of her, in his shirt.

He took in her every inch, and his hand clenched the excess fabric at her side, as if he was physically stopping himself from touching her skin.

"Touch me. Please," she said.

His own rules were forgotten.

She wasn't sure she was breathing as his fingers slipped up her leg, then beneath the waist of her underthings. His hand curled around her backside, his thumb stroked the inside of her thigh, so close, so *close*—

Isla looked from the sight of her body nearly exposed, his hand on her, to him, now just a few inches away. In his eyes, she saw torture.

She frowned. "Oro, if you don't want—"

Before Isla could finish, he flipped her around and gripped her hips. She gasped as he pulled her toward him, up against him and the proof that he wanted this just as much as she did. The pulsing heat within her became a wildfire. She arched her back and ground against him, making him curse.

Oro slid his hands up to her waist. He leaned down to whisper in her ear, in a deep voice that scraped against the back of her mind. "Knowing you've been wearing my shirts to bed, Isla," he said, "it drives me mad." His lips touched the edge of her ear. "That's what I'm going to think about when I'm alone." He pulled the shirt up, exposing her underthings. He looked and drew a sharp breath, taking in the lace. "You. In my clothes."

Her heart was going to break out of her chest. They both watched as his fingers slowly, slowly, too slowly, slid their way down to where she wanted him most. Finally, he reached her, and she closed her eyes tightly as he found the proof of her own desire. He stilled, his hand right there, right *there*—

She froze too, wondering if she should be embarrassed. . .

"Do you want this?" he asked.

She looked over her shoulder at him. She had never wanted anything more. "Yes."

He was a man unleashed. Suddenly, his shirt and her underthings were on the floor, and his hands were on her chest. In the dark, all her focus narrowed to the heat of his touch as his calluses lightly brushed across the most sensitive parts of her skin. She seemed to melt against him, making all sorts of sounds as he swept his knuckles down her bare stomach and murmured in her ear. "Tell me what you like, love," he said. "Show me."

"Here," she said, squirming. She found his hand and started to guide it down again. "Please."

But his fingers were long and practiced and needed little direction, even though he seemed to enjoy the sight of her hand over his. When he was right where she needed him, she reached back to weave her fingers behind his neck and said, "Don't stop. Don't you dare stop."

His lips were right over hers; his breath was hot against her skin, and he groaned as she began moving on him.

Her head fell back and she made a sound that he seemed to like, because he kissed across her pulse. He knew where to touch her, where to linger, where to explore.

It only took moments for her to be panting and at the edge of the world, and nothing had ever felt this good, this sweet. "Oro, I—" she said, because she could feel sparks traveling up her spine.

"Not yet," he said. He kept going, and she gasped as his teeth scraped lightly up her neck, until he reached her ear. "I want you so much I think it might actually kill me," he whispered, before he curled his fingers, and the world shattered around her. He held her close, both arms tight around her body. "Never doubt that."

She never would again.

ILLUSION

Isla fiddled with the petals on her bodice. That night was Copia. She had helped the Starling tailor make her dress. For fabric, she had bloomed hundreds of flowers, weaving their stems together, blanketing them across his shop floor.

A hand covered her own to stop the picking. It swallowed her own and pressed against her chest in a way that made her suddenly forget whatever errant thought was circling in her mind.

"Flowers don't pick themselves, remember?" he said, repeating her own drunken words from the Centennial. She hadn't known he had heard that part.

She smiled and turned to face him. He was golden, in his most official of outfits for the occasion. Isla smoothed the silk of his shirt that required no smoothing whatsoever. "What about kings? Do they pick flowers?"

Oro's expression was pure promise when he leaned down to say right into her ear, "Only when the flower picks them."

"Good," she said. "Because I'm pretty sure you're going to have to cut me out of this dress." She turned for him. "See? No strands. No buttons." In fact, she had molded the dress to herself. With Leto's instructions to his design, she had woven the dress around her, the flowers coming together, clasping tight, their stems locking her in.

Another fact was that she could certainly undo the dress herself as well, but the alternative was so much more enjoyable.

"Hmm," Oro said, his voice getting deeper. His mouth brushed against her bare shoulder. His fingers trailed down her spine, where corset ties might have been were this a traditional dress. They did not stop. She felt the heat of his hand sweep across the base of her back before gripping her hip bone. "That shouldn't be a problem," he said.

"Are you sure?" She blinked innocently at him over her shoulder. "If you're too busy with your kingly duties, I can ask someone else . . ."

He took her chin in his hand. Tilted her head up to his, so he could say right against her lips, "Tonight, my only *kingly duties* involve my mouth and whatever you wear beneath a dress like this."

Isla's eyes were still the height of innocence as she said, "So, your mouth and . . . nothing?"

Oro cursed, and heat filled the room. They were standing in front of a mirror. She turned her head and watched him look at her like she was the most precious thing in all the realms. And she . . .

She looked happy. She *was* happy. Her mind had emptied of most of its anxious thoughts. How had that happened?

Oro had happened. He had taken all her broken pieces in his hands and vowed to one day make them whole. He had been patient. Kind. Loving.

Inside, Isla now had a pocket of peace. A slice of sunlight. It was an anchor. If her thoughts ever spiraled, in her darkest hours, she would return here, to this moment she tucked away in that pocket.

Before, she had felt unmoored, betrayed, like she didn't truly have a home.

Now, *he* felt like home.

"Look," she said, fishing a thin golden chain from beneath her dress. The small golden rose hung there, in the center of her chest. She'd made a necklace of it. "It's heavy, but—"

"You kept it," he said, almost in awe, his brows coming together. Oro swept his fingers over it, and it became lighter, as if hollowed.

"Of course I kept it," she said. "It's us. A rose surrounded in gold."

Oro didn't seem to care that he was disrupting all the petals on her dress as he lifted her up.

Isla thought, as he leaned down and kissed her, that she had never been happier in her entire life.

The Mainland gardens were decorated with flowers Isla had bloomed herself. She'd spent all afternoon crafting the decor. The event was meant to showcase her abilities. It only made sense to have her power on display everywhere.

A hundred islanders and newlanders had been invited—not just nobles. In fact, some nobles would find that they were left off the list. People of every realm sat at the tables, and Isla had seated them all together, not separated, as they so often were.

The most surprising guest of all was Cleo. She had accepted her invitation, and Isla could only hope that it meant the smallest of peace offerings. The Moonling ruler sat perfectly postured, her chin as high as always. Her white hair was tied into a single long braid behind her. Her face didn't betray a single expression.

Oro squeezed Isla's hand under the table. *You can do this*, he seemed to say.

She could.

Isla stood. She was barefoot. Flowers bloomed with her every step to the center of the celebration.

She did not have to tell them to fall silent; they did that themselves. "Thank you for attending this banquet in honor of my realm," she said. "This day is meant to celebrate growth." Her voice sharpened with meaning. "Growth is not limited to our plants, or our realms, but *ourselves*. No matter what happened before, we can change. Our opinions can change. Hatred can become hope. And I sincerely hope, one day, Wildlings can return to Wild Isle, the way they lived for thousands of years." There was murmuring, but no one dared say a word against the idea to her face. Isla had to think that was some sort of progress. "On behalf of our realm, we wish you a season of growth . . . in the right direction."

This was it. This was the moment.

Everyone knew she had been powerless. They knew she didn't know how to wield.

Isla unraveled her hand, revealing a rare seed she had gotten from the newland. She tossed it in front of her, to the ground below, and everyone watched as it was sucked into the dirt. A moment later, the ground rustled, and a tree formed in front of them, years of growth in just seconds. The bark layered over itself, the branches thickened, leaves decorated, and then fruit blossomed. "This tree has not grown on Lightlark in centuries," she said. "Its fruit is often called enchanted because of its sweetness." She turned in a semicircle, and arches of vines and thorns and roses sprouted around the gathering, one after the other.

Whispers. Murmurs. Wide eyes. Curiosity.

Her demonstration worked.

Oro's hand was on her knee as soon as she sat down. His thumb rubbed down her thigh, and she was suddenly flushed, remembering his promises for that night.

The clatter of silverware against glass plates was a welcomed symphony. At first, conversations at tables between realms seemed quiet, perhaps even tense, but by the end of the dinner, there was laughter. Conversation. Joy, even.

Then, far too soon, everything went silent.

It was as if all noise had been plucked from the island. The candles lining the garden began flickering. Dimming.

Before them, Isla's tree wilted, branches dehydrating, until it was just a pile of dead leaves.

Then, in an instant, darkness smothered them all.

Everything in the garden turned to ash. Tables were toppled over. Shadows shot down from the sky like strikes of lightning, then raced across the Mainland like tornadoes that had fallen over, erasing everything in their path.

No screams, though mouths were open. No cries, though tears slid down Isla's cheeks.

She shot out her hand, but no power came out. It was as if everything within her had been extinguished.

No, no—

A blink, and everything returned to how it was.

Isla remembered Grim's demonstration of power at the Centennial. An illusion. This was an illusion.

Then, his voice was in her head.

It was in all their heads.

"Consider this a warning," it said. "A glimpse at the future. You have one month to vacate the island. In thirty days, I am coming to destroy it."

Shouts. Screams.

"Nothing will be left. You can choose to flee to your newlands . . . or join me in a new future. The choice is simple. Fighting is futile. The ruin coming is inevitable."

HISTORY

Isla flew down from the sky, carried by Ciel and Avel, who each gripped her beneath a shoulder. Before, she would have been afraid of the height. Now, she didn't have room for such a simple fear.

She landed on Cleo's castle steps and within minutes was surrounded by white-wearing guards. They had sloshing water pouches along their hips, water ready to wield into weapons.

Cleo came sweeping down from one of the highest balconies of the castle, on the back of a waterfall. When she landed, the water froze, a wide white halo around her feet. "The brave little Wildling," she said. "What have you come to crow?"

"Stay," Isla said.

The Moonling looked intrigued. "Here I was, thinking we were enemies."

"You're not my enemy," Isla said. "I've watched your every move. You always do what's best for your realm. Leaving Lightlark would be a mistake."

"Would it?" she said, seeming bored.

"Lightlark is the base of your abilities. If you leave and Lightlark falls, your people won't last."

Cleo almost smiled. Surprisingly, it didn't look cruel. Her expression, more than anything, seemed sad. "You know so little," she said, her voice empty of any contempt. "You assume you know my motivations. You assume your facts are truth."

Isla narrowed her eyes. "You found something out before the last Centennial. That's why you didn't attend. That's why you've been

building ships. That's why you are considering evacuating your people from Lightlark. Isn't it?"

Cleo said nothing. The Moonling only tilted her head at Isla, as if appraising a dull rock, searching for any hidden glint.

Isla took a step forward. "Answer me," she yelled, and thorns grew around her wrists, out of nowhere, trailing down to the floor.

A dozen Moonling guards surrounded her in seconds. Avel and Ciel were at her sides, each of their hands on her arms, ready to fly her to safety. She had her starstick just in case. She felt invincible.

The Moonling frowned at the thorns dripping from Isla's palms. "What a waste," Cleo said, then she turned toward the massive, frozen doors of her palace.

"We could work together," Isla said.

That made the Moonling stop in her tracks. She turned around, the hem of her white dress hissing across the iced-over stone.

Isla took her chance. "Wildlings and Moonlings are more similar than you might like to imagine," she said. "You have frozen, infertile lands. We have started to learn how to grow crops again. We could help you, so you don't have to rely on fishing. You can vary your diets." Lately, Moonlings weren't seen in the markets. They had almost completely cut themselves off from the other realms.

The Moonling's expression remained as still as the frost beneath her feet. Unconvinced.

"We are also healers," she said. "The elixir I demonstrated during the Centennial—we know how to make it. Between your people's natural healing abilities and the ones we can extract from nature, we could mend almost anything."

Cleo stared at her for a moment. Another. Then, she turned away again.

"What happened?" Isla asked. "What happened a century ago? Why didn't you attend the fourth Centennial?"

At that, ice swept across the isle. It rippled in every direction and hardened beneath Isla's feet. She had to sprout vines from her hands to root her in place, to keep from slipping. Ciel and Avel braced her sides, wind circling around their bodies to keep them still.

Cleo turned. "You dare ask me a question like that?"

Isla took a step forward, beyond her Skyling guards, her roots digging into the ice, keeping her grounded. "I do," she said. "Something happened. What was it?"

For the fraction of a second, Isla caught a sliver of real emotion that made its way past the Moonling's normally icy mask. *Pain.*

Cleo could feel pain?

"We both want the same thing. For our realms to survive. We can help each other." Cleo looked doubtful, and Isla growled. "I know you hate me, but you love your people. Do it for them."

To her immense surprise, the Moonling smirked. "I don't hate you," she said. Then she turned, and the ice around her retracted, curling back to its source.

Only when she was almost at the palace's front doors did Isla hear the Moonling ruler say, "I'll consider it," before sweeping inside.

Grim was coming to destroy Lightlark in twenty-nine days.

From her vision, she had figured an attack was inevitable, but that didn't help the pain of knowing someone she once cared about was set on destroying everything she now loved.

Oro was irrevocably connected to Lightlark, as king. If the island fell . . . so would he.

All representatives were called for a meeting first thing the next morning. Isla hadn't told Oro about her visit to Cleo the night prior. As she watched the door, her hope the Moonling would stay withered. Grim's declaration of an attack was the perfect excuse for Cleo to leave Lightlark once and for all, on her ships. The Moonling newland was well

established and not under threat. It would be so easy for Cleo to take her people and flee.

They couldn't leave. If the other realms went to war with Nightshade they would need Moonlings and their healers more than ever.

Enya was at her side, curling and uncurling her fingers. Anxiety spiraled through the room. The same people from the dinner were present now, but this time there were no floating foods or flame-trimmed goblets, or fish trapped in ice.

This time, instead of whispers, there was only silence.

The clock began to chime, marking the hour.

Just before the last ring, Cleo swept into the throne room, and Isla tried her best not to fall out of her chair in surprise. The Moonling ruler had listened.

She had stayed.

Soren's cane cracked against Cleo's icy wake as they both made their way to their seats.

Oro did not waste a moment. "We have twenty-nine days before Lightlark is under siege. Twenty-nine days to figure out how to stop Grim."

Silence broke open, and questions spilled over.

"Can he even do that?"

"Does he control the winged beasts from the coronation attack?"

"It's five realms against one; we can protect the island, can't we?"

"What did he mean 'new future'?"

One of Isla's necklaces sat heavy against her throat as she swallowed, seeing flashes of her vision.

Grim could do it. Grim could destroy them all.

She blinked and found Cleo watching her intently. The Moonling wasn't focused on the lively debate around her. She was just staring at Isla, the specter of a smile on her mouth, the look of someone who knew a secret.

"Yes?" Cleo said suddenly, responding to Oro, because apparently, she had been listening. Her eyes remained fixed on Isla's.

"Is the oracle awake?" Oro asked.

She shook her head. "I visited the moment I returned to the isle, and she refused to thaw."

There was muttering. Heat flamed from Oro, but he moved on to his next question. "How many healers do you have?" Oro asked.

"Nearly a hundred on Lightlark. Triple that on the newland," Cleo answered.

Isla jumped in. "Combined with our healing elixirs, we'll be able to heal almost any injury. We'll start producing more right away." Her back was straight. She glanced at Soren, daring him to question her the way he had at the last dinner. He said nothing.

"Both will be critical," Azul said. He trailed his gem-covered fingers across the table and shook his head. "If Grim is taking on all other realms, he must be well equipped, and determined. He must want something. This isn't just about destroying the island, or he would have done it during the curses, when we were most vulnerable."

For a moment, Oro's eyes flicked to Isla. She knew what he thought.

Grim wanted her.

No. If this was about wanting her, he could have appeared at this very moment and taken her. She agreed with Azul. There was a purpose for Grim's destruction. If they knew what it was, perhaps they could stop him.

Oro's gaze was pure fire. "Whatever he wants, his intent is clear. He is coming to destroy us. We need to use every resource we have, every bit of ability." He addressed them all. Heat scorched the room. "This is our home. It is our future. Our power lives here. Without the island, our realms will die. We have twenty-nine days to either save Lightlark . . . or lose it forever."

That night, Isla curled against Oro's chest and traced him in the darkness. His cheeks. His lips. She touched him gently, just the slightest brush of her fingertips, and felt him shiver. "Oro," she said. "Growing

up, I didn't experience seasons. It was always warm. But there were a few weeks in the middle of the year when everything felt the most alive. I called that summer, and I used to wish that it would last forever." She frowned against the memory of her vision. "You and me . . . we built an endless summer. And I won't let anyone destroy it."

The next morning, he was gone when she woke up. The clock had started counting down, and chaos ensued. Word of Grim's warning had spread, and people rushed the castle, frantic, looking for answers.

Every willing and able adult was expected to begin training.

It had been centuries since war. Many of the best fighters had died during the curses. Oro went off to Sun Isle, with Enya, to get their forces together. Azul assembled his flight force, a legion in the sky.

Isla felt uncertain about asking any of the Starlings to fight, given most were barely older than children. A few people on the Starling newland volunteered to fight, and the rest who could wield would make weapons and provide energy for a shield that could be used to protect parts of the island.

That night, before going to Oro's room, she went to her own. She didn't make it past the entryway before pausing.

There was a flicker of curling white fabric on her balcony.

Cleo.

The Moonling ruler stood there, hands gripping the ledge, facing the sea. Her white hair cut through the night in sharp strands. Her dress was a pale puddle across the stone floor.

Isla swallowed. She wondered if she should be afraid. She waited for the fear to come . . . but it didn't.

A greater danger was coming. *Grim* was coming. Fears were relative, she realized. They could feel smaller when placed next to bigger ones.

She wasn't afraid of Cleo. Not anymore.

The door creaked as it opened. From this angle, the full moon looked like a halo around Cleo's head. It lit her white dress and skin—she was

a candle without its wick. The Moonling didn't even turn around as she said, "It was a night just like this." Isla eyed the pool of water around Cleo's dress. "The worst night of my life. It was a full moon . . . just like this one."

Isla leaned against her door. "What do you want, Cleo?"

Cleo almost smiled. It was a sad expression. "Tonight? It might surprise you . . . but I want to help you."

Her eyes narrowed. "That does surprise me," Isla said. Vines crawled up the cliff, until they reached her balcony. They didn't stop until they wrapped around Isla's arms and down her palms. "Considering you tried to kill me."

Cleo looked from the vines dripping down her fingers to her face, and smirked. "Wildling," she said. "If I had wanted to kill you, you would be dead."

A massive wave crashed against the balcony, and Isla felt the force of it in her knees. Freezing water soaked her legs, and she tried her best not to shiver.

"I heard you were locked in a glass box of a room. Is that true?" Cleo asked. Where was she going with that? How did she even *know* that? Isla nodded warily and watched as Cleo turned back toward the moon. She stared at it as she said, "You are a young fool, but you remind me so much of him." Isla could have imagined it, but Cleo's voice cracked with emotion, splitting from its normal coolness. "My son."

The sea that had made its way through the teeth of the balcony pillars froze over. It nearly reached Isla, though she didn't move a muscle.

Son? Cleo had an heir . . . ? That couldn't be right; heirs weren't allowed at the Centennial—

"He died. The curse took him." Cleo looked down at the sea, sloshing and churning, and Isla saw a hatred there. "I did everything I could to protect him. I locked him up just like you, and I failed."

Isla would have thought it impossible to ever feel some sort of hurt for Cleo, though her eyes burned as she thought of her son, locked in his

room, and the mother who just wanted to keep him safe. "That's why you didn't attend the fourth Centennial," Isla said. "You had an heir."

"Our curse was well managed by then. It was more important to secure my realm's future. I had an heir, because, like you said, I do *everything for the good of my realm.*"

It wasn't just Isla who thought that. She remembered Oro during the Centennial saying Cleo was the most dedicated ruler of all of them. Though she'd had relationships with both men and women before the curses, she hadn't formerly been with anyone since becoming ruler. She put her realm's safety above all else.

"Something unexpected happened, though," Cleo said. "I . . . loved him. I had forgotten what that felt like . . . to love someone so much, it feels like drowning." She turned to fully face Isla, and the ice around her turned liquid, before crackling once more. Cleo had always worn dresses with a high neckline, but tonight she wore something more casual. Because of that, Isla was able to see a necklace: a simple ribbon with a light-blue stone that glistened in the moonlight. "I attended the last Centennial for him, so no one else would be taken by the curses." She looked Isla up and down, her expression still dripping in dismay. "And because of him, I'm helping you."

Isla didn't know why Cleo had told her all of this now, when she had been so defensive just days before.

Cleo wanted something from her. She just needed to figure out what it was.

"The oracle," Cleo finally said. "She's awake and has a message for you. You'll want to visit her soon."

The oracle was awake. They needed her now more than ever. Hope sprouted, but was tinged with suspicion.

The oracle was on Moon Isle. Cleo could keep Isla from accessing her if she wanted.

"Why . . . why are you telling me this?" Cleo said it was because of her son, but that didn't make any sense. Her son was dead. "Are you

agreeing to be loyal to Lightlark?" She needed confirmation before she could take anything the Moonling said seriously.

Cleo looked at her and frowned. "I'm loyal only to myself," she said.

She did not look at Isla again before a wave rushed up and took her away.

This time, Isla told Oro about her conversation with Cleo. They were rushing down the castle steps the next morning, on their way to the oracle, avoiding the craterous fissures from the drek attack, when Azul crashed in front of them with the force of a lightning strike. He was crouched, a jewel-covered hand balanced in front of him.

Ciel and Avel came down a moment later, flanking Isla.

Azul straightened, and for the first time, she could see traces of his true age in the heaviness of his expression.

"What's happened?" Oro asked, stepping forward. He reached almost absent-mindedly toward Isla, in a protective motion, and Isla watched Azul track it.

"See for yourself," the Skyling said, his voice grave.

In an instant, Ciel and Avel lifted Isla up, and the five of them shot into the sky. Azul's expression was serious, but he glanced down at her as he flew above, knowingly. Warily. Then, his gaze went back to the horizon.

Isla saw it before they landed, and her mouth went dry.

A fleet like dozens of swans, positioned in the shape of a diamond, cut through the ocean, riding against the current. These ships did not have or require sails. They made currents of their own. The sea parted from their path.

The ones who controlled the decks moved in unison, in practiced motions. They had been preparing for this. Training, just like her.

Cleo was on the front-most ship. Her white dress billowed, puffed up, the only thing resembling a sail on those vessels. She turned, staring right at them.

They were not the only ones watching. She heard the islanders on the beaches below and by the Broken Harbor witnessing history unfold. Moonling was leaving Lightlark.

"They're fleeing," Azul said, his voice still nearly unbelieving.

"No," a voice said, and they all turned around to find Soren standing there, watching the Moonlings fade away. "They're joining Nightshade."

PROPHECY

Moon Isle was melting. The previous labyrinth of ice and snow had lost its bite. The ice sculptures that had lined the walkway to the palace for centuries were nothing more than puddles. The woods were carved open, no snow to hide their inner workings. It was like the Moonlings had taken the cold with them, packed it in their ships.

Cleo had told her the night before to visit the oracle. Now, with Oro next to her, she needed to find out why.

The oracle was already thawed. She floated in the water of her glacier, edges melting.

Isla remembered what the oracle had told her and Oro months prior. *So many secrets, trapped between you. But, just like this wall, they too will one day give way and unravel and fall . . . leaving quite a mess and madness.*

Back then, there had been three women trapped in the glacier. Three sisters. Oro had said the other two had allied with Nightshade and hadn't thawed in over a thousand years. Now, they were gone.

"You're dying," Isla said. The oracle's power—a force in the air that Isla could almost taste now that she knew what to look for—was dimming. "Cleo injured you."

"Don't look so dour, Wildling. I'm ancient. We tend to die slowly. She left me alive long enough to tell you what you need to know."

It didn't make sense. Why would Cleo help her, then join her enemy? The oracle's white hair floated around her face, curling in the water. Her voice was a thousand voices braided into one, echoing, smothered

slightly by the wall of ice between them. "Though . . . you are the one with most of the answers this time. Not me."

"What do you mean?" Oro demanded. Isla wasn't sure if they could trust the oracle, but he would know if she was telling the truth.

"Her memories are the key. They unlock the world. Everything—why they are coming, what they will do with Lightlark, the weapon they already have, how to stop them—is in her mind. All she must do is remember. *Everything*."

No. The memories had only just stopped again, and she was happier than ever. She swallowed. "And if I can't?"

"Then Lightlark will fall. Forever."

Oro frowned. "Is the future not solid?"

The oracle's gown floated in the slight current of the water, her sleeves going far beyond her arms. "No, it is not. Not all of it." She looked beyond them, at the woods that had been far whiter the last time they had visited. "This much is clear: they are coming. If they succeed, there will be nothing left. And by the time they step foot on the island, I will be gone."

The ice started hardening again, and Isla pressed her hand against it. "I need to know. Is my vision real?"

The oracle nodded. "Very."

Chills snaked down her spine. That level of destruction . . . the death in her mind . . .

She had one more question. "The vault," Isla said. "Is it important?" Even though it had rejected her, she knew it was crucial. She could feel it calling to her, the connection stronger as her powers intensified.

"More than you know," the oracle said. "The vault will change everything . . . if you can find the strength to open it for good." The woman tilted her head at Isla for just a moment—and in that second, somehow, she spoke directly into her mind. The oracle said, "Before Nightshade arrives, you will visit me. Alone. Only then will I give my

final prophecy." Isla wasn't sure if it was an order or yet another telling of the future, but it didn't matter.

As soon as Isla nodded—the most imperceivable lowering of her chin—the oracle fell back into the last remaining ice and froze over.

"I don't want to remember," she told Oro as she sat at the foot of their bed.

They had shared it for over a week now. During that time, her mind had been blissfully clear of any memories of Grim. Oro had banished his presence. She was happy.

She should have known happiness was only ever temporary.

Oro shook his head. "There has to be another way."

"There isn't. The oracle was clear. I have to remember everything . . . and somehow find a way to open the vault."

Her knees were pulled to her chest. The memories she'd had so far were useless. Her being foolish enough to portal to Nightshade. Stabbing him in the chest. Grim nearly choking her. Their duel.

"I hate him," she said. "Not just for taking the memories away. But in the memories themselves. The ones I've already remembered."

Isla had already made up her mind. Of course she would remember. Of course she wouldn't put her own happiness above the safety of all Lightlark.

It didn't mean she was happy about it.

Tears streaked down her face. "I hate him, and I hate myself for even having these memories in the first place."

Oro's arms went around her back and under her knees. He hauled her against him. "This is not your fault, Isla. Whatever happened a year ago . . . you were not the person you are now. Do not judge yourself. Do not hate yourself."

After Oro was asleep, Isla sneaked into her room. She found a parchment and quill and wrote herself a note. No matter what she remembered. No matter what had happened in the year before the Centennial—

You hate him.
You hate him.
You hate him.
You hate him.
You hate him.
You hate him.

That very same night, Isla used her starstick to portal to the only person who might be able to get her memories back faster.

Remlar did not look surprised to see her. He was standing outside his hive. Isla didn't know if he ever slept. "Welcome back, Wildling," he said, purring the last word. He was surrounded by the other winged beings who lived in the hive. Their skin was light blue, and their wings were thin and silky behind them. Before, they hadn't worked. Now, they stood perched high over their shoulders.

"If my memories were taken by a Nightshade, how would I remember? Can you give them to me?"

The others flew away, up into holes in the giant wooden hive behind them, clearly not wanting to be involved in this conversation.

Remlar pursed his lips. "No. Memories are difficult to uncover. A skilled Nightshade could return them . . . but doing so all at once could be dangerous. The mind is so easily fractured . . ." He sighed. "The far better option is that they be restored by you." That, at least, explained why Grim hadn't simply given her memories back at the end of the Centennial. He had seemed so confident she would remember . . . and she had.

"How do I do that?"

"Assuming they weren't meant to be erased forever, the stronger your Nightshade powers become, the more the veil that has been put on them will weaken."

Isla frowned. "So, the more I master Nightshade power, the more I will remember."

He nodded.

Great. Now, she needed to learn yet another ability? She didn't want to wield death and shadows. She had been suppressing it. She didn't have time.

But if this was the way to save Lightlark . . . she had to try. "Fine. Teach me."

Remlar raised his brow at her.

"Please."

He shrugged a shoulder and pointed to the grass before them. "It's simple. Summon, Wildling."

"How?"

"Just try it. Focus. Reach, just like you do for your other abilities. But this time . . . look for the shadows."

Isla placed a hand in front of her. She could feel the Wildling ability inside, humming, ready to be used. Familiar.

Then, there was its umbra. It was harder to grasp—slippery, temperamental. The roots of her hair became sweaty as she focused, using all her usual rituals and tricks. Her mouth was a line. She reached for the power, over and over, until finally, she clutched it, for just a second—

Her hand pressed against the ground. Whatever her skin touched died. When she removed it, there was only her imprint, dark and sizzling.

"Is that good enough?" she asked.

Remlar didn't answer.

She turned—but she wasn't in the Sky Isle woods any longer.

BEFORE

She was in a market.

It had been a month since Isla had dueled with the Nightshade in the forest. She hadn't expected to see him again, of course. He was repulsed by her.

She was repulsed by *him*.

Her days were spent training with Terra and Poppy and meeting Celeste in secret.

She had a million things to think about, but sometimes, her thoughts would drift to the Nightshade ruler.

Grimshaw. In her mind, she called him Grim. It seemed fitting, given the dread his memory caused. Losing the duel meant Grim could slay her the first chance he got at the Centennial. It pained her to think one mistaken visit to Nightshade could cost her years of training and preparation. Especially since she was working with Celeste.

Isla had spent the last three weeks looking for an object that was central to her and Celeste's plan to survive the Centennial: a pair of gloves made of flesh that would allow them to absorb a whisper of power. She had searched every dark market in every newland, without success.

Except for Nightshade.

It had a famed night market that now operated during the day. A place where ungodly things were sold and traded. She had heard whispers of it in the darkest corners of the other agoras, which had been a bit like monsters whispering about even bigger monsters.

Skin gloves had to be made while a person was *alive*—they couldn't be taken from a corpse, which might have made attaining them slightly easier. According to the few merchants she had trusted enough to ask, they used to be far more common years before, when more power could be absorbed. Nowadays, after the curses, the amount of ability the gloves could muster was useless.

In most cases, anyway.

If any last pair of skin gloves still existed, they would be on Nightshade. She had promised herself she would never return, but—

Isla drew her puddle of stars, then it was done.

With mastery, one day, she might be able to portal anywhere she wanted. For now, she could only return to places she'd been before. The moment she landed in Grim's castle, she imagined he might step out of a wall and put his broadsword to her chin. But the hall was empty.

She didn't linger or explore—that was what had gotten her found out last time. With quiet steps, she made her way out of the palace and into the busy streets. Women wore clothes she had never seen in other realms' lands—boots that reached their thighs, dresses with chain mail woven through, pants that were glossy and shimmering. Compared to them, Isla was wearing far too much clothing. She kept her head down and her hood—a black one she had procured in another market— buttoned at its front, so as not to show what she wore beneath, the only other dark-colored clothing she owned, a deep-plum silk dress meant for sleeping.

Get the gloves and get out, she told herself.

The night market smelled of rotting flesh and boiled blood. Her black hood dropped so low it almost obstructed her vision as she wove through the crowds. No one paid any attention to her. She was the least interesting thing in the market.

One stand exclusively sold teeth. There were barrels of them—most looking distinctly human.

Another had skulls tied on strings. Some were small as fingernails, others as large as boulders—*what creature could possibly have such a large head?*

"Nightbane," someone whispered from a stall. She slowed in front of it, curious. There were small vials of something dark. The seller's face lit up at her attention. "Takes away all troubles and pain . . ."

Nightbane. She had never heard of it.

The seller reached for her, as if to place the vial in her hand, eyeing the gems she wore on her fingers, and she kept moving.

Crimson wine filled a cauldron a woman with fingers that looked suspiciously like claws stirred with what looked even more suspiciously like a femur. Poison. It had to be poison. The woman met her eyes, and Isla quickly looked away.

Gloves, gloves.

She looked for flesh, and—*gulp*—found it rather quickly.

A stand had skin spread out across racks, some still in need of more thorough cleaning. Isla nearly gagged. She parted the curtains of the shop and entered, sinking her face into the folds of her cape to try to mute the smell of decay. Disgusting. She couldn't fathom the type of people who could regularly visit the night market, let alone work here.

Gloves. Gloves. She searched, hoping to find them. If no shop sold them, she would have to find someone she could pay to *make* them for her. That possibility made bile crawl up her throat. No, the best thing would be to find some already made, preferably from the skin of a child murderer, or someone equally as deserving of such a cruel, torturous death.

She parted another wall of curtains. The shop was like a labyrinth, and some of its sweeping walls felt too thick—*skin?*—and she was suddenly sweating beneath her cloak. She tried to hold her breath as much as she could as she scoured the shelves and racks for something resembling human hands . . .

Until she did find human hands.

Or, rather, they found her.

Before Isla could scream, someone placed their fingers over her mouth and pulled her backward, straight through another set of curtains.

Into an alleyway.

She was shoved against a wall, her hood falling, the back of her head colliding with wet bricks. Something dripped against her forehead from far above and slid down her cheek.

A man whose flesh hung off his bones like the skins in the shop towered before her. He looked old, which meant he either had generations of children or had been alive more than a millennium.

Or . . . by the crazed look in his eyes and the faint yellowing of his skin, he had dabbled in something dark enough to have leeched away his life.

With a motion quicker than his appearance suggested he would be capable of making, he wrapped her hair around his other wrist and pulled.

Isla cried out behind his filthy palm. The man ignored her, inspecting her hair like it was a treasure.

"Yes . . ." he said, eyes sparkling. "This would fetch a pretty price . . . Wildling hair. Shiny temptress locks. Must get the root . . . that's the best part. The whole scalp, that will do nicely." He pulled a long, curved knife from his pocket.

Isla had a blade through his chest before he could point it in her direction.

It shocked her. The only other person she had stabbed was Grim.

The man's mouth turned into a curious shape, and his eyes were not on her but her hair as he crumpled to the ground.

A group of guards chose that exact moment to walk by the entrance of the alley. One stopped. Took a look at the man bleeding at her feet. That didn't seem to disturb him that much.

He might not have pursued her if she hadn't taken off, wielding the ruby blade she had just fished from the man's rib cavity. It was an admittance of guilt. But she couldn't stop herself.

She bolted, and he followed.

The group joined him.

Isla hurtled back into the market. She ducked and wove herself into the crowd, not turning around to see how close they were to catching her. She pulled her starstick out of her pocket and saw it was faintly glowing.

Thank the stars.

All she needed was to hide long enough to draw her puddle, and she would be gone, gloves be damned.

She ducked beneath a low-hanging row of axes, jumped over a tangle of snakes sitting in front of a shop—fangs not even removed—and tried to find a place to hide.

By now, everyone was watching.

Risking a glance behind her, she realized why. Many, many guards had joined the pursuit.

Did they have no one better to chase in this wretched market? she thought.

Then, she remembered what the old man had called her. *Wildling.* He'd still been alive when she left him. Had he told the guards?

Wildlings weren't supposed to be here. There weren't laws against it, but who would be foolish enough to travel to the infamous Nightshade lands? Her. She was foolish enough.

She ran faster. They were on her heels.

The boiling blood—she tipped the cauldron over onto the streets, and it sizzled as it burned their feet. They cursed, and she was off again.

She turned a corner, into another branch of the market, and searched desperately for another path, but they were too quick, right behind her.

Her blade gripped in one hand and starstick in the other, she wondered which one she would have to use as she turned and climbed up a short wall. She ran as fast as she could, turned again, and found a nearly empty part of the market, half abandoned. Without risking a glimpse behind her, she fell to her knees.

Mercifully, though her starstick seemed temperamental on Nightshade, it worked. It was a simple, practiced movement. Drawing her portal, watching it ripple, preparing to jump through—

Before it fully settled, she heard footsteps in front of her. The puddle shrank and disappeared.

She looked up, only to find Grim standing in the center of the road. "You," he said.

You.

The guards caught up to her then. She was roughly hauled to her feet, against one of them. He smelled of smoke and sweat. Before she could reach for her dagger, a dozen blades were at her throat.

Grim's eyes did not leave hers as he waved his hand and said, "Take her to the cells."

Her wrists were shackled to the ceiling. It had been hours, and her arms ached. The guards had taken her cloak, as if it had disgusted them that she dared wear their color. They had taken her starstick too.

Grim appeared in front of her cell and frowned. "Is that supposed to pass for black?"

He was looking at her silk dress.

She hadn't intended for it to be seen. She wasn't wearing anything beneath it. Her hands weren't available to cover up parts that she didn't want him to see, but he didn't even bother looking, giving her body the most cursory of glances before meeting her eyes.

"Demon," was all she said.

"Fool," he responded.

That she could not argue with.

She was the biggest fool in the realms for returning to this place when something bad happened every time she did.

With barely a move of his finger, the chains holding her to the ceiling melted into ash.

She fell to the ground in an undignified heap.

Grim studied her while she clutched her wrists, both raw and red. "You swore not to return."

Isla looked up at him. "No."

"No?"

"The promise from the duel was that I wouldn't return *here*, which, in the moment, meant your *bathroom*. Which I have no intention of ever doing again, don't you worry."

He looked at her with unfiltered disdain. "What are you doing on Nightshade?"

She said nothing.

Grim turned to go, and she rose to her feet. "You're keeping me here?"

He looked over his shoulder. "You appear in my realm, using a stolen relic. You stab me in the chest. You return and hide in my chambers. Then, you return yet again and attack an innocent man in the middle of the street."

She made a sound of indignation. "Innocent? He wanted to scalp me and sell my hair by the strand!"

Grim's eyes narrowed. "What type of people did you expect to encounter at the night market, Hearteater?" he asked. That last word dripped with mockery.

"My name is Isla," she said through her teeth, stepping closer to glare at him right through the bars of her cell.

"I will never call you that."

"Why?"

He looked down at her. "Calling someone by their first name is a sign of familiarity. Of respect."

Her nostrils flared. "You don't respect me?"

"You don't seem to respect your own life. Why should I?"

She scoffed. "Fine. Don't respect me. I don't care. You weren't why I came here."

"Clearly. Why *are* you here?" he demanded.

Isla crossed her arms, both in annoyance and to cover up her chest, inconveniently prickling in the freezing prison. "Why are *you* here?" she asked. "You clearly would love to see me rot. And it would benefit you at the Centennial." As soon as she said the words, she regretted them. What if he turned away and never returned? What would she do? Escape was impossible without her starstick. She would waste away far beneath Nightshade. Even Celeste wouldn't be able to free her. She didn't even know Isla was venturing here for the gloves, didn't know she had met the Nightshade ruler before—

"I believe . . . we might be able to help each other," Grim said.

Shock rendered her silent.

"We are looking for the same thing."

Isla frowned. "You're looking for skin gloves?"

He looked at her strangely. "No. You are looking for a way to survive the Centennial, are you not?"

Of course she was. She didn't say a thing.

"I have a deal for you, then."

"A deal?"

He nodded. "I'm looking for a sword. I believe you can help me get it."

"What sword?" And why would he possibly think she could help him?

"A powerful one that very few people know exist," was all he said.

"What exactly does it do? What does it look like?"

He bared his teeth. "Do you think I'll tell you so you can rush off and try to find it yourself?"

"I wouldn't do that." That was exactly what she was planning to do. "So, I help you get the sword. What do I get out of it?"

Grim looked pointedly at the bars. "For starters, you wouldn't freeze to death in this cell, in that flimsy dress." Isla had dropped her arms, but she covered her chest again. "And, if you can help me, I will not only agree not to kill you at the Centennial, but I will also be your ally."

"You—you've decided to attend?"

"Only if you help me find the sword."

His aid would be invaluable. With Grim by her side—along with Celeste—she might really have a chance of surviving the hundred days on the island.

Still. Grim couldn't be trusted. She and Celeste had a plan. She would find a way to get the gloves. "No."

Grim's shadows flared around him. "No?"

She shrugged. "No."

His fingers twitched, as if desperate to turn her to ash, just as he had done with the shackles. Instead, he said, "Very well," and turned to leave.

He made it to the end of the hall before she said, "Wait. You wouldn't leave me here, would you?"

"I would."

Her eyes bulged. No, no, he wouldn't.

Who was she kidding? He was the ruler of Nightshade. Famed for his cruelty. He had killed thousands in his lifetime.

His steps retreated once more, before she said, "Fine! Fine. But only if you return my starstick."

His lip curled back in disgust. "Your *what*?"

"My portaling device."

With a flick of his wrist, it was in his hand. "I feel strongly that I will regret this," he said, eyes narrowed, as he slipped it to her.

She grinned, cradling it in her arms. It was her most prized possession. Grim just frowned at her.

That was how she made a deal with a demon.

REVELATIONS

There is a sword."

Isla recounted her memory to Oro. It was the first one that seemed remotely helpful. "He said I could help him find it. He said it was powerful."

Oro's brows came slightly together. "Do you know anything else about it?"

"Not yet. But it might be the weapon the oracle says he has."

Oro nodded. "Then we need to find out what it does."

By the end of the day, Oro had dozens of people in every library and archive, searching for records of important swords.

Isla knew the answers would not be found in books but her own mind.

She just needed to remember.

The Wildlings didn't seem surprised at the idea of war.

"This is what we've always trained for," Wren said. There were nods around her.

"You—you want to fight?" Isla asked, doing her best to siphon surprise out of her tone. This was not really their battle. Wildlings hadn't been on Lightlark in five hundred years. None of her people had been alive before the curses. They had never even stepped foot on the island.

Asking them to potentially die protecting it seemed like a stretch.

"Are you giving us a choice?" Wren asked.

Isla hesitated. *Choice.* She was their ruler. She could have ordered them. *Should have*, probably. Now, Grim had Moonling. Cleo had been

building a legion. She had seen it herself during the Centennial, sneaking around the Moon Isle castle.

To defeat them, they would need as many warriors as they could get. Still . . .

"Yes," she said quickly. Once the word was out of her mouth, she couldn't take it back. "You have a choice." Isla studied her people. Some looked determined. Others looked wary. "I hadn't been to Lightlark until a few months ago," she said. "I could have returned here and ignored the threat on the island, but I know if Lightlark falls, so do we. Eventually, without that power . . . we will cease to exist. I see a future where we return and claim our isle again. I see a future where we use the power of the island to help regain everything we lost." She paused. "Who will fight alongside me for that future?"

For a moment, no one moved a muscle, and Isla's heart sank below her ribs. Wildlings were known to be among the best warriors. Without them—

One woman stepped forward. She had long hair tied into a braid and wore bracelets made from thorny vines.

Another.

Another.

Then, an entire group.

Isla wanted to smile, she wanted to cry, but she did neither. She nodded sharply and thanked them.

"For those who will not fight, I ask for something critical." She was honest with them. "Moonling joined Nightshade." There were a few murmurs. "They took their healers with them. To keep this war from destroying us, we need as many healing elixirs as possible."

"It's not something that can be rushed," Wren said. "We only have one small patch of the flower left."

Isla knew that. "We'll need to find more," she said. "We will need to search every inch of the isle for it." She sighed. "The elixir will be

the difference between life and death. We need everyone available to learn how to extract it."

Wren nodded.

She faced the rest of her people. "Grim is coming to destroy Lightlark." Her vision echoed in her head, and her heart started beating faster, each beat like the chime of a clock. "We are in a race to save thousands of lives."

Lynx was waiting for her in the woods outside the Wildling palace when she was done. Now that part of Wild Isle had been restored by her and Oro, she had contemplated bringing him to Lightlark.

With Nightshade approaching, however, she didn't know if it was the best idea.

"War is coming," Isla told him, wondering if he really could understand her. "I . . . I saw a vision a while ago. Of someone I used to care about, destroying the world . . ." She swallowed. "He's Nightshade, like my father."

Lynx's gaze sharpened.

"You must have known him, right? My . . . dad?"

The leopard blinked, and Isla didn't know if that was confirmation.

"The oracle said I'm the key. I'm the only one who can remember why he wants to destroy Lightlark, and how. I'm the only one who knows about the mysterious weapon he has. Some sword." She sighed. It was nice talking to someone, even if she wasn't sure he was listening. "I'm the only one who can open a door that has rejected me already, that is apparently extremely important in all of this." She laughed without humor, and Lynx just stared at her. "You know what? After the Centennial, I truly believed things could not get any worse. I was wrong. I . . . I was wrong about a lot of things."

Lynx didn't care. She knew that. She made to turn around, to leave him to his business, when he stopped her, with a quick nuzzle of his head that nearly sent her off-balance.

She turned around and found his head bent low. She reached out with careful fingers, and he allowed her to pet down his nose. His eyes closed, and he made a thrumming sound in his chest.

Her bonded didn't hate her. That was a relief. At least, he didn't hate her today.

Perhaps, Isla thought, it meant she had proven herself as a Wildling. Perhaps it meant she could finally open the vault.

Isla stood outside the hidden door. Voices echoed inside. It reminded her of being in the forest when her powers had first been released, a thousand mouths calling her forward. They were almost clear but muffled in meaning, like speaking underwater. She took another step and tried to listen. They became louder, more insistent.

A spark traveled up her spine, and she didn't dare move too quickly, in case it broke the connection. This was it all along, she thought. All she needed to do was connect to the vault, the same way Oro had taught her to form a link to her abilities. The same way she had begun to form a connection with Lynx.

Something in her recognized something in the hidden door. It pulled her forward, a hand gripping a thread behind her navel. It all felt so natural, so right, so fitting, just like the crown clicking into the lock, every twist and ridge lining up. Just like turning it, and pulling it—

Closed. It remained closed. It didn't move an inch, not even a sliver of an opening, like before. No force threw her across the room.

Just . . . nothing.

Isla ripped her crown from the lock and almost hurled it across the room. They had twenty-six days. Twenty-six days before—

Her vision flashed in front of her eyes, and she could almost smell the burning. She could almost feel the ashes landing on her bare arms as they swept over her in torrents. She coughed like the cinders were in her throat again, choking her. Screams sounded in her ears, followed by howls from dreks—

Dreks. That was new. She hadn't seen them in her vision before. They had suspected the drek attack was from Grim, but this was confirmation.

"We were right. He has dreks," Isla told Oro. She could still hear their howls in her head. "Last time was a bloodbath. How could we stand a chance against that many? Their skin is nearly impenetrable."

Oro sighed. "Ever since the first drek attack, I've had my best team looking for a special type of ore. It was mined a millennia ago and requires Sunling and Starling power to turn it to metal. When weapons were made from it, it's said that they could pierce even the thickest hides."

"Have any of those weapons survived?"

He shook his head. "If they did, none of us know where they are. We've already checked the castle's reserves."

So they would have to make new ones. "Who's looking for the ore? Have they had any progress?"

He looked at her. He seemed . . . almost nervous. "You've met Enya. Now, it's time for you to meet the rest of my friends."

Just an hour later, Oro led Isla into a room located in a turret at the back of the Mainland castle, with massive, curved windows overlooking the sea. A round table sat in its center, crafted from solid gold. It was a war strategy room. Oro walked to the windows and looked out at the horizon, in the direction of Nightshade.

Enya swept into the room at that moment. Her expression was pointed in concentration.

Two men who could not look more different walked in behind her. The only thing they shared was their significant height.

The much larger of the two was a Moonling. He had brown skin and a shock of white hair. His eyes were bright blue, framed by thick, dark lashes. He wore a sleeveless white tunic, and had the most muscled arms she had ever seen.

The other was Skyling. He was tall—though still shorter than the

Moonling—and lean. He had dark hair that tinted blue in the light, pale skin, and sharp cheekbones.

He narrowed his eyes at Isla and said, "So. You're the reason Oro doesn't see us anymore."

Enya gave him a look. "No, the reason he doesn't see us anymore is because the last time we got together, you called him an uptight wretch and asked when the last time he bedded someone was."

Isla raised an eyebrow. She glanced at Oro, who was glaring at his friends.

The Moonling sat down at the first available chair. "Well, he *was* dying," he said, shrugging. "He gets a partial pass on being a wretch."

"How generous of you," Oro said. He sighed and turned to Isla. "This is Calder."

The Moonling spoke up. "Cal, mostly." Despite looking like he could snap the table in half with his bare hands, there was something gentle about his demeanor. He had the kindest face she had ever seen.

"And Zed." The Skyling glared at her. He was studying her far too intently. Far too suspiciously.

Calder beamed. "Pleased to finally meet you." Isla took the hand he offered, her fingers laughably small next to his, and smiled weakly.

She shook her head. "I don't understand. I thought—"

"All Moonlings were like Cleo?"

She shrugged a shoulder.

He laughed, and it was a pleasant sound. "I can't blame you, after everything that happened, but . . . some opposed her. We are few, but some of us stayed."

"Like Soren."

There was a collective groan at the sound of his name.

"Cleo never trusted me in the slightest, of course. I moved to Sun Isle just before she cut the bridge."

Isla looked at the group and almost frowned. Enya was Sunling.

She understood how she and Oro had become friends. But from what she had seen, realms didn't often fraternize together. How—

"Wondering what we all have in common?" Enya asked casually.

She nodded.

"Him." Enya motioned to Oro.

Isla turned to him as he made his way to the front of the table. "You know that I was sent to train for years on each isle." He nodded at Calder. "He was the first in his class—in most subjects, anyway." He looked at Zed. "And he was the worst."

Zed grinned as if relishing the fact.

"He would have been the best, if the lessons were on anything he was remotely interested in," Enya muttered.

"What—what are you interested in?" she asked Zed, almost afraid to hear the answer.

"Thieving, for one," he said.

Isla frowned. "Who do you steal from?"

Zed nodded at Oro. "Him, mostly."

Oro sighed. "Zed likes to prove the supposed inadequacy of my guards every few years. He started breaking into the castle when he was a child. My father would have banished him from the island if he hadn't been my friend."

"No," Zed drawled. "He would have banished me, if he had actually been able to capture me."

Enya rolled her eyes. "He's the fastest Skyling in recent record, and rest assured, he will find an excuse to mention it at least three times during this conversation."

Isla raised an eyebrow at Oro. "Even with five hundred years of extra practice, you still can't beat him?"

Zed's eyes sparkled. "Perhaps he could. Let's check, Oro, shall we?"

Cal leaned back in his chair, making the wood groan. "You'll learn this, but they are annoyingly competitive."

Enya shook her head. "They are both annoying period, but Cal here has always preferred playing peacemaker to beating them both, even when they have definitely deserved it."

Zed raised an eyebrow. "To beat me, Enya, he would have to—"

"Catch you, we get it," she said, muttering something else under her breath. She shot a look at Isla. "See? I don't exaggerate."

By the time Zed turned back to face her, any amusement in his face had withered away. "So. You're Nightshade."

The air seemed sucked out of the room. Isla turned to Oro, who was staring at Zed like he was an enemy and not seemingly one of his oldest friends. "Zed," he said darkly, the word a warning.

"He didn't tell me," Zed continued, ignoring Oro. "A forest turned to ash on Sky Isle. The place next to it looked like a damned palace garden. It wasn't hard to put together."

"Zed—" Oro said.

"I am Nightshade," she said.

The room went silent.

Zed leaned back in his chair and stared at her. For a moment, he almost looked impressed. "I wasn't expecting you to admit it."

Isla sat straighter. "It is what I am. I can't control it more than you can control your dark-blue hair, or he can control the fact that he was born in a realm ruled by a witch." She motioned to Calder.

Enya nodded. "It's true," she said, looking at Zed as if to scold him. "All of us were born different, in one way or another. It's what brought us together."

Calder shook his head. He tried to smile at Isla. "Ignore him. He's just moody that Oro hasn't been joining our weekly games. The teams aren't even."

"Games?" Isla wondered.

Calder's grin grew. He opened his mouth, excited, but Oro stopped him.

"Enough interrogating Isla and talk of games," Oro said, setting his hands on the table. He looked pointedly at his friends. "We are at war, or have you all forgotten why I asked you to meet?"

That sobered the room.

Enya's expression became focused again. "Oro and I have the Sunling forces set up. Most are rusty, but our numbers are strong, and they are training as we speak."

"Do they need weapons?" Zed asked.

"No," Enya said. "All can wield. It's better they're not weighed down by swords or armor."

"Same for the flight force," Zed said. He glanced at Oro. "Is Azul coming?"

Oro nodded. "He's in a representative meeting, but he'll be here soon." He looked at Isla.

"Wildling warriors have volunteered. They can all wield and are training now. We have our own weapons." She looked at Calder hopefully. "Are you a healer?"

Enya made a choking noise, and Calder gave his friend a look. He smiled sheepishly when he turned back to Isla. "Currently the best on Lightlark."

"Because all the other healers are on Nightshade," Zed said smoothly.

Isla's smile faltered. Great. "We have healing elixir and are trying our best to make more of it. Starlings have volunteered to fight, but we see their best contribution as creating a shield around parts of the Mainland."

Zed nodded. "Smart," he admitted.

"I'm still trying to figure out how many talented wielders are on Star Isle, but I'm going to assume they're limited." She had asked Maren to get back to her with a list of the best, but so far she hadn't received it. "So, the shield will be small, but it might mean we can reduce where Nightshade can attack."

Calder nodded. "I can freeze parts of the sea around the island to limit where their ships are able to land too."

"He's not coming from the sea." Dread churned in Isla's stomach.

Calder frowned. "You think he'll arrive from the skies?"

"No."

That was when she told them about Grim's portaling flair. He and his army could appear anywhere, at any time. There would be no warning except for the one he had already given them.

Silence.

Zed paled even more. He bit out a curse word that almost perfectly encapsulated the situation.

"Exactly," Oro said. "To have any chance at winning, we need to be smart. We need to be ready."

"We need to find out why he's coming to destroy Lightlark in the first place," Zed said.

She agreed with him. All she had to do was remember. "Until we figure that out, Wildlings can work with the island's topography," she said. "We can cover the Mainland in barbs, or thorns, or poisonous plants, so they are forced to appear exactly where we want them." She remembered a grain of something helpful from her memories. "Bog sand, even. It . . . traps anyone that steps in it."

Oro nodded. He looked impressed. "We can fence them in."

"Exactly."

Zed leaned back in his chair. "That won't stop the winged beasts, though. We can only assume Grim will bring them."

Dreks. Her gaze met Oro's.

She knew she should probably tell them about her vision, but they were strangers. She couldn't trust them with the knowledge of her and Grim's history, or their memories . . .

It was a good thing Zed brought the creatures up first. He was right. She and the rest of the Wildlings could use nature to make the Mainland as uninhabitable as possible, but none of that stopped creatures that could fly.

"You haven't been able to locate the ore yet?" Oro asked.

Zed shook his head. "We're working on it, but the Forgotten Mines are tough to navigate, and the ores are almost impossible to extract. We should be able to get some soon, though."

"We need that metal," Enya said. "Making arrows for the Skylings should be the priority. They'll be crucial in the air, so those creatures don't pick us all off."

Yes. The Skylings would be critical. Without them at the coronation, many more people would have died.

Just then, Azul rushed in, wind on his back. "Apologies. The meeting went . . . longer than anticipated." Isla noticed Azul's typically jovial tone was completely missing. His expression was grave. He didn't even bother sitting down, before saying, "We have a problem."

"My people want to leave Lightlark," Azul said.

The world came to a halt. No one moved a muscle. Isla remembered how silent the Skyling representatives had been during their meeting.

No. They had already lost Moonling. They couldn't lose another realm. Wildling and Starling were the smallest; even with her people fighting, it wasn't enough—

"It's decided?" Calder asked.

"Not yet. But there will be a vote soon, and it isn't looking good."

Oro's eyes were raging amber. "We need you in the skies." His hands were pressed firmly against the table.

"I know," Azul said. "I want to fight. It is not my choice, however. My realm—"

"The island will fall," Oro said, his voice rising. "You understand that would be the end of your people. One generation, maybe two, and then the power you draw from would dry up."

Azul sighed. His eyes were bloodshot. He looked tired, like he had been up all night arguing with his representatives. "I know that, Oro," he said. "I do. But in the end, it will be their decision."

"How do we change it?" Enya said. "There has to be something they want. Something your realm needs."

Azul shook his head. "I spoke to them for hours. I don't think there's any changing their mind. There will be debates. Then, a vote." He didn't look hopeful. Azul's eyes were burning then, filled with meaning he hadn't put into words, as he looked at them. "I'm sorry," he said.

He left the room, and there was silence.

Heat swept across them all. Oro's brow was pinched. He ran a hand down his face.

"If we lose Skyling, we lose the war," Enya said. Her eyes were on the table. She was leaned back in her chair. "The winged beasts will decimate us, if Grim brings them, even if we do manage to find the special metal."

"Then we can't lose Skyling," Zed said.

She threw her hands up. "You heard him, Skylings cannot be bought or bartered with. Nothing we have could convince them."

Oro pressed two fingers against the side of his head. "The Skyling vote will take time. We have to operate under the assumption that we will lose the flight force and a large part of our legion."

"We need more soldiers, then," Zed said. He leaned farther back in his chair. "Calder and I already went to the corners of Lightlark. Gathered all the outside communities. Most have agreed to fight. Without Moonling and Skyling, it's still not enough though, and we've exhausted our allies."

A thought occurred to Isla. Oro's eyes met hers as she said, "Then what if we turn to our enemies?"

"Which enemies?" Enya asked.

"The Vinderland." The violent group they had encountered on their search for the heart of Lightlark.

"Absolutely not," Oro said.

"We're desperate, Oro," she said. "We just likely lost another realm."

"We're not that desperate," he said through his teeth.

"We need more warriors. *They* are warriors."

Oro shook his head, unbelieving. "Do I need to remind you that I watched them put *an arrow through your heart*?"

He didn't need to remind her. She saw the angry mark in the mirror every time she got dressed. If it hadn't been for the power of the heart of Lightlark, and Grim saving her, she would be dead.

Isla shrugged a shoulder. "That's in the past. We need them now. And we have a common enemy. They already hate Moonlings, right? They'll likely hate them more now that they've teamed up to destroy their home."

"Who they hate most is *Wildlings*," Oro said pointedly.

Isla knew that. Oro had told her during the Centennial that the Vinderland used to be Wildlings, far before the curses ever existed. She stood from her chair without breaking his gaze. "But I am not just Wildling," she said. She was also Nightshade. The Vinderland were not the only people who lived in the shadows of the island. There were other night creatures they had encountered during the Centennial. Perhaps she could convince them to fight.

Remlar had said it before—*she's one of us*. She had pushed her darkness down. Perhaps she could use it.

"No," Oro said.

Isla stood her ground. "Are you telling me I can't?"

A muscle in his jaw worked. "You are free to do as you wish," he said. "But this is reckless." His face softened. "We have time. We don't know if we're losing Skyling yet."

At the end of the meeting, Enya stayed back with Isla. When Oro was out of earshot, she said, "He is blinded when it comes to you. He forgets his duty." She placed a hand on her shoulder. "If you decide to go to the Vinderland for help, I will go with you."

With Skyling likely gone, Isla's memories became more important than ever. She trained with Remlar any chance she could. He taught her use of her shadows.

Now, he stopped in front of a tree. It was so wide five men would not be able to link hands and reach around it.

"This is a kingwood," he said. "It takes hundreds of years for it to get this big. This one has seen all the Centennials, Egan's rule, and even that of his father."

Isla pressed a hand against it. The thread between it and her was clear. Shining.

"Kill it."

She blinked. "What?"

Remlar's expression didn't change. "Use your Nightshade powers. And kill it."

"No." Her answer was immediate. She was the ruler of Wildling. Her allegiance was to nature, not the darkness. She was here only to pry the memories from her mind.

Remlar raised an eyebrow. "Have you killed people before, Wildling?"

She thought about the Moonling nobles, blood puddling on the abandoned docks. Countless others who were hazy in her mind . . . almost masked. By time. By *him.*

"Yes."

"Yet you won't kill a tree?"

Isla glared at him. "The people I killed deserved it. This tree has done nothing. Who am I to end it? For the sake of . . . practice?"

Remlar frowned. "Practice? I thought you needed answers. Answers to how to save thousands of people. A tree is but a small sacrifice."

"No," she said again.

Remlar grinned. "You have killed countless plants. When I untangled your powers, you destroyed an entire forest."

"That was an accident!"

"Does it change the fact that you are responsible for killing the woods?"

Isla closed her eyes tightly. No. It didn't.

Remlar sighed. "Nature is a flowing force," he said. "You destroy one tree, you create another. Pick one flower, plant another. The ash it turns into becomes fertilizer for another. It is a never-ending turning of a wheel, and there is no ending, or beginning, just constant turning, turning, turning."

"You're not making any sense."

"The tree does not care if you kill it," he said. "It will return as something better, something different. Everything that is ruined—especially by your hand, especially *here*—is reclaimed, remade."

Could that be true?

Remlar said it again. "Kill the tree. Leech it of its life . . . then create something new."

Create something new. If Remlar was right, she wasn't truly killing it . . . just turning it into something different.

Isla placed her hand against the tree.

Shadows curled out of her chest, flowing through her, turning liquid. They unfolded, and expanded, until she tasted metal in her mouth, and then, through her fingers . . . there was energy. Not only pouring out . . . but pouring in. Something vital, flowing out of the tree, and into her.

It was delicious.

Like gulping water after a day in the desert, Isla was suddenly desperately parched. The bark cracked beneath her fingers, split, shriveled. Branches and leaves fell and were ash before they hit the ground. By the time she was done, all that remained of the tree was a skeleton.

Isla was gasping. She was too full, a glass overflowing. She made it one step before falling to her hands and knees.

Life exploded out of her.

Dozens of tiny trees, just saplings, burst from the ground, breaking through the dirt.

She flipped over to her back, breathing like she still couldn't get enough air. Just a moment later, Remlar's head and the tops of his wings were blocking her view of the sky.

"I was right, Wildling," he said, sounding quite pleased with himself. She heard his voice before falling into another memory. "You are the only person living who is able to turn death . . . into life."

BEFORE

S he was doing it. She was really going to work with . . . him. The Nightshade appeared in the corner of her room, as if emerging from her thoughts, shadow melting into a ruler dressed all in black.

He didn't say a word. He just looked at her, frowning, as though he found every part of her disappointing.

Isla glared at him. "You do know *you* asked to work with me," she said.

Grim frowned even more. She hadn't known a frown of that magnitude was even possible. "I am aware," he said curtly.

With about as much revulsion as possible, he outstretched his hand. It was gloved this time, as if he couldn't bear having his skin touch hers.

He hated her. She didn't really understand why. Was it because she was Wildling? Was it because she had seriously injured him during their first meeting?

It didn't matter. She had been raised to hate him too. Nightshades were villains. Theirs was the only realm that drew power from darkness. Their abilities were mysterious, intrusive, vile. They had the power to spin curses. Most people thought *he* was responsible for them.

She reminded herself that working with him meant he wouldn't become her enemy during the Centennial. He could be the only reason she actually survived it.

"Wait," she said. "If my guardians come in and see I'm gone—" They usually granted her privacy after training, but it wasn't night yet. They could very well check in on her while she was away.

"I'm going to set an illusion in your room."

Oh. She supposed he had thought of nearly everything.

So why did he need her? It didn't make any sense.

"Great. Let's get this over with," she said, taking his hand.

Before the final word left her mouth, they were gone.

They landed on the edge of a cliffside made up of lustrous black rocks, crudely puzzled together. Ocean crashed hundreds of feet high, so close she could smell the sea spray. Rain instantly flattened her hair against her face in wild strands. It soaked her to the bone. She shivered immediately.

Isla heard the unforgiving sound of iron banging against iron, far above. They were on a ledge.

"Where are we?" she asked, gasping through the wind and cold. She wasn't sure where she was expecting Grim to take her first on their search, but it wasn't here.

"Before we look for the sword, I need to pay a little visit to its creator," he said simply. "The blacksmith."

From Grim's mouth the title sounded ancient.

"We'll have to climb the rest of the way to his forge," Grim said before stepping in front of her, toward the next wall of dark rocks. He didn't offer an explanation. Could he not use his abilities close by? Did he not want the blacksmith to sense him coming? With one gloved hand on the rocks, he suddenly turned as if in afterthought and said, "Don't let the rocks cut you."

Grim started up the wall. She reluctantly followed.

The rocks were slippery in the rain. Isla grabbed one and had to strain the muscles in her fingers just to hold on. By the time she moved a few feet, she looked up to see that Grim was already almost halfway up. Demon. He would leave her if she wasn't quick enough.

She squinted through the rain as she fought to grasp the next rock. The next. Her shoes were made with special bark at the bottom that had a good grip, at least. She climbed higher. Higher.

While she moved her feet into their next positions, her fingers

suddenly slipped, and her heart seemed lodged in her throat in the slice of a second it took to find another hold. She grabbed it desperately, without caring about the sharp corners.

Blood seeped down her hand, warm against the freezing rain. So much for not cutting herself. The rocks were sharp as knives. She risked a quick look down and swallowed. From this height, scraping against them would disembowel her before the fall would kill her.

Her gaze traveled up. And up. She was less than halfway done. There was no way she could make it, not without slipping again.

Isla closed her eyes. Her mind was running wild with fear and a thousand stressful scenarios that hadn't happened yet, so she focused on her breathing. This was unfamiliar terrain, but she had climbed her entire life. Terra would have told her that any climb could be broken into smaller steps. She started up again, concentrating only on the path right in front of her. And breathing.

She inched up the rock face, fingers carefully dodging the sharpest points of the stones. They were each long and narrow, a thousand giant crystals crushed together to form a wall. Her hand screamed in pain, and red kept streaming, even after the rain cleaned it, again and again. She would need to use her Wildling healing elixir when she returned to her room.

Almost there.

Before she could reach for the final few rocks, strong arms pulled her up the rest of the way, careful not to drag her against the cliffside. Then she was unceremoniously discarded on the ground. Mud squelched below her. She imagined she was now caked in it.

She glared at Grim, hovering above. His dark hair was plastered down his forehead, over his eyes, down half of the bridge of his nose. Even without his armor, he looked terrifying. She thought about the rumor that he had killed thousands with his blade, and the fact that this might have been their last sight. A towering shadow. "You are an exceptionally slow climber," he said. "I should have left you behind."

He turned on his heel and continued the rest of the way.

Isla muttered words that Poppy and Terra certainly didn't know she used as she followed him.

The banging of steel now rang through the rain, so loud, Isla winced as they got closer. Thunder rumbled above as if warring with the sound. The very ground seemed to tremble.

They climbed at a sharp incline, until finally, at the top of the hill, a structure came into view. Grim paused, his black cape whipping wildly in the wind.

The blacksmith's house was no more than a shed. It was made of the same stone that had cut her hand, and she could only imagine the type of tools necessary to be able to not just forage those rocks . . . but build from them.

The door was open, and flashes of red flickered through the entrance. Sparks from the molten-hot flames.

Abruptly, the banging stopped.

Grim slowly turned to face her. His eyes found her hand, still dripping in blood. "You fool," he muttered. "He will try to kill you."

Then Grim vanished.

Isla was alone. She looked down at her hand. It had already dripped a small puddle of blood below her. Could the blacksmith sense blood?

Was he a creature?

Her eyes searched through the rain, but she couldn't see anything. There was only one thought in her mind, carved from basic instinct and training.

Run.

She took off down the side of the hill, into a forest. She didn't know if nature was dangerous everywhere, but she would rather take the risk of the woods hurting her over a blacksmith who sensed blood.

Her heart drummed in her ears as she fought her way through the thicket. The branches cut through her clothes. She used her arms as shields, barreling her way through.

She felt the moment the creature entered the woods. All her senses seemed to heighten in warning. The forest itself seemed to still. Chills swept down her spine. It was as if her body knew there was a predator. And she was being hunted.

There was the crack of splitting bark as an arrow lodged itself an inch to her right, into the tree at her side. It was metal tipped. It would have gone right through her neck, with better aim. She gasped and took off again.

Another arrow whizzed by, and Isla didn't even bother to look where it went. She just ran and ran, crashing through branches and jumping over snaking vines.

The forest dipped low, and she lost her footing.

Suddenly, she was falling. She screamed out as her shoulder crunched painfully, her elbow scraped against a rock, her leg moved in an awkward direction. Her body tumbled quickly, only stopping when she hit a tree.

Then, silence as the world stilled and her pain caught up with her. She screamed soundlessly against the back of her hand. Dirt and mud caked her every inch. Her shoulder—something was wrong with it. Her entire body felt like a bruise.

Get up, that instinct in her mind said.

It was too late.

Footsteps sounded close by. Heavy steps that she heard even through the rain. Isla didn't dare move a muscle as the predator inched closer. Closer.

He stopped right in front of her.

The blacksmith leaned down, crouched to look upon the heap that was her broken body.

That was when she struck. She gripped the dagger she always kept on her and stabbed the blacksmith right through the eye.

He roared, and Isla scrambled to her feet. It took one step to realize something had happened to her ankle. She couldn't move—

She *had* to move.

Isla spotted a fence and limped forward. It was high. The gate was open. If she could just get through, maybe she could get it closed. Maybe she could figure out a plan.

She could hear the blacksmith getting up. He roared words into the rain that she didn't understand. She didn't dare turn around.

The whistle of an arrow, and she ducked low. It skimmed right above her head. She leaped to the side—her shoulder and ankle screaming in pain—behind a tree, and another arrow flew past.

She ran the last few steps, dragging her foot behind her, until she was past the fence. Her shaking hands hauled the gate closed and she collapsed against it.

Her teeth gritted against the pain. She closed her eyes as her body trembled against the gate. Hopefully it would hold. Her hands ran down its strange pattern. It was so smooth. Made of mismatched parts. So—

She opened her eyes. Looked behind her at the gate. And found that the entire fence was made of melded skulls and bones.

A yelp escaped her throat, and she scrambled back on the muddy ground, her fingers sinking into it. Her back crashed into something solid, and she screamed again.

Just then, the entire gate ripped off its hinges.

The blacksmith stood there, her dagger still lodged through his eye.

He was the most muscular man Isla had ever seen. His arms were enormous. He was holding a massive hammer that looked like it would go right through her body if she was hit with it. He had long, flowing black hair. Skin the pallor of a corpse.

Isla scrambled back against the other wall she had hit, a scream lodged in her throat.

The wall spoke. It sounded bored. "You can't have her, Baron. At least . . . not yet." She looked up and saw Grim frowning down at her. Not a wall. She had crashed into his legs. He raised an eyebrow. "I told you not to cut yourself, Hearteater."

The overwhelming urge to put a dagger through *his* eye filled her, but she couldn't stand again if she tried.

The blacksmith—*Baron*—hissed and returned the hammer to a holster on his back. "Ruler," he said, bending onto a knee. "To what do I owe the honor?"

"Black diamond hilt. Twin blades. You know the sword."

The blacksmith smiled proudly. Isla wondered if he was ever going to take the blade out of his eye. "I do. A very special weapon indeed. Among my best work."

Grim motioned toward her. "You've sensed her blood. Can she help me find it?"

The blacksmith pursed his lips. Considered. "She can."

This was why he needed her. Isla was trembling on the ground, but she found her voice long enough to say, "Why can't he find it himself?" She wondered if the blacksmith would answer her after she stabbed him in the face. Or if Grim would even allow him to.

The blacksmith met her gaze with his now single eye, and a shiver snaked down her spine. After a moment, he said, "The sword was cursed so no Nightshade ruler can claim it. If the sword so much as senses his ability, it will disappear."

So Grim couldn't use his powers to find it. This was why he needed her . . . though that didn't make sense.

Why not force one of his people to search for it? Why choose one of his rivals in the Centennial?

Before she could ask anything else, Grim said, "Do you know where it is?"

"Decades ago, I heard it had been stolen from a Skyling market. I sensed it return here, to Nightshade. Since then, nothing." He frowned. "I can't feel it anymore. Wherever it is . . . it's slumbering."

"Is there anything else we should know?"

The blacksmith opened his mouth again. His eyes darted to Isla. Then he closed his mouth. "Nothing else," he said.

"Good. Now, return the dagger. We'll be going."

The blacksmith roughly pulled Isla's weapon from his eye. What was left . . . Isla looked away to keep from retching.

He bent low to return it to her. Isla reached out with shaking fingers. Dark blood coated her blade. The rain only partially washed it away.

Before he handed it back, the blacksmith said, "You weren't supposed to be able to do that."

Then he walked back up through the forest to his forge, and Isla was left with burning questions.

And anger.

She turned on the ground to face Grim. "You *demon*. You almost got me killed. You—"

He rolled his eyes. "I was there. You were never in any danger."

Isla's entire body shook with her fury. "Never in any danger? My ankle—something is wrong with it. And my *shoulder*." She shook her head. "Why? Why let him hunt me?"

Grim shrugged. "I wanted to see how you would fare without me. Call it curiosity."

"Curiosity? Curiosity?" She attempted to stand, dagger gripped tightly in her hand, but her ankle rolled, and she nearly fell over.

Grim caught her beneath the arms. She tried to shake herself away, but it was no use. His grip was hard as marble.

"Why didn't you use your Wildling powers in the forest?" he asked.

The lie came easily. "You didn't portal directly to the house. You didn't use your own powers. I figured . . . there was a reason."

He just stared down at her.

She tried to move away again, then grimaced as pain shot down her shoulder. Grim held her still. He frowned. "It's out of its socket. I have to right it." Grim twisted her around, so her back was to him. He leaned down and said, "This will hurt."

Before she could object, his hands twisted, and she screamed so loudly, it hurt her own ears.

"Done," he said. "Now, there's nothing I can do about that ankle."

"Just—just portal me to my room," she said. The Wildling healing elixir would take care of the swelling, but it would be weeks before she walked the same again. She would have to come up with an excuse for Terra and Poppy. Pretend she had sprained it in training, or something else.

Her teeth gritted against the pain that roared again with their landing. She looked down at herself. She was a mess. Covered in dirt and mud. She would need about a thousand baths, and a quarter vial of healing elixir.

Tears stung as she closed her eyes. Was this what it would be like working with the Nightshade demon? Getting hurt? Running for her life from an ancient being for *curiosity's* sake?

She opened her eyes again and was surprised to see the Nightshade was still in the center of her room, leaking darkness everywhere.

"Can you not do that?" she snapped, watching the shadows uncurl, spreading themselves all over her stuff, only to return and repeat the process.

The shadows twitched, as if they had heard her and were offended. *Stupid. A shadow can't have its feelings hurt.*

Grim looked appalled. "You do not give me orders, witch."

She glared at him. "I thought I was *Hearteater*," she said, in about the most syrupy tone she could manage.

He glared back.

This was her chance to get answers. "Why did he have so many bones?"

"The blacksmith kills people with unique abilities and makes weapons from their blood and bones. He senses blood close by and kills anyone he can find, on the off chance they are useful." So why had he seemed desperate to have her blood?

Isla swallowed. She could have very well joined the fence of bones and skulls. Her people would have fallen. The blacksmith was ancient.

He'd seemed surprised that she was able to harm him. She had never been more grateful to have her dagger.

"So you can't use your abilities during our search. You will have to be powerless."

Grim said nothing.

Why was Grim the one looking for this sword? Not using his powers seemed like a massive inconvenience. Didn't he have people for that? Didn't he have far better things to do? She asked all these questions, in quick succession, and Grim's annoyance grew.

"You talk too much," he growled, and, for some reason, that stung.

Isla's chest felt as if someone were sitting on it. "I don't usually have people to talk to," she murmured.

His tone didn't get any gentler as he said, "This is too important for me to tell anyone in my court. I can't risk sending someone else or trusting them with any of my information." He hesitated before saying, "I've been betrayed in the search for the sword before."

Someone betrayed him? Why?

Would he betray her?

Isla turned to him, an eyebrow raised. "But you trust me?"

"Absolutely not." He took a step toward her. Another. "If you have any desire at all to survive the Centennial, you will not tell anyone in your court either."

Her court. She didn't even know what that was. Celeste didn't have a court, just her string of guardians who died every few years and were replaced, an endless cycle. Terra and Poppy were the only people Isla saw regularly.

As if she would ever tell any of them. They would all call her a fool for working with the Nightshade. They would ensure she could never leave her room again until the Centennial.

"What about the blacksmith? He knows we're looking for it."

Grim shook his head gruffly. "He won't remember."

She tilted her head at him. "Why?"

"Few people are foolish enough to visit him in the first place. But, in an abundance of caution, I took his memories away."

Isla blinked. "That's something . . . you can do?"

He nodded, as if it were not the cruelest power in the world.

"It's . . . permanent?"

"If I want it to be."

She shivered. There were still so many unanswered questions. If he needed the sword so badly, why didn't he look for it before? Why now? What had changed?

Isla wondered if she should back out. Grim was clearly using her. Now she wasn't even sure if what he had promised was worth the risk.

She and Celeste had a plan for the Centennial. She hadn't managed to find the skin gloves, but there was still time. Almost a year.

Isla looked around her room. The glass cage. Grim was insufferable, but the search for the sword promised something she had longed for since she was a child. Freedom. Escape, for just a while.

"So . . ." she said, wondering if she was making a huge mistake. The blacksmith had said the sword was stolen and last sensed on Grim's territory. "Who are the best thieves on Nightshade?"

PREMONITION

There was still no word on the Skyling vote. It had been pushed back, after much debate. Most Wildlings trained for war, and the rest worked nonstop to make more healing elixirs. Starlings on the newland were creating special armor for them, infused with energy.

Now, she needed to focus on the shield. Maren had promised Isla a list of the greatest wielders on Star Isle, to determine how large it would be.

Days had passed without her request being fulfilled. It was unlike Maren, who had managed all other aspects of preparing for the incoming war and evacuation with ease. Enya had helped Isla provide direct aid to Star Isle in the last few weeks—food, resources, guards at their bridge—and Maren had managed everything without issue.

She was clearly surprised to see Isla when she stepped foot on Star Isle.

"Isla," Maren said. "I wasn't expecting you today. We can get—"

"Who is the best Starling at wielding?" Isla asked. "Just—just take me to them." Her tone was harsh, but Grim was coming in only twenty days. They couldn't waste a moment.

Maren didn't meet her eyes. It took her several seconds to even say a word. "There are a few who are skilled. I can take you to them."

"No," Isla said. "Who is the best?" She frowned. "Is it—is it you?" Was that why Maren had been evasive?

Maren shook her head.

"Then who?"

The Starling met her eyes. The intensity there took Isla aback. "The king hasn't changed his mind about taking fighters who aren't volunteers?"

"No. No one is being forced to fight. We just need energy for the shield."

"Can . . . can the pooling of energy be anonymous?"

Anonymous? Isla was getting irritated. "I suppose so. Why?"

Maren's expression became more intense than usual. "Promise me," she said. "If I tell you, promise that you won't tell anyone."

Isla frowned. She was her ruler. She didn't have to make promises in exchange for information. Still, she saw the fierceness in Maren's face and nodded. "I won't tell anyone but the king."

Maren considered. She closed her eyes. "I will show you," she said.

She took her to a field of craters. They were holes in the isle like stars had fallen from the sky and left their marks. Someone stood in one of the craters' center.

Streams of silver shot from their hands in glittering ribbons. They whipped against the sides of the crater, piercing the rock, slicing through it like butter. Creatures formed from the sparks, and they slithered, jumped, flew around the crater, contained only by its perimeter. It was a dazzling display of power.

It was Cinder.

Isla's mouth had dropped open watching. Cinder wielded power like a master. Her stances, the liquidous movements of her arms—everything was so natural, as if she'd been alive for many multiples of her actual age.

She jumped down into the crater, and the little girl whipped around. A smile transformed her features. "Isla!"

"Who was your teacher?" she asked in lieu of greeting. "Are they still living?"

Cinder regarded her strangely. "Teacher?" She looked to Maren,

who had carefully made her way down one of the crater's edges. Maren only shrugged a shoulder.

"Who taught you to wield this way?" Isla shook her head in disbelief. "I was told there weren't any Starling masters left. How many can wield like you? You must have started training before you could walk! You must practice every moment."

Cinder laughed. "No, not really." She shrugged. "I'm just good at it, I guess."

I guess?

Isla looked to Maren, who seemed wary. She stepped to the opposite side of the crater, away from Cinder, and Isla followed. "When she was two years old, I heard her laughing in a room all alone. I came in to find her playing with a perfect ball of sparks. One she had created herself."

Isla's brows came together. "But that . . . that shouldn't be possible, should it? Someone who isn't a ruler being that powerful?"

"It is certainly unusual. She is the best wielder on the isle." She lowered her voice. "And she is the only reason any of us survived the fire that destroyed our homes."

Cinder was laughing as she created an animal with a crown of antlers out of sparks. It hopped on its haunches, jumping around her in a circle. Isla understood now. "That's why you've never let her leave," she said. "You don't want anyone else to know."

Maren nodded. "She is more a sister to me than a cousin. Having any family relation is rare for Starlings. She is my responsibility. She is everything to me."

Cinder blasted over, propelled by Starling energy shooting out of both of her palms. "Your turn, Isla! The crater is so plain and boring. Paint it with flowers!"

Maren gave her a look. "She is our ruler, Cinder. You do not command her."

"It's all right," Isla said, smiling. She raised her hand, and flowers bloomed across the ground.

"Pretty! Make a beast next! Make one like I do, but out of plants and sticks and stuff!"

Her expression faltered, just a little. "I—I don't think I can, Cinder."

Cinder frowned. "Why not?"

"I'm only now learning to wield. I'm not a master. Not yet."

Cinder tilted her head, her dark hair falling across her forehead. "You can't fully wield power?" A little crease appeared between her brows. "But . . . it's so easy."

"Cinder."

"Especially for a ruler. Right?"

"*Cinder.*"

"And you have *so much*, you—"

"Cinder!" Maren took her hand and began leading her away. "That's enough. And enough of this," she said.

Isla had the impression that Maren had restricted Cinder to use her power only during certain time frames and within the confines of this crater.

"Maren," Isla said, stepping forward while Cinder collected her things. Her voice was low. "We need her to provide energy for the shield." And possibly, Isla thought, to turn ore into the essential metal, if Zed and Calder managed to extract it. Maren looked from Cinder to Isla warily. "We're going to cover most of the Mainland with thorns and bog sand, but walls of energy will be critical to limit where Nightshade can strike."

Maren closed her eyes. "You promise to keep it anonymous?"

"I give you my word. She can form her part of the shield with no one else around."

"Fine," Maren said. Then, she called Cinder to her in a sharp tone. "We're leaving," she said. As she was taken away, Cinder looked over her shoulder and smiled. With a flick of her tiny hand, she sent a flurry of sparks to Isla that fell from the sky like glitter.

. . .

Isla told Oro about Cinder before bed. She was walking around the room, speaking with her hands, trying to demonstrate what the little girl had done.

"What do you make of it?" she asked, turning to face him when she was done.

"I think Cinder sounds like a very special child."

"Have those existed?" she asked.

"A few, over the centuries. There have been non-rulers born with flairs, even. Unfortunately, their tales often end in tragedy. Maren is right to keep her hidden."

Isla frowned. "But you're the king. Couldn't you protect her?"

"I could order an army to stand around her at all times. I could send for her to come live here, in the castle. Would you like that?"

"No," she said. Cinder's life seemed difficult, but in many ways she was free. The castle or legion would just become a thicker prison.

She took a step toward the bed, exhausted, when her vision suddenly went dark. Her limbs went numb—her body folded over. Before she hit the ground, she was in Oro's arms. Physically, warmth surrounded her.

Mentally, all she felt was cold.

It was her vision again, clearer than ever.

Darkness fell from the sky, night cut into pieces. It pressed onto her skin, got stuck in her eyelashes. Howls. Dreks.

Screams. People dying all around her.

Through it all, she saw Grim. The darkness touched everything but him. He was its source.

He was looking at her. He didn't look at the dying around him, he just looked right at her and stalked toward her with a concentration that cut through her like a blade.

Run, a voice inside her head said. *Leave. Save yourself.*

She either couldn't or didn't. She stayed there as darkness parted her lips and forced her to drink it.

She tasted death on the back of her tongue.

Then, in her chest.

Something was wrong. Something was very wrong.

Isla tried to fight it, but it was no use. In her vision, her organs began to shut down, one by one.

She felt it, as every part of her withered away.

She felt herself die.

Oro was cradling her in his arms. Apparently, she had been screaming. Tears choked her words, as she tried to explain what she had seen. Her vision, but more. It was clearer now. Longer. Before, she had seen only Grim's darkness and destruction.

Now, she knew how it ended.

"He kills me," she said. "In the future, he kills me."

Heat nearly set the room aflame. Oro's lip curled over his teeth. She had never seen him more murderous than she did now. "Then we will kill him first."

Her eyes rolled to the back of her head as she fell into another memory.

BEFORE

Poppy and Terra had sealed the loose pane in her room. She'd had to tell them about it in an elaborate story to explain her sprained ankle. For hours, Terra had screamed at her about how foolish she was.

Poppy wrapped her ankle in medicinal bark, and as punishment, Terra trained her harder in ways that didn't require putting weight on her legs. It took ten days for her to walk close to normally again. She wondered if Grim would look for the sword without her, but he waited until she was almost fully healed.

He didn't do it out of the kindness of his heart, she knew. It was because he needed her. She was integral to his search. She just needed to figure out how she fit into his plan.

Grim appeared in her room. He had a hold on his powers. The shadows that typically leaked from his feet were gone. His crown and cape were missing. He might not have worn his emblems as a ruler, but he was still unmistakably terrifying.

The blacksmith had told them the sword had been stolen, and, according to Grim, there was a notorious thieving group on his lands. They had a base on the other side of Nightshade. He wordlessly took her arm.

They portaled to the edge of a fishing town. The air was thick with salt and rotten catch. The streets were empty. Every curtain was closed. Of course, it was night—

Isla tensed. Panic gripped her chest.

"*Your curse,*" she said, words sputtering out of her. She pointed at the moon, like a fool, then, at him. "You can't—"

Grim wore a bored expression. "Go outside at night?"

She nodded.

"That won't be a problem." Then he turned back around.

Not a problem? "Even *you* are not powerful enough to escape the curses."

He sighed in clear irritation that she kept insisting on speaking to him. "No," he admitted. "But someone else was, and they made me this." He clutched at something below the collar of his shirt, some sort of charm, then instantly turned his attention away from her.

That didn't satiate her curiosity or confusion at all. How was it possible that a simple strand allowed Grim to be immune from his curse? It didn't make any sense. It should be impossible—

"While I am flattered by your concern about my well-being," he said, in about the most pompous tone possible, "focus on finding the sword. Not me."

She shut her mouth but wondered about the charm. Why didn't he make one for every Nightshade? Was it rare? Did he want his people to stay cursed?

A small boat with paddles floated at the docks, waiting for them. Grim couldn't portal them to the thieves, lest the sword be there and sense his power. Isla had asked if she could use her starstick, and he had said no.

She tried to grab one of the paddles, but he snatched it out of her hand. She sat behind him, watching his back as the muscles rolled. The sight should have disgusted her.

She wished it disgusted her.

It was miles to the isle. His paddling never weakened.

"It's surprising," she said, staring at him. The ocean was dark as ink around them. The moon was a paltry crescent.

She thought he was going to ignore her, but after a few minutes, he said in an annoyed voice, "What, pray tell, is so surprising?"

He was facing the opposite direction. She couldn't see his expression, and perhaps that made her bold. "Your flair is portaling. You can go

anywhere without lifting a finger. Yet . . . you climb quickly. You can paddle well. You are . . . muscled."

"Ogling my body, Hearteater?" he asked.

Isla's cheeks burned. She was suddenly extremely grateful they weren't facing each other. "Only in your dreams," she said.

He sighed. "Is there a question?"

"Yes. It's been hundreds of years since war. You can portal anywhere with half a thought. Why keep up with your . . . fitness regimens? Why . . . when you have so much ability?"

"I have never relied solely on my powers," he said. "A person's mettle is determined by who they are beneath them." He turned to look at her, lip curled in disgust. "And only a fool waits to prepare for a war until one is declared."

She was silent after that, until the boat roughly washed up onto the pebbled rocks of the isle.

He turned to look at her. "I won't save you," he warned. "If it's you or the sword, it will not be a difficult decision. I will find a way to get it without you."

"I am aware," she said through her teeth.

"Good."

The thieves' base was a tall structure with long and rectangular windows, all covered with thick fabric, which made their approach much easier.

"We look for the sword. If we don't find it, we get information," he said.

The first window they approached was unlocked and unguarded. Grim opened it from the bottom, and they slipped through without issue. Isla supposed the thieves weren't worried about any Nightshade visiting their isle at night. Who would be able to?

Inside, there was only silence.

"I'll search the top floors," Grim said. He swept past her, leaving her alone. The room was unremarkable. Just a place to store supplies,

by the looks of it. She removed the top of a barrel and found some sort of alcohol. Before she left, she listened.

There wasn't any noise in the hall either. Maybe the thieves were asleep?

She crept along the first floor, going from room to room. One looked like a kitchen. One had a few tables. The walls were stone. Wind whistled through large cracks. It was freezing.

Isla finally reached a hall, lined in windows. She carefully pulled part of one of the curtains away. The sea crashed nearby. The slice of moon illuminated the water. She saw its reflection in the waves.

She pushed the curtain back into place, then walked backward, admiring the high ceiling. Wondering if Grim was almost done searching the top floors.

She didn't even hear them coming until a blade was already against her throat. "I wonder what you might go for," the voice in her ear said.

Training overruled panic. In a flash, she grabbed his arms with both hands and pulled, giving some distance between the blade and her neck. She curved her shoulder up, bent under his arms, hands still gripped on his wrists, twisted to his side—and stabbed him with his own dagger, over and over and over. Terra had tested her in this exact scenario.

The man slumped to the ground. He looked surprised to see blood puddling next to him. He was still alive, just in shock. She couldn't afford to be. She took a step, and two more Nightshades were on her.

She reached for her blade, and they reached for theirs.

They struck first. Isla dodged the first man's blows, steel echoing through the room. More would come. She knew that.

Where was Grim? Had he searched the floors already? Had he run into his own trouble?

She remembered his words. He wouldn't save her. She needed to save herself.

The next man struck, and Isla raced to defend from both sides. Sweat shot down her temple. She had never fought like this before. Training was one thing . . . real fighting was another. One of the Nightshades aimed for her head and just barely missed.

Her fingers felt around the side of her pants, slipping into the specially designed pockets that held her throwing blades. It wasn't her dominant hand, but Terra had ensured she was proficient in both. She gripped the blades between her fingers and threw them at one of the men, just as he was going for another blow.

One landed in the middle of his chest. The other landed in the middle of his throat. He looked down briefly before falling forward, accidentally impaling himself on his own sword.

Nausea rolled through her stomach. She had just killed her first person that she knew of . . . Should she feel guilty? He had been attacking her. But she had invaded his home . . .

The blow came out of nowhere. The other man struck the side of her head with the hilt of his blade, and she immediately fell to the floor. Her ears rang. Blood dripped down her temple.

He could have killed her, but he didn't. Which meant he was thinking of other uses for her. Anger and fear made her breathing uneven.

In the fall, she had dropped her sword. The Nightshade approached. He kicked her weapon out of reach, and the metal clattered against the marble floor. He smiled as he walked toward her. His eyes roamed down her body in a way that made her want to retch.

"I think I'll keep you for myself," he said. "I like them with a little fight."

Grim. Where was he? Was he coming?

The man stepped forward. From this angle, he was framed by the window curtain behind him. He grinned as he approached. He wanted to be closer to her. He wanted to be pressed against her.

She decided to give him exactly what he wanted.

Before she could have second thoughts, Isla rushed to her feet and shoved herself against him with a roar, his blade slicing her arm in the process. He tensed in confusion. She pushed as hard as she could—

And sent them both crashing through the window. The curtain ripped away. Glass shattered.

The man screamed for half a second before his entire body melted into ash beneath her. She gasped and accidentally inhaled some of it. The rest stuck to the blood on her arms and face.

Isla stood on shaking legs, caked in what was left of the man. She turned very slowly to see Grim standing in the hall, staring at her through what remained of the window.

She bent over and retched.

Grim just watched her as she walked through the open hole in the wall. She used one of the other curtains to try to get the ashes off her. "Did you find it?" she asked before heaving again.

"No," he said. "But I found him."

That was when she noticed the Nightshade on the floor, bound and gagged. "I've asked you three times about the sword," Grim said. "I've described it in detail. You know what I am referring to. Now, for the last time. Where is it? Is it here?" He ripped the fabric from the man's mouth.

The Nightshade made a sound like a whimper. He shook his head.

Grim sighed. "I really didn't want to get my sword dirty," he said. Then he cut off the man's hand.

The Nightshade screamed a wild sound. She watched the man's hand spasm on the ground and felt like she was going to be sick again.

"It's already dirty now," Grim said, frowning down at his sword. "Your limbs are next."

He lifted his blade, and the man said, "Wait. Wait." He trembled. "If I tell you, will you let me go?"

Grim considered. He nodded.

"Do you swear it?"

"We swear it," Isla said, eyes darting to the man's injury. He needed to cauterize the wound soon, or he would bleed to death in front of them.

The man swallowed. His words came out in just a rasp. "It hasn't been here in decades. We stole it, but one of us went rogue. He took the sword and lost it to someone else. Only he knows where it is now."

"Where can we find him?" Grim demanded.

"His name is Viktor. He's been seen near Creetan's Crag."

"How will we know it's him?" Isla asked.

The man let out a wheezing noise. He was pressing his wound against his body to try to stop the blood. It was getting everywhere. "He has . . . he has a snake. Takes it with him everywhere." A snake?

"Thank you for being so helpful," Grim said, sounding genuinely sincere.

Then he slit the man's throat.

Isla gasped. She watched the man choke on his own blood before he collapsed on the floor.

"You promised," she said, turning to him.

Grim frowned down at her. "No, Hearteater," he said. "You promised." Tears stung in the corners of her eyes. They swept down her cheeks. He looked at her with disgust. "Don't tell me you are crying for that filth's death."

"Filth?" she asked, incredulous. "He is one of your people."

"Don't speak about my people when you don't know the first thing about your own. Locked in a room with the glass painted over . . ." Grim bared his teeth at her. "He was a thief and sold much more than just rare objects," he said. "He deserved to die, and I was happy to be the one to end him."

Isla swallowed. She turned to the other dead body in the room. Then to the man she had stabbed in the side with his own dagger. He was dead now too. And the man who was now no more than ashes . . . A sob scraped against the back of her throat. "I—I've never . . ."

Grim just stared down at her. His expression did not soften in the slightest in response to her tears. He watched her cry for a few more seconds, before saying, "It gets easier."

Then he took her arm and portaled them back to her room.

She had to close her eyes against the sudden rush of nausea. She didn't want to retch again. She didn't want to think about what she had just *done*—

"There is a celebration on Creetan's Crag in two weeks," he said. "That's when I'll return."

Her eyes were still closed when he left.

I DO NOT DIE TODAY

The outcome of the battle was not set in stone, that was what the oracle had said. Those were the words Isla clung to as her own death replayed in her mind, over and over again, and as she watched Oro rage against the vault.

He had tried to use her power to open the door, but it remained closed.

"Oro," she finally said, placing a hand against his tensed back. Only then did he stop.

He pulled her into his arms and said, "He isn't going to kill you. I will rip him limb from limb before he ever hurts you."

The floor seemed to tremble with his promise. She had never seen him so disheveled, so . . .

Afraid.

She was afraid too. "I need to know. You and me . . . we have a love bond. Does that mean if I die . . . you can take my abilities? You can save the Starlings and Wildlings?"

Oro's eyes flashed with fear. "You're not going to die, Isla. But yes. I should be able to."

Her relief must have been visible because Oro became more distressed. She placed her hands against the sides of his face. "You aren't going to lose me," she said. "I'm not going to die." She would make sure she kept that promise.

Which meant they needed to make sure they won the war.

"I'm going to see the Vinderland with Enya," she said. "And you need to be okay with that." The Sunling was waiting for her now. They were going immediately.

More fear and pain had hardened in Oro's eyes, and she understood, she really did. If he was set to do something reckless, she would feel the same way. She thought of her guardians then, and Cleo with her son.

It was possible to love someone too hard. It was possible to turn love into a prison.

He finally nodded. "You're right," he said. He walked her over to Enya, who was waiting beyond the Mainland woods. Before they left, he pressed a hand against her arm. Sparks erupted from his touch, shimmering, covering her entire body from the neck down. It formed onto her as closely as her clothes. Besides the faint sparkle, it was nearly invisible.

"It's a Starling shield," he said. "Like the one you're creating for the battle, but smaller. Can you take it over?"

She focused on the energy. Breathed in and out. Slowly, under her command, it dripped down her fingers, past her skin. Keeping the shield in place took effort, but she was grateful for its protection.

"It's not invincible," Oro said, "but it will stop an arrow."

"Thank you," she said, before lifting on her toes to kiss him. At first, it was soft, but then Oro grabbed her like he was afraid she wouldn't be able to keep her promise, like she might be gone any day now. His fingers ran through the back of her hair, tilting her head, giving him a better angle. His other arm curled around her waist, and she felt her shield ripple there. She pulled him closer.

Enya cleared her throat, and Isla tore herself away. The Sunling shook her head at them while Isla drew her puddle of stars and portaled them to the people who had split her heart in two.

Wind howled in her ears. Her cheeks went numb. The air was white, coated in a thin layer of snow. They were on flat land, yet fighting against the current of the snowstorm made every step forward feel like climbing up a mountain.

211

"What a charming place to live," Enya bit out, before her body was coated in reddish gold. It wrapped around her like Isla's Starling shield, then spread beyond, warming the air around them until Isla could feel her nose again. "That's better, isn't it?" she asked. The snow below the Sunling's shoes melted and sizzled.

Isla searched the blank horizon. There were a few monstrous mountains, covered in sharp panes of ice that looked like scales. "I don't know how they survived out here," she said. She remembered coming to Vinderland territory with Oro, during their search for the heart. It was hard to imagine, but back then, it had been colder. Ever since the Moonlings left, Moon Isle had increasingly gotten warmer.

"Are you . . . are you afraid?" Isla asked, wondering if she sounded like a fool.

Enya only glanced over at her. "No. Not at all."

"Why not?" she said. "The Vinderland are warriors. I've seen how well they fight"—which was why they so desperately needed them in battle—"They don't just kill their enemies . . . they *eat* them." And not because of a curse. Simply for pleasure.

Enya stared at her for a long while. "I'm going to tell you something only Oro, Cal, and Zed know."

Isla blinked. She was surprised Enya would tell her anything personal. They weren't necessarily friends. It had been clear from the beginning that Enya was like a shield around Oro, protecting him at all costs. Her loyalty was to him, not her.

She waited.

"I know exactly when I will die," Enya said.

Isla stopped and was instantly drenched in cold, now outside of the dome of warmth Enya had created.

She thought of her vision. Her own death.

"What? How—how could you know that?"

Enya motioned for her to keep moving, and she did. "The day I

was born, a Moonling sent for my mother. The oracle wanted to see her. She hadn't thawed in a while, so it was considered important. She visited her, holding me. The oracle told my mother she had seen my death."

Isla realized they had more in common than she'd thought. For a moment, she wondered if she should tell Enya about her vision. Who else would understand?

In the end, all she said was, "That's . . . awful."

Enya shrugged a shoulder. Bits of snow fell above them and melted inches away, raining onto their heads. "Most mothers might think so, but mine wasn't like that. She said, 'Well, are you going to tell me?' The oracle did. When I was old enough to understand, my mother gave me the choice. Know how and when I will die . . . or don't. I've been told I'm a lot like her . . . and you already know which choice I've made."

"Does Oro know?"

"When I die?"

Isla nodded.

"No, though he used to ask me incessantly when we were younger. I think he wanted to know so he could somehow keep it from happening. He's like you, in that way. He carries guilt around that doesn't even belong to him." She lifted a shoulder. "I think of it as a gift. I know when I die, so I can spend every day until then living to the fullest. You and Oro seem to get lost in your minds, thinking about the past, future—I spend most of my time in the present." She sighed. "The reason I'm telling you this is to explain why I'm not afraid. Not even in the slightest."

Just as the words left her mouth, a legion of Vinderland appeared on the horizon, wearing metal helmets with massive tusks, fur around their necks, and intricate armor. They were holding swords and axes longer than her limbs.

Enya casually turned to Isla, winked, and said, "I do not die today."

. . .

A flurry of arrows struck Isla and ricocheted off the Starling shield glittering along her skin, humming with energy. It took every ounce of focus for her to hold it in place, and she winced with every hit. They might not have pierced her skin, but they would certainly leave bruises.

At her side, Enya formed a wall of fire, charring the arrows before they reached her. Her movements were smooth, casual even, as she melted all ice and snow around her and turned their weapons to ash.

There was a battle cry, and Isla leaped to the side as an axe was thrown right at her body. Its blade missed her by inches, and then the warriors descended.

They bellowed words she didn't understand and rushed forward, moving surprisingly quickly with the heavy armor they wore. Thick furs peeked through the gaps in the metal.

"Red hair," one of them yelled, staring at Enya. "You're going to make a lovely stew. Charred and zesty." He smiled, revealing teeth sharpened into points—better to tear flesh with.

"And you're going to make a lovely pile of ashes," Enya replied, her fire bursting forth, burning his beard. The man screamed as the rest of him caught fire. He rolled onto the snow.

A sword came for Isla's neck, and she ducked, then hit the man in the temple, knocking him out. They needed these warriors—they were worthless in battle dead.

Enough.

She flung her arms to either side, and trees sprung up from the lifeless land, breaking through the ice.

The Vinderland went still. If they didn't recognize her before, they certainly did now.

One towering man stepped forward, his armor clanking. He took off his horned helmet, revealing a sharp face with a

diagonal scar across it. "How dare you come here, after killing so many of us?"

Isla bared her teeth. "You all almost killed me. You tried to eat me. You put an arrow through my heart."

His eyes narrowed. "Yet here you are. Do you think you'll be so lucky to escape death a third time?"

She almost smiled. *Escape death*. That was exactly what she was trying to do.

"With your help, I hope so," she said.

The man laughed. It was hoarse and made her skin crawl. The rest joined him, their laughs echoing in their helmets. "We would sooner die than help any of you."

"Then you will die anyway," she said, stepping forward. "Nightshades are coming to destroy Lightlark. There will be nothing left. Every inch will be decimated. Everyone will perish, including you."

The man's eyes narrowed at her. "Lightlark has survived thousands of years, several wars—"

"Not like this one," she said. "I know the future, and it is destruction."

"The oracle—"

"She says Lightlark's fate is in the balance. Everyone must protect it." She curled her lip in disgust. "I hate you," she said. "And you hate me. But we have a common enemy, and that is anyone who would destroy Lightlark. I'm sure you've noticed Moonling has left."

He nodded.

"They have joined Nightshade."

The warriors behind him began talking to each other.

"We need you," Isla said. "We need every warrior on this island to defend it. Say you will fight alongside us. If we can make peace, then there is hope for the future of Lightlark."

The man considered. She waited. Finally, he put his helmet back on and said, "No."

Then, he gripped his battle axe and aimed for her head.

Her focus wavered; her shield fell away. Time seemed to slow down as she watched the axe swing toward her face. Her hand instinctively raised to block herself, fingers half an inch from the metal. In her mind, she knew, logically, her hand would be cut in half, and the axe would bury in her brain. She would die.

But that's not what happened.

The moment Isla touched the blade, the axe turned to ash.

BEFORE

Isla counted down the days until her visit to Creetan's Crag. She often waited up past midnight, in case Grim might make an appearance. Maybe there would be a change in their plan, another place to go.

He never came. She started to turn their last conversation around in her mind. *Don't speak about my people when you don't know the first thing about your own.*

He was right. All she knew about the Wildlings was what Terra and Poppy had told her. Her people were strangers. She only ever saw them during ceremonies.

That night, so late that she was sure Poppy and Terra were sleeping, she grabbed her starstick and portaled to the other side of the Wildling newland. Before, she'd never dared. The cost of getting caught was too great.

Tonight, she just wanted to see them. Understand them.

She had been to one of the villages before, for a short, closely monitored visit. That was where she went.

The forest scraped against her skin as she landed, purposefully trying to mark her. She stayed on its outskirts, eyes on the village. From here, she could see the backs of houses. They were worn and leaned together like a group of old friends.

Something in her burned. Her only friend was Celeste, who was currently angry at her. Since Isla had started working with Grim, her visits had become more infrequent. Celeste had noticed. Isla had made excuses, of course. Lies. With each one that slipped out, they got easier to tell. Just like Grim said about the killing.

A light burned up ahead. Someone was awake. Isla wondered if she could creep around the edges of the village, just to overhear a conversation. Just to watch. She wondered if perhaps she could try to blend in. Maybe they wouldn't recognize her. The dress she wore was not elaborate. The only times they would have seen her would be in full costume, barely recognizable as a person underneath so many flower petals.

Just one step out of the woods. Just a few minutes walking around the village. It couldn't hurt, could it?

She was very close to taking a step out of the forest when the choice was made for her.

"Now," she heard, and she turned around, in time to see the hilt of a sword before it hit her forehead.

When Isla awoke, she was bound. Her hands were tied behind her, at the base of her back. Her ankles were roped together.

There were voices.

"I don't recognize her. Do you?"

"No."

"Good. Get your dagger."

There was a pause. Then, "She's Wildling."

"So? We're starving. There haven't been hearts in weeks."

Isla's vision was still blurry, but she regained consciousness quickly. *Starving.*

She didn't understand. Terra and Poppy hadn't mentioned a shortage of hearts. She knew her people were steadily weakening since she was born powerless, but she was under the impression they still had a decently steady supply.

The women left the room she was being kept in, and Isla saw her chance. She wrestled with the restraints, but they were tied tightly. With a roll of her spine, she realized they hadn't found her starstick. It was still tucked into the back of her bodice.

She stretched her fingers up as far as they could go, twisting her wrists painfully, seeing if she could reach it. But there were still a few inches between them.

And the women were back.

"She's awake," one said uncertainly. There was regret in her tone.

"Doesn't matter," the other replied.

The one who had reservations was her last chance. "You don't have to do this," she told the woman. Her vision was still blurry from the hit, her forehead pulsed in pain, but she could make out the Wildling's features. Large, dark eyes. Small nose. Long limbs, and hair down to her waist. "I'm Wildling. Please."

She turned to the other woman, as if to say, *See?* but the second one simply stuck something firmly in her mouth. A gag.

No.

Then she produced a dagger.

What a fool. She should have used her few words to tell them she was their ruler. Then they would understand her death would kill them all. She had been too worried about revealing her identity—

Too late now. With little ceremony, the woman ripped her bodice down the center. Then she began to carve through her chest.

Isla screamed an animalistic noise that made it past even the gag and scratched the back of her throat like sharp nails. She was on fire. The pain was a flame consuming her, eating her from the inside out. She could smell her own blood, and the Wildling kept sawing, through skin and tissue—

When the blade went deeper, Isla arched unnaturally, and that was when her bound fingers grazed her starstick. She screamed to the heavens, wondering if it might make it across the realms to Grim, not even knowing if that was possible.

With renewed hope, she fought against the restraints, the rope burning her wrists, until she could finally grasp the device. She wrestled one hand free, then drew her puddle behind her. She hurled herself off the table and was gone in an instant.

She couldn't go home. Terra and Poppy couldn't know about this. With this pain, it would be almost impossible to keep quiet. One moment she was being carved. The next, she was bleeding out in the middle of Grim's room. He was standing in its corner, without a shirt on, clearly getting ready to sleep.

Shadows raced across the floor. He pulled the gag out of her mouth, and his eyes widened at the state of her chest.

"Sorry. I shouldn't have . . . I didn't—I didn't know where else to go, I couldn't go home," she said, and then his arms were lifting her from the floor. "My guardians—they can't know I—"

He made a sound like a growl and said, "You are a fool."

"I am very much aware."

"Who am I killing tonight?"

"What? No one."

He looked down at her. "I don't know how you're still conscious," Grim said like an accusation. Then, "Why won't you stop bleeding?" almost to himself. The remaining rope around her wrists turned to ash.

"I just need you to do one thing for me," she said. "Well, two." Her breathing was labored. "I need you to get my healing elixir from my room." She described it to him, and he was gone. A moment later, he returned with it. With a shaking hand, she poured the liquid over her chest.

Her scream would have woken up the entire Wildling castle. She shook as she applied more, until the skin began to slowly grow back. It did nothing for the pain. Grim silently offered her a roll of bandages, which she took and wrapped around herself, making a makeshift top. It soaked with blood immediately, so she added more. When she peeked over her shoulder, she saw the Nightshade was gone.

That was fine. She knew he didn't care about her injury, so long as she lived.

He returned a little while later and all but shoved a mug at her. "Here. Drink this."

She winced as she took it from him. "Medicine?" she asked.

"No. This has sugar that will keep you conscious. It . . . helps." She glanced down and saw it was dark brown, and thick. Was he lying to her?

Isla dipped her nose to it to smell.

"I could kill you a thousand different ways, Hearteater," he said flatly. "Poison would not be one of them."

True. She took a sip, and he was right. Pain still consumed her, but this made her feel the littlest bit better.

Chocolate. It was melted chocolate and tasted like molten divinity, poured into this stone mug. The best thing she had ever tasted. She'd had chocolate a handful of times in her life, from the chefs in the Wildling palace during special holidays and from the Skyling market. But not like this. Not in a *drink*.

"So, I take it you like chocolate."

"Yes," she said, voice coming out like a croak. "Do you have something else for the pain?" she asked, desperate. "How about that Nightshade substance?" She remembered the vials in the night market. The seller had said it would take away all pain. "Nightbane?"

Grim went still. In a voice that chilled the room, he said, "You will never know nightbane."

"Why not?" she asked. Why did he get so upset about it?

"It's a drug."

"What does it do?"

He frowned. "It makes you the happiest you've ever been and takes away all suffering."

She blinked. "I want it."

He gave her a scathing look. "It kills you slowly, methodically, efficiently, until you die with a smile on your mouth. With continued use nightbane is a death sentence, and everyone who takes it knows it."

Never mind. "So why take it?"

Grim shrugged a shoulder. "I will never understand. I suppose they feel the pleasure . . . however short-lived . . . is worth it."

Isla moved, and pain ripped down her middle. "Alcohol. Do you have . . . alcohol?" She had never tried it, but it was rumored to help with pain.

In a moment, a bottle was in her hands, and she drank a large swig.

She immediately choked. Her throat burned. It was as if the liquid was eating through it. It turned out alcohol tasted exactly like it smelled. "Why don't you have anything but alcohol in your room for pain?"

"Pain is useful," he said quietly. He didn't elaborate.

"It doesn't feel very useful now," she mumbled.

Grim looked down at her. It seemed to surprise them both when he said, "When I was seven, my training consisted of being cut and skinned until there was barely any flesh left on my back."

Isla's jaw went slack. Her training could be painful . . . but to do that to a child? "That is barbaric."

He only lifted a shoulder. "It was a custom here, for a very long time. Meant to toughen the body and mind at the height of its growth. The place I trained as a warrior . . . we were punished for the smallest of infractions. In public. Shadows can turn into the sharpest, thinnest blades."

"That's humiliating."

"It wasn't. It was a chance to prove we didn't react to the pain. Standing there, being cut, and not moving a muscle in your face . . . It was seen as strength." His eyes weren't on her when he said, "My father would come and watch. It was an honor to show him that I had no reaction to the pain."

She crinkled her nose. "You know how awful that sounds, right?"

He nodded. "It's why that doesn't happen anymore. Our training is still ruthless . . . but not as cruel."

Isla swallowed. What he had said about the punishment . . . "But . . . you don't have any scars." He only had one. And she had given it to him. "You have a Moonling healer, don't you? Or Moonling healing supplies?" It didn't make sense. "Why is Cleo helping you?"

Grim just looked at her. After a few moments, all he said was, "You should leave."

She felt a bite of hurt and didn't know why. He was asking her to leave his quarters, when she was injured. Why was she shocked? He didn't care about her.

The second thing she needed from him. Isla collected her torn top from the floor and said, "Can you . . . destroy this? I can't bring it home. All the blood . . ."

A moment later, the top was only ash.

She grabbed her starstick and, without another word, portaled back to her room.

In the middle of the night, she woke and almost screamed.

Grim was sitting across from her bed, watching her.

"What are you—"

"I'm making sure you don't bleed out in your sleep," he grumbled.

Isla looked down at her bandages. Blood was already peeking through again. She got a few rags she used to clean her swords and pressed them to her, so she wouldn't stain her sheets. She would need to ask Grim to destroy them before he left.

"I'm fine," she said, though she certainly wasn't. All she could do was hope the bleeding stopped by the time her training started. "You can leave."

Grim gave her a look that made her think he didn't believe her for a second. He leaned back in the chaise he had decided to sit on. It was decorated with roses, and far too small, but he made himself comfortable and stretched his long legs out in front of him. "Your death would be most inconvenient. I'll stay a little longer."

"Inconvenient?" she said, scoffing at him.

He didn't look fazed. "Inconvenient," he repeated. "You are an investment."

Her voice raised to a high pitch. "An investment?"

He continued as if she hadn't spoken. "My time is valuable. I have a lot to do. Choosing to work with you . . . fitting you into my plan. You are an investment. You're no good to me dead."

She glared at him.

Fine. Let him stay. If he wanted to watch her sleep, that was his decision.

She made it ten minutes this way, willing sleep to come down and find her again. It did not, and the only thing more uncomfortable than having him sit and watch her was the pain pulsing like a second heartbeat in her chest.

When she carefully sat upright and pulled her knees to her chest, she found him still watching her.

"I can't sleep," she said.

His chin rested on his hand. "Clearly." He studied her. "If you weren't going to sleep, I suppose I could have allowed you to stay at my palace. Let you heal there."

"I hate your palace," she said.

That seemed to surprise him. "Why?"

"Besides the fact that you live there?" Grim looked faintly amused. "There's no color. It's so . . . dark. I could never live in a place like that." He said nothing. "You know," she said, staring at her glass wall. "My guardians closed my window because of you."

He raised an eyebrow at her.

"There was . . . a loose pane. You saw it when we dueled. It was the only way I could sneak out. I had to tell them about it, to explain my ankle injury."

"Can't you use your portaling device to go outside?"

Her eyes found the floor. "I—I'm awful at traveling short distances with it. And I can only reliably go places I've been before."

The portaling device was born of his own power, which he clearly had complete mastery of. She wondered if he would think less of her than he already did.

"I'm sorry," he said suddenly. Her eyes abruptly met his again. "About the window."

Isla asked a question she'd had for a while. "If you created my device, then how did it get to Wildling?"

"I'm not entirely sure," he said.

All at once, a thought gripped her mind and chest. "Did you . . . did you know my mother?"

Grim frowned. "No. I haven't met a Wildling since the curses," he said.

So how had her mother come to possess the starstick?

They just stared at each other. Isla watched him watch her and wondered if he would be the first to look away.

"Do you always play with your hair when you're uncomfortable?"

It wasn't until then that she realized she was raking her fingers through her damp hair like they were two combs. She immediately put her hands in her lap. "No."

"Liar. I've watched you do it on no less than three occasions."

She narrowed her eyes at him. Without breaking his gaze, she made her way to the end of the bed, so she was sitting right in front of him. "Here I was thinking that you couldn't even bear to look at me, and you've apparently been studying me quite carefully."

Grim's expression did not change. "You are my enemy. Of course I study you carefully."

"Right. Tell me, Nightshade," she said. "What do *you* do when you're uncomfortable?"

"I rarely am."

"You seemed pretty uncomfortable when I stabbed you in the chest."

Grim looked bored. "I'm used to being stabbed."

"By someone you were trying to bed?"

That got a reaction from him. His jaw tensed. "You tricked me. Had I known who you were, I never would have touched you." The disgust in his tone was clear.

Isla scoffed. "Had *I* known what was about to occur, I never would have joined that line."

"Why were you there, then?" he snapped.

She recoiled, taken aback by his sudden rush of anger. "I accidentally portaled there with the starstick. It wouldn't work, and I was chased by your idiotic group of guards. The head woman grabbed me, and the next thing I knew I was in that line."

Grim crossed his arms. "I should take that thing away from you. All it's bringing you is closer to death."

"You could try," she said, her voice as threatening as she could make it.

Grim looked at her and said nothing.

"So. You have a harem?" she asked. Since that night, she had wondered who those women were. Their function was clear.

"No."

Isla laughed, disbelieving. "So, women just line up to sleep with you? They volunteer for the honor?"

Grim glared at her.

He had the reputation of an accomplished killer. There was no way the women didn't know about it. "Who would want to sleep with you?"

Grim stood from the chair, until he was right in front of her. He towered over her, his shadow even bigger behind him, filling her wall. "I don't know, Hearteater," he said. "You seemed pretty willing."

Isla swallowed. He was so close. She was breathing too quickly, and it only made her wound more painful. "No. I was disgusted."

Grim grinned. "Is that so?"

She nodded, even as he placed his hands on either side of her on the bed and leaned down so his face was right in front of hers.

"I can feel flashes of emotions," he said. *He could?* Now that she thought about it, it was a rumored Nightshade ability, one only the most powerful possessed. The blood drained from her face. "And yours were very, *very* clear—"

She wasn't breathing.

"—just as they are now."

Her heart was beating wildly. She told herself it was because she could feel the power rolling from him in waves. She told herself she was afraid. "Your powers are wrong."

He tilted his head at her. She watched his eyes move from her collarbones to her neck to her lips. "No. I don't think so."

Then he went back to his chair. "Go to sleep," he said.

She crawled back to her place and covered herself in bedding so he wouldn't see the heat of her face.

LINE BETWEEN
LIFE AND DEATH

I sla blinked. She had just had a memory. It didn't seem as though any time had passed, however.

Was it because her Nightshade abilities were getting stronger? Had it always been this way?

The Vinderland warrior was frozen in front of her. She had just demolished his weapon with a single touch. "What are you?" he asked. "You're . . . Wildling."

"I'm more than that," she said, stepping forward. Suddenly, she had Enya's confidence. She had seen her own death too.

She would not die today.

"You are going to join us in battle, or we are going to all perish," she said, her voice taking on an edge. "It's as simple as that."

He looked down at the pile of ashes that had once been his weapon. They mixed with the snow, then blew away in a flurry. The warriors at his sides spoke to each other in low voices. Their eyes were wide. They looked stunned.

"A Wildling who is also Nightshade," the man in front of her said, his tone completely different than before . . . almost reverent. He seemed to turn the words around in his mind before he reached for another weapon—a sword this time—and held it high in the air.

Isla might have been afraid that he would try to behead her, but she knew the positioning of his sword. She raised her own, and the swords clanked together loudly—a warrior's handshake.

"Singrid," he said, sheathing his weapon.

Isla shot a look at Enya, who shrugged.

"You . . . you will fight with us?" she asked.

He shook his head. "No. We will fight with *you*."

Isla should have celebrated, or left while she was ahead, but she didn't understand. "You . . . you tried to kill me. Just moments ago."

Did her being Wildling and Nightshade really mean that much?

"Apologies," he said, looking like he truly meant it. "I should have known. You survived an arrow to the heart . . . we have stories about people like you. Those who stand on the line between life and death."

Isla shifted in the snow. If only he knew that she had seen her own demise.

She wasn't about to tell him that. Instead, she said, "How many of you are there?"

Their numbers didn't seem significant the last time she had encountered them, but she hadn't seen their base or full population.

"Hundreds," he said, and hope swelled. "Most cannot fight, however."

Hope withered. "Why?"

"They have a sickness," he said. "The last few decades, it has spread. Incapacitated most of us."

A sickness? Isla almost asked why they hadn't seen a healer, but she stopped herself. No Moonling would ever treat part of the Vinderland. They were known for their viciousness and appetite for human flesh.

"What if we could heal them?" Isla asked.

She felt Enya staring at her.

Singrid took a step forward. "You have a healer?"

"Yes," she said, avoiding Enya's look. "If they could recover in time . . . could they fight?"

Singrid nodded. "We are all trained."

Good. "I'll be back, then," she said. She raised her sword and clashed it with a weapon from every one of the Vinderland in front of her.

She had a legion, she thought. If she could just find a way to heal them.

"Please tell me you can help," Isla said to Calder. The Moonling frowned as she told him about the sickness. "You . . . you *are* a healer, right?"

He gave a weak smile.

"The worst," Zed said. "He's the *worst* healer."

Enya shot him a look. She turned to Calder. "We know you're not the best . . . but you're who we have. And Isla here might have exaggerated your skill set."

She had a thought. "Oro's a healer, isn't he?" He had healed her injuries before, during the Centennial.

Enya moved her hand back and forth in front of her. "He can heal physical wounds, but only straightforward ones. As far as I'm aware, he's never tried sicknesses." She looked at Calder again. "You have, though, Cal. Right?"

Calder swallowed. "I . . . I *have*, but—"

"I'll bring you to the Wildling newland," Isla said. "Our healing elixir is made from a flower. Perhaps if it was boiled, made into a tea, that could help them as well. I can show you."

Calder agreed, and that was when she told him and Zed about her starstick. The look the Skyling gave her could only be described as withering.

The three of them went through the puddle of stars.

At Isla's request, Wren showed them the patch of flowers where the healing elixirs came from.

"These are magnificent," Calder said. Isla hadn't ever seen them in their original form before. They were deep violet in color, with sharp petals. Beautiful. Vicious.

"The flowers are so rare, we use them only in emergencies. We've never tried them for sickness," Wren said. Her eyes darted to Isla. "We . . . we have only been able to find a few more additional patches."

They didn't have many to spare.

Isla sighed. This was the hard part of ruling, she decided. Was it better to use a portion of the flowers now, to ensure the help of the Vinderland warriors, knowing there would be less healing elixir later, which could save lives?

Though . . . having more warriors would save lives too, wouldn't it?

She closed her eyes tightly and decided. "Let's test with just a few flowers. If we see meaningful results . . . we can determine how many we would need to heal all of them."

Calder nodded. Wren began to pluck the flowers. The moment they were pulled from the ground, the color became darker, almost black.

There was a rustling in the woods by the patch and Zed froze. He looked up, and up. His hand inched toward the weapon on his belt.

"Don't you dare," Isla bit out, before breaking into a smile.

Lynx. She had missed him.

He bowed his head begrudgingly, as if acknowledging he had maybe missed her too.

She jumped as high as she could and threw her arms around his neck. That was apparently taking it too far, because the massive leopard shook her off.

When she turned around, Enya, Calder, and Zed were gaping at her.

"That is the largest cat I have ever seen," Enya said.

Lynx uttered a sound that made it clear he did not like being referred to as a cat. She placed her hand against his side. "He's a leopard, thank you very much," she said. Lynx didn't even acknowledge her.

Zed narrowed his eyes at Lynx. "I . . . I don't think that's a leopard."

"Of course he is," Isla said. "Look. If you squint, you can see the patterns."

Calder stepped forward to get a closer look, and Lynx bared his massive teeth. The Moonling held his hands up. "Never mind. I can see from here. Very pretty."

Zed just shook his head. "Are there more of them?" he asked.

"More of what?"

He motioned at Lynx. "Your *leopard*."

She looked at Lynx, whose eyes slid to hers. Somewhere deep inside of herself she knew that meant no.

Was that part of the connection between Wildling and bonded?

"No. Why?"

Zed shrugged. "We could use creatures like that. The Skyling vote's in a few days. I'm not holding my breath."

He was right. Isla wanted to bring Lynx to Lightlark for the battle. If she could manage to ride him, it would be a considerable advantage.

When they returned to Lightlark, Calder joined Isla to visit the Vinderland, with the flower. If it worked, she would be adding hundreds of skilled, ruthless warriors to their army.

The next day, she would visit Cinder on Star Isle to begin practicing the walls of energy that would keep the battle enclosed. She had already started learning to create the defensive nature that would cover other parts of the Mainland. Confined, the Nightshade soldiers would be easier to defeat.

They had a plan.

As Isla fell into another memory that night, though, she couldn't help but think it still wasn't enough.

BEFORE

Grim was gone in the morning. Her chest still burned in pain, but the healing elixir had worked. Her skin was nearly completely healed.

That night, after her training, he appeared in her room again. Any trace of humanity she had seen from him the night prior was gone. He looked furious.

"If you are going to insist on keeping my device and portaling anywhere you wish, I will teach you how not to be an idiot."

Isla glared at him. "Or what?"

"Or I will take it back," he said, eyes darting to the floorboard where she kept her starstick.

Her hands clenched. She knew he wasn't kidding. "Fine," she said. "When are you going to teach me?"

"Now." He grabbed her arm, and the world turned. When it righted itself, they were in a long hall.

"This . . . is in your palace," she said, looking around.

"It's a training room," he said.

"I didn't bring anything," Isla said. Grim made a motion, and her starstick fell through the sky, right into her hand.

"How did you—"

"The first thing you should know is your device is unreliable," he said. "I did not pour much power into it. Around other portaling ability, it won't always work." That explained why it had failed her during their first meeting. "Portaling power is all about visualization. That is why you believe you can't go anywhere you haven't already been."

"So how do I go somewhere I can't visualize?"

"Maps help," he said. "It's easier to go places when you have a sense of the distance and relation to other locations." Grim clearly didn't rely on maps anymore. Hundreds of years of mastery seemed to mean he could travel nearly anywhere he pleased. "Now," he said. "About the short distances."

Grim was there. Then he wasn't. He appeared right behind her.

"It requires far more control. And control is developed through practice." He nodded at her starstick. "Try to portal across the room."

Isla planted her feet firmly against the ground. She drew her puddle and focused on the small distance. Visualized the other side of the hall.

She landed on dark volcanic sand. The tide washed in, soaking her hands and knees. She heard a tsk above her. She looked up to see Grim standing there, frowning. His castle was a monstrosity above, overlooking the beach. "You overshot by a bit," he said.

He portaled them back.

"Again."

The next time, she landed in the night market. Grim swept her away before anyone noticed.

The time after that, she appeared in his bedroom. It was immaculate. Grim sighed. "You are, surprisingly, getting closer."

After five more disastrous attempts, she appeared in a throne room. It was long as a field. The throne was made up of what looked to be calcified shadows, melted together, moving.

"The training room is the next one over," he said behind her.

She turned around to face him. "Where are your people? Your attendants? Your nobles?"

"In other parts of the castle," he said. "Most parts are restricted only to me."

Grim was free, but he seemed almost as enclosed as she was. "How often do you see them?"

"Whenever I command it." He motioned behind her. "Close your eyes." She did. He took a step forward. He was so close she could feel his breath on her cheek. "Focus."

It was hard to focus on anything with him this close to her, but she tried. She made a map in her mind of all the places she had mistakenly portaled to. The distance between her and the training room became clearer. She kept her eyes closed as she reached for her starstick and formed her puddle. She fell through.

"Good," Grim said, her only indication that she had done it. She opened her eyes. She was in the center of the training room. "I was beginning to think you were incapable of being trained."

Isla glared at him.

"Now," he said. He made a motion, and one of her favorite swords fell through the air. She caught it. "You are tolerable at swordplay, but your defense needs work."

She scowled at him. "My guardian is an excellent teacher."

He raised an eyebrow at her. "Has she seen war? Has she encountered creatures who could swallow her whole?"

Isla flattened her mouth into a line. Terra and Poppy had both been born after the curses were spun. As far as she knew, they had never left the Wildling newland. "No," she said through her teeth.

"Then it seems I have a few more lessons to teach you," he said. In an instant, he had his own blade in his hand and he was on her, sword moving so rapidly, she could barely keep track of it. He grunted commands while he fought, criticizing her technique, chastising her every move.

"Dead," he said, slicing the thinnest of lines across her chest with his sword. It cut through the fabric of her shirt but did not pierce skin. That kind of control was extraordinary. One inch off, and her insides would be spilling out. She reached out to block him again.

His blade sliced against her stomach, forming another slash in her clothing. "Dead," he said again.

She tried her best to cut *him*, but no matter how hard she fought, how much she tried to trick him, his blade was always there, sending hers away.

Isla gasped as his sword swept across her throat. This time, he *did* cut her. The smallest drop of blood dripped down her neck. "Very dead," he said, his voice just a whisper, far too close.

A growl sounded deep in her chest. The demon could have killed her by accident. Enraged, she fought harder, advancing, cutting the air between them to pieces. She wanted to cut *him* to pieces.

He blocked every blow, but there was an opening. She saw it, and took it, and cut the smallest rip in his shirt.

Isla grinned and was unceremoniously knocked on her back. He had kicked her feet out from under her.

She made an awful sound as she fought for breath. Grim leaned over her. "Another lesson. Sometimes your opponent will let you get a hit in, as a distraction." His blade traveled up her chest, right to the center of her breast. He tapped once and said, "Dead."

Isla glared at him. "I get it. You could kill me any number of ways, including with a sword. Teach me to be better."

He did. They spent the rest of the night dueling in that room. He taught her moves that were ingenious. He taught her how to fight without a sword as well.

"Always go for the nose," he said.

By the time the sun came up, and Isla was due in her quarters for even more training, she was dripping in sweat. "Thank you," she said, even though she knew he wasn't training her for any other reason than because he needed her to find the sword. *You're no good to me dead*, he had said.

"The celebration on Creetan's Crag is in three days," he said. He stepped close, narrowing his eyes. "Before then, do me a favor, and don't die."

CREATURES IN
THE WOODS

Grim had taught her to defend herself. She blinked away tears
as she wondered if he would ever guess he would become her
greatest threat. In the future, he killed her. She saw it clearly.

Why would he hurt her, after taking such pains to keep her safe? It
was counter to everything she knew about him.

Though, perhaps she had never truly known him at all.

When Isla crossed the Star Isle bridge, the air felt taut with energy.
It smelled faintly of metal. Just like when Celeste used to get worried
and upset.

She ran the rest of the way to the ruins where the Starlings lived,
and there, she also smelled blood.

"What happened?" Isla demanded.

"The creatures," Maren said. "A little girl . . . about Cinder's age . . ."
Her voice cracked at the end.

Leo was there, a reed sticking out of his mouth. He chewed it with
nervous fervor. "She went into the woods, and this is all we found."

A cloak sat on the floor. It was soaked in blood. Someone cried out.
A sister, or friend, she didn't know.

Isla shut her eyes tightly. She had promised to protect them.

She looked around at the Starlings. They were young. Scared. They
were staring at her, and she remembered what Ella had said. *You gave
us a chance to live. To most of us, you are a god. A savior.*

It was her duty to see if she could possibly save the little girl.

With more resolution than she felt, Isla asked, "Where can I find these creatures?"

None of the Starlings would walk beyond the first silver stream of water that cut the isle in half. It looked like a piece of ribbon, glittering below the sun.

Everything was silent.

Ciel and Avel circled above. She told them to keep their distance. Surprise would be an advantage.

"If you see them, you're already dead," one of the Starlings offered, and she expected fear to curl in her stomach.

It did not. She had seen her own death in her head. She had faced many dangers already. Those thoughts kept her moving forward, through the stillness of Star Isle.

A bird with silver wings cut through the sky like a pair of swords. She recognized it immediately. Celeste—Aurora—had told her about the bird. A few of them had made it to the Starling newland. It was a heartfinch, named so because they always traveled in pairs and often leaned their beaks together in a manner resembling a heart.

This one was alone.

Isla's fingers slipped down the hilt of her blade at her waist, by habit. The ability in her chest thrummed, as if in warning, and she let it warm her, like drinking a hot cup of tea.

The crumbled wall is your last chance to turn around, Leo had told her around his reed. *After that . . . you belong to them.*

They looked nervous that Isla was going to confront the creatures. She would show them she was capable of protecting them.

The wall was no more than a few scattered silver stones, with an arch that had partially collapsed. There was a puddle of something at its entrance. She leaned down and dipped a finger inside.

She didn't need to smell it to know it was blood. It had gone cold.

Just as she straightened, squinting behind her to see Ciel and Avel circling in the distance, it began to rain.

Of course, she thought, glaring up at the sky, wishing she was a Moonling so she could at least direct the water around her. She was no such thing, so she shook her head and resigned herself to being soaked. Water splashed in the puddle of blood, overflowing it, making it run down the mossy cobblestone, through the gaps between them in lines like veins. She studied it for a moment, her stomach turning, then stepped through the remaining half of the arch.

Isla walked for nearly an hour without incident. She had reached the forest where the creatures were said to live. It was nothing like the other Star Isle woods she had visited during the Centennial. Where that one had been sparse, this one was overgrown. Wild. The silver trees had leaves sharp as blades. Their trunks were braided together into thick knots, their roots were the width of her arms. Thorned brambles made up much of the space between them. She would have exerted much of her power to clear a path, but she didn't need to. She happened upon a wide, clean pathway cut right through the forest, as if made for her. There were no roots or errant flowers or weeds on it. It was smooth. Recently used.

That didn't make sense. Was there a community living out here? Were they like the Vinderland? Outcasts who had renounced all realms a millennium ago?

Isla gripped her sword hilt again.

She felt little connection with this place. It seemed defensive, a fortress. Lightning struck, slicing the sky in half. Thunder clapped, and more rain showered down, pelting her through the treetops.

She whipped around.

Out of the corner of her eye—she swore she saw movement, far above. Her sword made a high-pitched scratch as she unsheathed it and leaned into her stance.

Seconds passed. Nothing moved. The flash of motion she had seen had been high above her, past even the treetops . . . She squinted through the rain, but the trees were empty. The leaves were too sharp, she reasoned. No people or animals could comfortably climb them. They would cut themselves. Right?

She did not re-sheathe her sword as she stepped forward, into a clearing. A massive lake sat in its center, a slice of silver in the shape of an eye. Its surface vibrated with a million raindrops, tiny circles everywhere, overlapping.

As she walked toward it, she tripped. A root—how did she miss it? No. Upon closer inspection, she saw it was not a root. It was a snake. Its metallic scales shined brightly. It writhed below, lifting its head as if to strike her. She took a step back and noticed a new shadow, casting long in front of her, all the way across the lake. It was too large to be a tree.

It hadn't been there before.

Chest constricting, Isla slowly turned around.

Lightning struck again, reflecting off the scales of a coiled, hundred-foot-tall serpent.

Isla resisted the urge to scream.

There was the creature. One of them, at least. It was large enough that it could swallow her without any trouble at all. It could swallow a *tower* without any trouble. She took a step back—

It struck.

At the last moment, Isla rolled to the side, and its fangs sunk into the wet, silver-speckled ground.

Move. She needed to move. Avel and Ciel weren't far behind, but by the time they got to her, it would be too late.

Before she could react, the serpent recovered and reared back, ready to strike again.

It launched into her, throwing her into the lake.

For a moment, there was silence as she fell through the ice-cold water, a thousand needles through her limbs. Bubbles exploded from the surface—

Then, there was the snake head. She cut her hand as she gripped both ends of her sword in front of her body, to keep it from swallowing her whole. The snake's massive jaw only widened. Her arms shook as she struggled against its strength, as it pushed her farther and farther down into the water.

Her vision began to lose its sharpness. Her hands and feet began to lose their sensation. The options were clear. Either the serpent was going to eat her, or she was going to drown. Potentially both. She called to her power, but there was no foliage here, in the center of this lake. She tried her shadows and watched them dissolve in the water, useless.

Without warning, the serpent pulled back and she heard a muted roar through the water.

Mind spinning, chest pulsing in pain, lungs begging for air, she crashed through the surface, only to see that Ciel had dug his sword through the space between the serpent's thick scales. It roared and raged, striking at the Skylings in the sky, as they battled with torrents of air.

She raced out of the water, dripping, freezing, in time to see the snake spin and strike Avel with its tail. She fell from the sky and landed in a heap on the ground. Her twin cried out, distracted, and the snake took that opportunity to attack—

It hit a wall of thorns instead.

Slowly, very slowly, the serpent turned around. Isla stood there, panting, arm raised. She had power.

She would use it.

Isla kicked off her shoes. She dug her feet deep into the muddy ground and focused. Found her center. Cleared her thoughts. The connection clicked.

She had been practicing.

Her eyes opened, and the forest raged. The woods rose around the serpent, so quickly it was trapped before it could move an inch. Thick roots acted as chains, tree trunks curled around its body, vines pinned it in place. By the time Isla was done, it couldn't wriggle even an inch

out of its prison. She expected the serpent to roar again, or try to strike, but it just watched her.

She was panting. Her chest felt hollow. Too much power had been used in too short of a period. Her gaze shifted to Ciel, who was cradling Avel's head. Relief rained down her spine. The Skyling was awake.

Isla was about to tell Ciel to get his sister help, when the serpent suddenly slipped out of its confines. She watched, frozen in place, as the snake shrunk, turned, and uncoiled—

Until it became a woman.

She easily walked through the tower of restraints Isla had made, tilted her head, and said, "Wildling?"

Isla didn't breathe as the woman stepped forward. She was wearing a long dress that trailed across the floor, made up of the same scales she had just worn across her body.

As a *snake.*

"What are you?" Isla demanded. She had never heard of a person being able to change into an animal before. It was an impossible ability.

The woman tilted her head at Isla, the movement purely serpentine. "You don't recognize your own people?"

She . . . used to be Wildling? Had she somehow, like the Vinderland, abandoned her realm?

How was that even possible? It clearly wasn't anymore, or most people would have abandoned their ties to their realms during the curses.

The woman nodded. "You're putting it together, I can see it . . . your face is very expressive . . . not a very good trait as a ruler, is it?" She stepped forward, and it took everything in Isla not to recoil.

"The little girl," Isla said, her voice shaking. "Is she—"

"She's gone," the woman said quickly. "Not me . . . but . . . all the same, there's nothing left."

Isla's bottom lip trembled. Her eyes stung. Poor girl . . . she should have been here to protect her. "You . . . you kill children," she said, her voice full of disgust.

The woman's lip curled away from her mouth, baring teeth that were far too sharp. "Oh, and other Wildlings didn't?" she took a step forward. "We have done what we needed to survive. We needed food. We're no different from you."

We. Were there more like her? Serpent-people? Or were the other ancient, deadly creatures different?

"It ends now," Isla said. "I rule Starling, and you will stop killing them."

The woman just looked at her. "Tell them to stop coming to this part of the isle," she said. "We never hunted; we simply took whatever came wandering in. We could have killed them all, you know."

Killed them all.

Isla wanted to kill the serpent-woman right then . . . but she thought about Zed's words. They could use beings like her in battle.

"Nightshades are coming to destroy the island," Isla said. "You will fight with us." It was a command.

The woman looked at her. Then, she laughed. It was too loud, like the roar of the serpent, like the clap of thunder that sounded above. "Now . . . when you asked that, did you really believe I would say yes?"

Isla stepped forward. She worked every bit of command into her voice as she said, "You are Wildling. I am your ruler, and I am ordering you."

The woman bared her teeth. Before Isla's eyes, her dress became a tail. It took her half a second to be upon Isla, growing larger and larger, rising, serpent part piling beneath her. "I *was* Wildling," she said. "I will not fight for you or anyone else on this island." She leaned back as if to strike again. "I will let you live today, and you should take that as a gift."

Avel was on her feet. Blood dripped down the side of her head, but she looked capable of flying. Before Avel and Ciel lifted her between them, Isla said, "You will not kill another Starling."

She could hear the woman laughing as they took to the air and left.

It was only once she was in bed that night that Isla remembered a very different encounter with a snake.

BEFORE

Music thrummed through the day. Drums, everywhere. Laughter. Jeers. The sharp smell of alcohol that was so concentrated, it burned her nostrils.

Some people walked through the streets nearly naked, covered only in scantily used body paint. There were designs painted across their chests, their legs, their stomachs. Others lined the sides of the road, shouting. They all had blades on their belts and drinks in their hands.

Everyone was wearing masks.

Her own was tight to her face, but she reached to put her hair behind her ear, just for an excuse to touch its edge, to be sure her mask was secure. Grim had thrown the mask and a scrap of fabric at her the second he had appeared in her room.

"Today's the longest night of the year. There's a celebration at Creetan's Crag. During the day, obviously."

She had caught it and frowned. "Masks?"

"Everyone wears them."

Isla had scowled as she let the dress unravel in front of her. "Does everyone wear *this*?" It was black and gave her Wildling clothing competition for impropriety. It hung by two thin straps that looked one wrong move away from snapping, had the lowest-cut bodice she had ever seen and a slit so high, there was very little fabric in the middle holding it all together.

Grim didn't meet her eyes. "Most people do choose to wear little clothing, yes. At least, at celebrations like this. Some just wear paint." He stared at her then, an eyebrow raised. "Would you prefer I get a pot of ink and a brush?"

That had sent her behind her dressing curtain without another complaint. She didn't have a full-length mirror in there, so it wasn't until she was in front of him that she saw herself clearly.

Her breasts were pressed together and spilling over the top. The slit was so high, she'd had to forgo underclothes altogether.

Grim stared at her and looked, more than anything, horrified.

"Do I look Nightshade?" she asked, a note of panic in her voice. She smeared bright paint across her lips, the same way she had the first time she had met him, which seemed to be a Nightshade fashion. Then she put on her mask. He hadn't answered, so she turned back to him, only to find his eyes still on her. "Hmm?"

"It'll do," he had said gruffly and extended his hand.

Now, as they walked through Creetan's Crag, Grim looked straight ahead. Even if he wasn't looking at her, others were. She felt their gazes on her and resisted the urge to press her hand against the slit, to ensure it didn't expose more than her leg.

Grim seemed more on edge than usual. He couldn't use his powers, on the off chance that the sword was close by. They'd had to portal far away and walk for nearly an hour as a precaution.

"How does it feel?" she whispered.

He looked over at her. "How does what feel?"

"Not being the scary, all-powerful Nightshade ruler anymore. In a crowd like this."

Grim gave her a look. "I could still kill everyone here with my sword."

"Not me."

His eyes were back on the street. "Are you forgetting the results of our duel?"

"I didn't hate you as much as I do now. I'm sure that very fact would help me win."

"Is that so?"

"Absolutely."

Speaking of the crowd . . . "How do you know a celebration like this will draw him out?" The mysterious thief. The one with the snake who had been seen nearby.

"I don't. But if he is here, all this . . . distraction will be useful."

Distraction was one word for it.

Thousands of people made currents through the streets and filled each shop to the brim, so much so that she watched someone fall through an open window in a bar and land right in a pile of vomit.

Demonstrations, shows, and betting rounds were going on. Cards were being played. By the sounds coming from alleyways, every type of desire was being fulfilled.

"We know he has a snake. How else are we supposed to find him?" She looked over at him. "Do you know how to get information without cutting off hands?"

Grim glanced over at her. Not a minute later, he stopped in front of a woman. She had five drinks in her hands and looked about to take the order of a group of people sitting outside a bar.

Isla watched the woman's entire face change as she took him in. His wide shoulders, his height. Her expression went from annoyed to curious in an instant. Even from a few steps down the street, she couldn't hear what they were saying over the music and drunken jeers. The woman was saying something, and then she placed a hand on his arm, and he *let* her. Something uncomfortable that she didn't want to name curled in her stomach.

When Grim returned, he looked far too smug. "I know where to find him."

Isla didn't give him the satisfaction of looking surprised or impressed. "Good. Lead the way."

They didn't have to walk far. Minutes later, they entered a massive tent. "That's him." The *him* was a man wearing his shirt completely open, revealing a muscular chest. He had pale skin, hair cut close to his head, and, most remarkable of all, a viper wrapped around his shoulders.

The thief was with a group of people—his collaborators, no doubt—sitting front row at a very . . . interesting show.

People with fabric draped over them—and little else underneath—danced in front of bright lights, turning the sheets they held completely sheer. Every inch of their bodies was visible. Some wore nothing underneath; others wore limited underclothes. The man was watching them intensely, elbows on his knees.

All right. There he was. Somehow, they would have to get information from him. "He seems preoccupied. How are we—"

Grim looked from the dancers to Isla. Then back again.

She scoffed. "Absolutely *not*, you cursed demon—"

He shrugged a shoulder. "Then we'll find another way. I just thought, you being a temptress and all, you could use *your* powers, since I'm unable to use mine."

Powers. She was supposed to be a cursed hearteater, able to tempt a person with a single look. Capable of bringing anyone to their knees with her seduction. Somehow he hadn't seemed to notice her powerlessness, beyond a few pointed statements. He couldn't find out she didn't have ability. What if that was why he was working with her in the first place? Would he rescind his offer to help her during the Centennial?

Roaring began filling her ears. They hadn't found the skin gloves. She and Celeste needed him. *Her* people needed her. They were suffering.

"Can't you just torture the information out of him?" she asked. Suddenly, that option sounded a lot more appealing.

Grim looked amused. "Of course I can, Hearteater. But one of the most infamous thieves, one of the only people who knows about the sword, turning up dead in such a violent fashion? It would be suspicious . . ." He shrugged a shoulder. "I suppose, if you are unable to actually *use* your powers—"

"Of course I can," she said quickly.

Grim looked unconvinced. "It's fine. We'll find another—"

"No." She was suddenly intent on wiping that look off his face. She reached back into her dress and shoved her starstick at him. "Take this from me, and you'll see my *other* Wildling curses in action," she said.

Then she turned on her heel, toward the tent behind the stage.

All her previous bravado was gone. She had traded one of the girls in the show a ruby from her necklace in exchange for her extra set of clothing. Now, she stood just offstage, trembling. Her chest was covered only by a thick strip of black fabric. Her other parts were covered only by a skirt that truly had not earned that description, for it barely concealed anything.

The sheet was over her, but she had seen it at work in the light. Everything would be revealed. *She* would be revealed.

Get it together, she told herself. Her people were starving. The mark above her heart was only the faintest scar now, but the encounter had left more than torn flesh behind. She had seen the women's desperation. They looked guilty, but they were hungry. She was their ruler. It was her responsibility to do whatever she could to survive the Centennial and break their curse.

With her people in mind, a stupid dance in front of a thief seemed easy. She had a plan. Seduce him, bring him to a private place, and feed him the bottle of liquor she had also bought off the dancer.

"A drink of this, and any man will be flat on his stomach," she had said. "Lets us accept payment without doing most of the more unsavory acts."

Finally, Isla had asked for advice. "Do you know the man with the serpent?"

She had rolled her eyes. "We all do, unfortunately."

"How do I get him to notice me?"

"Easy," she said. "He likes attention."

All she had to do was dance in front of him.

How hard could it be?

She was wearing a mask. Anonymous. No one knew her here—except for the cursed demon, who she doubted would even be watching.

With a burst of confidence, Isla stepped onto the stage, wrapped in the cloth she knew was made completely transparent by the lights behind, casting her body in full shadow.

Gazes were brands searing her skin. At first, she rejected it, felt disgusted, but then . . .

This was a choice. She was not being forced. They were here to watch, and she had agreed to be part of the entertainment.

She positioned herself right in front of the man with the snake, making sure to give a smile just for him, and she began to dance.

The music was a rush of drums and strings so fast and intoxicating that her body moved to its rhythm, matching the routine of the others. Her hips swayed, dipped, her arms reached above her head, she ran her fingers down her stomach, touching her body through the fabric . . .

And met his gaze. *Him.*

Grim.

He was watching her like she really had power and could seduce a man with one look. He was staring like a man entranced, standing predatorially still. She met his eyes, and he did not look away—no, if anything, he looked more intensely. His eyes swept down her body, and up, and lingered, and she felt it in her blood, in her bones, *him*—

His gaze broke away, narrowing on something right in front of her, just a half second before she felt a pull on her fabric.

She heard a hiss.

The thief. The snake around his neck flicked its tongue out. The man offered his hand, which was full of coins she had never seen before. "Might I have a private show?" he asked.

Bile worked its way up her throat. She gave her most convincing smile. "Of course."

The man helped her off the stage, and she led him to the back of the tent, where she had watched other dancers take their clients. Before going into one of the private areas, she scooped up her bottle of liquor.

"For you," she said reverently, and he smiled. The snake hissed again, and he petted its head. "Apologies—she is a jealous woman," he said about the serpent.

The curtains made a scratching sound as she opened them. They were in a building now, with stone walls. The sounds of music and yells were muted here. In their room, there was only a chair, some candles, and a table with awaiting goblets.

She uncorked the bottle and poured him a glass.

He took it immediately, and Isla thought he was a fool for not even smelling it before gulping it down. He must not have viewed her as a threat.

Perhaps this was how he'd lost the sword.

"More," he said, offering his goblet. She happily obliged, and he downed the drink again, before loudly leaving it on the table. "Now," he said, smiling, teeth shining in the limited light of the few scattered candles. "Dance."

Isla did. She danced in front of him, smiling coyly when he made to reach for her, turning around strategically, so he didn't think she was denying him.

When she turned around again, she saw his eyes were drooping. He fought to stay awake, his head lolling, then straightening, again, and again.

This was her chance.

"Come here," he said, patting his leg. She felt a bout of nausea but complied, sitting on his lap, far from where he wanted her.

The snake lunged for her, and Isla startled, but the man just laughed, head lolling to the side. "Don't worry, she doesn't bite," he said. "I had her fangs removed." Though she was grateful for it now, Isla thought that was very sad. For a moment, she felt pity for the snake.

"I'm looking for something," she whispered.

"Are you?" he said, his voice slurring.

"A sword. The one your group stole from the Skyling market and that you stole from them. Where is it?"

He laughed, his eyes rolling back. "That sword ruined my life," he said. "It's nearly killed anyone who's tried to use it. I suppose none of us were powerful enough for it." He laughed some more.

She leaned closer, clutching both sides of his open shirt in her hands. "Where is it?"

The man smiled. His eyes were nearly closed now. His very pale cheeks were now flushed. Perhaps the drink had worked too well. "A thief stole it from me. Ironic, isn't it? Some call her the best thief in all the realms."

"What's her name?"

"No one knows."

"Where can I find her?"

He lifted a shoulder.

That wasn't helpful. She shook him by the sides of his shirt. "Where do you think the sword is now? Would she have traded it? Sold it?"

"Oh, I *know* where the sword is."

Isla stopped shaking him. "You do?"

He nodded as much as he could manage. "The thief has a favorite hiding place."

"Where?"

"Here, on Nightshade."

Hope bloomed. "Close by?"

He shook his head. "No, no. Far."

"Where?"

"The Caves of Irida."

Isla stopped breathing. That was a very specific location. She didn't know where it was, but Grim would.

Suddenly, her hope began to deflate. "Wait. If you're so sure you know where it is, why haven't you stolen it back?"

He laughed, but it sounded faded. He was moments from sleep. "Besides the fact no one will go near it? Because it's impossible," he slurred. "The thief has a monster."

"*Monster?*"

"It guards her bounty."

"What kind of monster?" she demanded.

But the thief had succumbed to the liquor. She let him go, and he crumpled against the chair, making a snoring sound. The snake slid across his face, as if trying to wake him.

Isla only realized that in her fervor to get information she had climbed atop the man when Grim opened the curtain to the room. She stood quickly, grinning, mouth opening, ready to tell him everything they now knew, when she abruptly shut it.

Grim looked furious. He looked at the man, sleeping peacefully, then at her.

"Don't kill him," she said.

He gave her a look.

"You look like you want to kill him."

"I want to kill a lot of people," he said, like that made things better. He looked her dead in the eyes. "I *kill* a lot of people."

She swallowed, and his gaze went straight to her throat.

He stalked toward her, and Isla backed away. Her spine hit the wall. Her heart seemed ready to beat out of her chest, but she smirked. "I got the information. I know exactly where the sword is. Seems like I'm a perfectly good temptress." In the most mocking tone that she could manage at the moment, she said, "Tell me, nonpowerful Nightshade. Was I able to tempt you?" He frowned down at her, and she grinned. She stared up at him through her eyelashes. "Did I make you fall hopelessly in love with me?"

Isla gasped as he pinned her against the wall. His hands were rough against her hips. His fingers traveled up the sides of her stomach, to her ribs, to her breasts. She arched her back, groaning as his thumbs made wide sweeps across them. She knew he could feel her emotions, her want.

"No," he said against her parted lips. "You are not something special to me. You are not something I want to love." He reached up to her lips and smeared her red lipstick with his thumb. "You are something I want to ruin."

Then he ducked his head to her throat and bit her.

It was a light bite, just a scraping of his teeth, but Isla gasped, which turned into a moan as his tongue swiped across the same spot. She wanted him so much—she wanted everything.

In a single motion, he turned her around, so her chest was pressed to the wall. His hands raked up her thighs, until he gripped her hips.

Before she could move against him or do any of the millions of things that were racing through her mind, he made a portal with her starstick against the wall in front of her and pushed her through it.

SPLIT

S he woke up next to Oro and couldn't even look at him. When
she was in her memories, it was as if everything was happening
to her, *again*, and—

It felt like a betrayal.

Oro would tell her it wasn't her fault. That these things had already
happened, months before she ever met him.

But now, reliving them . . . sleeping next to someone else . . .

It was a poison she was feeding herself. Forcing herself to swallow
it down, even though it was killing her inside.

She felt like she was being split apart. Past Isla, a person she barely
even recognized. Current Isla, who had slipped back into pain, into
anxiety, into hurt, due to the memories.

A person could take only so much.

Midnight was a comforting time of action. Perhaps it was the quiet,
or the fact that the chances were low that someone would stumble upon
her, or the indulgence of patting herself on the back that she was going
above and beyond by even being awake at this hour, let alone working,
or maybe it was all of that encapsulated into one.

Maybe it was because she was part Nightshade.

She used her starstick to portal herself to Wild Isle. There, she went
through the Wildling movements. She began practicing forming the types
of defensive, thorned plants that she would create across the Mainland.
She made patches of bog sand.

Isla visited her room before she went back to bed and watched
herself in the mirror. There were dark circles beneath her eyes. Her lips

were raw and chapped. Her skin was rough in some places where it had been smooth. She looked too thin.

Her eyes slid to her neck. It looked bare.

It was not.

She touched a hand to the necklace, which only she could feel, and anger built inside. Of course Grim would gift her a necklace impossible to take off. Of course he would make sure she couldn't forget him, even though she *wanted to*.

She remembered his words when he had gifted it to her, at the ball. *Should you ever need me, touch this. And I will come for you.*

Enough. Isla got one of her blades and positioned it precariously against the necklace. One slipup and she would be dead, but she would not slip. She began trying to cut the damned thing off.

The blade didn't even make a mark. She tried pulling the back, nearly choking herself in the process, but the necklace stayed firm, undisturbed.

She tried wrapping Wildling power around it. Sawing it. Burning it with her fireplace poker. Even summoning a handful of Nightshade shadows and sharpening them into weapons.

Nothing worked.

Thirteen days before Grim was set to destroy the island, the Skylings finally held their vote. The meeting on Sky Isle was well underway. For hours, different sides had debated the issue. Isla, Oro, Enya, Calder, and Zed sat watching as they discussed the very good reasons why all Skylings should leave Lightlark.

She had seen it in her vision—dreks were coming. Without Skylings in the air to fight them, it would be another bloodbath. Hundreds of Skyling soldiers had been trained in the flight force. They made up a large part of their numbers.

"We can't lose them," Enya whispered, almost to herself.

The sides were almost evenly matched—just a few votes were undecided. Still, it seemed clear that it would tip toward leaving the island.

Before the final vote was cast, Oro stood to address them. "We all know the value of your flight force and numbers in this battle. You might believe you can flee the danger, but it will follow. If Grim wipes out Lightlark, what is to stop him from taking out the Skyling newland as well? For all we know, he wants to wipe away the world." There were whispers. A few people nodded. "Regardless, without Lightlark, Skyling will fall. Every generation will become weaker. People will die. Power will dwindle. Your ruler's ability and your own stem from the power that is buried deep within Lightlark. If the island is destroyed . . . so are we all."

Oro sat down. It was a good speech. There was murmuring. Still, something in her chest said it wasn't enough. Something told her how the vote would go—

She stood, and the whispers quieted. She looked at Azul, who had organized the meeting. "May I speak?" she asked.

Azul nodded.

"This isn't just about the battle," Isla said. "This is about *after*. The future we build after saving the island. Building a better Lightlark." She looked at the committee, including Bronte and Sturm. Then, at the Skylings sitting in the room, watching her.

She needed to offer something to the Skylings. They didn't value much . . . but they did value something above all else.

She hesitated, before saying, "If we survive this attack, I plan on implementing a democracy for Starlings." Murmurs. Zed shot her a look. She straightened her spine and continued, "I will hold a vote, and if someone else is more capable of being ruler, I will step down." She meant it. She had always admired Azul's rule, and the truth was, the Starlings deserved to be ruled by one of their own. Maren, for example. "Anyone who stays and fights is battling for a better future. One where more people have choices and rights. We need Skylings, or we will lose, and that better future will have been just a dream, extinguished."

Oro placed his hand on hers for a split second as she sat down, and she felt better, knowing he had agreed with what she had done.

She didn't think it would shift the vote, but it could encourage some Skylings to stay and fight. She only knew she'd had to try.

Azul's voice thundered through the room as he said, "We will now conduct our vote."

Isla waited for the results with Enya and Calder, in the war room. Oro was at the vote. Zed was casting his own.

At first, the group used the time to catch each other up on their progress. Enya determined the Lightlark civilians would have to be evacuated between the Skyling and Starling newlands. She was preparing infrastructure and supplies for them to be able to comfortably live there for however long the war went on.

Calder had been visiting the Vinderland every day, tracking their progress. So far, the flower wasn't working. Perhaps their preparation had been wrong. They would have to figure out another way to heal them.

Then, there had been hours of quiet, as they waited.

The moment Oro walked through the door, Isla knew it was bad news. She could feel it in her core. Zed was right behind him.

"We lost Azul," Oro said. Enya gasped. "The Skylings voted not to allow him to fight." His eyes found Isla. "Part of the flight force made their own choice, though. If you pledge to make Starling into a democracy, they will stay."

"How many?" Enya asked.

"One hundred."

Mixed emotions battled within Isla. Azul was the strongest of the Skylings, a ruler. He held most of the ability in his realm. Losing him would incapacitate them significantly.

Zed shook his head. "It's not enough. It's not nearly enough."

Azul walked in, then. He looked devastated. He closed his eyes and said, "I do not agree with this choice. I—I am truly sorry."

Zed turned to him. "I'm staying here. I've made my choice. Yet you're leaving us. For what? Democracy? Does democracy even matter, if we're all dead?"

"Zed," Oro said steadily. The Skyling sat down, but his glare did not diminish.

Azul shook his head. "I am truly sorry." He looked at Isla, and she remembered the words he had once told her: *It is an honor to rule but not always a pleasure.*

She didn't want to be mad at him. She *agreed* with his way of ruling. How could she fault him for upholding his people's wishes?

Their wishes, though, meant she and the people she loved most might die.

Later that day, she portaled to a deserted part of the Wildling newland and raged her shadows across the dirt, letting her anger scorch the world, until she collapsed into another memory.

BEFORE

It had been a month since Grim had pushed her through the portal, along with her starstick. He hadn't followed her into her room, so she assumed he had portaled himself back to the castle after taking the thief's memories of their meeting away.

She had been left feverish, wanting, consumed by need—

Now she just felt empty.

Why had he left? At a time when she had most wanted him to stay?

Isla might have assumed he had gone off to find the sword without her—if he hadn't left before she could tell him where the sword was. She knew exactly where to find it now. He *knew* she knew.

So why had he gone weeks without seeking her out?

Her confusion and anger soon turned to dread. What if Grim had . . . died? Word wouldn't reach the Wildlings of Nightshade's demise for weeks. Months, maybe.

It was this thought that made her do something careless. That night, she finally reached for her starstick, intent on finding Grim herself.

His room was empty and just the way she remembered it.

Part of her itched to draw her puddle of stars and leave again, but she decided to wait. It had been a *month*. She was tired of staying up late at night, wondering about his absence.

An hour became two. Then three.

Finally, the door to his room opened.

It was not Grim.

It was a woman.

Isla stood from the chair she had been lounging in, and the woman froze. Then, her eyes narrowed. "Who are you?" she demanded.

Who was *she*?

The woman, mercifully, closed the door, as if she had walked in on something private, and Isla portaled away.

Isla felt inexplicable rage. Had he decided to start looking for the sword with someone else? Had he cut her out of his plan? No. She wouldn't let him. She needed him to fulfill his side of their deal.

She knew where the sword was. She would find it herself, and he would be forced to help her at the Centennial.

Isla put on the only black clothing she had—the unfortunately flimsy dress from Creetan's Crag, with her black cape atop it, which conveniently covered the sword strapped to her back—and portaled away.

Grim's lessons had been useful. She needed a map to find the Caves of Irida. Then she could work on trying to portal there.

That was how she ended up in the night market.

It was less than an hour to sunset, and the place was still surprisingly busy. A few carts began packing up for the night. Some people ventured inside large buildings that looked mostly abandoned.

They made a good vantage point. All she needed to do was spot a map shop from above and wait until sunset to sneak inside and find what she was looking for. That way, she wouldn't risk running into trouble again.

She left the market and entered the closest building. The ground floor seemed to be an extension of the shops, a place to trade when the sun went down. It was bustling with the sounds of carts being pushed inside from out, haggling, and whispers.

No maps sold, though. Higher. She needed to go higher and get a better view of the market outside.

The stairs creaked but were empty. So was the second floor. There were just a few boxes and barrels lining the large room, all the way to

windows caked in dust. She rubbed her cape against one and peered outside. Shops were folding closed.

In the corner of her vision, she spotted it. A stall with elixirs sold at the front and parchment in the back. A large map took up its entire back wall—

Footsteps sounded behind her.

Then, "What do we have here?"

Isla turned to see the room was now quite occupied. A dozen Nightshades stood around. Had they been invisible when she walked in? Or had they soundlessly followed her?

She drew her sword. One of them laughed. Her own shadow behind her whipped like a viper and knocked her blade away.

Shadow-wielders. Her chest filled with dread.

Isla quickly turned, deciding to take her chance on the window. She was only on the second floor—

Before she could break through the glass, shadows wrapped around her ankle and dragged her across the room.

Her cheek hit a snag on the floor and tore open. Broken glass stabbed through her hands and her thin dress.

When she was forced to her knees, blood dripped down her chin and chest. She couldn't even move her fingers.

Her cape was ripped away from her by invisible hands, and she gasped at the cold. The man was circling now, a predator leering at his prey.

"Who are you?" he asked.

She spat at his feet, and one of his shadows slapped her in the face. Blood trickled down the corner of her mouth.

"I'll ask again," the man said. "Who. Are. You."

Why did he care? Why was he doing this to her?

She didn't say a word and cried out as another shadow struck her. It was sharp as a blade. Blood dripped down her shoulder. If she didn't heal her cheek soon, it would scar. Another hit sent her crashing to her

glass-filled hands in front of her. She screamed as the glass embedded itself deeper. Another flash of shadows, and she gasped for air.

The man bent down and grabbed her face roughly in one of his hands. Her entire body was shaking. She was going to die. She was such a fool. Hadn't she learned her lesson with the Wildlings who'd tried to carve out her heart? Why had she believed that she could do this herself?

Tears blurred his face in front of her. "You shouldn't have been able to cross the threshold," he said very carefully. "You're going to tell me who you are, or I'm going to skin you alive."

Her blade was on the other side of the room. She hadn't brought any of her daggers or throwing stars with her. The man's shadows were creeping toward her again, across the floor.

She remembered what Grim had said—go for the nose—and head-butted him in the face with her forehead.

He staggered back and called her an awful word, but Isla didn't look to see if she had broken his nose.

She pulled her starstick from her leg holster and drew the puddle of stars. It formed.

Just before she could dive through, the man dragged her away by her hair. She cried out. He ripped her portaling device from her hand and shoved her against the back wall.

The puddle sat there, rippling, in the center of the room. A few of the other Nightshades inched closer to it, murmuring.

"It's . . . a portal," one of them said in awe. More of them rushed to get closer.

The man frowned. Blood got into his mouth. She had broken his nose. "Go see where she was running off to," he ordered.

One of the Nightshades fell through her puddle. It closed after him.

Her only escape, gone.

The only relief was that she hadn't been trying to portal back to the Wildling newland. No . . . she had been trying to portal somewhere else entirely.

"The rest of you," the man yelled, "get out your blades. Let's see how quickly we can skin her. Make sure she stays alive. I want her to feel every inch of this."

She tried to run, but the shadows behind her became restraints around her legs and ankles. One tied around her mouth, muting her screams.

Some of the Nightshades laughed at the sight of her struggling. She heard the scrape of metal as they took their daggers out of their holsters. Some were caked in rust. Others in dried blood.

The man in front of her plucked even more shadows from the room. They inched up her neck, then sharpened into knives.

"Let's start with your face, shall we?" he asked.

Isla winced. Braced herself for the first strike of pain.

His shadows fell away.

The man frowned. He tried his shadows again, but they didn't cooperate. The Nightshades went suddenly quiet.

They slowly turned around. Isla looked through the gaps between them.

Grim stood there, holding the Nightshade who had gone through her puddle by the neck, high above the ground. Her portal had led to Grim's room. There was a crack, and he released him. The man fell in a heap at his feet, dead.

He looked murderous.

In front of her, the man's trousers turned dark, dripping down his leg.

Grim wore his crown and armor. He looked like a demon come to life, spikes on his metal-covered shoulders. Shadows leaked from his very form, snaking through the room. Some of the Nightshades scrambled to kneel. Others tried to flee.

At once, they all jerked high into the air, feet dangling, clawing at their throats.

Grim's eyes never left hers as he stalked over to her. He scanned her body. The cuts across her chest. Her ripped-open cheek. The long marks across her shoulders. Her hands covered in glass.

Grim's voice was lethally calm as he said, "Which one?"

She opened her mouth, but no words came out. Her eyes darted around the room. With them all floating at this angle, she couldn't see their faces clearly. Which body was he? Tears blurred her vision.

"Isla," he said carefully, like he was trying very hard to keep all of himself reined in. He had used her first name. "Which one did this to you?"

She didn't know what he would do, or if she wanted to be the one responsible—

"Fine," he said. "All of them, then."

There was a chorus of cracks as all their necks were broken in tandem. They all fell to the floor. Grim opened his hand, and her starstick flew into his grip.

"You idiot," he said before reaching down and taking her into his arms.

He was furious. He had portaled them into his room. He set her down on a couch and growled, "I'll be back," before vanishing.

Her head fell against the back of the chaise, and she groaned. She had truly believed she could find the sword herself. How wrong she had been.

He reappeared, holding about a dozen different types of bandages and a bowl. He motioned for her to lie down, then went to work, placing the gauze over her shoulders, where she had been injured. They were cold as ice. At their contact, she bucked, cursing.

Grim kept her down with a firm hand on her lower stomach that made her feel shockingly feverish.

"These are Moonling," he said. "They're good at healing cuts."

She was right. Cleo was helping him. Or, at the very least, he was stealing from the Moonlings. "Do you . . . trade with them?"

Grim didn't answer.

His brows were drawn in focus as he plucked pieces of glass from her chest. She closed her eyes tightly against the pricks of pain.

"Let me see your hands."

They were a wreck. She didn't even want to look at the damage. She held still.

He snatched one himself and cursed under his breath. "This will take a while," he said. She imagined there were dozens of pieces buried deep beneath her palm and fingers.

Without warning, he lifted her in his arms again. And set her on his lap.

Isla tensed. She was still in her far-too-revealing Nightshade dress. "What are you doing?"

"You need to keep still," he said. "Or the glass is going to move while I'm working and make removing all of it almost impossible. I can make you pass out if you prefer."

Isla balked. "I most certainly do not prefer that."

He looked down at her, waiting for approval to continue. She gritted her teeth and said, "Fine."

"So charming," he said coolly. Then he snaked his arms around her, pinning her in place, while he gently opened her fingers.

She wasn't breathing. She was engulfed by him. He was cold as bone. She shivered.

He plucked the first piece of glass from her hand, and she bucked again. This time, though, his arms were around her, hard as iron, keeping her in place. She breathed too quickly, pain shooting up her arm. She watched him expertly remove piece after piece.

She gasped at an especially deep incision. He was tall enough that he rested his chin against the top of her head, and said, "There are about a dozen more on this hand alone, so I would find a way around the pain."

She peered up at him. He glanced down at her for half a second before focusing back on her hand.

"Where were you?" she demanded.

A muscle feathered in his jaw. It had been a month since she had seen him. "I was preoccupied," he finally said.

"With what?"

He said nothing.

She scoffed. Unbelievable. "What could be more important than finding the sword?"

"Not more important, simply more . . . pressing." He had hinted at trouble in his realm. Was that what he was referring to?

"You could have told me. You could have visited at least once . . . allowed me to tell you what I had learned."

He raised an eyebrow at her. "Miss me, Hearteater?"

She huffed. "No. Every time I see you, I get injured, or insulted."

Grim frowned, just the smallest bit. He focused solely on her hand. "What were you thinking?" he said harshly.

She sighed, wincing at another shot of pain. "I was thinking I could find the sword without you," she said honestly.

Isla leaned against his chest, gritting her teeth against the pulling of the glass. Some shards were small, but others felt like knives being plucked from her palms. She tried to breathe past it. The same pain, over and over, she could almost get used to. She had learned that during the hours she had spent preparing for specific Centennial ceremonies.

"I went looking for you, before," she said, voice just a rasp.

"I know."

The woman must have told him. Her cheeks suddenly heated with embarrassment. And . . . something else. Her next question bubbled out of her. "Who was that woman?"

"She's my general," he said.

His general. "Does she suspect . . . ?"

"I told her you were someone I had found to bed from another realm."

Isla swallowed. He said the words so simply . . . was that what she was to him? A girl from another realm he had clearly, at Creetan's Crag, wanted to bed?

Inside, she felt like shattered glass, but she closed her eyes and said as smoothly as she could manage, "I know where the sword is. The thief in Creetan's Crag told me."

"Where?"

"The Caves of Irida."

"I know it."

She expected him to look happier about this development; they were so much closer to finding the sword, but his focus was still pinned on her hand. The last piece of glass on that hand clinked against the bowl. He leaned down and whispered right near her ear, "This is going to hurt," before he poured alcohol over her hand.

Grim pressed his palm against her scream. She was grateful. It was an anchor in the sea of pain.

It was blinding. She writhed against him, and he cleared his throat. One of his hands pressed against her hip, holding her still.

"If you can help it," he ground out, "please stop that."

Oh.

She froze.

She was suddenly far too conscious of his body pressed against her as he reached for her other hand and began again.

Underneath her, Grim had tensed completely. His eyes were trained on her palm. He looked intent on his task.

She was not. What was wrong with her? The pain slowly muted as she focused on every graze of his callused fingers against hers. Every part of her was too sensitive. She was now very aware of every place they were touching. The chin against the crown of her head. The muscled torso behind her, hard as rock. Beneath her . . .

She drew a shaky breath.

Grim seemed to rush, because just a few moments later, he said, "Done." This time, he easily lifted her off him before pouring the alcohol on her hand. She closed her eyes tightly and didn't open them again until the Moonling remedies began to reduce the pain.

He was staring at her.

"Thank you," she said.

He said nothing.

"When can we go to the caves?"

"Once you can properly hold a sword again." It wouldn't be long. By morning, with her Wildling elixirs, most of her wounds would be healed. They would still hurt, but not enough for her to want to delay their search.

"Tomorrow," she said.

He nodded. He reached to portal her back to her room, when she said, "Wait. There's one problem."

"Problem?"

She told him about the monster supposedly guarding the sword.

His eyes narrowed. "What kind of monster?"

"I'm not sure."

Grim didn't look too worried. Monsters weren't scared of other monsters, were they? He offered his hand again to portal her back to her room. "Then I guess we'll have to find out."

ASKING FOR HELP

W_e found the ore," Zed announced during their next meeting. He had been searching the Forgotten Mines for days, with Calder, navigating through their dangerous tunnels. Most of the passages had collapsed over time. His face turned from smug to wary as he looked at Isla. "We need your help," he said simply.

Enya was peeling citrus fruit, the smell brightening the room. She raised an eyebrow, and Zed shot her a look.

He didn't particularly like Isla. That much was clear.

"With mining it?" she asked.

He nodded. "I tried using air, but the ores are almost impossible to move. But you . . ."

Control rock. Isla almost smiled, thinking how far she had come from glaring at the stone Oro had placed in front of her on Wild Isle. "Lead the way."

Breathing was difficult in the mine. Zed kept having to move fresh air down deep into the tunnels, which only barely muted the smell of dirt, dust, and sulfur.

She held the fabric of her shirt over her nose. Zed walked in front of her, carrying an orb of fire he had gotten from Enya.

"I would say you get used to it," Zed said. "But you don't. Just feel lucky you haven't been trapped down here for weeks."

She suddenly felt extremely lucky.

They were mostly quiet as they walked. It was a mutual silence—both were happy not to speak to each other. After several minutes, though, she had a thought. "Why does everyone hate Soren?" She remembered how he had questioned her in front of the others, seemingly intent on proving her unworthy of being a ruler. "Beyond the obvious, I mean."

Zed chuckled lightly. He looked over at her. She bet she looked ridiculous, half of her face hidden in her shirt. "He thinks Moonlings are superior to all other realms, and he acts like it. Under his guidance, healers closed their shops in the agora. Less Moonlings started visiting the Mainland at all. They became more closed off and guarded. He used the curses as an excuse to isolate their realm from the others."

He was more awful than she had previously given him credit for. "If he believes that, then why did he stay? Wouldn't he be happy to leave?"

"Perhaps he hates Nightshade more than he hates all of us," Zed mused. He shrugged a shoulder. "Or he stayed behind as Cleo's spy."

She didn't trust Soren in the slightest, but something occurred to her. "Is . . . is Soren a healer?"

Zed nodded, and hope felt like sparkling wine in her chest. He frowned. "You're not seriously going to ask him to help you with the Vinderland."

"That's exactly what I'm going to do," she said.

Zed finally stopped. He motioned to a wall, and all the rock looked the same, save for a tiny flicker of color. She pressed her hand against it and closed her eyes. Beyond, she could feel it—ore buried deep within the wall. It would take concentration to ensure she wouldn't completely bring the entire mine down atop them, but she felt confident she could extract it.

"You might want to make a shield with your wind," she said, before her hand burst through the rock wall.

The entire tunnel trembled—rock fell from the ceiling and was deflected by a stream of wind above them. She felt around in the wall, looking for the bundle of ore. Her fingers broke through stone like a blade through butter. She finally gripped it and pulled her hand back through. "I think this is what you're looking for," she said. It was the first of many. It didn't look very special, but Zed had explained that

with a Starling's energy and Sunling's flames, it could be turned into the drek-defeating metal.

Zed stared at her, the wall, then the ore, eyebrow slightly raised. "That's one way to do it," he said.

Isla found Soren on Moon Isle, looking quite comfortable roaming the palace. She didn't know if he was a spy or had his own agenda, but she would soon find out which side he was on.

He seemed pleased to see her, which only made her more suspicious. He scraped his ice cane against the floor with a sound that stabbed through her brain. She got straight to the point. "Which side are you on? Ours? Or Nightshade's?"

Soren blinked at her. "I assumed it would be obvious by my presence, here on Lightlark."

"Good," she said. "Then you wouldn't have any problem healing potential warriors for our fighting effort?"

Soren's eyes narrowed. She tried to look as innocent as possible. "I . . . suppose not," he said.

She smiled sweetly. "Great. Because . . . if you had said no . . . I would have had to assume you were a spy for Cleo, or somehow working against us."

Soren smiled in the least friendly way possible. "Who am I healing?"

Isla found particular pleasure in his expression after she said the words, "The Vinderland."

The hardest part about getting Soren to heal the warriors ended up being convincing the Vinderland not to kill him.

He showed her how to correctly steep the Wildling flower for tea without losing its healing properties, then began healing their sickness in conjunction with the elixir. The results weren't immediate, but Isla was hopeful that enough of the warriors would be doing better in time to join her in battle.

She had extracted several ores for Zed. Later that night, Isla visited the Wildling newland and found Lynx waiting outside the woods for her.

Her lips twitched. "If I didn't know any better, I would think you were worried about me," she said.

Lynx made a sneezing sound that felt like a denial.

She stood in front of the creature and offered a slab of meat she had gotten from the kitchens.

He sniffed it . . . then, for once, accepted her gift. Progress, she told herself. It was progress.

When Lynx finished eating, she asked, "I've told you we are going to war. Will you fight with me?"

She searched his eyes for a response.

He bowed his head, almost all the way to the ground, and something inside her chest constricted at the clear *yes*.

So often, she had been betrayed. Put her trust somewhere dangerous. The fact that Lynx, who liked to pretend he didn't care for her much, was willing to go to battle with her . . . it meant everything.

She threw her arms around his neck, and he let her hang there. He lifted his head, and she held on, legs dangling.

"We'll get you armor made." She was floating just inches from Lynx's eye as she said, "First, though, I need to learn how to ride you."

As the days before war dwindled, it became clear that there was not enough of anything—time, soldiers, resources, energy.

They sat at the round table again and planned their strategy. They had limited everything, which meant they needed to figure out how to be strategic—how to force Grim and his soldiers to fight exactly where they wanted them to.

They had crafted a map of the Mainland with the mysterious ash Isla had used before, on Sun Isle.

Oro and Zed had been arguing for hours about where they would have the best advantage.

"Here, over the mines," Zed was saying. "We can have warriors in the tunnels. It could work as a trench."

"It would work well for the Nightshades, who could demolish the ground and bury our forces alive," Oro said.

"How about between the Singing Mountains? Nightshades don't know how to fight in mountainous terrain."

"Sunlings don't either."

In the end, they agreed the best place to fight was on the west side of the Mainland, in the space between the agora and Mainland castle. That way, the Mainland woods would naturally frame their fighting area, along with the Starling walls and Wildling defensive nature.

"Can you manage to cover that much territory?" Zed asked. "In nine days?"

"Yes," she said, because there was no other option.

At night, she practiced riding on Lynx. She fell off so much, they had started moving their lessons to the river. The leopard was tall enough that he could easily walk through even its deeper parts, and Isla wouldn't risk a serious injury every time she fell.

She fell a lot.

Each time, Lynx looked at her in a way that could only be interpreted as unimpressed, and then he would fish her out of the water with his great teeth and throw her on his back again.

If only they had more time, she thought. The days were slipping through her fingers.

She needed to get the Wildlings on Lightlark, to start coating its surface in poisonous plants. She needed to start portaling civilians onto the newlands. That alone would take days and much of her energy.

She needed a shortcut.

She needed to remember something useful.

BEFORE

Monster was a kind word for the creature that lived in the cave, housed at its mouth.

It was a dragon.

When Isla was a child, Poppy used to tell her stories of beasts large as hills, with scales like peeling bark and claws at the ends of wings so large they blocked the sun. Isla used to be afraid one might find its way to the Wildling palace and break her room apart with a single shrieking cry.

Don't worry, little bird, Poppy had said. *All the dragons are gone.*

No. Not gone. Just hiding.

"It's asleep," Isla whispered. The dragon was curled in the mouth of the cave, its head facing the opposite direction. Its body rose and fell in a steady rhythm.

She squinted. The cave was not deep. There was a sliver the dragon wasn't covering, and she could see behind it, farther inside—

"No," she said, blinking quickly. "That can't be—no, that's too easy, it can't—"

"It's the sword," Grim said.

Just behind the dragon, the sword was sitting on top of a pile of other relics. It was made of two pieces of metal, braided together like lovers, until they formed a single joined tip.

She made a sound of relief. "We just have to sneak past it without waking it. That's it."

Grim didn't look convinced. "And if it does wake, it will char us alive," he murmured.

They approached the cave slowly, silently, keeping to its very edge.

This would be easy, she reasoned.

The dragon was sleeping soundly. The sword was *right there*; she could *see it*.

The moment Isla stepped foot inside, something flew through the sky. She felt a howl of pain in her leg.

Grim moved fast as lightning. He knocked her off her feet and pinned her against the ground, hand coming down behind her head to soften the fall. Less than a second later, half a dozen arrows went right through his body.

Isla opened her mouth to scream, but before she could make a sound, Grim's other hand smothered her lips. It stayed there, cold and solid as ice. Her eyes were wide, and they stared at each other, faces inches apart, as more arrows stabbed him through his arms and legs. His body lurched with every new hit until they finally stopped.

There was a moment of tense silence, both waiting to see if they had awakened the dragon. She was panting, her chest nearly meeting his own.

No movement.

Her eyes dropped to his wounds. Twelve arrows. It was a wonder none of them had gone through his heart. Blood soaked his clothing, dripping onto her body.

He had shielded her from the attack, without a moment's hesitation.

She dragged his hand down from her lips. "Portal away," Isla mouthed, lips shaking around the words.

Grim shook his head.

If they used his power or the starstick, the sword would disappear. They might never find it again.

Somehow, Grim had to make it out of the cave.

Isla wasn't even sure how *she* was going to make it. The one arrow that had pierced her before Grim had made himself into her personal shield had gone straight through her shin.

With more strength than she could imagine, Grim somehow got to

276

his feet. She quietly stood too and had to bite her hand to keep from screaming from pain. She tried to walk a step and nearly crumpled back down to the floor.

With one quick motion, she was off her feet. Grim, twelve arrows still sticking through him, held Isla in his arms and somehow walked steadily out of the cave and through the field until he could portal them away.

The moment they landed in his room, Grim collapsed, sending Isla sliding across the floor. She gasped as she made her way to her feet, toward him. No. To the cabinets. She opened them all, hurriedly looked for healing supplies, and found Moonling gauze. She used her starstick to portal back to her room, grabbed an entire vial of healing elixir, then returned.

Before she could help him, her own leg needed to be dealt with or she would lose too much blood and pass out. Bracing herself for just a moment, she snapped the end of the arrow and pulled it out. She screamed against the back of her hand. Her wound stung as healing elixir dripped onto it. Her fingers trembled as she quickly wrapped her leg with the bandage.

No time to wallow in the pain. She limped over to where Grim had barely managed to sit up and knelt before him.

"I'm going to—"

"Do it," he said, his breathing labored.

She snapped the first arrow, and he swore. She slid the first arrow out, and when she poured healing elixir over the wound, he bellowed. "Well, you have about another dozen of those, so you better toughen up," she said, partially echoing his own words, only because she knew it would bother him enough to stay awake. "Or did you forget that pain is *useful*?"

"Don't mock me," he said, teeth bared. "It's true."

She rolled her eyes.

"I'll tell you a secret, Hearteater." He flinched as she removed the next arrow. "Pain makes you powerful."

Isla let out a sound of disgust. "It does not," she said. "Though I suppose that's a very Nightshade thing to believe."

"No," he said, mouth curling in amusement even as he suffered. "It isn't an ideal. It's truth. Emotion feeds power. And pain is the strongest."

Isla frowned. That couldn't be true.

"It is true," he said, likely sensing her doubt.

If it *was* . . . "Have you . . . have you ever *purposefully* . . ."

"Yes," he said quickly. "I have purposefully caused myself pain to access deeper levels of power. That was a long time ago. Now, it isn't so necessary." As if in afterthought, he said, "And . . . there are many different kinds of pain."

Isla still couldn't believe it was real. Did every ruler know about it? Why wouldn't it be widely used, then?

No. It couldn't be.

Grim shook his head, reading either her face or her emotions. He tsked, then braced himself as she pulled another arrow out. "Still doubting me," he said. He looked her right in the eye then. "How, Hearteater, do you think I am so powerful?"

That made her hands still around one of the arrows for just a moment. He had experienced deep pain. That was what he was telling her.

It surprised her, but . . . she wanted to know what had made him this way. Who or what had hurt him.

He stared at her. She stared back.

She removed one of the arrows from his chest, and he roared.

By the time all the arrows were out, she'd heard every curse word she knew and over a dozen she didn't. He helped her get his shirt off so she could apply the healing elixir. She caught sight of the small charm beneath his clothing. The one that kept him immune from the Nightshade curse. When his chest was bare, she winced at the sight of the dozen wounds.

Grim laughed darkly.

Laughed.

"I've never had a woman wince at my naked body," he said.

She shook her head. "It must be exhausting carrying around such a magnificent ego."

He laughed faintly as she began applying the serum. The first press of the liquid to his skin, and he hissed. His normally cold body was feverish.

"Your leg," he said, even as he was bleeding from a dozen places.

"Is already bandaged," she said before moving on to the next wound. She worked quickly and diligently, brow creased with focus as she made sure all the splinters were out of his skin and that each place was thoroughly cleaned. Through it all, she could feel him studying her.

"What?" she finally said.

Even in what must have been knee-wobbling pain, the demon still managed to sound pleased. He smirked. "I just think it's ironic that the hearteater who stabbed me through the chest is now tending to my injuries."

She gave him a look. "*I* think it's ironic that the demon who claims he has no shred of humanity left used himself as a blockade against an army of arrows to save me."

He said nothing.

When she was finished with the last injury, the healing elixir was halfway gone. The gauze was on its last few rounds.

Now that he was taken care of, Isla looked at the mess in front of her: his blood-soaked shirt, the pile of broken arrows. She threw up her hands. "Seriously. Why did you *do* that?" she said, exasperated.

Grim's head was lolling to the side. He looked half a moment away from passing out. "That's an interesting way of saying thank you," he drawled.

One of his bandages was already soaked in blood, so she moved to make it tighter, to stop the flow. Once she got it in the right position, she went to remove her hands, but one of his own came over both of hers, pressing her fingers to his chest. "The cold, Hearteater," he said before closing his eyes. His head fell back against the wall. "It helps the pain."

She sat like that for a few minutes, the only movement the steady beating of Grim's heart somewhere near her hand. His eyes remained closed the entire time. After her hand warmed against him, she took it back and sat against the wall next to him.

"What happened?" she asked. The arrows had come from nowhere. "I didn't see anyone, or even where they were coming from—"

"It wasn't a person; it was a weapon. A mechanism designed to go off against intruders. I've seen it before."

"Where?"

"My own castle."

Isla turned to look at him. His eyes were still closed, and the crown of his head was still leaned against the wall. "You believe the thief stole it from your castle?"

Grim shrugged a shoulder. "If she did, she really is the best."

"I take it there aren't any ways around it."

He shook his head. "Infallible, unfortunately."

She sighed. "What do we do now?" There had been yards between them and the sword. Even if they could lure the dragon out of the cave, who knew how many other enchantments the thief had protecting her bounty?

Grim groaned as he straightened himself. "Tonight? I drink my entire store of liquor. Later? I suppose I continue to play shield until we get past all the protections."

PAIN

Power was metal in her mouth, in her nostrils, down her throat, in her stomach. It lit every inch of her up and through; she was a shining beacon, a blade of power carving the world to her desired shape and measurements.

In her memories, Grim had taught her something no one else had bothered to. To win, she needed more power.

Grim claimed *pain was the strongest emotion.*

Pain could be useful.

Trees rose from the soil in bursts of dirt. Ground broke and built until it formed the beginnings of mountains. Flowers blanketed in front of her, so many, so quickly, they fell right off the side of the island.

More. She needed *more.*

Barbed plants, the same ones that had stabbed her everywhere during the Centennial, rose up in thick brambles. Plants with poisoned leaves sprouted. She painted the Mainland in them both, all the parts they needed to block off.

Isla sank her hands into the dirt, fingers in wild shapes, and bellowed, until the ground broke open and more plants formed all around her. Thorn-covered, monstrous plants that would fight back and defend themselves.

It might have been minutes or hours later, but she felt him, a ray of sunlight landing behind her. "Isla?" he said. Her name was a question.

"I finished it," she said. It had seemed almost impossible to create so much nature in nine days, but she had done it in a single night. "Look,

I made walls to block their paths. I covered all the open spaces. Grim can only portal them where you and Zed decided." She was beaming.

He did not look proud.

He looked . . . horrified. She didn't think she would ever forget the way he now looked at her. Like she was something wrong.

Like she was a monster.

"What have you done?" he asked.

She tracked the direction of his gaze and saw it. Blood dripped down the front of her dress. Her hands reached up and touched it, coming from her eyes, her nose, the sides of her mouth, her ears.

Power . . . tasted like blood.

It tasted like blood.

She was saying it over and over, or maybe it was just in her head, or maybe she lived in her head, maybe she never had to leave, maybe she should open herself completely up to the world and let everything in her finally pour out—

"*Isla.*" His hands were rough against her shoulders. He was shaking her. He looked angry. Upset.

Disappointed.

She ripped her power back into herself, and the world steadied before her.

The voices stopped.

It was only her and Oro. And still . . . he looked displeased.

"What did you do?" he said again. His voice was harsh. It was the voice of the king, not of the man who slept beside her, who swept his hands along her back to help her sleep.

"I found a shortcut," she said. "And tested it."

Oro studied her hand, and she winced at what she had done. She had carved a thick line through its center. That was the shortcut. Doing what Oro had warned against, months before.

Using emotion to spur power.

Pain can be useful.

Pain makes you powerful.

"It's fine," she said, fishing her healing elixir from her pocket. She put a drop on her injury and watched the skin grow back. "Look. Like nothing happened."

"Isla," Oro said carefully. "I told you. Wielding power through emotion is dangerous. The power might be immediate, and strong, but it comes at a cost." His hands were in fists; he was practically shaking. "I told you that this could kill you! It *is* a shortcut," he said, spitting the words out. "A shortcut to death."

Heat blanketed the air. It was suddenly sweltering. Then, it was all ripped away.

Realization made him predatorially calm. "He taught you this. In your memories."

Isla did not deny it.

Oro looked at her . . . and shook his head. He studied her face, covered in blood, then her now healed hand, and said, "I don't recognize you, love."

Her hands trembled. She didn't recognize herself either. She didn't recognize the girl in her mind, the one who had made decisions she didn't understand . . .

"I know you want to get into the vault. I know you want to defeat Grim. I know you want to save yourself and everyone," he said. "But this isn't the way." He looked at her. "Promise me you won't try this again. Please, promise me."

"I promise," she said, because he looked so concerned. Because he was just trying to protect her.

She didn't want to tell him that though she was bleeding, she felt stronger than she had in a long time. She felt in control. Transcendent.

The blood tasted like power, she wanted to say. Power—

It tasted like blood.

. . .

Over the next few days, Isla did not sleep. She began portaling all the civilians to the newlands. She recognized some of them.

None of them sneered at her or called her names. Not when she was their only quick way off the island before the attack.

She was about to leave the Starling newland for the tenth time that day, when she did something she had been avoiding for far too long.

She stepped into the room almost as familiar as her own. She almost expected Celeste—*Aurora*—to be waiting there, braiding her silver hair, just to do something with her hands.

The room was empty.

Memories were everywhere. The pile of silver blankets in the corner that they always used to bundle themselves in. The peeling paint that revealed another color beneath, left over from a previous era. The stone floor in front of the fireplace that had been worn over time, soft enough to lie across. They used to joke that the Starlings before Celeste had loved that spot just as much as they did. Now, Isla supposed, it had always been Aurora, sitting in front of that fireplace. Changing the room color. Alone, until Isla came along.

The flames were gone now. Only cinders remained.

A collection of orbs sat on a shelf. They were some of Celeste's most prized possessions. Each held something mysterious. Celeste had claimed they had been passed down through generations and she didn't know what each contained.

Liar.

Isla grabbed the largest and threw it to the floor. It shattered, glass going everywhere. Angry tears prickled the corners of her eyes. "You must have thought I was such a fool," she said.

She hurled another against the wall. "Did you laugh when I left your room? When I told you my greatest secrets, and all you gave me were lies?"

Another orb hit the door. "Was any of it real?" She threw another. She thought of the little Starling girl who was killed by the creatures. All the people who had died in the last five centuries. Her voice shook as she said, "I killed you, and it wasn't enough. The curses didn't die with you. They are still felt." She clenched her hands in fists. "Did you know you were going to kill thousands of people? Did you even care?"

Shadows exploded out of her, tipped in claws. Gashes ran down the walls, cutting through the paint. There was a halo of black around her feet.

Isla panted, the anger and sadness stuck in her chest. She closed her eyes tightly as tears swept down her cheeks. She flung her arm to the side, and shadows destroyed the rest of the orbs.

All were empty, except for one. When it shattered against the wall, something slowly floated down to the floor.

A single silver feather.

Isla stepped forward. She leaned down to take it between her fingers. It had a sharpened tip, almost like a quill for writing.

Why would Aurora put a quill in an orb?

There wasn't any ink on its bottom, but Isla tried to write on a piece of parchment anyway. Nothing.

The room was in ruins. It looked like a giant beast had broken in and tried to claw its way out. It pleased some part of her to see it destroyed.

"I hate you," Isla said to what was left of the bedroom.

She took the feather with her.

It was late afternoon, when shadows were the longest. The ones the trees cast were uniform, and pliable under her command. Remlar sat on a high branch as Isla turned in a circle, roping them all together. Once they were tied, she flicked her wrist and snapped them like a whip. Their sharp edge cut a row of trees down.

"Learn that in one of your memories?" Remlar called from above.

Isla ignored him. She replaced the trees that she had destroyed with new ones. That was her rule. Replace everything she ruined.

"Now that war is almost here, I feel the need to remind you that not all life can be restored," Remlar said. "At least, not on Lightlark."

Her teeth came together. She was aware of that fact, and it ate at her.

If Oro was right, and Grim really was declaring war over her . . . that would mean every death would be on her hands. She couldn't take it—couldn't live with it.

She still didn't understand. In her memories . . . they didn't love each other at all.

Darkness pooled out of her as she flung her hand out. It shot through the forest, destroying everything in its path. Something about using her Nightshade abilities was therapeutic. It was like letting the worst part of herself out.

Remlar floated down from the tree, landing firmly in front of her. He looked pleased. "Your darkness is blooming," he told her, eyes trailing over the path her shadows had made. She had obliterated part of the forest.

"It is," Isla agreed. She had felt it, inside. Uncurling. Awakening. She was remembering more and more. "That's what I'm afraid of."

"You shouldn't be afraid," Remlar said. "You should use it."

"Use it how?"

"War is days away. Me and my people"—he nodded at the hive—"plan to fight. There are other creatures on Lightlark touched by night that would join you, if you asked."

She shook her head. "No, they wouldn't. I *have* asked." She thought of the serpent-woman on Star Isle.

"Have you asked all of them?"

No. She hadn't.

"How would I convince them?" she asked. "What would I offer them?"

"You," he said simply. "You would offer you."

"Me?"

Remlar nodded. "It has been thousands of years since a single person wielded both Nightshade and Wildling power. You cannot begin to understand what that means." It reminded her of the reverence with which the Vinderland had treated her.

"Tell me what it means," she almost begged.

"You don't need me to tell you," he said. "You will see yourself." He motioned around him. "The creatures as old as me on the island will join you. They will immediately understand what you are."

"And what is that?" she asked.

He looked at her, and she saw a gleam in his eye. "Hope."

"Hope?" she asked, before turning toward a sudden trickling sound. A column of water was impossibly falling from the sky.

She blinked, and the rest of the forest fell away.

BEFORE

The bath was almost full. The water was murky, darker than a bog. She could see the pillar of water from his bedroom.

"Medicinal," Grim said gruffly. "Helps with healing." He began to shed his clothing, revealing deep gashes that would have been deadly for anyone without a ruler's power.

They had visited the cave five times. Each visit, they uncovered another enchantment designed to keep thieves out. Grim always took most of the impact, but that day, when a million ice chips had rained down from the ceiling, some had cut down her arms, face, and back before he'd pulled her out of the way.

Isla winced as she reached to pull her starstick from its place against her spine. Her skin was coated in blood. Her vial of healing elixir was steadily running out. She would have to sneak into Poppy's quarters while she was sleeping if she wanted to get more.

"Stay."

The word was followed by silence. It was said matter-of-factly. Flatly.

"Stay?"

Grim was down to just his pants. His chest was a canvas of gashes, blood, and, of course, the mark oh so close to his heart. "The bath is big enough for two. It will help you not scar."

Isla just stared at him.

He didn't leer or make a suggestive comment. It seemed he was too tired to even say anything worth glaring at him over.

"I'll face the other direction."

Isla found she was too tired to turn down the offer of a warm bath with healing properties. But . . .

"I can't," she said. "Remember?" It seemed like years since they had dueled.

Before she could say another word, Grim said, "I take back my win. You're welcome in every part of my palace."

Isla told herself it was shock that made her step into the bathroom. True to his word, at least this time, Grim turned around. She did too.

The sound of his pants being discarded seemed to echo through the vast bathroom. Then, the sound of water parting, letting him in, settling around him.

She didn't check to see if he was facing away as she peeled her own clothes off. It was a painful process. Fabric stuck to her wounds, blood making a most inconvenient adhesive. She made a small sound of pain and hoped he didn't hear it, though she knew he heard everything. The shuffling of her pants being rolled down past her ankles. Her fingers unraveling her braid.

The groan as she placed a leg into the tub, chills sweeping up the back of her calf and up her spine, burrowing into the crown of her skull.

Grim was very still as she lowered herself completely. All she saw was his back, tight in its rigid posture, his shoulders nearly as wide as the tub itself. Everything else was hidden beneath the dark water, swirling with healing enchantment.

"You can turn around," she said. He did not move an inch. "The water . . . it covers everything." It was true. The only part of her that was visible was her head, framed by wet hair, her shoulders, and collarbones.

Seconds passed. Tripped over themselves. Finally, though, he turned.

She was pressed against one side. He was pressed against the other. The tub was enormous; they might as well have been on opposite sides of the room. They just stared. No words were exchanged, but she saw an understanding there. Two people who had fought back-to-back for something they both wanted more than almost anything. A chance to save their people.

The water became clearer and clearer, the medicine dissolving, until Isla crossed her legs, pressed them to her chest, and looked away when Grim did no such thing.

Isla was still looking away as she heard him stand, the water scattering just like anything in Grim's path always did, and he left.

ARMOR

It was time to have armor made for Lynx. She had practiced riding him in the forest, up hills, down steep cliffsides. With every session, his disdain for her dimmed, little by little. He almost seemed pleased that she was now able to stay tethered to him, no matter how fast he ran.

"See?" she had told him the last time. "I can hold on now."

He had promptly taken a hard turn, which had her falling straight into a stream.

As long as he wasn't intentionally trying to throw her off, she felt confident she could bring him into battle.

Wren was training with the other Wildling warriors when she found her.

"I want to have armor made for him," Isla explained. "I was hoping to get your advice on what that would look like."

Wren frowned. "You don't need to have it made," she said.

"I—"

"Lynx already has armor."

Isla slowly turned to look at the leopard, and he just blinked at her.

"He does?"

Wren nodded. The light in her expression suddenly dimmed. "He fought bravely. With . . . your mother."

"Fought who?" she asked, bewildered.

The Wildling smiled. "It's quite a story. I would be happy to tell it to you."

She wanted to hear it more than anything . . . but not now. Not when every hour mattered. Less than a week remained before the battle.

"Another time, I would be very grateful to hear it," she said. "Do you know where the armor is?"

Wren led her to a store of weaponry. There were dozens of swords, sets of armor, and shields. In the very back were enormous sheets of metal that could only fit a very specific, easily annoyed creature.

Isla had to focus for several seconds before she was able to shakily use her Starling energy to move the armor onto Lynx. It included iron plates down his sides and around his front and neck. It even had small holes for his pointed ears and a place for her to sit. Wren helped her put the piece together, and once they were finished, Isla took a step back.

"Don't you look menacing," she said.

Lynx made a sound of approval. He seemed to like being back in his armor. He lowered his head, motioning for her to get on his back, and she did.

"Thank you!" she told Wren, as Lynx took off.

He raced out of the structure, into the forest. Isla gripped the strange saddle, finding it made holding on infinitely easier.

She bent her head down low as they shot through the brush. The first few times, she had felt afraid of being so high up, but now she felt safe. Protected.

Lynx slowed in the middle of a clearing. He bent his head, his silent request for her to jump off. She did.

There was nothing around. What did he want to show her?

Usually, Lynx would have straightened by now, but his head was still bent. She touched between his eyes, silently asking what he wanted, and went rigid.

Her sight was taken away. No—replaced. She was in the same clearing, but it looked different. There were more trees. The grass looked healthier.

There was a girl. Her? It looked just like her. But she didn't have those clothes . . . she didn't often walk with her hands on her hips.

The image became clearer, and her voice shook as she said, "Is that—is that . . ."

Her mom.

She had never seen her mom before. There weren't any paintings of her. Terra and Poppy hadn't given a description, beyond once commenting that she had her mother's face.

Now, she saw it clearly. Lynx was *showing* her.

Her mother was far more beautiful. She had tanner skin and thicker hair. It was shinier. Her eyes were a lighter green. They had the same lips, though. Same high cheekbones. Slightly different noses.

"Lynx, come on," her mother was saying. "Terra's going to have both our heads."

The image disappeared, and Isla started to protest, until it was replaced by another one.

It was her mother again, but this time, there was someone else too. A man with black hair and lighter skin. He was looking at her mother the way Oro looked at Isla. Like he would gladly lay his life down for hers.

The image shifted, and there was crying. Her parents were holding a little bundle between them, looking like they might burst from happiness.

Isla fell to her knees. Tears streamed down her cheeks, into the grass in front of her. She could barely speak. "You—you met me," she finally said.

Lynx had seen her as a baby.

That was right before her parents were killed. He must not have been there, because Isla knew for certain that he would have done everything he could to protect her mother.

Did he feel shame? Guilt? Had he partially blamed Isla for her mother's death? Or did he blame her father?

Lynx made a soft sound as he bent down and wiped her tears away with his fur, on the parts that weren't covered by iron. He ended up swiping his wet nose across her face, and she sputtered.

"Thank you for showing me," she finally said. She wasn't sure how exactly the bonded connection worked, but she felt grateful for it. "I never knew her, but . . . I think this would have made her happy. Us . . . finding each other."

Lynx closed his eyes for a long time, and she could feel his grief like it was her own. She pressed her cheek against his and for a while, it was just them, in the clearing, sharing a memory between them.

When the sun went down, Isla portaled them back to her room. Lynx sat curled in his favorite corner as she stared at her swords, contemplating which ones to bring into battle. There was a whisper of movement behind her, and she turned, mid-sentence.

Only to see that Lynx had been replaced by someone else entirely.

BEFORE

Grim was standing in front of her. She was ready to go to the cave again, but he said, "Not tonight."

"Why not?"

"I have a commitment."

She frowned. "What is it?"

"A ball." He said it with venom.

Isla laughed. "A *ball*?"

"Is that amusing to you?"

She lifted a shoulder. "*You* hosting a ball? Decorations? Dresses? Clinking wineglasses?" Isla had never actually been to a ball, but that was the picture painted by Celeste and the books she'd read.

"Hardly," he said coolly. By his reaction, he made a ball seem like a death sentence. "I would cancel it, but it is a good distraction."

"From?" she asked.

He didn't answer, but she imagined he meant whatever danger was threatening Nightshade. The threat that could mysteriously be solved by the sword. The reason there were often long stretches between his visits. The *more pressing* matter he often needed to attend to.

"Can I come?" she asked.

He looked at her as if she had asked if she could have his throne. "Absolutely not."

Then he vanished.

Late that night, Isla was bored to death on her bed, reading her latest book for the tenth time. She had already filled the margins with notes.

With a sigh as dramatic as she could manage, she flipped onto her back and flung the book to the other side of her bed. She wondered what the ball was like. Were women throwing themselves at Grim? Of course they were. And he was probably accepting them with open arms. The thought made her more than a little nauseous.

She had already changed into her pajamas and was ready to go to bed when her starstick glimmered from beneath her floorboard. It was almost like an invitation.

One she accepted.

A quick, thieving trip to the night market later, she was dressed in about as little fabric as possible to still be considered clothed.

She doubted Grim would even see her. She would stay out of sight. Even if he did see her, so what? He would have to pretend not to know her, to keep up appearances. It was late enough into the night that most of the people at the ball were probably too intoxicated to notice. They couldn't leave until daytime. The party was meant to last until the morning, she realized.

Isla portaled to the Nightshade castle.

If the word *debauchery* had been a place, Isla was looking at it.

The halls of the castle were filled with music so loud and fast it drowned out the moans she could hear only when she passed by the dark halls, people moving furiously in the shadows. Inside the ballroom, all pretense of propriety was abandoned.

People danced with long ribbons of black silk, on platforms lining the room between full suits of armor. In the darker corners of the rooms, couples were coupling, not seeming to care in the slightest that they had hundreds of people as their witnesses.

Before, Isla had felt embarrassed by the amount of skin she was showing, but now she saw she was wearing almost the most fabric in the room. Her dress was black gossamer, with a dipping neckline, two

pieces covering her breasts, then coming together in the middle. It had a slit up to her hip.

Eyes were on her immediately. At first, she panicked, wondering if they somehow recognized her.

No—their gazes were not threatening. They were hungry.

Tonight, she embraced it. It felt good to be seen and wanted.

Isla assumed the party would be crowded and raucous enough that she wouldn't even see Grim, but—

He found her immediately.

She felt his gaze like a brand, and when the crowd naturally parted at the sound of a new song, there was a direct path, across the room, from him to her.

Even from far away, she could see he was furious. Women fought for his attention, barely clothed, but he was watching her, eyes blazing with so much anger, he looked ready to wage a war.

Isla did the most foolish thing possible in response to his anger, which was smile and blow him a mocking kiss.

Immediately, he stood, knocking over some of the goblets that the women had placed around his throne. He didn't even look down; all he did was take a step forward, as if he was going to portal to her and send her straight back to Wildling.

No. She knew it wouldn't do much good if he really wanted to find her, but she ducked into the crowd. In the center of so many people, Grim wouldn't dare appear and whisk her away. She was unknown in the court—it would lead to too much notice and too many questions that Grim had gone to great lengths already to avoid.

That was what she told herself, at least.

The music seemed to get louder, and Isla danced, just one person in a crowd. She met gazes that looked her up and down and seemed to like what they saw. One pair of eyes never left her as she moved until the song ended, and the man walked over.

He was tall and had a scar across his cheek and hair cut short to his head. He wasn't shy with his notice. "You are the most beautiful creature I have ever seen."

Creature seemed like a strange term, but she had never been spoken to so boldly, and she felt her skin prickle. "I am?"

He took a step closer to her. "I've never seen a face like yours," he said. "Not ever."

Isla could feel herself blush. It was so stupid, but the compliment made her feel like a puddle.

"Would you dance with me?"

The crowd behind the man shifted, and Isla saw Grim clearly, sitting back on his throne. His gaze was set on her, expression fuming. His eyes narrowed, as if daring her, just *daring her* to say yes.

She smiled. "I would love to," she said, watching as Grim's grip on his throne tightened.

The dance started off innocently enough. The man stood a respectable distance away and led her through a series of moves that corresponded with the quickening beat of the drums. Then the Nightshade offered her a drink, and she swallowed it down in a single gulp, hoping it would give her the nerve to have the night of her life while she still could. Within moments, she felt light as a feather, and the beat of the music seemed to be synchronized to the beat of her heart, both quickening.

Keeping her eyes right on the Nightshade ruler, she stood in front of the man and danced. Grim's knuckles became skeletal white as he gripped the sides of his throne.

He watched her like he could see right through her, like he was a moment away from turning the entire crowd of people before her to ash.

Still, he did not move to stop her. When the man asked her if she wanted to go into the hall—and Isla had seen *exactly* what happened there—she said yes and let him lead her there.

Isla expected Grim to follow, but he did not. Just a few steps out of the ballroom, she shifted her focus to the man leading her away.

She decided she was going to kiss him. Grim was the only person she had kissed before. Every time she was near him, she felt covered in sparks. Even when they were apart, she felt somewhat empty, like he had taken a part of her with him.

Maybe that was what it was like with every man. Maybe she would kiss this one and see that it felt the same. Better, even.

It would be a relief. Grim was her enemy. She *shouldn't*—couldn't—be attracted to him.

They found an empty corridor, and the man didn't waste any time. He pressed her against the wall, and his mouth went straight to hers.

Nothing. Her skin didn't prickle. She didn't feel heat traveling through her core. He tasted of smoke and alcohol, so she turned her head, not wanting to taste him anymore. He took that as an invitation to continue a path down her neck.

Maybe she just needed to get used to him. She stood still as he explored her, hoping a connection would click.

It wasn't like with Grim at all. The man palmed her chest in a way that should have made her groan. She felt nothing.

His hand started making its way down her stomach, and she watched it, knowing she could stop it but wondering how it might feel. He was so close. Maybe, if he touched her there—

Just as he reached the bottom of her stomach, he froze. He did not blink. His shoulders were hiked up in shock.

That was when they both looked down to see a sword sticking straight through his chest, its tip an inch from her own. The blade was quickly removed, and the man crumpled to the ground, revealing Grim, standing right in front of her.

"Don't worry, Hearteater. He's not dead. I will make sure of it," Grim said in response to her expression of horror. He leaned down to whisper, very slowly, "Because I'm going to bring him to the brink of death a thousand times before I will finally allow him the mercy of dying."

Isla stared at him in shock. "Because . . . he kissed me?" she asked, chest still heaving.

Anger flashed in his eyes, then disappeared. "No, Hearteater," he said. "Because he poisoned you."

She shook her head. "What?"

"The drink he gave you. A few minutes more and you would find yourself paralyzed, a motionless vessel for his pleasure."

Even as he said the words, Isla felt her muscles tightening, like every part of her was hardening into bone.

"How do you know?"

"I didn't until you were leaving. Your face and chest are flushed scarlet. It's a sign." He tilted his head at her. "You feel it, don't you?" he said. He offered her a small vial. An antidote? She swallowed it down. "Better?"

Better. The tightening loosened.

All softness left his expression. He looked down at her, at every inch of her dress, the fabric wrinkled in the places that had been gripped by the man now gurgling on his own blood at her feet.

"Hearteater," Grim said, voice mocking, "who knew you were so desperate for pleasure?" She glared at him, and he only grinned. "If you wanted someone to bed you so badly, all you had to do was ask."

She took a shaking breath. "I would rather die than have you touch me, demon," she said.

He frowned down at her. "Is that so?" He dipped his head, so his cold breath was against her mouth. "All right. I will not touch you again until you ask me to. I won't touch you again until you *beg* me to."

"That will never happen," she spat. "I hate you."

"You can hate me, Hearteater, and still want me in your bed."

She laughed in his face. "In your dreams, demon."

"All of the best ones," he agreed. His eyes seared through her as he looked her slowly up and down. "We do such depraved things, in my dreams."

300

Isla opened her mouth. Closed it.

Grim leaned closer, so they shared breath. "When you finally do beg me to touch you—and you will—you won't want anyone else to touch you ever again, Hearteater." His voice was a dark whisper against her ear. "Late at night, you will think of me touching you. With my hands. My mouth." Isla's chest went tight at his words, his proximity. Her insides puddled; she was hot everywhere. "And you will dream of me too."

Isla closed her eyes tightly, trying to force herself to be repulsed by his words.

When she opened them, both Grim and the Nightshade who had poisoned her were gone.

NEXUS

Five days remained. Isla was back on the Wildling newland. Enya was helping her make the final arrangements for the warriors to travel to Lightlark. The Sunling had already found space for them in the castle, close to Isla. They catalogued the healing elixirs that were left, after she had given a great portion of them to Calder and Soren. Reluctantly, Soren had agreed to let Calder shadow him as he treated the Vinderland. Calder was an eager learner, writing notes, which only seemed to annoy Soren.

Every remaining drop of elixir was crucial.

They both worked without speaking, exhausted, but there was no time to rest. She finished her remaining tasks and, at the end of the day, portaled them back to Lightlark.

In Isla's overstuffed chairs, they were finally still. After a few minutes of companionable silence, Isla asked, "Do you have anyone? Anyone you're . . . worried about, beyond Oro, Zed, and Cal?"

"You mean, do I have a partner?"

She nodded.

"Not at the moment. I've loved many women through the centuries, but it always seemed selfish to take a wife, knowing . . . what I do." Knowing when she would die.

The Sunling tilted her head at Isla. Her red hair was vibrant against her pale skin. "You are different than I thought you would be. I like you, Isla, I really do," she said, and Isla felt the same way. She wanted to tell her, but in the same breath, the Sunling said, "But I don't like you for him."

For him.

For Oro.

Isla's previous love for the Sunling woman hardened into rock. "What do you mean?" she said slowly.

Enya sighed. "May I be honest with you?"

Isla nodded, even though her teeth rubbed together, painfully, behind her lips.

"Oro is king of Lightlark. His duty, from the moment his brother died, was to his people. Not himself. Not me. Not anyone he cares about. I used to hate it. I used to hate that one of the people I loved most would never truly know happiness. Now, I accept it. Because his happiness, and mine, are not more important than the happiness of everyone else on this island."

Enya filed her fingernails against her pants. "He loves you, and that love is making him weak. If he's not careful, it will be the death of Lightlark."

Isla felt her face twist. "How can you say that? How can you paint love as the enemy?"

"Because I've watched thousands of people die, I've watched devastation for five centuries—all in the name of love." *The curses.*

"This is different," she said.

Enya smiled, and it was sad. She didn't look cruel, or mean, and that made her words sting even more. "I believe those words have been spoken by every person in love since the beginning of time."

You don't know anything about us, Isla thought.

It would have been easy, so easy, so *convenient,* to ignore Enya's words as jealousy or misguided advice.

Deep inside, if she really thought about it, she knew Enya was right.

Isla was almost done portaling the rest of the civilians. By tomorrow, only warriors would be left on Lightlark.

She was walking across the Star Isle bridge when she got the feeling she was being followed.

She focused on the ground beneath her, and she could sense the footsteps far away. Walking. Waiting.

She was about to be ambushed. She knew it, and she understood that only one group of people would be so bold, so close to the day of battle.

Isla let them capture her.

She braced herself, and the strings on the other side of the bridge snapped. It swooped down like a pendulum, and a force plucked her from the air, into a carved opening in the side of the Mainland cliff. The ones who had been following her swung in after her.

She rolled inside, her ribs screaming in protest as she tumbled before nearly hitting a wall.

When she opened her eyes, a dozen red masks looked back at her.

She smiled. "I don't think this is going to go the way you're hoping," she said. Then, she twisted her fingers, and the ground grew teeth, trapping them all against the ceiling. She hadn't killed them.

Not yet.

"Wait," someone said. One of them fought to get their arm out between the ceiling and rock, to remove their mask. "Before you kill us, please just listen."

Isla didn't listen. She lashed out, the ground beneath her shook—

The person got their mask off, and Isla went very still.

"Maren," she said.

Isla imagined she look crazed. Another Starling she had trusted, betraying her—

"How could you?" she asked, voice shaking. Maren had Cinder. She was a *leader*.

She had tried to kill her—

"We didn't mean to hurt you before," the Starling said quickly. "The Moonling who performed that did not consider the fact that you might . . . drag across the balcony. It was supposed to be simple—"

"What do you want?" Isla demanded. "You have five seconds to explain before I bring this cave down all around us."

"Do you agree with the system of rule, Isla? You each make decisions that affect us all, whether you intend them to or not. The system of rule is a curse. Our lives being tied together is a curse."

"No." Her answer was immediate. She didn't think it was fair that rulers were born with the bulk of power. "That's why I'm implementing a democracy on Star Isle."

Maren nodded. "We heard, and we appreciate it," she said. "But the current system of rule goes beyond just votes and voices. We have all historically been tied to rulers' lives, because of the power they alone channel. Do you know why, Isla?"

She shook her head.

"Because thousands of years ago, the king's ancestors had a Nightshade create a series of curses called nexus, designed to keep the people weak. Everyone—except for his line—was cursed to only be born with a single ability. And people were cursed to be tied to their rulers, so power could never be overthrown. Nexus was meant to keep us all weak. Subservient. Loyal."

Nexus? She had never heard of it. "How do you know any of this?"

"History was buried. It took centuries for our group to finally gather this information. It started during the curses. You six were the stars of the Centennial, but we regular islanders also worked to break them. We learned that it used to be possible for a person to denounce their power and leave a realm."

Isla thought about the Vinderland and the serpent-woman, who had left Wildling many centuries ago.

"We believed that if we could figure out how they did it, we could give up our powers and not be bound to the curses. It was a sacrifice many of us were more than willing to make. That led to researching why the ties between the people and their rulers existed in the first place.

"We failed to figure out how to properly denounce our realms, but, after you broke the curses, we realized you could be the answer to all of our problems. You could break the current system of rule."

Now, Isla was lost. "How could I possibly do that?"

"We believe you have a flair, Isla."

She didn't. If she did, she would know it by now, wouldn't she?

"We believe you are immune to curses."

"What?"

"You were not cursed, even though you did indeed have power. And you were born with two abilities, Wildling and Nightshade."

Isla took a step back. How did they know—

"We have members in Skyling," Maren said. "You practice in the woods." She should have been more careful. "If we are correct, then you have already inadvertently freed two realms from being tied to your life. Wildling. And now, Starling."

Her death wouldn't be the death of everyone she ruled.

She shook her head. She wished more than anything that it was true . . . but none of this made any sense. "Why wouldn't you just tell me then? Why kidnap me? Why be so secretive?"

Maren glanced at the others. They were all still crushed against the rocks, and Isla loosened her hold on them, just a little. "Because to free all the realms from nexus would require the death of the king. We needed to talk to you without him finding out."

Isla laughed. She actually laughed. "No," she said, the word final.

"We haven't even told you how—"

"I don't care," she said, baring her teeth. "I won't do anything that requires the king dying."

Maren just looked at her. "Even if it means potentially saving thousands of people?"

She knew how it looked. How could she possibly choose one life over thousands?

Perhaps she wasn't as good as she thought she was, because she said, "Yes. Even then."

Without another glance at the rebels, she carved stairs out of the side of the cliff with her power and climbed out of the cave.

That night in bed, Isla wondered if she should tell Oro about them, or ask about the nexus. She quickly decided against it. They were days away from battle. There was enough to deal with.

Isla shifted in the bed and startled when a loud thud broke through the silence.

BEFORE

The noise had come from the center of her room. It was the middle of the night, and something heavy had just thumped against her floor.

She was up in an instant, the long dagger she kept between her bed frame and mattress fisted in her hand.

Squinting through the darkness, she found someone slumped over in front of her bed, their blood staining the stone.

"Hearteater," he said.

She threw her dagger down and rushed to his side. "Grim?" It had been days since the ball.

He grinned. "I believe you'll be pleased," he said, his words labored.

"Will I?" she said, eyes searching his body for where he was bleeding the most, for signs of what could have possibly happened.

"Something got very close to killing me."

The sinking feeling in her stomach was like a boulder dropping into a river. This information did not please her at all, and she knew he could feel it. "Oh? That is wonderful news," she whispered.

He nodded. "It is with great regret that I share it did not succeed."

She shrugged a shoulder. "Not yet, at least."

He barked out a laugh, then groaned.

Her arms circled his body, and she pressed him against the floor with all the strength she could muster. Shaking hands—from worry, of course from worry—began unbuttoning his shirt.

He made half-sensical comments about her undressing him, but she shushed him, eyes studying the constellation of wounds across his torso. They weren't like anything she had ever seen before. His skin had turned ashen; the marks were dark. Black veins like roots from a decaying tree wove across him.

"What is this?" she asked. He glanced down at her hands pressed against his chest, and she slowly removed them.

Grim ignored her question. "The elixir, Hearteater. The Wildling flower," he said.

Then his head fell into her lap and he ceased speaking.

Isla tried to undress Grim properly, but he was too heavy to move all that gently. Instead, she took her knives and cut the clothes off him. She could only imagine what he would say about that.

She nearly gagged at the sight of him. The wounds were eating through his skin and bone, ruinous and sinuous. It was as if the darkness was still feasting, even now.

"What is this?" she said to herself. And why wasn't Grim healing quickly, the way he did with typical injuries?

Isla hoped the elixir would help. If it didn't, would the shadows spread until Grim was nothing more than ash? Was the entire fate of the Nightshade realm in her hands right now?

With determination, Isla applied the elixir to every wound. On his neck. His chest. His stomach. His arms. His thighs. When she was done, her vial contained only a few more drops.

She sat next to him as he slept and was there when he gained a sliver of consciousness. "Isla," he said.

She nearly jumped, looking to see what he needed. But his eyes were closed.

It was only a little while later, knees to her chest as she watched him, that she realized what he had called her. *Isla.* He had sworn never to call her by her first name . . .

Yet there it was again, falling so effortlessly from his lips.

. . .

Isla portaled them both to his room, where he soon dozed off again. Luckily, she was able to transport them to his bed in his groggy state, or he would have woken up on the floor. His ruined clothes were a tattered pile nearby. Isla toyed with the idea of dressing him again as he rested but settled on simply covering most of his body with one of his dark sheets.

Slowly, like clouds clearing after a storm, the elixir had eaten through the wounds. His skin had grown back. He still wasn't in perfect condition, but he would live, and for that, Isla found, she was grateful.

Strange. Months ago, she'd wished him dead.

Now, the thought of him dying—

She was sitting at the edge of the bed, legs crossed in front of her, when his eyes snapped open. This time, they were more alert and found her immediately. "You healed me."

Then he studied himself. Lifted the sheet. Raised an eyebrow.

"It isn't the first time," she said. "And . . . you have healed me too."

"Thank you," he said then. He leaned forward before she could stop him, wincing from the effort . . . and did something so unexpected, she didn't move a muscle. He kissed her on the forehead, then leaned back against the pillow.

Watching him shift uncomfortably, her expression turned serious.

"What happened?" she asked. Then, her eyes narrowed. "Are you— are you looking for the sword without me?" Were those somehow wounds from the dragon? Had he awakened it?

"I'm not," he said. She must not have looked convinced, because he added, "I am the ruler of Nightshade. Do you truly believe working with you is the only opportunity I have to be wounded?"

"Yes," she said. "Because only in the cave can you not use your powers. With them, you just do . . ." She waved her hands in front of her face dramatically.

Grim raised an eyebrow at her. "I do *what*?"

"You know what I mean," she said, shaking her head. "Shadows. Death. Stuff. You know."

He sighed. "Well, the creatures I face often are mostly immune to *shadows. Death. Stuff.*"

Creatures? "Grim. What is going on in Nightshade? What could possibly be strong enough to wound you like this? Why do you need the sword?"

There were too many questions spilling out of her mouth, but she couldn't push them down any longer. Things between them had changed. Before, she'd agreed to work with him only because of his promise to help her during the Centennial.

Now . . . she wanted to help.

He studied her. It was a minute later when he looked down at his hands, still partially covered in marks from the attack. "It is treason if I tell you. It is one of the greatest secrets of our realm."

Isla just looked at him. "Everything about this is treasonous."

He frowned. "I suppose you're right." He shifted his position and winced. "Centuries ago, after the curses were spun, a scar opened up across Nightshade. Winged beasts began escaping from it. They look like dragons, but smaller, and their scales are nearly invincible. They're called dreks, and they have already killed thousands."

They sounded terrifying. "Do people live near the scar?"

He nodded. "Near the parts that are inactive. The attacks have been concentrated to one area in the last century."

Grim rubbed a hand across his forehead. He looked exhausted.

"Dreks used to be people, millennia ago. My ancestor Cronan cursed his warriors to become unbeatable beasts. He had the blacksmith make him a sword, imbued with his power, so his later generations could control the drek army. Also . . . so they could make new ones. After his death, one of his descendants predicted the dreks would lead to the end of the world, so she cursed the sword to be unusable by a Nightshade ruler." How was he going to get past that curse? Was he hoping *she* would use it for him? "Dreks had ravaged both Lightlark and Nightshade. After Cronan's death, they were all banished below. Now . . . they've started rising up again."

"So . . . the sword controls the dreks. That's why you want it? To stop them?"

Grim nodded.

"My father was obsessed with finding the sword," he said, seeming to surprise himself, because he frowned.

"Why?"

"He wanted to use it to invade Lightlark. It would have been easy, with the dreks."

Grim's father sounded awful. Good thing it seemed like Grim was nothing like him.

She wondered . . .

"What was your mother like?"

He seemed shocked by her question. She was shocked she had asked it. Eventually, he said, "I wouldn't know."

Her brows came together. "She—died? In childbirth?"

Grim frowned. "No. On Nightshade, rulers don't take wives," he said. "They don't ever even bed the same woman twice. Or, at least, they're not supposed to."

"What? Why?"

"A precaution," he said simply. "Love makes our power vulnerable. It is a weakness."

She just stared at him. "You don't actually believe that, do you?"

"I do. If I love someone, they have access to my ability. It's a liability. My ancestors never cared to take the risk."

Pieces came together. "That's why you had the line of women," she said. "The volunteers. To make sure . . . to make sure you never sleep with the same person twice."

He nodded. "Not that I would remember them, but the palace has records. It's a precaution. It's been that way for generations."

Isla realized something. "You're trying for an heir, aren't you?" She remembered the women talking about being involved with the ruling line . . .

Grim did not deny it.

She swallowed. "I'm guessing . . . it hasn't worked?"

He shook his head. "Bearing children as a ruler can take time." He looked at her. "No, I haven't continued since we made our agreement."

Good. If he created an heir, he couldn't attend the Centennial. Still, there was only one reason why he would want to have a child that she could think of. "You think the dreks will eventually kill you," she said. "You want to ensure your realm survives."

If he was dead, he couldn't help her at the Centennial. It was in her best interest to not only help him find the sword . . . but also help him use it.

Grim nodded, just the slightest bit. "It's my duty."

"And if you did eventually have a child, after the Centennial, you wouldn't want to know the mother? You wouldn't . . . allow her to help raise the child?"

"No," he said.

A precaution. Love makes our power vulnerable. It is a weakness.

"That sounds . . ." she said, "very lonely."

Grim made a face. "I've never felt lonely in my life," he claimed.

The way he said it made her feel like he really believed it. Still— everyone got lonely. "Maybe you just don't know what it's like to miss someone, then," she said quietly. "Because you don't open yourself up long enough to let them in."

He shrugged a shoulder. "It doesn't matter," he said. "Love is for fools, anyway. It makes people do foolish things." He looked at her and said, "I do not intend to become a fool."

She was the fool, she knew. Because something about him saying that made her heart break.

LOYALTY

I know what the sword does," Isla told Oro. He immediately called a meeting.

Azul was not fighting with them, but he had remained on the island, to help in any way they needed him.

He was there, in the war room, when she told them everything. Her history with Grim. The oracle's words. The fact that she had important memories. Azul looked pensive. Zed looked furious. Enya looked curious. Calder looked from Oro to Isla, then back again.

They might have been angrier if she hadn't immediately told them about her latest memory.

"Dreks used to be people. Cronan made a sword that controls them and can make more." She pressed her lips together. "I believe Grim now has that sword."

Heat flooded the throne room.

"It's done, then," Zed said. "It's—"

"Wait." Azul held up a hand. "You don't remember finding it, though, right? Perhaps you never did."

It was a good point.

Zed laughed without humor. "The oracle said Grim has a weapon. The dreks flew toward Nightshade after the attack. It's obvious he controls them. And now, with the sword . . . perhaps he has created more. We must prepare to face an army of endless dreks."

Calder was the one who said what they must all have been thinking: "How do we possibly prepare for that?"

Even before learning about the sword's use, winning seemed impossible.

Now, she wondered if it was foolish to ever think they could stand a chance against Grim.

"We're dead," Zed said, after a few moments of silence. "If he really has that sword, and can create dreks at will . . . we're dead."

Enya stood. "No. Not yet. What we are now is desperate. We need to find more power. We need to find another way to win."

"We only have four days left, Enya," Calder said.

She whipped around. "So, we give up? We let this army destroy our home? The one our own parents loved and protected?" She shook her head. "No. I refuse." She took a step, and wings of flame burst forth from her back. They curled open, sizzling behind her. She looked like a phoenix. "I didn't live five hundred years in the darkness, dreaming of the day I got to feel the sun on my skin again, to have my home taken away."

Enya was right. They couldn't give up.

And she was right about something else. They *were* desperate. Which meant Isla was about to make a very bad decision.

Grim was coming with an endless army of dreks. Loss felt almost certain, but she couldn't give up.

There had to be a way to save the island. There had to be a way to save Oro and herself.

Isla used her starstick to portal to the edge of the Star Isle forest. It didn't take long for the serpent to find her.

She watched as the snake turned into a woman and walked toward her, her long green scale dress trailing behind. "I let you live last time," she said. "It seems you have rejected my gift."

Isla didn't have time for games. "We need you," she said. "The destruction coming . . . We have no chance against it. Not without you and the other ancient creatures."

The woman glared at her. "We are outcasts. No one has ever cared about us. How dare you ask for our help?"

Isla let her shadows loose. They swept across the silver ground, swirling like ink. "Because I'm an outcast too," she said. She stepped forward. "I understand if you can't trust anyone on this island. I understand what it's like to be hated and abandoned." She took another step. "Don't trust them. Don't believe in them. Believe in me."

The serpent's eyes sharpened.

"I will not abandon you. I will fight by your side, and when all of this is over, I will make you a place on Wild Isle. You won't have to hide or kill innocent people for food. You will be part of the island again. I promise. I extend that promise to whatever else lives in this forest."

She meant it. With every part of her, she meant it.

The serpent rejected her anyway.

Isla didn't let the rejection stop her. There were other night creatures on the island. She went to each isle and sought them out.

Remlar was right. Most, when she showed them who and what she was, bowed their heads and joined her.

Her. Their loyalty was to *her.*

All this time, she had rejected the darkness within her. Now, she wondered if it was her greatest strength.

By the time she left the last isle, the shadows of the island tilted toward her, as if called by her presence.

She took one in her hands, felt it glide across her fingers. It slipped away, and she turned to grab it again—

But she wasn't on Lightlark any longer.

BEFORE

Grim had made her an illusion of the cave. They had gotten past every single obstacle until the last—the dragon itself. Its tail now sat between them and the sword, too spiked to climb, and impossible to get through without power. If they couldn't get past the dragon, they would have to lure it out.

They were thinking of ways to do that when Grim suddenly said, "I want to show you something."

She took his hand, and they were off.

They landed in a field of flowers so beautiful, they looked like melted night. Deep purple, with five sharp petals. Stars.

Grim picked one and gave it to her. At first she was surprised, and touched, but he said, "Smell it, Hearteater."

She did and frowned.

"Familiar?"

She would know the smell anywhere. "It has the same scent as the Wildling healing elixir," she said warily. It smelled sweet. Syrupy.

"I think they're the same flower."

What? That didn't make any sense. Isla turned around in a circle, eyes focused more closely around her. There was supposedly only a small, coveted patch of the flowers that produced the healing elixir in the Wildling newland. There were entire rolling hills of these here, a sea of nighttime sky. "What even is this?" She didn't know the name of the flower that produced the serum.

"It's nightbane."

Nightbane. The drug he had talked about. The one that made people endlessly happy while killing them from the inside out. She felt like an idiot shaking her head so much, but none of this was adding up. She felt the need to spell it out clearly. "But the Wildling flower doesn't kill . . . it *heals.*"

"We extract the same nectar. In Nightshade hands, under our own extraction process, it turns into a drug that produces euphoria," Grim explained. "I suspect under a Wildling's touch it turns into a healing elixir instead."

She stared down at the flower Grim had given her. Her fingers ran across its petals. They were as soft as velvet and didn't fold beneath her touch.

Both poison and remedy. Opposites, like her and Grim. The ruler of life and the ruler of shadows.

The flower connected them.

"We can make a deal," Isla said quickly. "We—we don't have much of this flower. If you can give us some of yours, we can provide healing elixirs." Isla said it and wasn't sure how to even make that happen. Terra and Poppy had no idea she had spent the last few months with Grim. It wasn't as if she could tell them out of nowhere that they were making a trade agreement with Nightshade, but her people were dying and desperate. "In exchange, we need hearts," she added. "From . . . from people you are already going to kill. And other stuff I can't think of right now that we need."

Grim stared down at her. The corner of his lips twitched in amusement. "It's a deal, Hearteater," he said. He held out his hand, and she took it. They shook on it. By the third shake, he had portaled them back to her room.

He didn't drop her hand. She didn't drop his.

Isla swallowed, and his gaze traveled down her throat. Lower. Lower. She took a step back, and her spine hit the wall. He stepped forward.

Grim had told her more about himself than ever, the last time she saw him. He'd let her look beneath the mask of death and darkness. Underneath . . . there was a man. Someone who had been through pain.

Someone she had started to understand.

Their gazes were locked. Isla had the sense that the room could come crashing down around them and they still wouldn't break eye contact. Grim stepped and stepped, until he was right in front of her. She had to crane her neck to watch him.

He leaned down. He dipped his head slowly, tentatively. He was the greatest warrior in all the realms, but Isla could have sworn he was trembling. She felt his breath against her face. His breathing was labored.

"Please," he said, sounding pained. "Please, tell me you want this." He waited for her to nod. He traced her body with his eyes and said, "I know if I touch you again it will kill me . . . but I think I might die if I don't."

She didn't dare move as he gathered her in his arms and ducked to meet her.

An inch from her lips he stopped. Cursed.

She straightened. "What is it?"

"There's been a breach in the scar," he said.

Then he vanished.

GONE

When Isla awoke that morning, she startled out of bed. Oro was next to her in a moment. "What's wrong?" he asked.

"Not wrong," she said, frowning. "Just . . . a development. The Wildling healing flower, the rare one?"

He nodded.

"It's *nightbane*." She said it like it was the biggest news in the world, but Oro just looked at her.

"What's nightbane, love?" he asked.

Oh. She sometimes forgot that he wasn't in her head. There was an entire life she was currently living internally that he didn't know about.

She closed her eyes. Breathed. "Nightshade has fields of the Wildling flower." Isla didn't know what to do with this information; she just knew it was important. "I—"

Suddenly, her head was pounding. She bent over and felt Oro race to her side. She blinked, but she wasn't seeing in front of her.

No. She was seeing a forest.

She knew that forest. It was right outside Wren's village. There was a pull in her chest, a desperation, a call.

Lynx.

Somehow, she was seeing what he was seeing right at this moment.

Just as she wondered about the connection between bonded, she saw him.

Grim.

He was in the Wildling village. *No.* Fear gripped her chest.

Lynx leaped forward. He raced through the trees, to the village. Before he could reach any of the villagers, though, the vision vanished.

"I need to go to the Wildling newland," Isla said, her voice just a rasp, her hands shaking.

"I'll come with you."

She portaled her and Oro to the village, the same way she had done almost every day for weeks.

Silence.

Isla portaled to another, smaller village, which had been filled with singing and laughter and the snap of weaving with wood and vines the last time she visited.

It was empty.

She went to another. Empty.

Every house was vacant. Crops that should have already been collected that day remained untouched.

She portaled back to the outskirts of Wren's village, where the small patch of deep-purple flowers had been planted and extracted. It was where she and Enya had just finished cataloguing it all.

The healing elixirs that they had spent weeks producing were gone. *Gone*.

"Isla," Oro said, putting a hand on her arm. Lynx broke through the brush. His eyes were wide, angry.

No.

She'd finally faced her people, gotten to *know* them—

And they were gone.

It was in her room in the Wildling palace that she finally found a note. Its seal was as black as melted-down night sky, and bile rose up her throat. It confirmed what Lynx had shown her.

I've brought them to Nightshade, it said. *They're waiting for you, heart. We're all waiting for you.*

A chill dropped through her stomach. Darkness bloomed.

The paper disintegrated in her hands, blowing away in a few pieces of ash, and she raged. The stone in her room rippled with her anger. Her wooden door flew off its hinges, collapsing against the opposite wall. The spot beneath her was tinged with darkness.

Lynx made an angry sound as Isla broke down completely in front of Oro, sobbing into his chest. "He took them," she said. "They're gone. They're all gone."

BEFORE

Grim was gone. One moment, he was there, so close to her, and the next, she was alone. There had been a breach in the scar, he said.

How did he know? Could he feel it?

It had been hours since he had vanished, and she began to worry.

A part of her, a whisper in her mind like a shot of ink tainting all other thoughts, imagined the worst. It spun possibilities. What if the dreks had defeated him? What if he was stuck on the battlefield, slowly being consumed by the darkness that only her elixir seemed able to heal quickly?

What if he needed her?

She told herself she was worried because if he died, he couldn't help her at the Centennial. Only for that reason.

Night bled into early morning, and Isla decided she couldn't sit in her room and wait. She had to do something.

She was wearing one of her nightdresses. Isla considered changing, then forgot it. Grim could be dying. He could be in his room, bleeding out, not able to portal to her . . .

She portaled in secret to Poppy's room to steal more serum and drew her puddle of stars.

Isla had been waiting in his room for half an hour, sitting perched on the edge of his bed, when he finally entered.

Relief filled her, then rushed away.

He looked like a demon.

Grim wore a helmet with spikes that curved down over his nose, his temples. His shoulders had barbs like blades. Touching him anywhere would draw blood. His armor resembled dozens of scales, plated together. He looked like a creature of the night, a monster in the dark. Shadows puddled at his feet, circling.

Isla didn't dare breathe. She told herself she should be afraid. If she had met him like this for the first time, she might have been.

But when the demon shed his layers, there was a man beneath. His helmet cracked against the floor when he dropped it. He stripped the armor off, with the tiredness of someone who felt suffocated, who wished to be free.

His shirt beneath was black and tight, fabric wrapped around and around. Isla didn't know how he hadn't noticed her yet.

All she could do was sit in shocked silence as he took off his shirt. Only when the fabric was over his head did his back tense.

And he slowly turned around to face her.

Isla felt her face go scarlet. He was unharmed. She felt foolish. Of course he was unharmed. Last time must have just been a fluke. He was the ruler of Nightshade; he knew how to defend himself. He didn't need *her*, of all people, looking after him.

Stupid. She felt her face heat. She stood from his bed—*why had she decided to sit there?*—and smoothed her hands down her silk dress. Grim's gaze dropped. She felt it like a flame, heating her from her collarbones, down her chest, her stomach, to places that made her dress suddenly feel too thin. "I—I just wanted to make sure you were fine," she got out.

He motioned toward himself. "I'm fine," he said.

Isla swallowed. "I can see that." She straightened. Opened her mouth. Closed it. Her gaze slipped down his bare chest. She had seen him without a shirt before, of course she had, but she hadn't ever allowed herself to truly study him this way. Now, she took all of him in.

He looked etched out of marble. Every muscle was defined by

training, cut perfectly. His shoulders were wide. She studied him, and part of her ached to keep watching, to get closer, to touch him—

His words from the ball were right. Late at night, she sometimes thought of him, of his hands, rough against the softest parts of her.

In her imagination, she followed the muscled lines of his stomach, lower, lower, only to awake gasping.

Now he was right here, and he wanted her. She could see the evidence of it, right there in front of her.

She looked away. Suddenly the wall behind him looked very interesting. There was a mirror there, and she saw herself, standing very stiffly in her red dress. She studied her reflection, wondering what could have possibly made him want her in that way when she wasn't doing anything special, she was just standing there, in a dress she often just wore to sleep.

The straps were thin; the bodice was overflowing. Her dress clung to her. It was more revealing than she had previously realized.

Isla looked to Grim. He was looking at her like she was the world, and he wanted to conquer it. For a second, she felt brave. Powerful, in a strange new way.

She stepped toward him.

Grim stood unnaturally still.

Her hand pressed against his chest. Her fingers were trembling. His skin was cold and hard as stone. Isla wasn't sure if he was breathing. His eyes were hungry, devouring her, taking in every inch of skin. She bit her bottom lip.

He studied her mouth, and she didn't want him to keep looking, she wanted him to *do* something.

She stepped forward, until every part of her pressed against every part of him. Her fingers did not shake any longer as she traced the large scar in the center of his chest. His reminder of her. Her hand ran lower. Lower.

Lower.

"Hearteater," he said, voice strained. The word was a warning.

She met his gaze. His eyes held all sorts of dark promises, and she wanted them all.

He was too tall. Too far away. She went on her toes to reach him, but she still could not.

She frowned and fell back onto her heels. He desired her, that much was clear. She felt like a flame, like she might just simply burn away if he didn't extinguish this feeling building inside her, this insatiable want—

Grim had told her he wouldn't touch her unless she begged. Back then, she had promised herself that wouldn't happen.

Now, she was ready to go on her knees before him.

"Touch me," she said, her voice just a whisper. "*Please*."

Grim didn't move an inch. He stood almost impossibly still.

Isla frowned. Did she have to say it again? She ran her hands lower, as if to show him exactly what she meant. Until she could almost feel all of him. "*Please*, Grim, would you just *touch*—"

Before her sentence was over, his mouth was on hers. The kiss was punishing, exploring, unrelenting. He tilted her head back, hands cradling her neck, thumbs brushing across her throat.

She made a sound into his mouth, and he seemed to like it, because he growled and bit her bottom lip before swiping his tongue over the hurt. She was on fire; everything burned, some places more than others, and she needed those hands, that tongue, everywhere. Now.

He broke their kiss and looked down at her. She looked down too. Her nightdress was pulled so low, she was nearly spilling out of it. Her chest was heaving.

Grim looked at her body like he was committing it to memory. "You know, I really like this dress," he murmured. He traced the neckline. His fingers slipped beneath the fabric and Isla gasped at the cold, then moaned as he traced every inch of her chest. "But it's in my way."

He gripped the silky fabric with both hands. He paused, looking

at her as if for approval, and when she gave it, he ripped it right down the center. Stitches broke; fabric was torn.

He kept going, until her nightdress was nothing more than shreds of fabric on the floor.

And she stood naked in front of him.

No one had ever seen her this way. Isla was burning, ready.

But all he did was look at her. For far too long, he just stared.

Was something . . . was something wrong with her? Was he not attracted to her? Had they gone too far already?

Isla began covering her body with her hands. She sat on the bed and crossed her legs, embarrassment heating her face.

"Is . . . something wrong?" she finally asked.

Grim laughed. It made her want to crawl into a hole. But then he said, in a tone so earnest and gentle that she believed him, "Nothing, absolutely nothing, is wrong with you, Hearteater."

He removed her hands covering her chest and replaced them with his own. She stood and groaned as his calluses stroked against the softest and hardest parts of her skin, as his hands pulled and explored. Then, he lowered his head and did the same thing with his mouth.

Isla's head fell back. She had never felt so sensitive, all her senses zeroing in on the strokes of his tongue on the peaks of her chest, on his mouth taking everything in.

His hand traveled down her stomach. Before he reached the place she wanted him, he paused, again waiting for her approval.

She parted her legs, giving it, then gasped as his fingers finally touched her *right there*—

He felt her own want for him and made a deep sound that rasped against the back of her mind.

"Are you always like this around me?" he asked.

Isla gasped again, then glared at him. He only grinned.

"You certainly think highly of yourself," she said, breathless. Grim explored her with his hand, and she moaned.

"It's hard not to, when I can feel the effect I have on you. Tell me, Hearteater, has anyone ever touched you like this?"

He knew the answer. He must. The demon just wanted to hear her say the words. She ignored him. Her eyes fluttered closed, as he pressed—

"Is it just me who elicits this response?"

Her head fell back as he kept circling. Her chest was bare to him.

"No need to reply," he said. "The sounds you're making are all the confirmation I need."

She scowled. "You just like to hear yourself talk, don't you?" His fingers slid lower, and her breath hitched.

"I do. But I like to hear *you* talk more. So, tell me." He stopped suddenly. Withdrew his hand. "Are you always like this around me?" he repeated.

She scoffed at him. "Are you always this desperate for validation?"

"No. Not from anyone. Only you."

She blinked, surprised by the admission.

"If you want me to continue, answer my question," he said. He was breathing just as quickly as she was, chest heaving. "Please," he added.

Isla knew he wasn't used to saying that word at all. Yet, now he had said it to her multiple times.

Part of her wanted to portal away. Leave them both unfulfilled. But right now, the way he was looking at her . . .

She felt truly powerful for one of the first times in her life.

"Yes," she said, and took great pleasure in watching his eyes burn even brighter in intensity. She wrapped her arms around his neck. Leaned in until her lips brushed his ear as she said, "Always."

Grim was unleashed.

His hands gripped her waist, lifting her into the air with little effort. He hooked her feet behind him and brought them to the bed. Her back hit the sheets, and his hand returned to where it had been. Their chests were flush, just as they had been when he had shielded her from the arrows. He leaned down and looked her right in the eye, like he wanted

her to hear every word. "Next time, I'll use my mouth," he said. "And then, after that—"

She needed to feel him. Her hand shifted below his waist, to the evidence of his desire, and all thoughts eddied away.

He filled her with all sorts of want, and she didn't know what to do, didn't know how to make him feel as good as he was making her feel, but just having her hand on him made his breath catch.

At least, until he gently removed her hand and laced their fingers together. He pinned her hand above her head. "Let me focus on you," he said. "I don't want to miss a moment of this."

He filled her more than she ever thought possible, and she met him movement for movement, eyes fluttering closed. "That's it, Hearteater," he said. "Make it good for you."

"*Grim*," she said. His name caught in her throat and she clutched his shoulders.

He looked her right in the eyes and said, "Remember this, Hearteater, the next time you want to stab me through the chest."

He swallowed her final moans with his mouth and pulled her into him, lifting her to his chest with a hand against her lower back. He held her closely, so closely. Only minutes later did he set her down.

Lost for breath, lost for sanity, she managed to say, "I'll remember."

REUNION

Isla didn't want to remember anything else. He had stolen her people. He had forced them to his territory. How afraid they must have been. How unwilling.

It was time to bring an end to this.

At midnight, Isla sneaked back to her room. Oro would hate her if he knew what she was about to do. Everyone would. None of them would trust her again, because what she was planning was so traitorous, so foolish—

She stood in the center of her room, the moon wide as a judgmental eye through the window in front of her.

She pulled her necklace.

If she had feared he wouldn't come, that he wouldn't drop anything he was doing and rush to her, she was wrong.

Barely a second after her fingers left the black diamond, she heard a step behind her. Then, "Hearteater."

She turned and he immediately swept her into his arms. He looked crazed, hungry, relieved, *so* relieved. He was an inch from pressing his lips against hers, and she was an inch from letting him—*she was confused*, she told herself, *the memories were messing with her*—before he saw her expression. Sensed her emotions. There was no thread between them. From her side, anyway.

He went still.

"You heartless *demon*," she said.

Grim's eyes had been pleased, delighted, but now he looked devastated. "You don't remember."

"I remember plenty," she said, stumbling away from him. Her eyes glimmered with tears. Angry, angry tears. "How could you?"

"You got my note."

"Yes, I *got your note*," she said, spitting the words out with disgust. "How could you take them? How could you *make them* go with you?"

Grim raised a hand. "I didn't *make* them do anything," he said. "They chose to come with me."

No. Liar. "Why would they ever go with you?"

At that, Grim went silent.

He wasn't telling her something. But he didn't have to. Pieces came together, questions finding answers.

She shook her head, unbelieving. Hoping she was wrong. "You have Poppy and Terra," she said, her voice a whisper. "You took them in."

Grim nodded, and her tears fell freely now. The betrayal . . .

"You know what they did to me. What they did to my *parents*—"

"It is unforgivable," he said. "But you need them. You need—"

"I don't need anyone!" The words exploded out of her. The vines on her balcony rushed through the open door, spreading like fingers, devouring the room. Shadows leaked from her feet, from her hands.

Grim's face broke in half, into the biggest smile. "Heart, you are radiant," he said.

Her shadows lunged at him, but he stopped them with a simple wave of his hand.

Her voice shook. "You are a monster."

Grim frowned. "Am I?" He took a step forward. "Tell me why I'm a monster. Because I brought your people to a place with more comfort, more options, more chances of survival? Because I have them all waiting for your return?"

Her return. He made it sound like a certainty, and she nearly laughed in his face.

"Because I helped them forget what they did?"

Isla froze. "You . . . what?"

"Some of your people were suffering from endless guilt. They couldn't get past the actions they had committed during the curses. I . . . took their memories away."

Shadows exploded out of her. She heard the mirrors in her room shatter, but they were just white noise compared to the anger that surged through her. "How could you? Haven't you learned?"

"They asked me to," he said. "Are you denying your people their own choices?"

She shook her head. "Why would anyone ask you to do that?"

His face hardened. It seemed he wanted to tell her something, but instead, he changed the subject. "We made a deal . . . remember? Wildling help with nightbane, in exchange for a very vague assortment of whatever your people needed." He shrugged. "I was simply making good on it."

Isla curled her lip in disgust. "I suppose you think that makes you generous, don't you? Helping my people? You are not. You are a monster. You portaled the dreks here. They killed *dozens* of people, innocents—"

Grim bared his teeth. "I did no such thing. I told you before, dreks were buried below Lightlark and Nightshade. They must have started rising up, the same way they did on Nightshade."

"They went to your land, like they were called—"

"I didn't call them. They must have sensed their kind."

"You control them," she said. "I know you have the sword."

At that, Grim studied her. "I do. But I did not order them to attack Lightlark. I swear it."

Her mouth went dry. There it was. Confirmation that Grim had gotten the sword. And, somehow, he had found a way to use it.

Even if he didn't order the attack, she had endless reasons to hate

him. "You are coming to kill everyone on the island. You will murder thousands of innocents just to get it. You sent a message of ruin, of destruction—"

"No. I'm not. I warned everyone here, which is more than they deserve. They can either leave . . . or join us. It is their choice. No one has to die."

It was almost heartbreaking how he really believed this. If only he knew what she had seen. All the death that would result from his own hand.

Her own death.

"Do you really think anyone would give up their home without fighting?"

"When fighting is futile . . . I do."

Isla was filled with rage. Hurt.

"Heart," he said gently. "If I wanted to take the island by force, I could. Right now. Destroy all of it and everyone, in a matter of seconds. The curses are over." She could feel the power of him, especially now. Every ounce of it, so much waiting to be unleashed.

His eyes dipped to her neck, where her necklace had become visible, where her fingers had instinctively gone, and she ripped her hand away. "Take this off," she said.

A wicked grin spread across Grim's face. "You remember, do you? No . . . No," he said. He prowled closer. Closer. "If you did, you would know I cannot."

Talking to him wasn't working. She could see in the set of his mouth, his eyes, he was intent on invading Lightlark. She shook her head. "Grim, *please*. If you care about me at all, please don't do this."

Grim smiled softly then. He reached out. "Heart," he said, his voice as gentle as she had ever heard it. His fingers traced her cheek, from her temple to her lips. She was trembling—why was she trembling? "It's *because* I care about you that I'm doing this."

And then he was gone.

. . .

Isla knew what she needed to do.

Remlar was having tea in his hive. A tree grew beneath her, taking her to its highest floor, and she walked through the gaps, right to his makeshift throne. Vines were crawling in her wake, mixing with shadows.

"You look determined, Wildling," he said, putting his cup down. "You look ruinous."

"I want you to train me in something wrong. Something treacherous."

"Oh?"

"I want you to teach me how to cut off someone's power through a love bond. At least, for a few moments."

Remlar's lips crawled into a wide, wide smile. "It would be my pleasure," he said.

Grim had the Wildlings. Three days remained. She convened everyone in the war room once more.

"I summoned him," she said, and Oro turned to look at her. His expression was unreadable.

Zed stood roughly. "You what?"

"I thought I could reason with him," she said. She knew it was risky. Stupid. Still, at any moment he could have portaled into her room and taken her. He hadn't, which meant Grim wanted her to remember everything. He wanted her to go back to him willingly.

And he needed something from Lightlark, beyond her. She just needed to figure out what it was.

Zed's look was incredulous. "That . . . that's treason," he said. "You summoned our enemy to the Mainland castle. The person who is hell-bent on destroying all of us." He looked to Oro, whose expression had hardened.

"Let her speak," he said, though his voice did not have any hint of the warmth it had developed over the last few months with her.

"When I was with him, I could feel . . . I could feel that he still loves me."

Azul leaned forward. "You felt the connection?"

She nodded.

Zed still glared at her. He wouldn't ever trust her, she knew that. If she were him, she wouldn't trust her either.

Still, he was wrong about her. She loved Oro. She was loyal to Lightlark. She closed her eyes and said, "I know how we can win." They waited. No one moved an inch. "Grim is too powerful. It makes him nearly impossible to defeat. Especially with the sword. But he loves me—I can use the link and take away his powers long enough for us to overpower him."

Silence.

Enya was the first to speak. "Have you ever tried doing that before?" Isla shook her head. Not that she remembered. Yet. "Have you ever tried . . . even accessing his powers?" Again, she shook her head. Not that she remembered.

Yet.

She turned to face Oro. "But I've done it before . . . Accessed powers through the link."

It wasn't easy to do. Especially for someone like her, who had only recently wielded power at all.

"It requires an intense . . . connection," Oro said. He wasn't looking at her. He shook his head. "It would be too big of a risk. If you couldn't steal his powers immediately, he would know what you were trying to do and would portal away."

Calder said, "Oro. This could change everything. It could change the entire tide of the war. Though . . . we would be sentencing all Night-shades to death."

"Maybe not," Enya said. "If Isla took all his power, it would spare his people, wouldn't it?"

"It should in theory, though something like that has never been tested through a love bond," Azul said. "This is a very . . . unique circumstance." Azul studied her. "You would be willing to kill him?"

The words hit Isla like a stone in the chest, even though she had been the one to suggest it.

Kill Grim.

The thought sounded poisonous in her mind, but she remembered her vision in front of the vault. If she didn't stop Grim, he would kill innocent people. He would kill her. Oro had been right. Grim's words in her room had confirmed it. *It's because I care about you that I'm doing this.*

Grim was really going to war because of her. She didn't know his main reason for destroying Lightlark, but his purpose was clear. Which meant every death would be her fault.

He had stolen her people. Her memories. Her happiness, the last few months.

She wouldn't allow him to steal anything else.

"Yes," she said.

Oro met her eyes. She expected to see relief, but all she sensed was concern. He reached across the table for her. She watched Azul track the exchange. By now, he must have known. Oro didn't seem to care that everyone else was watching as he said, "You don't have to do this."

Isla remembered Enya's words. She saw her meaning clearly now. Oro was putting her own well-being above that of the entire island.

She wouldn't let him. "Yes," she finally said. "I do."

She was going to kill Grim.

Remlar taught her the basics of taking power. It required a complete hold. Pinching the thread between her and Grim between her fingers and being strong enough to stop the flow of power within him.

"It will be painful," he warned. "And difficult. Grimshaw is a most talented wielder," he admitted. Isla wondered if Remlar had ever met him.

They had almost run out of time. Only two days remained. Grim clearly needed something on Lightlark. If she could remember what it was, they could shift their plan to make sure he didn't get it.

She just needed a shortcut.

"I need you to help me speed it all up," she told Remlar. He had warned her it would be dangerous to force the memories. It could break her, mentally. At this point, she didn't care.

"Are you sure?" he asked. "Even knowing the risks?"

"I'm sure."

Remlar began making tea.

Isla's mind was a battleground.

She didn't want to remember—*she had to remember*. She didn't want to feel anything but disgust at the Nightshade—*she had felt* everything *with the Nightshade*.

The more she saw, the more she knew . . .

"What is the opposite of night, Wildling?" Remlar said, as he poured the tea into her mug.

Isla frowned. She was convinced Remlar just liked to hear himself talk. "Day?"

Remlar shrugged. "If you say so."

Isla narrowed her eyes at him. "What do you mean? What's the answer?"

Remlar took a sip of his own tea. It looked scalding. "Very few questions in this world have only one answer."

Isla wondered what the point of this conversation was.

"What is *your* answer?" she asked. She watched as her tea became more saturated in color.

He didn't say a thing. These were mostly one-sided conversations. "What does power feel like to you?"

She lifted a shoulder. "Like a seed. Behind my ribs."

Remlar nodded, excited by her response. "A very pretty way of seeing it," he said. "Very fitting, for a Wildling."

"What does it feel like to you?"

This time, he answered. "Like nothing," he said. "I've been alive for so long that my power is as much a part of me as my blood and bones."

She dared ask a question she had wondered since the first moment she had seen him. "Are you truly Nightshade?"

"Labels are so unproductive," he said. "Though, I suppose you would call me a Nightshade. In terms of my power."

"You wield darkness?" Isla asked. "How have the islanders not banished you?"

"They fear me too much," he said.

"Why?"

"Because my knowledge surpasses theirs. I have survived when kings have risen and fallen and died. I have remained. We, the ancient creatures, remain. And some of us remember."

"Remember what?" she asked. She finally took a sip of her tea. That was all it took. Within seconds, her mind began to slip away from her. The past bled into the present. She blinked and watched Remlar fade far away.

The last thing she heard him say was, "Home."

BEFORE

They had a plan to get past the dragon. Grim would lure it out of the cave, and Isla would get through all the protections herself before the dragon returned. She practiced going through each one, with the help of Grim's illusions. He watched as Isla finished the entire circuit for the tenth time successfully. She turned to face him when she was done, and he actually looked impressed.

They were standing in his training room. She leaned against a stone wall and slid all the way down it. "I'm exhausted," she said.

"I can imagine."

Grim had clearly just come from the scar. He was covered in ash. "You look awful."

"*That* is harder to imagine, but I will take your word for it."

Magnificent ego, indeed. She sighed. "I'm ready. Why don't we celebrate?"

He lifted an eyebrow at her.

"Tonight is the Launch of Orbs in the Skyling newland," she said. She had attended the previous year, but only barely. She had hidden in the shadows, watching. Wishing to be part of it all. "It's to celebrate the new season of hot-air balloons being unveiled."

Grim scowled. "They are always finding an excuse to celebrate. I bet they celebrate tying their own shoes."

"I've always wanted to ride in one," she said. She looked pointedly at him.

His eyes slid to hers. He looked like he would rather do absolutely

anything other than be launched into the sky in a balloon. "Don't you have anyone else to go with?"

Isla stood. She gave him a withering look. "You know what? I'm sure I can find someone else to spend the evening with me," she said. She turned on her heel, but before she could take a step, he was up in a flash, holding on to her wrist, stopping her in place.

"Don't even think about it," he said, his voice a growl in her ear.

She turned to face him and found him towering over her. His shadows were spilling everywhere. She lifted her chin in defiance. "Let go of me," she said.

"Never."

Isla was breathing too rapidly. He was too close. Her voice came out brittle. "Might I remind you that there is nothing between us. I do not belong to you. And you do not belong to me. If we decide to have . . . fun . . . then that is all it is. Momentary entertainment. Nothing more."

Grim's grin was wicked. "Oh, Hearteater." He leaned down, until his lips were pressed right against her ear as he said, "If we do decide to truly have fun, there will be nothing momentary about it."

Isla swallowed. He traced the movement. His lips were dangerously close to her neck. "Take me to the festival," she said, her request breathless.

"Fine. Get dressed."

Grim was right. Skylings did truly seem to think up any excuse to celebrate. She loved it.

At the Launch of Orbs party, everyone wore glitter. In their hair, on their outfits, dusted upon their shoulders. She asked Grim to buy her a few things in the market to wear, and—with more than enough complaining—he surprisingly complied.

She got ready in her bathroom, and, after an hour, there was a loud knock against her door. "Are you preparing for battle or for a foolish party, Hearteater?" he asked.

"Both, if you're going to be so insufferable," she said before she opened the door.

Grim went silent.

Her dress was tiny, sky blue, and strapless. She had glued little gems around the sides of her eyes. Glitter dusted her collarbones and shoulders. He had bought her each of these items—with very specific instructions—but he still looked surprised.

They were about as mismatched as possible. She was glittering, and saturated, and he wore his typical all black, cape and boots included.

"How do I look?" she asked, smiling, turning to see herself in the mirror.

Grim frowned. "You look like a Skyling."

"Good. That's exactly what I was going for."

The sky was filled with balloons. Light-blue baubles floated close to the stars, looking like daytime sky peeking through the night.

"It's beautiful," Isla said, smiling.

She could feel Grim's eyes on her. He was looking at her face, not the sky. "No," he said. "It's not." She frowned and moved to turn his head toward what they were here to see, but he didn't budge an inch. "When you've seen something truly beautiful, everything else starts to look painfully ordinary."

Isla took his hand. His fingers immediately tensed, as if he was about to recoil. Then, after a moment, he gingerly cupped his hand around hers. "Come on," she said. And he did.

Crowds were stopped, listening to something. A speech. She heard a rich, pleasant voice, moving airily through the crowd, as if his voice had grown wings. When they got closer, she saw a dark-skinned man dressed in a thousand glimmering jewels. He wore a crown.

"Azul?" she said, and Grim grunted in response.

She was suddenly grateful that he had formed an illusion around them, disguising them—even if she had spent an hour getting dressed.

What would Azul, ruler of Skyling, think, seeing the ruler of Night-shade and the ruler of Wildling here, in his territory . . . *holding hands?*

Truly . . . what was she doing?

The thought made her drop his hand. Grim frowned and immediately grabbed it again, locking her fingers in his. The action made her inexplicably warm everywhere, made her remember how he had touched her—

Grim glanced at her, and she knew he could feel her emotions. She swallowed and quickly changed the subject. "What do you think of Azul?"

"He runs his realm as a democracy. Everyone has a say. It's foolish."

Isla's brows came together. "That doesn't sound foolish to me."

Before Azul's speech was over, he led them toward where the balloons were taking off. There was an entire field of them, all painted slightly differently. All magnificent.

"Choose," he said.

Isla frowned. "I don't think we can choose, and I think there's a line—"

He followed her line of sight, to the one she thought was the prettiest. It looked like a light-blue egg, with a white swirl in the center.

In less than a moment, they were standing in its carriage. Somehow, he was starting it up. And then they were flying.

Isla gasped, watching the ground suddenly push away from them, and she stepped back. Right into Grim's chest.

He looped an arm around her waist, tethering her. It made her feel safer. Grim—for as much as he had claimed he had no interest in riding in the hot-air balloon—was peering over the edge, watching the newland with interest. Isla looked too, but she suddenly felt afraid.

"I don't think I like heights," she said. Her stomach shifted uncomfortably. Her heart was in her throat.

Grim made a calming noise that couldn't have possibly come from him. He leaned his head down, so his chin rested where her crown would have been if she had worn it. "I can portal us anywhere, remember?" he said.

It did make her feel better. She took a step toward the edge and leaned over, just a little. The world was beautiful. It was mountainous and wide, and she felt suddenly free. For nearly half an hour, they just watched the world in comfortable silence.

As she moved back again, her foot knocked against something she hadn't noticed before. It must have been included in each of the carriages for the night. A bottle, with transparent liquid filled with bubbles. Water?

"Skyling wine," he said, frowning. "Disgusting."

Isla uncorked the bottle and tentatively sipped it. She grinned. "This is the best thing I've ever tasted."

Grim sighed.

It was sweet, and sparkling on her tongue, and—

Grim plucked the bottle out of her hands after her second sip. "You might want to wait a little while before drinking more," he said. "Unless you don't want to remember the night." He offered her the bottle, letting it be her choice.

She shook her head. No. She didn't want that at all. She wanted to remember all of this.

Isla turned to face Grim and tilted her head.

"Can I say something honest?"

He looked taken aback. Nodded.

"You are the most unpleasant person I've ever met."

Grim raised an eyebrow at her. "And you are the bane of my existence."

She took a step toward him. "I was disappointed when I didn't kill you."

Grim ran his hand up her thigh, taking her dress with him. She bristled at the cold, at the fact that soon, if he continued, anyone around would be able to see her undergarments . . . but they were in the sky. The next balloon was yards away. "And I'm disappointed you haven't tried again."

His hand curled around her waist. His lips traced her neck. Her back arched, and she moaned as he began kissing her across the glitter on her shoulders, her chest, as he started licking it. "I don't think it's edible," she said.

"I don't care."

And then she was kissing him. Their lips crushed together, and his hands were instantly everywhere. He swept his tongue into her mouth, and she groaned. With one rough motion, Grim lifted her into the air, then placed her on the edge of the basket. Isla's eyes flew open, wind dancing behind her back, roaring in her ears.

"Relax, Hearteater," he said, and his breathing was uneven. Her legs widened, and he settled between them. His hand gripped beneath her knee, and she wanted more, more—

"Portal me to my room," she said.

Grim pressed her fully against his chest—and pushed her over the edge.

Before she could scream, the world tilted, and she landed on Grim. He was on her bed. She was straddling him.

A thousand violent words in her throat, but all of them withered and died when she felt him—every inch of him—against her. Her hips rocked back and forth, ever so slightly, and the friction made her head fall back, her shoulders hike up.

Grim laughed darkly beneath her. "The sight of you, on me . . ." He stopped her, with two hands curved under her backside. He lifted her off him.

She was desperate for his touch, aching—

He gently set her down next to him. He seemed faintly amused by her bewilderment.

"Not tonight, Hearteater," he said, tucking hair that had fallen across her face behind her ear. "Sleep."

Isla was flushed with need, with want—

He was too.

Grim chuckled into the darkness. He pulled her toward him, tucking her into his side. "Remember to dream of me," he said lightly, and she wondered if he knew how often she did.

344

BEFORE

They stood just out of view of the cave.

"Are you ready?" Grim said.

"Yes. Are you?"

He nodded. While she trained, he had researched the dragon. He had a plan for distracting it.

All Isla had to do was make sure she made it through the trials and to the sword without dying. She crept silently toward the entrance of the cave. The dragon was curled, asleep. She waited, at the edge, for Grim to wake it.

There was a noise outside. The dragon opened an eye and roared.

A massive leg peeked out first. She didn't even look at Grim or what he was doing. She focused on the thin sliver of opening the dragon offered.

Another leg.

Then the dragon shot out of the cave like a strike of lightning.

Now, her mind said, and she leaped into the cave.

First, the arrows. The ones that had wounded Grim in a dozen places. As soon as she triggered the trap, she moved, hurtling for the opposite side. She watched arrows pierce the ground, exactly where she had been.

Isla swallowed. So close. No time for fear. The dragon was still distracted, but who knew how long it would take for it to realize it was being tricked?

Boulders fell from above, and Isla rolled out of their path. A thousand shards of ice were next, too many to miss, so she lifted the metal shield she had brought with her over her head. It made a torrential sound, and Isla winced, knowing the dragon would hear it.

Faster. She had to be faster. As she hunched over, waiting out the last of the hail, she locked eyes with the sword.

It was sitting in a pile of spoils. Just one of hundreds of relics. She didn't even look at any of the rest; she just focused on the blade, shining, as if winking hello.

Only a few more steps.

Isla leaped to the side, just missing a hidden pile of spikes.

A spear flew, aimed at her side, but she was faster. She ducked, missing it.

Just two more steps.

A foot before the pile, a tunnel of wind suddenly burst through the cave, a storm blasting. That, she could not duck to avoid. She faced it, full-on, shield in front of her, jaw clamped tight, fighting against its current, barely making it an inch forward. Another inch. She gritted her teeth, groaned, fought forward—

Until it stopped, and she went tumbling. The sword was in her reach.

Just one more step.

She heard a great roar behind her.

Now. It had to be now.

Her hand reached for the sword. The moment she had it in her grasp, they could portal away. The dragon was coming. Her fingers brushed its hilt. It felt cold under her touch, before warming. Waking up. She turned around, to see where Grim was, to tell him that she got it.

Only to see a flood of fire filling the cave.

It was too late. She wouldn't reach her starstick fast enough. Flames poured in to the brim, hurtling toward her. There was only time to turn her head. The sword sparkled prettily. She hadn't even gotten the chance to fully grip it. Isla prepared to be burned alive.

Before the flames caught her, shadows filled the cave. They wrapped around her, shielding her. Saving her.

The fire cleared. The shadows fell away.

And Isla watched the sword vanish.

Grim had saved her. He had used his powers, knowing it would mean giving up the sword. And it had disappeared.

"Why did you do that?" Isla said. She had bathed and changed into one of her dresses. Grim had gotten changed in his own chambers and returned here, to her room in her castle.

She was grateful he had . . . but it didn't make any sense.

Grim's eyes locked on hers. "You think I would watch you die, for the sword? Did you think I would make any choice that wasn't you?"

"Yes," she said, incredulous. "You said so."

He just looked at her. "Things changed."

She realized then that she would have done the same. She would have chosen him.

"But your realm . . . you said you need it. For you, it's the most important thing in the world."

"My realm does need it," he said. He traced his fingers down her temple and said, in the quietest of voices, "But it is not the most important thing in the world."

She looked at him, really looked at him. Saw pain in his eyes, as he assessed her for any injuries, even though he had already done so before she had bathed. Saw patience as she scowled and told him again that she was fine.

She didn't see regret.

"I touched it. For a moment, I touched it. Maybe I'll be able to find it again now that it knows me."

"Isla," he said gently. "I don't want to use the sword anymore."

Her brows came together. "What? Why?"

"Its cost is too high," he said thoughtfully.

It seemed Grim had changed his mind about the sword in the time between entering the cave and saving her. It didn't make any sense.

"How are you going to save your realm now?" she asked. "How are you going to stop the dreks?"

Grim lifted a shoulder. "I'm going to use my power, the same as always. Use myself as a shield." He grinned, and she knew it was solely for her benefit, to make light of a devastating situation. "I make a decently good one, wouldn't you agree?"

The thought of him, shielding his entire realm from the dreks. Only his power against theirs . . .

"Will you still keep your promise?" she asked, attempting a smile back. "To help me at the Centennial?"

Grim grinned wider.

"Of course, Hearteater," he said. "It's going to be fun pretending not to know you. To introduce myself to you."

He was right. No one could know they were allies. No one could know they had known each other for months. They would have to pretend to be strangers.

"To pretend I don't know that you love chocolate, and touching your hair, and that you blush when I look at you for more than a few seconds. Or that you hate the cold and love to dance and you frown when you lie." His words were so soft. So unlike him. He tucked her hair behind her ear. "You really do, by the way," he said. "You should work on that before the Centennial."

She blushed, because he had been looking at her for more than a few seconds. She felt tears stinging her eyes, because he knew her.

He really knew her. He'd been paying attention.

What a thing, to be known.

Isla's voice was thick with emotion when she said, "And it will be fun pretending like I don't know the shadows at your feet puddle when you're happy. Or that, for some reason, you've had healers remove every one of your scars, except for the one I gave you. Or that you have a magnificent tub in your bathroom, and an even more magnificent ego." She bit her lip. "And that, even though I hated you, *really*, really hated you . . . whenever I'm not with you, whenever I'm with anyone else, I feel hopelessly alone."

He took her hand, and she said, "At the Centennial . . . we're going to be strangers."

"No," he said. "We could never be just strangers."

"So what are we then?" she asked. "If not strangers? If not . . . enemies?"

"I don't know," he said. "But I want to be the only person you glare at, Hearteater. I want to be the only person you insult. I want to be the only name you speak in your sleep." His eyes darkened. "I want to be the only person who knows how to make you writhe against a wall." He studied her. "You know what? I want everything. I want to be greedy and selfish with you. I want all your laughs. All your smiles too." He frowned. "I would rather die than watch you smile at anyone that isn't me." Grim closed his eyes slowly. He looked almost pained.

Why pain? It didn't make sense.

When he opened them, he said, "There's something I need to tell you."

"No," she said. "There's something *I* need to tell you."

He had saved her life. She hadn't ever trusted anyone this much, other than Celeste. For some reason, she wanted him to see all of her. She didn't want to hide it any longer.

She swallowed. Her guardians would have her head if they knew she was about to tell the ruler of Nightshade her greatest secret. "I—" she said. "I'm—"

Grim watched her struggle to get the words out, and he grabbed her hand, to keep her from touching her hair. "Hearteater," he said, the word so gentle now in his mouth. "I know."

Her brows came together.

What did he think he knew? What did he think she was talking about?

"I know that the curses don't apply to you," he said. "I know that you have never wielded power."

She stepped back. Time had been wounded; it wasn't moving, it was dead—

Part of her wondered if she should run, or hide, or be afraid—

"I've known for a while."

He's known for a while. And he hadn't tried to kill her. He hadn't shared her secret. He'd continued to work with her. He knew how meaningless her life was, how weak she was, how in trouble her people were, and yet . . . he hadn't used it to his advantage.

"Nightshades can sense curses. I didn't realize it at first, but I couldn't sense yours. Then, when the Wildlings were able to attack you in the forest, to try to get your heart . . ." Of course he would have questioned why Isla hadn't fought back. Why she hadn't used even a drop of power the entire time they were working together.

Tears fell freely now. "Grim . . . what—what is wrong with me?"

He took her face in both his hands. "Nothing, absolutely nothing, is wrong with you, heart." He said it for the second time, and it directly contradicted everything she had ever thought about herself.

She went on her toes and kissed him. It was clumsy and too forceful and caught him by surprise. She fell on her heels, wondering why in the world she'd done that, but she didn't wonder for long.

Hands still pressed to her face, he ducked and parted her lips with his own, kissing her like she might be leaving, like he might never get to do it again. His tongue swept across the roof of her mouth, and she groaned. This was impossible—it was impossible to feel this good.

She was a burning flame, and there were too many clothes, too many layers between them. She had always been told that her body didn't belong to her, it belonged to the realm, but *no*, right now she wanted to feel everything that was possible. She wanted Grim to *show* her.

"I want you," she said, breaking their kiss, breathing too quickly. "I want everything."

Grim looked like he might be losing his mind. Like he couldn't have

possibly heard her correctly. His chest was heaving. He blinked. Again. Said, "Are you sure?"

"Yes," she said, and she meant it more than she had ever meant anything else.

Grim swallowed. "I'm not gentle," he said gruffly.

Isla opened her mouth. Closed it. The thought of him not being gentle . . . it unexplainably made her feel hot everywhere.

"Could—could you be?"

He hesitated. Then nodded.

The way he carried her to the bed . . . it was as if she were made of glass. He laid her on her sheets like she was mist and might just slip away if he wasn't careful. Isla's eyes darted to the closed door.

"We're hidden," he said. And Isla had never been so grateful for his illusions.

He was over her now, completely clothed. No. She didn't want anything between them.

She yanked his shirt up, and it didn't move at all. But Grim reached back and tore it over his head in one smooth movement, making his shoulders flex, and Isla couldn't see enough of his body, couldn't touch enough.

"You are perfect," she said, and she couldn't believe the thought had reached her lips. "I didn't know—I didn't know someone could look like this. It's unfair, really."

Grim only laughed. "You're doing very little to discourage my *magnificent ego*."

Her hands stroked down his hard chest. He radiated pure power, strength. She traced the scar just half an inch from his heart, and his eyes fell closed for a long moment. She could have sworn he shivered. The shadows in her room melted across the floor, puddling.

His gaze locked on her chest, prickled with need, aching like every part of her, and the silk of her dress did nothing to hide it. His hands

went to the bodice, to rip it like before, and Isla made a sound of protest. "Demon," she said. "I'm not going to have any dresses left if you keep destroying them."

"I'll buy you new ones. I'll buy you a market. I'll get you your own tailor."

"Fine," she said, and the dress didn't stand a chance. It was ribbons in a second, and then his mouth was on her chest. He bit her, lightly, and she made a rasping noise, her back arching.

His hand trailed down her stomach, below her underthings, and when he touched her, he cursed. "*Isla,*" he said against her chest, "you are truly going to kill me."

"I will," she said, "if you don't keep touching me."

She was burning, aching, desperate for more.

"Please," she said. "I want everything."

Grim took the rest of his clothes off, and Isla went still. She had felt him before, but now . . .

He climbed over her again, his hips settling between her legs, and her breath hiked. He pressed his lips against her shoulder, her chest, her neck, her cheek. "I think you'll find we fit perfectly," he said, as if reading her thoughts.

Then he looked at her and asked one final time. "Are you sure?"

"Yes," she said, and he reached down between them.

For a while, there were just their shared breaths, his forehead pressed against hers. He was leaning on his arms, holding himself over her, shaking slightly as he exercised every ounce of control.

At first, there were flashes of pain. She winced, and Grim always stopped. Always waited for her to tell him to go farther.

He went farther. And farther. *Farther.*

Her nails dug into his shoulders, and she breathed through it as her body got used to him. He was gentle, so gentle, fisting the sheets in his hands, cursing words into the place between her neck and shoulder.

Suddenly, it all seemed to go so much easier. Suddenly . . . Isla's head was falling back as she groaned, and Grim was making a sound like a growl. His arm curled below her spine, and he hauled her fully against his chest. Her legs locked behind him.

Isla saw stars, gasped his name, said all sorts of ridiculous things, and then she was whimpering, because she had never felt this good, this close to the stars—

She pressed her cheek against the sheets, and he kissed up the length of her neck, until he gently turned her head, fingers curled around the back of her neck, until their eyes locked. He seemed fixated on her every expression, the way she drew breath when he reached down to raise her hips higher, the way she bit her lip to keep from making more noise.

He tugged her bottom lip from between her teeth and kissed her.

She cried out against his lips as she shattered, and Grim kept going, and going, until he joined her over the edge.

For minutes, he just held her, tightly, as if someone might take her from him. Then, he rose to look at her face, emotions battling across his own. Unexpected ones. She wanted to tip his mind over and play with the contents.

"Hearteater." He leaned down and pressed a kiss to her lips. "You are both curse . . ." he whispered against her skin, lips traveling down her neck, to the center of her chest, ". . . and cure."

After the first time, she didn't want to stop. It was as if an entirely new world had been opened, and she wanted to explore every inch of it.

Hours later, she woke up sprawled on top of Grim. Her cheek was against his chest. One of his arms was wrapped around her, the other was hanging off the bed.

The things they had done in this bed . . .

She lifted her head, to look at him, and found him already awake. He met her eyes and smiled.

Smiled.

She had never seen him smile, not like that.

"You have a dimple," Isla said in disbelief. It made him look boyish, and adorable, and she couldn't believe it.

"Do I?" he said.

He didn't even know.

She crawled up his chest, to rest her chin on her arms, right below his face. She just looked at him, up through her lashes.

Suddenly, something occurred to her. He had told her Nightshades didn't keep the same partner for long. Soon, would he leave her? Would he forget her, like the rest?

Grim sat up. "What's wrong?" he asked, expression filled with worry.

"You—you aren't going to disappear, right? Now that we . . . now that we—"

He laughed. He folded over, shoulders shaking with it. She pinched him below the ribs, and he kept laughing. "Hearteater," he finally said, breathless. "I said Nightshade rulers are typically forbidden from bedding the same person more than once. Last night alone . . ."

Multiple times. Relief filled her. It didn't look like Grim was going anywhere. She rose until she was straddling him. She ducked her head, so she could say right into his ear, "Good. Because I want to do it all again. Immediately."

Grim groaned. His head fell back, and he closed his eyes again. "Hearteater," he said. "You are a bane." She remembered his words from before: *You are both curse and cure.* "It's never . . ." He sighed. "For me, it's never felt like that."

She wondered if he really meant that. He was her first; she didn't know what it felt like, other than last night. And last night . . . "So, you won't be entertaining other women lining up for the privilege of sleeping with you anymore?"

She expected Grim to make a joke, or at least look amused, but his expression turned serious. "No." He shook his head. "You have

ruined me." He swallowed. "I have a thousand things to do, but all I want is to lock us in this room . . ." He traced his hand down her spine, and she shivered. "All I want is to claim you so thoroughly, that there won't be a part of you that doesn't have a memory with me."

Isla was going to burst into flame. "Do it," she said. She was ready, she wanted it—

Grim closed his eyes again. His chest quivered with restraint. "A curse," he said.

Then he took her into his arms.

And he did.

She portaled to Grim's room a few days later. Within a moment, she was in his arms. He kissed her like he hadn't seen her in years, even though they had seen each other that morning. He leaned down, slid the bridge of his nose down her neck, and whispered in the place between her neck and shoulder, "You are an addiction." He bit her lightly, and she gasped. "You are my nightbane."

Isla was glad he was in such a good mood. "Don't be mad."

Grim immediately tensed. It took him a moment, but he eventually stepped away from her. "Why would I be mad, Hearteater?" he asked. His eyes were studying her, as if searching for injury.

"I went back to the cave—"

His eyes widened. He took a step toward her. "Are you—"

"I'm not hurt," she said. "But . . ."

He crossed his arms across his chest. "Yes?"

She tried to give him her best smile. "It's nothing bad! Don't get upset."

His expression didn't change. He looked down at her and said, "Hearteater, what is it?"

She opened her mouth. Closed it. Then, she said, "I should probably just show you." She pulled out her starstick, but before she portaled

away, planning to bring her discovery to his room, Grim grabbed her arm, taking himself with her.

Which meant he portaled right to the tree where she had leashed her—

"Dragon," Grim said, staring down at the little bundle of black scales. "Hearteater . . ." he said. "You didn't."

Isla knelt next to the little dragon. She had found it wandering alone, near the cave. "I think he was abandoned by his mother," she said. "Because he's small. Or injured. I'm not sure yet."

The dragon was small enough that she could hold him in her arms. His black scales glimmered like a collection of dark gems. His head was rounded. She hadn't seen him spread his wings yet.

"Think of him as . . . a pet." Her eyes darted to him and back to the dragon again. "For you."

He looked at her like he was trying to evaluate her mental condition. "You think I am going to keep this creature in my quarters?"

"Yes," she said. "I think you are. Because I am asking you to."

His eyes flashed with disbelief.

"Please, Grim," she said.

Isla knew he would refuse. Her mind sifted through different places she might be able to take the dragon on Wildling. Maybe she could hide it in the forest and visit between trainings? Maybe she could find someone who would make a good caretaker?

But without another word, Grim frowned, picked up the tiny dragon, held it as far away from his body as he could manage, and portaled them away.

"We need a name," she said after a week.

"A name? It should be grateful it has a home."

"Grim."

"Yes, Hearteater?"

"Stop being so cruel. Look, it just dipped its head. You made it sad."

Grim whipped around to face her with a look of pure incredulity. "You think that animal can speak?"

She glared at him. "No. I think just like another *beast* in this room, it might be able to sense emotion. Or, at the very least, tone." Isla sat down and scooped the dragon into her lap. She stroked a finger between its eyes, and it sighed. "It's okay," she cooed. "He's mean to everyone."

Grim raised an eyebrow at her. "Is that what we're calling what I did to you last night? Mean?"

Isla felt her cheeks flush. The dragon tilted its head at her in curiosity, and she wondered if it really did understand them.

"That thing keeps flying into my bed at night," Grim said.

"That's adorable!" Isla exclaimed.

Grim looked at her in a way that could only be described as a fusion of disgust and horror. His favorite expression. She looked at him and thought she had never been happier.

FORGIVE ME

I t hadn't worked. None of those memories had been useful. If anything, they had been ruinous. Now Isla felt far more conflicted
about what she had to do.

Oro met her in the Mainland woods. She had practiced dipping her
hand into the link between them and attempting to hold his powers.
She could only ever do it for a moment at a time.

"It will only take me a moment to kill him," Oro said. "You won't
have to hold for long."

Kill him. Some echo of her past screamed against the words. She
pushed the doubt away.

"You must hate me," Isla said.

Oro's brows came together. "Hate you?"

"Yes," she said. "I summoned Grim. It—it was reckless."

"It was," he agreed, "but it helped you come up with your plan. It
could save us, if it works."

She looked at him, incredulous. He *should* hate her. His endless patience
and forgiveness was infuriating, because it couldn't possibly be real.

Enya was right. Oro deserved better than her. She wasn't good for him.

"I'm broken, Oro," she said. "You should really—you should really
find someone else to love."

He raised an eyebrow at her. "Do you think that's how this works?"
he asked. "Do you think love is something you can control?"

She put her hands up. "I'm a mess. I see the way you look at me. I
can imagine the things you want. A future. What if I—what if I'm not
ready for any of that?"

His gaze did not falter. "I have waited hundreds of years for you," he said. "You have no idea how patient I can be."

Tears burned her eyes as she looked at him. "I don't deserve your love."

"Is that what you believe?"

She nodded. She really did. "You don't know," she said. "I—I'm awful inside. My mind is a mess. *I'm* a mess." She shook her head. "One day I'm going to do something, and you're going to see. You're going to see me. The real me. The worst me."

"I see everything, and I love you. Is that what scares you?"

"Why?" she demanded. "Why do you love me?"

He looked at her. "For hundreds of years before I met you, I don't think I smiled or joked or laughed more than a handful of times. Nothing excited me. Nothing made me feel *anything* anymore." He took her hand. "Meeting you was like remembering what I was like before the curses," he said. "Loving you is remembering what I once loved about me."

He leaned in closer.

"You feel so strongly. You *care*. I went centuries without feeling a single thing. Until you. Don't you see? You brought me to life."

Isla pressed her hand against his chest, over his heart. She heard it beat under her palm. The love between them was a bridge. It went in both directions. She could feel where their forces met as much as she could feel his heartbeat.

She dipped inside the bridge. She felt Oro there. His power. Sunling. Starling. Moonling. Skyling.

She gripped a bit and opened her palm. Fire curled out of her fingers. It was tinged in blue, just like his flames.

She had never felt closer to him. Sharing power was intimate, she knew that.

Darkness had clawed its way into her heart, but for this moment, all she could see was light.

All she could see was *him*.

She went on her toes and kissed him. He startled for just a moment before kissing her back. She clung to his neck, nails digging into his skin the same way they had the first time he took her flying.

"I'm not going anywhere," he whispered against her lips. "My heart is yours for as long as you want it."

"I'm not going anywhere either," she promised.

Isla told Oro she needed to train alone for a while, in preparation for the battle. She asked him to supervise the Starling barrier being built. Earlier that day, Cinder had started the shield, summoning enough energy to make an entire shining wall herself. The rest of the Starlings were now going to build a second one, on the other side, securing their position.

When he was gone, and she couldn't feel the connection between them at all, she sighed.

Remembering hadn't worked.

She walked to the Wild Isle bridge. Crossed it. Made her way to the Place of Mirrors. She stopped in front of the vault and produced a blade.

"Forgive me," she said to Oro. Then, she broke her promise to him. She sliced a long line across her palm. The skin parted, blood flowed, pain bellowed—

She turned it into strength.

All the Wildling power within her—the seed—melted down, dripped through her bones like liquid gold.

Isla stuck her crown into the lock, turned it—

And forced the door completely open.

No surge stopped her.

She took a step into the vault.

UNLOCKED

The vault was starless black.

And it was empty.

No. That was impossible. She could feel the power everywhere, metal in her mouth, enough to nearly bring her to her knees.

Where was it coming from?

Blood from her hand dripped onto the smooth stone floor. Her bare feet slid across it as she desperately searched every corner.

Nothing.

Roaring filled her ears; the world seemed to tip to the side.

There were footsteps behind her.

Isla whipped around and nearly dropped to the floor.

Terra said, "Hello, little bird."

Her guardian stepped forward. "Do you feel proud, little bird?" she said. She smirked at Isla's hand, still bleeding profusely. Isla didn't even feel the sting of pain any longer. Power was still gathered in her bones; it still honeyed everything it touched. "Do you feel proud, when you should feel ashamed?"

Grim must have portaled her here. It was the only way. He must be watching her.

Did Terra steal whatever was inside?

No. She couldn't have. Isla's crown was the only key.

So why was she here?

Isla laughed without humor, the shock slowly wearing off. *Ashamed?* "You, who lied to me my entire life. You, who trained a girl to fight but

planned for her to seduce a king." She took a step. "You—" Her voice began to shake uncontrollably. "Who *killed my parents* in cold blood." Another step, until she was out of the vault and standing in front of her old guardian. Her old teacher. Her old *friend*. "You, who warned me my entire life about Nightshades and have now joined them."

Terra stood and listened, chin raised, almost in challenge. "I did what I needed to in order to protect our realm. To protect you. And I will continue to." She outstretched her hand. "Come with me, little bird," she said. "Before you make more of a mess of things."

A mess?

She spat at Terra's feet. "You are a traitor," she said. "Don't speak to me about making a mess."

The vine came out of nowhere.

Isla was slapped across the floor. She slid for a few feet, then stopped. Her shoulders curved. She panted. Then she smiled.

"I'm not the powerless fool you raised anymore," she said. Then she brought the entire force of the forest through the ceiling of the Place of Mirrors.

Trees blew through the remaining windows, and branches snapped, twisting into mangled shapes.

Vines lunged at Terra in every direction, enough to drown her in their grip, but the fighting master sliced her arms through the air in practiced movements, and they were all cut down.

Isla's power was everywhere; it flooded her every thought, every sense, the pain in her hand feeding its frenzy. She bellowed, and the stone floor shattered as spiked trees erupted from below, right where her guardian stood.

Terra leaped from side to side, just barely missing every one right before it impaled her on its thorns. She tsked. "Little bird, your form is dreadful." She shook her head, moving effortlessly to the side as a boulder broke through the ceiling, cracking into a thousand shards. "And far too predictable."

Predict this, Isla thought before sharpening the trunk of a massive tree into a blade. She flung it at her old teacher, the drumming in her ears, her power, eager to see her cut down. She wanted to see her dead, bleeding out on the floor.

Power tastes like blood.

Before her sword could skewer Terra against the wall, her teacher made her own blade, cut from the side of a cliff. It raced through the broken windows of the Place of Mirrors. Both of their weapons now floated between them, two massive swords ready to duel.

Isla grinned. "Just like old times," she said through her teeth. She tasted metal. She tasted blood.

She attacked.

Their blades crashed together, making a sound that rumbled across Wild Isle. Isla wielded hers with her mind, faster, faster, using all the techniques her teacher had taught her. But now, she was stronger.

She was a ruler. She ruled over *everyone*, not the other way around. Not anymore.

And Isla didn't care about playing fair.

She created another sword, this one crafted out of a thousand gems. She made them from thin air, her power hardening into crystal and ruby and diamond. It took so much effort, enough that she felt her power scraped to the very bottom, getting every last shred. It was her anger, hardened into a blade, glimmering, remembering, about to make her guardian pay.

It sliced through the air behind Terra, ready to plunge through her back, to destroy everything she ever was.

But before it could, Terra turned her hand into a fist, and it all shattered.

Isla was sent backward, flying. She hit the ground with a crack. She slid until she hit the wall.

Her power had been drained to the ashes. All her fury and sadness and pain had lashed out—and had been defeated.

She was powerless to move a muscle when Terra walked over and frowned down at her. "Little bird," she said, "your emotions always were your greatest weakness. You are still so foolish. Have it your way." She bent down to say, "Thank you for opening the portal for us." Her footsteps echoed as she left the Place of Mirrors.

What? What portal?

Terra's last words were a key, unlocking a memory.

BEFORE

Isla was polishing her throwing stars after training with Terra when she felt it. Something calling to her from the forest.

She frowned. It didn't make a noise, but it was like it was tapping her on the shoulder with its presence.

Grim was supposed to meet her soon. She should wait for him.

But the calling beckoned, more desperate now.

She tucked her throwing stars and daggers into her pockets and used her starstick to portal into the woods.

The sun was getting close to setting. Gold peered through the tops of the trees. It was a dangerous time to be in the woods. They were bloodthirsty and known to lash out.

Still, she followed the call.

She followed it until she reached a spot the eldress had shown her before she died. A river framed by cliffs, and waterfalls that fell in transparent sweeps. Stones larger than her skull lined the edge, smoothed over time.

And sticking out of the dirt, as if thrown down from the heavens, was the sword.

The sword's double blades refracted light in twin shimmers. A bright-red stone sat buried in its hilt. It was heavy in her hand.

Grim portaled into her room and paled.

"Hearteater," he said. "Where did you find that?"

At first, she was happy. Excited, ecstatic that the sword had presented itself. It would help *Grim*. He would help *her*.

Then she began to ask questions.

"You said you had something to tell me," she said, remembering the night he had first taken her to bed. "Before I interrupted you. What is it?"

Grim swallowed. He looked almost . . . afraid. He took a seat in one of her chairs and beckoned for her to sit across from him.

"I'll stand," she said sharply, already feeling betrayal rooting itself inside her chest.

Grim was silent for a few moments, eyes on the hands in front of him, and then he spoke. "More than twenty years ago, I began my search for that sword," he said. He looked at it for just a moment before bringing his eyes to hers. "I had help. My best general. One day, he went to follow a lead, taking my relic I had made to get there." *Her starstick.* "Then . . . he was gone."

She remembered Grim saying he had been betrayed before, by someone else he had hunted the sword with. It was why he had always been so secretive, so stingy with information.

"I assumed he died in the attempt to get the sword. For over two decades, I believed that to be true. Until you portaled into my palace."

What did his general have to do with her?

"Guards found your clothes, the ones you had left behind. When I discovered you were Wildling, I knew there was only one way that you could have gotten to my palace so quickly. Then . . . when I realized you were uncursed, everything made sense."

Isla took a step back. The tip of the sword shrieked against her floor. "Wh—what do you mean?"

His eyes softened. "It's rare, but non-rulers can have flairs," he said. "My general had one." His voice was gentle. "He was impervious to curses."

The one who had made his charm.

Tears stung her eyes before she even knew what he meant, like her body had put everything together before her mind could process it.

"He was your father, Isla," he said.

"No."

That would mean—it would mean—

"I'm not Nightshade."

Grim smiled. "But you are. You *are*."

She shook her head. "That doesn't make any sense—"

"I believe your father did find the sword. But he always feared I would one day share my father's ambitions and use the dreks to conquer Lightlark." He frowned. "He must have met your mother. And clearly . . ."

"Why would he think that?" she demanded. Her father had gone to great lengths to make sure Grim couldn't get the sword. He must have had a good reason. She remembered what Grim had told her. "Why did your father want Lightlark so badly?"

"Lightlark is a miniature," Grim said. "The creators of the island fled a world made up of different countries. Moonling, to the very north, buried in the ice. Sunling at the center, where the sun shined brightest. Wildling close by. Skyling, then Starling, then Nightshade at the opposite end, where it was darkest and coldest. They took thousands here, to another world, and created a smaller version of the one they left behind."

She had never heard of that. It sounded impossible.

"Cronan, my own ancestor, wanted to go back, after he was cast out from Lightlark. But the portal is built into its foundation. Using it successfully would mean destroying the island."

"Why doesn't anyone know about this?" she demanded. Poppy and Terra had never mentioned any of it in her history lessons.

"Only the ancient creatures remain from that world. Over time, the information was lost, but not by Nightshade. Though, my people never attempted to try to seek out the portal again until I was born."

"Why?"

"I have the same flair as Cronan. Portaling. The portal doesn't work on its own, it requires someone with my skill."

The destruction of Lightlark . . . it would doom thousands of people to death. "Why would anyone ever want to go back to that other world?"

"I don't," he said. "We went to war over the portal, but after the curses, when my father died, I abandoned the search myself. I only needed the sword after the dreks became a problem, to stop them."

"Does anyone else know about the portal?"

Grim nodded. "Only one other ruler that I know of. Cleo. She is . . . very interested in using it."

That was how Grim had the Moonling medicine. Cleo was helping him for a reason. She was trying to persuade him.

"Why would she want that?"

"I don't know," he said. "She wants to go to that world, for some reason."

"You won't do it, though, will you?"

"No. Even if I wanted to, I couldn't. The portal is in the Wildling palace on Lightlark. Only a Wildling ruler can open it."

She would never do that. Tears stung her eyes. She would never doom an entire island of people.

Her throat felt tight. She finally had answers. Though, part of her wished she hadn't asked any questions. She was happier, she thought, living in ignorance.

"Here," she said, flinging the sword at him. She wanted to stab him with it.

Grim caught the sword and leaned it against her wall. "I told you. I don't want to use it anymore."

"Right," she said, her voice cruel. "The cost is too high. Tell me the truth now," she demanded. "What was the cost?"

"Your life."

He said it so matter-of-factly, all she could do was stare at him as tears slowly fell down her cheeks. "My . . . *life?*" Her voice broke on the last word.

"I needed you to use your flair to break the curse on the sword," he said. "It was an ancient curse. Breaking it would have either killed you on the spot, or significantly shortened your life."

Her world had just smashed against a rock. Everything she thought she knew was shattered.

"You knew from the very beginning," she said. Tears were hot down her cheeks. "You knew when we made the deal. *That's* why you made it. You knew it might kill me. You probably weren't even planning on going to the Centennial at all."

He didn't try to deny it. "That was before I knew you," he said. "Before . . . all this happened."

She didn't care. She could barely even see; her tears had made everything look distorted, and she didn't mind, because she didn't want to look at him. "Goodbye, Grim," she said. "I never want to see you again."

Silence.

"You mean that?"

"I do."

He closed his eyes against the words. For a while, he didn't say anything. Then, very slowly, as if he was still trying to make sense of his own emotions, he said, "I've been stabbed a thousand times . . . but none of that hurts more than hearing you say goodbye."

And then he vanished.

PORTAL

Oro didn't say a word about the cut on her hand. He didn't get angry. All he did was scoop her from the ground of the Place of Mirrors and bring her back to their room. He cleaned her wound, and fed her broth, and brought her medicine. Ella was in the Skyling newland now, almost everyone was, so he went down into the kitchens and made everything himself.

Oro had found her through their link. She had called to him, her essence just a whisper . . . and he had answered.

He had always answered.

He deserved so much better. Enya was right.

Why didn't she ever listen? Why didn't she ever learn?

When she was back to her previous strength, she said, "I need to tell you something."

The castle was empty. The attack would happen the next day. Azul, Oro, Isla, Zed, Calder, and Enya stood on the stairs in front of it for their meeting. The legions had their orders. They had their plan.

But something had changed.

"I know why he's coming," she said. She told them everything. About the other world. The portal. The fact that using it would completely destroy Lightlark.

"Why would he want to go to a different world?" Azul asked.

Isla didn't know. That part didn't make any sense. In her memories, he had told her about the other world without showing any interest in visiting it.

What else wasn't she remembering?

Zed paced up and down the stairs. "Whatever his reason is, we have to make sure the portal stays closed," he said. "We must—"

"It's already open," she said, tears streaming.

A storm cracked the sky in half. Wind howled around them. "What do you mean, it's already open?" Zed demanded.

She felt everyone's eyes on her.

Terra was right. She was still so foolish. She had been so blinded by her need to get the vault open, by her desire to prove herself as a true Wildling, that she had given her enemy the key to destroying everything she loved.

Her voice was just a rasp. "I opened it for him."

FATE DIVIDED

It was the morning of the war. The oracle was leaning against the ice, as if she couldn't hold herself upright. She smiled when she saw Isla.

"You left it until the very last moment, didn't you?" she asked, her voice echoing. "My very last prophecy, the most important yet . . . and you almost miss it."

Tears were dried on Isla's cheeks. She was numb. She had ruined everything. The oracle had demanded she return. "What do you want?"

The oracle hummed against the ice. "My desires matter very little, actually," she said. "Yours, however . . . Yours will decide the fate of the world."

Isla shook her head. "Fate has already been decided," she said. "I opened the portal." Her voice shook. She had tried to close it again, but the door had not moved an inch.

Wrong. She had done everything wrong.

The oracle looked at her curiously. "Fate has not been decided," she said. "The battle hasn't even begun."

No. That couldn't be true.

"Wildling," she said. "You need to understand, the future is split in half. There are two possibilities, not one greater than the other. I see you choosing each path. It changes almost every minute."

"What paths?" Isla asked.

"Your heart decides the future of the world," she said. "Your choice decides."

"What choice?" she practically screamed.

"Oro and Grim."

Isla froze at their mention.

"You will kill one of them. That much is certain. Which one lives, and which one dies . . . that has not yet been decided."

She planned to kill Grim that very day . . . but the oracle said it was just as likely she would end up killing Oro.

It couldn't be true.

Now that she had most of her memories back . . . she didn't want to kill either of them.

"*Nothing* is decided," the oracle repeated. "Both possibilities are just as likely. You *will* kill one of them, with your own hand."

This couldn't be her fate. She couldn't be the one to decide the future of the world. Why her?

"You, whose heart has been split in two in more ways than one, are capable of both life and death. You are both curse and cure."

Grim had said those same words to her—

Isla sobbed into her hands. Her mind was at war. The more she remembered—

"They're almost here," the oracle said. "Go, now. Make your choice."

The oracle smiled, one last time, before the wall of ice cracked and fell, water forming a wave that Isla only missed by rising above, using her Wildling abilities.

When the water cleared, the oracle was gone.

Isla raced across the Mainland on Lynx's back. He was wearing his full armor, scuffed with marks from previous battles with her mother. Lynx hadn't needed much time to get used to the island. She held tightly as he expertly avoided the brambles she herself had set up, to block the Nightshades. Wind whipped her face. Tears were briny on her cheeks.

You will kill one of them.

No. Days before, she had declared she would help kill Grim. She

would put a hold on his powers. But now . . . she remembered so much more.

He was her enemy. He was coming to destroy the island. He was going to kill innocents, kill *her*, if she didn't stop him. So why did the idea of hurting him hurt so much? Why did it feel like she was being torn in two?

Their army was lined up and ready, spread across the only clearing left on the Mainland. Skyling warriors glimmered like ornaments, armor shining as they waited above. Ciel and Avel were among them. Each were supplied with dozens of metal-tipped arrows. Zed and Calder had worked hard to make sure of it.

Before Azul had left, hours before, he had given them a gift. A violent storm raged high above the island, contained between rows of clouds, as a fence to keep the dreks from being able to escape once the Skylings began using their special weapons.

Azul had looked devastated to leave. He had clutched her hands in goodbye and she had slipped one of her rings onto his finger, the same way she had the first time they ever saw each other. "Keep it safe for me," she said. "Until we see each other next."

Lynx came to a sudden halt in front of Oro. The traitorous creature greeted him with about ten times more fondness than he had greeted her.

Enya stood next to Oro in rose-gold armor, looking determined. She nodded at Isla, then at Lynx, who tipped his head in greeting.

A Sunling called to her, and she excused herself. Isla watched her go and—

"Be—be careful," Isla said, surprising herself. She didn't realize how much she had come to care about the Sunling, even after what she had told her.

Enya grinned over her shoulder. "Don't worry about me, Wildling," she said, winking. "I do not die today."

Isla wondered if she could say the same.

She slipped off Lynx's back and landed in front of Oro. She couldn't meet his eyes, after what she had just learned. "They'll be here soon," she said. She wouldn't tell him how she had visited the oracle. How could she explain that the woman had predicted she had just as much chance of killing Oro as Grim?

No. Impossible. She would kill Grim today and end the prophecy. There would be no chance that it could ever be Oro.

"Are you okay?" he asked. His hand was warm against her arm.

"No," she said. "I'm afraid." She had never been in a true battle before. And certainly not one of this scale. "I'm afraid I've already ruined everything."

Oro shook his head and pulled her fully to his chest. "We have a plan," he said, lips pressing against her forehead. "The portal being open doesn't change that."

No. But it certainly made the stakes higher.

Their plan had slightly shifted, now that they knew Grim was targeting the portal in the Place of Mirrors. Nightshade power didn't work there, which meant Grim couldn't portal directly inside. Isla had covered every inch of the isle in poisonous plants. The closest he could get was the bridge, where she would be waiting.

That was where they would battle.

"Isla," Oro said softly. She looked up at him. He traced her lips with the tip of his finger and smiled. Then his face became serious. "If something happens to me, I want you to leave. I want you to take all my power and leave."

She frowned. "Oro, *nothing* is going to—"

"Love," he said, smiling again. He looked almost happy . . . almost at peace. He tucked away a stray hair and said, "It's all for you." He took her hand and pressed it over his heart. His eyes closed, for a moment, and he kept smiling. "All these years, I saved it for you."

Isla didn't know why she was crying.

"It's yours. It will always be yours. Protect the people of Lightlark."

No. She didn't know why he was talking like that. All she could say was the truth. "I love you."

Oro smiled wider, and this was too perfect, too much joy to fit in a person, too good to be true, like a sunny day right before a storm. He produced a rose in his hand and said, "I know."

She reached beneath her shirt and showed him her golden rose. The necklace she wore below the one she couldn't take off.

He took her into his arms and kissed her.

That was when she started to worry.

His kiss was desperate, like it might be one of the last things he would ever do. He leaned down and whispered in her ear, "One day, I'm going to take you to my favorite place." She remembered him telling her about it. A beach on Sun Isle with water the green of her eyes. "And I'm going to lay you upon the rocks." Her pulse quickened. "And I'm going to make it your favorite place too."

Isla smiled. She wanted that, desperately. She could see it so clearly—Oro pressing her against the sand, waves washing around them while he wrung pleasure from her, the same way he had in their bedroom.

And she could see beyond that too.

"Tomorrow," she said. "We're going to do that not *one day* but tomorrow. We're going to win, everything is going to be fine, Lightlark is going to survive, and we're going to go to the beach tomorrow."

Oro smiled. Nodded. But she knew him now. She could see the tiny signs.

He didn't believe her.

One moment, the Mainland was empty, save for their own soldiers.

The next, Grim's army was everywhere.

Isla's blood went cold. Grim had portaled them all—*thousands*—at once. She knew how much power that required.

Shadows and ash erupted across the Mainland and were met by lashes of fire. Wind swept down from the sky. Metal clashed against metal. Screams, cries, bellows—

"Tomorrow," Oro said, pressing one final kiss to her lips. Then he jumped into the air, straight into the battle.

His effect was immediate. Isla watched in awe as Oro's fire became a wave that washed over dozens of Nightshade soldiers. As he pulled water from the sea and flooded an entire unit, washing them right off the side of the island. He made a sword of Starling sparks and began fighting, and anyone who dared approach him died.

Lynx knelt, and Isla pushed the ground beneath her to propel her onto his back. She slipped into her saddle. "Let's go," she said, and he raced forward.

A group of Nightshades stepped into their path, but before they could draw a single shadow, Lynx plowed through most of them and tore the rest apart with his mighty fangs.

From his back, Isla had the perfect vantage point. She turned in both directions, her arms moving wildly, burying some Nightshades in the ground, and covering others in a sea of poisonous plants. The flora she had created previously also fought back, almost extensions of herself, stabbing with their barbs and thorns.

Near the coast, Isla saw what looked to be a moving wall of water. It was Calder. He swept across the land inside a massive wave with a dozen serpent heads coming out of it. They each lashed out, swallowing Nightshades, drowning them. Calder looked deep in meditation. It seemed contrary to his peaceful nature to kill, and she knew every death would haunt him afterward.

Nightshades fought back with relish. Unlike Calder, most of them seemed to enjoy the killing. Darkness was everywhere, ink turned over, just like in her vision. She watched a Sunling turn to ash. A Skyling was sliced in half by a ribbon of umbra. His pieces fell from the sky, landing amid the barbed brush.

She shot her arm to the side and sent a line of Nightshades hurtling toward one of the Starling shields. Their bodies broke against it. She propelled another group into the center of her poisonous plants. Their screams quickly turned to silence.

No sign of the dreks. Not yet.

Perhaps she had been wrong. Maybe Grim hadn't found a way to use the sword. Maybe the dreks wouldn't be a threat. They would be in battle by now, wouldn't they?

In a flash, the world went sideways as Lynx was struck. Isla just managed to encase them both in a shield of energy, and together they slid across the Mainland, raking through all the plants in their path.

"Lynx!" she yelled as soon as she was on her feet. She raced to the leopard. He was on his side. He wasn't moving.

She threw herself atop him, guarding him with her power.

No. If he was hurt, if he was—

He made a sound of irritation below her, as if annoyed that she was scrambling to feel for his heartbeat.

She buried her face in his fur, relief cold through her blood. Shadows had eaten through part of his armor. If he hadn't been wearing it, that would have been his skin.

They could have killed him.

Rage shot through her veins—energy filled her limbs. Oro's voice was in her head, telling her to calm down. Telling her that being emotional would make her lose control.

She tried to breathe through the anger, but it only intensified, until her power was so saturated, she could feel it like a weight in her chest.

Before she could stop herself, her hand struck the ground before her, and the island shattered. Its terrain rippled, swallowing any Nightshade in its path, until they were buried beneath rock. More of them rushed forward, and she almost smiled, something wicked uncurling inside her chest.

They called their shadows?

She called her own.

They streamed from her fingers, and she gathered them up just like she had in her training with Remlar.

"Get down," she told Lynx, and he ducked just as she turned her stream of shadows into a scythe that cut all the Nightshades around her down.

She was panting. She had used too much power too quickly.

But all the enemies around her were dead now.

More were joining them.

Skylings shot powerful gusts from above, forcing Nightshades toward the center. Sunlings created walls of flames. Grim's army was slowly being boxed in, Lightlark's legion advancing from all sides.

Now, she thought, grabbing her starstick from its place along her spine. "I'll be right back," she told Lynx, who bowed his head, before she portaled to Sky Isle, where her own legion was waiting.

"It's time?" Singrid asked as soon as he saw her, grinning, clearly eager to join the battle. The Vinderland stood ready behind him, hundreds of warriors clattering their weapons together. Nearby, Remlar watched with curiosity, along with his people and the other night creatures she had recruited.

Their plan was simple. Oro's armies would surround the Nightshade forces. Trap them. Keep moving them to the center of their battlefield. Then, Isla would portal the second wave of warriors right into the middle, so Grim's forces would be enclosed in all directions.

"It's time."

Isla drew her puddle of stars as large as she could make it. And, with all her remaining strength, she kept it open as the hundreds of soldiers rushed in. She was the last to fall inside.

Battle cries pierced the air. Nightshades were now being smothered. Sunlings, Skylings, Vinderland, and night creatures all fought side by side.

Isla marveled at them. Enemies, united.

She was lifted off her feet by Lynx, who threw her onto his back without stopping. She gripped his saddle and joined the fighting.

The Nightshades didn't stand a chance. They were almost easily overpowering them.

Then a woman came from the sea, on the back of a swell that dwarfed even the Singing Mountains.

The water crashed across the Mainland, and soldiers were covered, then frozen where they stood. They couldn't move their legs. Lynx only avoided the ice by jumping at the last moment. His paws cracked as they landed on the frozen ground.

Suddenly, Cleo was right in front of her. She wasn't wearing a dress. No, now she wore a fighting suit that covered every inch of her body except for her hands and face. It was white, with dark-blue detailing. She frowned at Isla and Lynx. "What a pleasant . . . pet," she said, tilting her head. "You're on the wrong side, though, Wildling. You said you wanted your realm to live, didn't you?"

It wasn't lost on her that Cleo hadn't killed the Lightlark soldiers. She could have frozen them solid, but she didn't. There was still a chance she would change sides.

Isla understood her now more than ever: A woman who had dedicated her entire life to leading her realm. Who had allowed herself one happiness. Who had lost it.

"Why are you doing this?" Isla asked.

"For him," she said. *Her son.*

"I don't understand."

Cleo reached down into her collar and pulled out the necklace she wore. The blue stone shimmered. "The other world has power we can't begin to fathom. Souls can rise once more."

She understood now. Cleo believed there was a chance to see her son again.

"I can't let you use the portal," she said.

Cleo frowned. "I hoped you would see reason," she said. "We really do need you."

The Moonling raised her arms, and the ocean rushed to wrap around her body, curling, alive, forming her shape. She rose into the air, on a swirl of sea.

She shot her watery hand out, and her arm became a rope of water that sent Isla flying back, right off Lynx. Her leopard roared. Before she cracked her head against Cleo's ice, a bed of flowers bloomed behind her, bursting through the frost, breaking her fall.

Cleo laughed, the sound muted and distorted by the water surrounding her. "Flowers won't help you."

Isla slowly rose. She took a step, and the ice broke. Flowers sprouted in her wake. Vines formed down her arms, long thorns growing against her knuckles.

She had been watching the Moonling fight. She used her hands. She needed them to wield water.

It was impossible to grip Cleo's wrists in her water-covered form. Isla's restraints would slip right off the sea.

Cleo was too busy staring Isla down to notice that Enya had become a living flame behind her. An understanding passed between Isla and the Sunling.

Isla charged. Cleo watched her, water swirling, towering.

So did Enya. She jumped, wings made of flames uncurling from her back and wrapping around the Moonling ruler.

Cleo was quick—she sent Enya backward with a thick stream of sea. But, for just a moment, Cleo's water shield had melted, weakened by the flames.

It was all Isla needed. Roots flew up from the ground and tied around the Moonling's wrists in seconds. They trapped her legs next. One wrapped around her neck for good measure. Flowers bloomed on the restraints. Isla plucked one.

"The flowers helped," she said.

Isla didn't see any more Moonlings. Cleo had a legion. Was she saving them for after Grim's own army was finished?

Part of her feared that Wildlings might fight alongside Nightshade . . . but her people were nowhere to be found.

Isla wondered if that was better or worse.

She was back on Lynx in a moment, hurtling through the battle. Hope bloomed once more. Much of the Nightshades were dead.

They had a chance, Isla thought. It looked like they could win.

Until a crack sounded through the world, and dreks filled the sky. There were hundreds of them. So many, they looked like nighttime sky ripped to flying shreds.

They were everywhere. Skylings fought back, with their metal-tipped arrows, and some of the creatures were shot down, but they were quickly replaced.

A flash like a bolt of lightning shot above her—someone was twirling a special metal-tipped sword and traveling so quickly, they went through one of the dreks. The creature died instantly and fell, crushing a group of Nightshades.

Zed.

He really was that fast.

Isla breathed in and out, trying to focus her energy to the sky. She had one of the metal-tipped blades in her belt. With a shot of power, she might be able to take one of the beasts out. Just as she was about to try, a drek dipped low, and she was knocked off Lynx with the force of its wings. She hit the ground, and the air was stolen from her lungs.

Lynx lunged for her but was immediately surrounded by Nightshades. She gasped for breath, watching helplessly as he was surrounded in shadows.

No.

Two figures came crashing down from the sky.

Ciel and Avel.

Relief rained down her spine. "Thank you," she croaked as Ciel reached a hand to help her up.

Even now, they were still watching out for her. Even—

Ciel's kind face twisted in shock as a drek's talon went clean through his stomach.

Avel's scream shattered the world. She rushed to catch her twin in her arms, her hands shaking as she tried to keep all the parts that were falling from him together.

No. With a roar, she turned the drek to ash. She fished in her pockets for one of her last remaining vials of Wildling healing elixir. She poured it all over Ciel's injury, hand shaking.

It was too late.

His eyes were cold and unblinking.

Avel cradled her brother in her arms and screamed.

This was her fault. Ciel was trying to help *her.*

Dreks landed all around, tearing limbs.

"You need to get up," Isla told Avel. "They're going to—they're going to—"

She refused. She cradled her brother and wouldn't even look at her. Tears swept down Isla's face as she created a small dome of Starling energy around them both, hoping it would hold.

She heard a growl. Lynx. He was fighting off too many soldiers. Isla gathered her power and raged against all of them, until they were nothing but dust.

Her energy was drained. She fell to her knees, and Lynx shielded her with his body.

Through his legs, Isla watched, helpless, as death drowned everything around her. The dreks were endless. Grim must have made more.

It was just like her coronation. Limbs being torn. Screams turning to silence. Bodies fell from the sky more than dreks did. The flight force had been reduced to just a few units.

They didn't stand a chance.

The island would fall. Oro would die. She would die.

A deafening roar sounded across the Mainland. Even the Nightshades stood still. They watched as a serpent with its jaw pulled all the way open swept across the land, swallowing all the Nightshades in its path.

The serpent-woman. *She came.* She stood on her massive tail and picked dreks off from the sky, stabbing them through with her fangs.

The dreks attacked the serpent, but their talons could not penetrate her scales. The storm Azul had created kept the dreks flying low, and she took out a dozen in a few seconds, hitting them with her tail, piercing them with her teeth.

Oro fought nearby, charring the skies with his flames. Zed sped through multiple dreks. Enya was a phoenix, fire-wings curling behind her as she fought.

It still wasn't enough.

Isla looked around. The dead were everywhere, from both sides. Grim still hadn't revealed himself, but this had to be put to an end.

Lynx helped her onto his back, and they raced across the Mainland, passing battling Vinderland, and Remlar, who had been fighting near the woods. He brought dreks down with the smallest movements. They shared a look.

The forest flew by in a flash, and then she was at the bridge. She slid off Lynx.

He would come to meet her. She knew he would. Isla waited for minutes, wincing as she heard the battle raging, willing Grim to come find her.

When more minutes passed, she almost pulled her necklace.

Then, the woods filled with shadows.

At once, the bridge was blocked by a new wave of the Nightshade army. They drew their shadows. They were everywhere.

A howl broke the air in half.

"Even think about touching her, and I'll kill you," a voice said. Steps sounded behind her. "Hello, heart."

BEFORE

When Isla finished training, Grim was waiting for her in her room.

It had been weeks since he had told her the truth. She hadn't sought him out, and he hadn't returned.

"I told you I never wanted to see you again," she said. The betrayal was still raw.

She didn't mean it. She had missed him so much, but she needed time before she could think about forgiving him.

Grim tried at a smile. "I might have good news for you, then," he said.

"What do you mean?"

He looked so serious.

Grim swept across the room and took her in his arms, and she let him, because she knew something was wrong. He studied every part of her face, as if trying to commit it to memory.

Her starstick was hot against her back. It was glimmering in his presence, as if in warning. *Something isn't right*, it was saying. She gripped his chest and said, "What's wrong?"

"The scar has opened. In a place it never has before. A place previously deemed safe." Isla's stomach sank. He had told her about the scar, about how he didn't think Nightshade could survive much longer. "Hundreds of people live near it."

Isla gasped. She opened her mouth, but he beat her to it.

"Whatever happens to me, heart, I want you to know something."

"What?" she said. She tried to shake out of his arms. "Grim, nothing is going to happen to you, nothing—"

"Let me talk, heart," he said, pressing a finger against her lips. "Interrupting is very rude." She could tell he was trying to distract her. Trying to make her smile. She did not.

"I need you to know that you changed everything." He ran his thumb down her cheek. "The gods don't listen to people like me, but I would go on my knees and beg them to let me keep you. You were once the bane of my existence . . . and now, you are the center of it."

He couldn't possibly be saying this, not him, demon in the shadows, ruler of darkness. Not him, looking at her as if she was the answer to all his dreams. "My entire world was night, and you lit a match. No matter what happens to me in this life, I'll find you in the next one. I'll always find you. What I feel for you can never be extinguished. Like the nighttime sky, it is infinite. You and me . . . we're infinite."

Tears streamed down her face. Why did it sound like he was saying goodbye forever?

"No. Don't go," she said. "I can help you. We can figure this out, whatever it is, Grim, *together*. Let me go with you. We can try the sword. Let me go."

"Okay, Hearteater," he finally said. "You can come."

He kissed her. It was quick, and brutal, and then soft—

She didn't even notice when he slid a hand down her spine. By the time she did, it was too late.

He had taken her starstick and vanished, making sure she wouldn't be able to follow.

DAY AND NIGHT

Grim stepped onto the bridge. Exactly where they needed him. He was wearing his full armor, the one she had seen in her memories. Spikes everywhere. On his shoulders. On his helmet. He looked the part of a demon. Shadows swirled and lashed out around him.

But the ones at his feet puddled. "This is obviously a trap," he said, taking a step forward. "You knew I'd find you." He smiled. "You knew nothing could ever keep me from you."

"Even certain death couldn't keep you away?" she asked, voice trembling.

He smiled wider. "Oh, Hearteater," he said. "You and me . . . we're infinite. Death doesn't stand a chance."

Isla couldn't breathe. She was drowning from the inside out, knowing what was about to happen. Knowing what she must do—

Oro landed in front of her, and power rumbled across the island.

Grim only smirked at the king. "And neither do you."

And then he struck. A burst of shadows erupted from him, right at Oro, but the king shielded it with a covering of flames so saturated, they were tinged in blue.

Isla prepared to block herself from the shadows too, her Starling shield forming, but they moved around her almost gently, like extensions of Grim himself.

Oro burst forth with a thick cord of power—a mix of silver energy, water rushing from the sea, and flashing flames. Grim met it with a chain of pure darkness.

Their powers clashed and reverberated in waves. The bridge below them shook. Isla barely kept herself on her feet. She felt the force of their strength in her bones.

Both were too powerful. They roared, fighting, each with equal hatred clear on their faces.

Grim was gone—then, he was right behind Oro. He hit him with a wave of shadows, and Oro only just barely blocked it with a shield of crackling Starling energy. Still, the impact knocked him onto his back.

Before Grim could take another step, Oro's arms went wide, and the sea rushed from hundreds of feet below. It hit Grim, then hardened, then cracked as he fought to melt through it with his shadows. He couldn't move his arms. Oro shot enough fire to char Grim through the ice, but, at the last moment, he portaled away, leaving the frost behind. It fell back onto the bridge and shattered.

"Behind you!" Isla shouted, and Oro turned just in time to block Grim's blade. Oro created a sword out of Starling energy, and they dueled across the bridge.

Grim grinned as if he was having the time of his life. "It's been a long time since we fought, Oro," he said, advancing. "What a shame that it will also be the last time."

Oro let his sword disappear and shot up into the air.

Grim followed. He portaled so quickly that it was as if he were also flying, appearing then disappearing in wild spurts. They dueled in the sky, this time with streams of power.

Isla watched from below, finding herself cringing at every blow the other landed. She bit the inside of her mouth, dread churning in her chest.

There was no winning.

A rumble sounded before the sea below spiraled up, becoming a massive snake that lunged at Grim. In response, he spun a wolf formed of shadows. The creatures battled, mauling each other, protecting their creators.

Oro shot out his hand, releasing a dozen throwing blades made from flames. Grim blocked them with a dark curl of smoke before that shield became a dozen arrows all aimed at Oro's chest.

They ricocheted against Starling sparks, and both of their attacks quickened. Grim was portaling so fast, she could barely track him in the sky, and Oro was creating so many weapons, she missed half of them by blinking.

Finally, Oro paused for a moment, as if gathering his energy. This was it. It was about to be over. The air seemed to go taut in anticipation before he shot out his hand—and released a strike of lightning. It raged across the sky, charged with energy, a combination of his abilities.

It all happened so quickly.

Before the lightning could hit Grim, he was gone, then replaced—With Oro.

Grim had portaled him there, using his power, in that fraction of a second. Isla watched helplessly as Oro's own lightning struck him.

And then, he was falling.

He landed on the bridge with a force that threatened to make it crumble away beneath them. She raced forward, but Grim landed between them.

"No!" she screamed.

Shadows burst forth from his palm, but before they turned Oro to ash, he came to and lifted his own hand. Fire, energy, and wind wrapped around and around. Their powers met in the middle.

Oro was injured. He looked like he could pass out at any moment. She knew what she had to do.

It was time.

Don't do it. The voice was firm, speaking from the past. Her own voice.

She didn't want to. But the oracle had made it clear—it was either Grim or Oro. Her choice would define the world.

She had to decide. As Grim and Oro dueled, so did past and present Isla.

Don't do it—

She had to do it.

DON'T DO IT—

Her fingers shook. Tears blinded her. She closed her eyes and followed Remlar's instructions.

She reached for the link. The one between her and Grim. It held every memory of them together, like beads on a bracelet. She saw them in her mind. The first time they met. The first time they kissed. The first time they were one. The first time she made him smile. A sob scraped the back of her throat, and Grim's eyes went to her. A stream of power was hurtling toward him, and he didn't seem to care. He looked at her.

It nearly broke her to reach for their thread. To reach for his power.

And take it.

BEFORE

No.

Isla's chest was ripping in two. She was helpless. Stuck here, on the Wildling newland. It would take months to sail to Nightshade, and even then, even if they let her in—

It would be far too late.

No. This wasn't happening. She hadn't finally found someone who understood her only to lose him.

Tears and salt and gasps turned into a predatorial silence. All her senses sharpened like a dagger.

Grim was a demon. He was the feared ruler of Nightshade.

But he had become her friend. They had faced countless challenges together. He had touched her in ways that made her feel alive, and like the space between stars, and she had felt, for once, that her body belonged to her. Not the realm. *Her.*

For all his remarks and attitude, he had believed in her. He had trusted her.

And she trusted him.

He had saved her.

She was not going to give up on him.

Thousands of miles were no space at all, not for them. He was right. They were infinite. She reached out, looking for her demon, for *him.* The one who had pressed shapes against her skin, the one who didn't know he had a dimple because he so rarely smiled.

Her mind emptied of anything other than him. She could see him in her head, could smell him, could feel him.

She reached out with every ounce of herself, threw her marrow through the world—

And found him.

When everything else cleared away, the universe fading like ash and smoke, only a link remained. She could feel it now, tying them together.

Isla didn't think about what it meant. Not then. The thread was wrapped in power, and she didn't know how to use it; it slipped through her fingers, but she had one ask—one request.

Take me to him.

With the sword in her hands, she grasped Grim's power to portal with every inch of herself and vanished.

She landed on her knees.

Dreks were falling from the sky like pieces of night smelted into rain. Hundreds. Thousands. Grim had told her about them, but nothing could prepare her for seeing them—hearing them.

They were far smaller than the dragon, but whereas the creature was graceful, these were like throwing stars, shooting across the sky, falling to the ground, talons first.

Grim was at the center of it all.

There were others. They did not last long. She watched Nightshade warrior after Nightshade warrior be plucked up and away. Some were torn in half in the sky; others were eaten whole. Blood, everywhere, screams, men twice her size yelling for their lives.

Grim. He was rumored to be one of the strongest rulers.

Shadows erupted from him, and where they struck, everything died. He was seeping, everywhere, roaring—

It was not enough. The curses had dimmed his power. There were too many. And some seemed immune to even his shadows. They barreled toward him, and Isla knew how these injuries worked. They rotted flesh and bone and did not heal. How many times had he already been struck?

The scar ran across the ground, for as far as she could see. Grim said it went across all of Nightshade. Right there, so close, was a village Grim had told her about—the one that had been deemed *safe*. Dreks swooped down into the streets. Cries. *Children.*

Grim looked up, as if sensing her. And Isla had the feeling that no matter where they were, even on a battlefield, he would always be able to find her.

Horror. Pure, unfiltered horror, and devastation, to find her here, in a place where everything would soon be dead.

Then—surprise.

Understanding. He had taken her starstick. There was only one way she could possibly be here.

They stared at each other, and for just a moment, it was like no one else was there. Just them. No dreks. No soldiers.

He looked at her like she was the beginning and end of his world, and he *smiled*—smiled because he had found love, even if it was just before he died.

Grim closed his eyes, and she knew what he was going to do. He was going to portal her away. He was going to *die*.

Before he could, a drek pierced his chest. Its talons went right through him.

She screamed, and it didn't sound human; it sounded like scratching the night sky with a blade, like pain spun into a sound.

Other dreks shot down. Grim roared, and they all descended, seeing their chance. They gripped him by the shoulders, and his head went limp. They were going to tear him in two—

No.

No.

Isla didn't hesitate before she took the sword in her hands—and dug it deep into the ground before her.

Nothing happened, not right away. She didn't know how to break the curse, she didn't know what to do, but she was desperate.

And there was something there. Something strange and twisted. Isla grabbed it.

Her pain provided passage. Everything she was made of spilled out. The sword shook beneath her hands. Then, her fingers slipped, and when her hands hit the ground, death was unleashed.

From her poured an endless wave of shadows. The dreks shriveled and died. The soldiers became clouds of blood. Everything that wasn't him disappeared.

Her darkness ate the world, and it had no limit. It kept going.

You and me . . . we're infinite.

She felt infinite.

Power poured out of her like the ocean tilting itself to the side, unstoppable, uncontrollable; it raged and raged, and Isla kept screaming until it finally ran out. Because her love might be infinite, but her abilities were not. Her life was not.

It felt like she was saying goodbye, but she didn't really care. Because he was there, and he would be okay, and she loved him, she loved him so much, she just hoped he would take what she was offering, all of the Wildling power she wasn't supposed to have, because she knew he would take care of her people. Just like he had taken care of her.

Grim roared, and Isla sent her Wildling powers across the thread that bound them together. It was the last thing she did as she stumbled and fell.

Into his arms. He had portaled and caught her, and she knew he would survive his injuries, but he was searching her face like he was the one dying, and he was yelling at her, but all she could do was smile.

"Isla, come back to me. Come back."

He shook her, and she could barely feel it; there was barely anything left.

Her body stiffened. Her breathing stopped. Grim roared.

"Wake up," he said. His voice was thick with desperation. He was *crying*. "Stab me through the chest again if you have to, just wake up."

She wanted to. She really did.

"Grim," she said to him, the last of her life leaving her. She remembered what he told her. *Pain could be useful. Pain was the strongest emotion.* "Pain is not the strongest," she said.

Then, her heart went still.

SACRIFICE

Isla took his powers. Grim's shadows ceased, and he was hit by the full force of Oro's fury. He landed on his back. Isla didn't know how he wasn't immediately killed.

Or how he slowly inched up, gasping for air. His hand lashed out as he tried to summon his shadows once more. He could not.

He frowned and turned to look at her with an earnestness that made her want to sink to the ground. "What is this, heart?" he asked.

She was sobbing, and he didn't look betrayed—he looked devastated that she was crying. He was *upset that she was upset at the fact that she had stolen his powers, readying him for Oro to kill—*

She couldn't do it. Her concentration wavered.

Still, she didn't stop her hold on his powers.

Oro made a sword out of Starling energy. It crackled with strength, and he lifted it over his head. Grim wouldn't be able to defend himself. She had weakened him. In one moment, he would be dead. He would be dead. *He would be dead.*

That was the first moment she had ever seen Grim afraid.

Just before the blade found his neck, he bellowed, "If I die, *she dies.*"

It wasn't even his death that he feared. It was *hers.* Her death was what made him rabid, shaking, yelling, eyes wide and desperate.

Oro froze, just an inch from ending the Nightshade. "No," Oro whispered, disbelieving. Furious. Understanding something Isla still hadn't. "You didn't."

BEFORE

This is wrong, was Isla's first thought. She shouldn't be alive. Her body recognized it. Its life force had been drained away completely.

She opened her eyes, and Isla had never heard such a sound of relief.

Grim was kneeling in front of her. Her hand was in his. "Heart," he said. "You're here, heart." It was like he still couldn't believe it.

She had been somewhere else.

Now, she was back.

"How?" she asked.

His head lifted, and she saw tears in his eyes. His face was covered in dirt and blood, but he was here, kneeling before her, like she was something to worship. "You died," he said, the word cracking. His voice was raw, like he had been screaming too. "You died in my arms."

Grim closed his eyes, and tears fell. They made lines in the dirt and crusted blood. She reached for him on instinct, clearing them away. She *had* died. Were her people okay? Had giving her power to Grim through the thread that connected them worked?

She couldn't cheat death. Grim couldn't either. It didn't make sense that she was still living.

"How?" she asked again.

MISSING PIECE

Y ou bound her to you," Oro said, voice shaking with anger. With shock.

She remembered now. Grim's explanation in the past. She knew binding someone to oneself meant sharing a life. Not just powers, but life itself.

One could not die without killing the other.

That was why, when the arrow had split her heart in two during the Centennial, she hadn't died immediately. Not just because of the power of the heart of Lightlark . . . but because Grim was keeping her alive.

"It was only a temporary solution," Oro said, voice shaking with anger, but also fear.

Grim nodded. "The other world offers a permanent one."

That was the reason for this war. That was the reason for all this death. She remembered what Cleo had said. In the other world, *souls can rise once more.*

He wanted to open the portal to save her life.

Oro hesitated, sword still in his hand. If he killed Grim, she would die too.

"Do it," Isla said, because she was willing to die if it would save everyone else. Even if most of them still hated her and thought she was a blight on the world. The same way Oro had said he would give her his power, she would give him hers, in case the rebels were wrong.

Oro looked at her, and she saw fear and fury and disappointment—disappointment in *himself* for not being strong enough to make the right choice for his people. Enya was right. Isla had made him weak.

"I can't," he said, the words so soft.

"*Kill him*," she said, her voice getting hysterical. "He's going to kill innocent people. I told you about the vision. He's going to *kill children*. He's going to kill me."

Grim looked at her. "Heart . . ." he said, so gently. "What do you mean?"

She saw flashes of her vision again. The darkness, eating everything. Skin sliding from bone. Bone reduced to ash. Death, everywhere, and Grim standing in the middle of it—

It looked familiar now.

Isla started sputtering. "The village. The people. Their skin melting from them, the shadows. Then the—the darkness came into *me*—"

No.

The world went silent.

The vision was not a look at the future. Not an example of the lengths Grim would go to get her.

It was a memory.

And Grim wasn't the one who had summoned those shadows, wasn't the one who had killed those hundreds of innocent people.

"It was me," she said. "It was me."

She saw herself, returning to the place where it had all happened, where she had offered all her power she didn't know she had to save Grim. She saw the village, on the outskirts of the scar. Charred. There were only shapes of people—of children—where they once stood.

She saw herself collapsing on the ground, sobbing. Screaming, "I did this. I did this."

Oro was in front of her now, hands pressed against her face, taking her out of the memory. "You are not a monster." Was that what she had been saying over and over? "You are not defined by one mistake."

But it was not *one mistake*.

Isla had used emotions to wield her power multiple times. Recklessly. Even after Oro had warned her, she hadn't been able to help herself, she had done it again and again.

She was not to be trusted. She was reckless, dangerous, a *monster.* Enya was right. Oro deserved so much better.

"Get away from me," she screamed. She tried to step away, but Oro took her hand. "Let me go."

She understood now how it was even a possibility that she might kill Oro. Just by *proximity* to her, he was in danger.

She had no control of her emotions. Of her powers.

She would kill him. One day, she would be overcome with emotion, she would lose control yet again, and she would kill him. She saw it so clearly now.

"Let. Me. Go," she bellowed, her voice thick, tears falling into her mouth.

She tried to wrestle herself away, but Oro didn't budge. He didn't understand; he didn't know how much of a danger she was to him—

Grim's voice seemed to rumble the world as he said, "Let go of my wife."

There it was. The final missing piece.

BOUND

That word, *wife*, unlocked a door in her mind that had been stubbornly jammed.

She saw it. Hands joined together, before an altar. Then, against a bed frame.

She saw months of suffering with guilt for having killed so many innocent people. She saw herself begging Grim to take the memory of what she had done away. She saw him refusing.

Memories fluttered, until they snagged on one last moment. She saw herself wearing her Centennial dress. She watched Grim take a necklace out of his pocket and present it to her. One with the biggest black diamond she had ever seen. "In Nightshade, instead of rings, we give necklaces," he said. "I should have given this to you before. It's a sign of our commitment. Once I put it on, it is on forever. Only with your death will it be released."

She saw herself smiling and telling him to put it on her. She saw her move her hair, clearing the way.

Instead of clasping it forever, she saw him slip it back into his pocket.

She heard him say, "Please, heart, forgive me for this."

She watched understanding come over her face as she said, "Grim, no—"

But it was done.

She watched him take her memories away, return her starstick, and send her back to the Wildling realm.

Isla knew what happened next.

TRUTH

O ro let her go. Out of shock, or disgust, or because he was finally listening to her, she didn't know.

You will kill one of them. That much is certain.

Screams sounded from the battleground; power rippled through the air. Out of nowhere, more dreks appeared, screeching. Arrows shot through the sky, and the creatures fell, but there were too many. They picked Skylings off, one by one. She watched helplessly as more Skylings dropped from the sky, limp or in pieces.

Death, so much useless death. Pain and blood painted the island. It made her remember what she had done. What she had done—

Her voice was trembling. "If I go with you, will you leave? Will you stop the attack?" she asked.

"*No*," Oro said, the word a plea.

Grim's answer was immediate. "Yes."

He held his hand out, the same way he had countless times before, and the echoes of it reverberated in her mind.

Isla reached for Grim's hand. She was a monster, just like him. She needed to get away from Oro and this island. She looked at Lynx, and Grim said, "Don't worry, he's coming too." She watched her leopard vanish.

"Don't," Oro said. His voice broke on the word. She knew he wouldn't let her go. He didn't understand; he didn't know about the prophecy. He would think there was another way.

So before Grim could portal them to Nightshade, she turned and said, "I love you, Oro." She closed her eyes tightly. Felt tears sweep down. She took Grim's hand. "But I love him too."

And, because of his flair, he knew it was true.

ACKNOWLEDGMENTS

I want to start by thanking you, the reader, for supporting this series. When I wrote *Lightlark,* I never could have imagined that people around the world would love this story and these characters as much as I do. Your excitement for this book got me through every deadline. I am endlessly grateful for you. *Thank you.*

I have many people to thank for helping to get *Nightbane* out into the world. Thank you to Anne Hetzel, my editor, for believing in *Lightlark* before everything, for your editorial guidance, and for your infinite championing of me and this series. Thank you to Andrew Smith, who saw *Lightlark*'s potential, and has made so much possible. Thank you to my literary agent, Jodi Reamer, who read too many versions of this book, and was my guiding star during this entire process. I am so grateful to have you in my corner.

To everyone at Abrams, including Megan Carlson, Micah Fleming, Maggie Moore, Marie Oishi, Ashley Albert, Abby Pickus, and Angelica Busanet, for all your hard work on this series. To Chelsea Hunter and Natalie Sousa, for designing the book covers of my dreams. To Kim Lauber and Hallie Patterson, for everything you have done for me and *Lightlark*—it is truly a joy to work with both of you.

To my incredible team, who has made all this possible. To my entertainment lawyer, Eric Greenspan, for taking a chance on me. You have been one of my biggest supporters from the very beginning—thank you. To David Fox, Chris Maxwell, and Debby Sander. To my Film/TV agents at CAA, Berni Barta and Michelle Weiner, who have made some of my wildest dreams come true. Also, to Ali Ehrlich—thank you for

everything. To Denisse Montfort and Allison Elbl, for all that you do. To Cecilia de la Campa, for everything to come. To Katelyn Detweiler—I am so grateful that you believed in these books first. Your kindness and sincerity are a gift. To Sam Farkas, who has made it possible for *Lightlark* to be published around the world. Seeing the foreign editions of *Lightlark* has been one of my greatest joys—thank you for everything.

To Anqi Xu, for reading this book early and for giving me great notes. To Sean, for being one of the first to read all my books, including the early drafts, even when you're busy—I really appreciate your help. To Kaitlin López for your last-minute assistance that saved the day. To Annika Patton, who has become one of my dearest friends. You were the first person to read this book, back in January (and the first to react to the ending!).

To my heart, Rron, for supporting me, even when I had to write through the holidays and weekends. Eight years together means you knew me as a teenager writing books and dreaming of becoming an author. This book is for you. I love you. To your family as well, for their love and support, and for bringing me snacks while I worked on this book.

To my parents, who always encouraged me to chase my dreams. Mom—I hope one day I can be as strong as you. Dad—thank you for teaching me that the harder you work, the luckier you get. To my twin, Danny, who used to sit with me after school in the bookstore as I looked up literary agents to query. I am so proud of you. To Angely, a second mom to me; Carlos, who is always there for me; and JonCarlos and Luna, for being the lights of my life. I can't wait to watch you both chase your dreams. To my grandma Rose, for telling me stories before bedtime and inspiring me to become an author. To my grandpa Alfonso, for teaching me resilience and a strong work ethic. To Maureen, Uncle Buddy, and Aunt Patty for always believing in me. To Leo, Bear, and Truffle, for bringing me so much joy.

To my author friends, who have helped me navigate all of this. To Adam Silvera, who always answers the phone, even when he's on

deadline, and is the Honest Friend. To Chloe Gong, who doesn't get mad when I talk more than I write at "writing sessions" in coffee shops and is the fastest reader I know. To Dustin Thao, who is always there for all of us. To Sabaa Tahir, Marie Lu, Brigid Kemmerer, and Zibby Owens, for your support. I am so grateful to know you. To every other friend—you know who you are, and I am so lucky to have you in my life.

Finally, thank you to everyone who follows me on social media, or has ever recommended my books. Your messages mean more to me than you will ever know.